I0671445

Thomas Haftmann, Private Eye:

The Short Stories

Book 2

Thomas Haftmann, Private Eye:

The Short Stories

Robb White

NEWPULP PRESS

NEW PULP PRESS

Published by New Pulp Press, LLC, 926 Truman Avenue, Key West, Florida 33040, USA.

For information contact:
Publisher@NewPulpPress.com

ISBN-13: 978-1945734090 (New Pulp Press)
ISBN-10: 1945734094

For my son Matt

Author's Notes On Stories:

"The Kneeling Woman," by Terry White, pseud., was the first Haftmann story in print in *Words of Wisdom* 14 (1994): 19-26. "The Riding Boy" was first published in *Rock Falls Review* (Summer 1996) and republished in *The Thrilling Detective*. Nov. 2, 1998. "No Escape, No Turning Back" was first titled "Nocturne for Murder" and published in Gary Lovisi's *Hardboiled* in March 2005: 25-42. This was followed by "Strawberry Girls" in Allen Guthrie's British webzine *Noir Originals* (Issue No. 6, May 2005).

Of several Haftmann stories published or reprinted in 2010, these were among them: "The Last Outlaw," first published in *The3rdegree* webzine on Oct. 2003, was republished in *Sex and Murder Magazine* June 2010 (the webzine's subtitle: *A Magazine of Extreme Horror, Dark Fiction, and Splatterpunk*. Vol. 1, Issue 11) under the pseudonym Robb White, was first published in *Sex and Murder Magazine* in 2010 and then reprinted in *Sex and Murder Magazine's* print anthology. (Ed. Douglas Rhodes. S.A.M., 2010. 2-11). Also in that year were published: "The Slave Master's Dungeon" was published in *Powder Burn Flash;* "A Woman with Tea-Colored Eyes" in *A Twist of Noir; and* "The Dog Returneth to His Vomit" in *Thrillers, Killers, 'n Chillers.*

"Welcome to the Piggy Palace" was published in Jessica A. Weiss' Wicked East Press anthology: *Under the Stairs*, 2011. "Rock Me to Sleep" was accepted by *Darkest before the Dawn* (Jan. 2011), but to my knowledge was never published. "The Last Case of James Revelle" was published in Issue Seven of *Pulp Modern: Thieves and Liars.* (Uncle B., 2014: 84-99).

Thomas Haftmann, Private Eye

"She Played Bach in the Piano Bar" by Robb White, pseud., was published in *Sex and Murder Magazine* Vol. 1, Issue 15. Dec. 2010.

"The Bride from Paradise Park" was first published in *Midwest Literary Magazine* and included in the anthology *Winter Canons* (Ed. Anthony Shields. Midwest Press, 2011) and, finally, republished in *Jack Hardway's Crime Magazine* Vol. 2, No. 1 Jan./Feb. 2015.

- Robb White

Thomas Haftmann, Private Eye:

The Short Stories

The Kneeling Woman

Haftmann wasn't sure he had heard right. Millimaki was just then emerging from the squad room, the cheroot coming from his mouth with a wet, plopping sound and immediately followed by the braying yawp of his laugh. As Haftmann approached, Millimaki turned abruptly toward the dispatchers in the room and waved the cigar about like a baton to punctuate his remarks: "Couple hundred stab wounds with a serrated steak knife. Harris said she's exsanguinated, not a single artery left he didn't puncture and there wasn't any place for the blood to collect. Forget lividity. She looked like a side of beef thrown into a wood chipper."

Haftmann watched as the blue cloud of Millimaki's smoke wafted above the heads of the captive dispatchers, then swirled and nosedived, arcing downward between Millimaki's legs; once in the corridor the backdraft sucked the blue smoke and, like a python grabbed firmly by its tail, led it gently in Haftmann's direction toward the stairwell he had just come from.

Haftmann loathed his boss' ham-handed crudeness in general and his bullying in particular – of the men under him as well as the harassment of the women civil servants employed at the station house. One reason why he was retiring as a detective sergeant, second-grade to open up his own P.I. office. Not for the first time Haftmann wondered if life was hell and this was his pre-vision of it: Millimaki, an obese lesser devil always sucking up to the bigger demons, looking for new souls to torment. Haftmann thought he knew it for what it was: misfired synapses of childhood terrors about hell and damnation. He knocked a clump of dirty snow free from beneath his heel. He heard Millimaki grunt in his general direction.

Millimaki saw him and hitched his pants up over his gut and shuffled toward him in that awkward, rolling gait – a skiing accident in his youth. "Well, look what the cat drug in. You're late. Daywatch briefing in the muster room ended, uh, (squinting at his watch) fifteen minutes ago."

"In case you haven't noticed, chief, there's a snow squall outside. Makes driving –"

"Yeah, I noticed that, Haftmann, and I accounted for that fact when I got up this morning (cigar coming loose with that sickening wet noise) and I made allowances for it just like everybody else (cigar-jabbing around the room for audience benefit) who managed to get here on time."

"What's the real problem, Millimaki? Augie's bagman delayed by the snow? I can buzz him for you, see if he'll send it with Nickie DeAngelo. DeAngelo owes you anyway, right? Gave him the whole township's police force for traffic detail at his daughter's wedding last month."

Mllimaki loomed close. The smoke haze like a blue halo under fluorescent lighting. "You do what I say, when I say it, Haftmann. I can put your plans to open your lousy little agency out of business before you get out the door."

Trouble is, he was right. I knew he was right. That didn't stop me from hating his slimy rat face.

I said: "You put that cigar any closer to me and I'll stick it in your face."

Millimaki blinked. Haftmann watched Millimaki's dewlaps quiver and the bloated face of his chief suffuse with blood. Haftmann felt a vein pulsing in his neck. *God, he was too tired for this*. The corridor had grown quiet; the typewriters had stopped clacking and a few detectives were looking up from their cubicles. Guys he used to work with eyeballing him hard now and probably wishing they could get away with the same kind of insubordination. Millimaki was universally hated. Pete smirked at him from behind a computer. He'd be telling this anecdote at Tico's Place tonight. *Then Haftmann says to the chief . . .* Good for a laugh, he was. Not much else.

Haftmann brushed past. "Hey, where you think you're going?"

"I'm working the runaway case with Meldrum."

"Not anymore, ace. You and your buddy Wendel got a date with the Kneeling Woman. Somebody made a pincushion out of her last night. Harris is posting her right now at county morgue. You and Meldrum check out the house. Techs are on their way back. Fact, you might ask Doc where he was last night. Looks like one of his jobs." This produced feeble snickering from a few dispatchers and squad detectives. Millimaki, putting on the dog, cigar tip glowing salmon-pink-orange.

Haftmann tasted coppery bile. Cottonmouth and homicide on a snowy Monday morning in February.

Six weeks ago one her neighbors on Erieview said lights were always on and called 911, who called Jefferson Township, who in turn called the station house. Wendel Meldrum called Haftmann because he was his former partner, broke him in on cases, and because Haftmann had helped the old lady out a few months ago by getting some itinerant contractor to return the money he'd ripped off for painting her with silver brite from the local Walmart and calling it a roof job. Haftmann had grown fond of the old lady, proud and stiff-necked, making it on her own in the shabby gentility and neglect of a decrepit resort town that catered to teenagers, dropouts, low-riders, and assorted kooks and drifters. They found her in the living room of her Cape Cod kneeling on the carpet. She had been on her knees since Christmas. Even Doc Harris, who rarely saw one live these days, felt compelled to stop by her room to

3

catch a glimpse of the human oddity the papers had tagged the Kneeling Woman. Harris told Haftmann her condition was "deplorable" and that she'd probably lose both legs to gangrene. But she didn't. She spent five weeks in the county hospital and was sent home a week ago, the story of the Kneeling Woman all but forgotten.

Apparently, a stroke or freak hip injury had caused her to drop to the floor and she was unable to rise. The flesh of her skin had rotted into the carpet and Haftmann had to cut around her to free her; the rank smell of gangrene and feces had sent Haftmann's rookie partner reeling across the floorboards with his hands covering his mouth to keep from splashing the scene. The woman had urinated and defecated in that posture for weeks, and Haftmann had finally to pull shreds of the fouled carpet loose with his hands. What they never discovered, though, was who had visited the Kneeling Woman. *Who had come time after time put food in her mouth and water to her lips to enable her to survive all that time?* Someone had watched this woman's incredible agony in silence for a long, long time.

Haftmann snapped to, noticed that Meldrum had joined the crowd gaping at him, all waiting for Millimaki's punch line. "Yeah, Haftmann, you might say something's happened to her. That is, if you call a couple hundred stab wounds . . . *something*." Haftmann stepped around the puddle of melted snow and walked to his desk while their laughter booted him from behind. *Lousy cop humor.*

He took the runaway's file he'd brought from his office that morning and dropped it off on Mookie's cluttered desk and told Wendel to meet him in the lot. Outside the arctic air had blurred the landscape to a pockmarked whiteness that blasted the eyes and seared the tear ducts. Haftmann found small comfort looking over the cars, like multicolored windbreaks against the drifting snow. He questioned his own sanity lately and found comfort in a world that refused to conform to its outlines. *The furniture blurs sometimes when I try to focus on it. The little psychiatrist in Cleveland with the owlish eyes: So much is written about schizophrenia, so little is actually known . .*

The frozen lake was a couple hundred yards in the distance. Haftmann and his brother as boys used to clamber about the piled ice and sand heaved upwards into pyramids and hollowed ice caves. The wind stropped their foreheads with its razor keenness. He was thinking of Chaz and his cousin Spider when a candy-apple Cherokee roared into the lot and nearly sideswiped an Acura before lunging into a drift-filled slot beside Haftmann's Plymouth.

He recognized her as Jefferson-on-the-Lake's female new-hire – Sheila, Sherelle – a dispatcher whose partially disabled husband owned a small food concession on the Strip in summer. She leaped from the driver's side and scissor-walked through the drift piles. She cut her eyes to Haftmann, recognized him and mouthed the words *Late, damned weather* but the shrieking wind tore the sound away. Haftmann nodded.

He had heard that Millimaki was scouting her, sizing her up for seduction as he did with all the new women. "New fish," Millimaki called them. *Convict slang.* "Hey," Haftmann said as she stomped her boots on the concrete steps.

"You say something to me?" Her voice up close was raspy from early-morning cigarettes.

"Yeah," said Haftmann. "Stay away from that slob Millimaki. He can't fire you no matter what he says."

Her face contorted; she opened her mouth to say something, turned abruptly flung open the door. It seemed to Haftmann that she was sucked inside its vortex: another lost soul.

"That's OK," Haftmann said to nobody. "I

5

understand."

Haftmann heard Meldrum gunning Vice's unmarked Tercel, a piece of crap that the dope-pushing kids on the Strip knew by sound before they saw its approach. He waited for him to bring it around. He stepped around to the passenger side. Then he remembered something old Jack had said to him on patrol many years before, long before he joined the Jefferson Sheriff's. Before Micah had divorced him. Before a lot of things had happened. He was still a rookie working out of a westside substation. *Men have feverishly conceived a heaven only to find it insipid, and a hell only to find it ridiculous.* Not realizing he had said it aloud, he looked into Wendel's brown eyes. Haftmann rubbed at the open wound and then licked at the sere oozing from his palm.

"Haftmann, Mookie and those guys on third trick got a running bet that you'll never make it as a gumshoe."

"Fuck him."

"You know 'bout that other bet?"

"Yeah." Augie the Dwarf was taking action since Haftmann's celebrated retirement from the force, one that culminated in a three-day, on- and off-the-job booze binge that the moody loner would eat his gun before the year was out.

"Well, Thomas," said Wendel, "a lot of your former fellow officers are gonna have a tough time pretending to be sad at your wake if you lose that bet."

"But you'll cry, right?"

"Fucking-A, Thomas."

Haftmann looked over at his former partner, saw nothing in his wide brown face to say whether he was serious or joking and rolled down the window to spit. The February sky was pewter, full of stars yet; the Seven Sisters overhead, high and distant. "I heard about it yesterday," Wendel said. "Millimaki told Mookie he wanted to get

6

down for a couple more yards." Wendel stared at him, bunching his neck muscles in that familiar way he did in anticipation, but all he said was "Thomas, Thomas. That's why he don't give you the bum's rush every time you sashay into the station house, looking like you ready for a little workplace violence. He wants to see how his money doin'." Haftmann grunted. For some reason, he remembered that the full moon in early February was known as the Wolf Moon.

~ ~ ~

The Kneeling Woman's house looked mushroom in the muted light of dawn, but there was nothing else to distinguish it from the others on this quiet end of the street. Mostly retirees. The other end abutted the Strip, which in high summer teemed with lights and crowds. The drugs and drunks stayed at the lake end, mostly, although Vice had been keeping watch because of "unusual activity lately." Except for the yellow crime-scene ribbon snapping in the wind, it expressed nothing but the smug, tidy respectability the Chamber of Commerce worked so hard to promote. Cozy, decorous, a nice place to finish up your golden years watching the gulls flash and dive over the lake. One of the techs must have pulled the venetian blinds over the picture window and the horror within.

Inside Meldrum took a plastic bottle of talc out of his pocket and dusted his fingers and then pulled on a pair of latex gloves. It was a station house joke because he was very cautious around blood. He offered Haftmann an extra pair and returned them to his coat pocket when Haftmann shrugged. Wendel had once caught Millimaki doing an imitation of him for some detectives in the squad room. Millimaki was aping a black man's speech in the manner of a minstrel-show buffoon: "Oooooh, Lawdy, some ob dem AIDS bugs can jump nine feet! Das why I's gots to wear muh gloves!" In his college football days as a defensive end

7

at Ohio State, a sportswriter had described blocking Wendel Meldrum as the same as trying to block a bear with short arms. Haftmann had seen angry men grow suddenly quiet when Meldrum featured his special look. Wendel merely walked away.

"Wendel. Here. Kitchen." Haftmann pointed at some blood spatter at the bottom of the refrigerator and along the baseboard.

There were three large blood pools. The smallest, almost congealed, at the near corner of the refrigerator and two larger ones where the flow of blood had followed gravity's tug across the skewed floorboards in an eastern and southerly direction. The tile lozenges were smeared; someone had wiped up after, but the blood had collected at opposite ends of the kitchen and the tiny rivulet that fed the pools had traversed the mailman's line of sight in the early morning hours and he called it in. The blood must have been crimson then. Easy to see. Impossible to explain except one way. She was 68 years old. Haftmann thought she was in her nineties at the time he helped load her into the ambulance – dehydrated, bones showing through skin and noxious ammonia reek. One of the paramedics stood back and let Haftmann work on her. She was incoherent but conscious. *And that other smell too. Death, how people smelled when they were about to die of cancer or some awful disease.*

Haftmann touched the surface of the pool that had collected nearest the kitchen table just enough to jitter the surface. The sinuous thread of blood connecting the pools had already oxidized to a crusty brown.

Haftmann flipped through the crime-scene officer's preliminary report.

"Who caught it?" Meldrum asked.

Haftmann cut his eyes to the bottom of the page. "Boomhower. He's OK."

"That means he signed every page, right? Got all that forensics jargon right too, I'll bet?"

"You know it. We'll be working for him one of these days."

"No we won't either, Thomas. And you know why. Millimaki's got too many fingers in too many pies."

"So, Wendel, what about it?"

"This much blood. It looks like frenzy to me. You remember that case four, five summers back? Old-timer laid off from Reactive Metals said his wife always used to stack the refrigerator full of vegetables, hiding the milk. Said he wasn't going to take that shit anymore."

"Yeah, I remember. His boy called us in. Not this time. No family. You worked drug detail then. What about the usual lowlifes we have hanging around all year? Maybe a loser looking to score an old lady's retirement stash."

"Could be. I don't know. We had only a few cases this far away from the Strip. Nobody on Neighborhood Watch reported anything. Usual drunken teens turfing lawns. Crap like that. We may have us a real psychopath here, Thomas, but since everyone says you know the Kneeling Woman, why don't you just save us some time and tell me what you're thinking?"

"Later. Let's finish the house first. You want up or down?"

"Whichever. You pick."

"I'll take up. Bedrooms are my specialty." He winked into Meldrum's large mocha face with a fake leer, and realized with a hollow gutwrench that *that* was exactly and all he was, finally: a voyeur of other people's tragedies.

Two hours later, they met in the dining room and compared notes. "OK, we did the drill," said Meldrum, "now give. What's the story?"

Wendel wanted his take. It was unofficial, of course. Haftmann's imminent retirement meant, by departmental regs, he was no more a cop and shouldn't have been let onto the crime scene.

He hadn't even been cleared formally as a suspect or a wit.

Haftmann told him what he knew about the Kneeling Woman. After packing her off to the county hospital in Jefferson, Haftmann figured she wasn't going to make it – he'd seen a lot of dying and he figured, with an ex-cop's cynicism, Wendel would be doing all the paperwork once the death certificate was issued. So he went inside and poked around, riffled through paper in drawers, cabinets – still not convinced that this wasn't just another sad joke nature inflicted on the species – a woman knocked to her knees by a near-fatal stroke, and some halfwit Good Samaritan drops by to spoon a little food into her from time to time. He'd seen crazier things in his years as a cop.

But something stuck in his craw right from the start. *Her silence, the appalling suffering. Who witnessed it? Who put baby food in her mouth and held a glass of water to her lips while she quietly rotted into the floor?*

Haftmann had to be grabbed by Meldrum's thick hand before he went after Mookie back at the station house because of one crack too many about cheap carpeting. No photos on the wall, no family. One odd, personal item in the living room: Haftmann found a cheap plywood easel in the wrong position to catch light. There was a reproduction of an artist's sketch on it that Haftmann was to learn after visiting the head of the art department of the local college was a Goya, its title (Professor Burton Timkin, bearded like D. H. Lawrence, trilled the *r*'s): *El sueño de la razon produce monstruos.* Like most Lake cops, Haftmann spoke pidgin Spanish because of the influx of migrant workers who came to pick grapes for Welch's: "The dream of reason produces monsters." *Monsters.*

("Well," said Wendel, "No doubt about one thing. She

had a monster somewhere in her past and it sure as hell caught up with her last night.")

Haftmann filled in the rest on their way to the morgue to see Doc Harris and get the autopsy report. Her name was Birgit Helga Frömm. She was born in Kleinmachnow near what used to be considered East Berlin before German Reunification. Haftmann had seen her naturalization certificate (Americanized to Brigitte Frome) and dated just three years ago. He also saw a university degree from Jena, dated fifteen years ago, with a specialty in German literature. The bedroom was spartan with the same familiar exception: no photos, no portraits, no tokens of memory. He remembered the air from the first time – cloying, sulfurous, rancid like the smell of menses. The air upstairs was stifling but no blood smell wafted upwards.

~ ~ ~

Haftmann knew Doc Harris wouldn't release an official M.E. report this soon, but he knew there were two salient facts: ligature marks around her neck had almost severed the strap muscles. The killer used a coathanger wire; black paint flecks were visible in the folds of skin. The knife wounds were postmortem. Haftmann guessed that because of the telltale blood spatter – or lack of it. Arterial spray is messy and leaves distinct tracks, especially when a victim is in death throes. This blood had one-way spatter insignificant to the volume of blood released.

Haftmann accounted for it this way: someone wanted to screw up forensics and assumed draining the body of blood would do it. The killer must have spent time squeezing the torso of blood to keep it from settling in the trunk.

Haftmann could not figure it: walls without photos, a Goya sketch, a house with secrets. Folded behind the

painting and crimped into a corner that the easelback
would hide were two pieces of paper. The top one was a
torn portion of cheap newsprint with a circled horoscope
for Pisces. It said this:

> PISCES *(Feb. 20-March 20): A lot depends
> on your willingness to take another's
> lack of charm, consideration, and coop-
> eration in stride. Personally and
> financially you certainly appear to be on a
> knife's edge. However, Friday's Full Moon
> in Cancer must bring a decidedly unhappy
> and costly cycle to a close.*

The other was a receipt from a Cleveland
dermatologist specializing in laser surgery who charged
$1,200 to remove a tattoo.

Back at his office on the Strip Haftmann called in a
favor and ordered up all personnel records from the
previous November to the past week. He wrote down what
he needed and called Wendel: "Get your gun. You and I are
going to see a state cop I know. Call Judge Stevens at the
Court House and tell him we're coming to see him. Then
you have to make an arrest."

~ ~ ~

Three continual hours of telephoning overseas enabled
Haftmann to backtrack through the dead woman's long,
unhappy life. The Bureau of Naturalization in Washington
D. C., The Justice Department's Office of Special
Investigation (Haftmann's last and biggest favor called in
for this), Interpol in three European capitals and, finally,
the Simon Wiesenthal Center in Vienna.

He didn't know it all but he knew enough from these
sketchy conversations in broken English and pidgin
German, thanks to a stalwart German grandmother and a

capacity to pick up languages (*another trait of incipient schizophrenia*, said a Cleveland psychiatrist, after Haftmann's first good shooting as a rookie), to put together a sketchy outline of her past. At the age of 25 she had been sent on to Auschwitz from Sachsenhausen, where her parents were taken and, presumably, killed. She never found them after her release. She entered KZ Auschwitz, Barracks F in the spring of 1943 and was assigned work at the hospital run by the infamous Angel of Auschwitz himself, Dr. Josef Mengele who, among other atrocities, spent much time cross-matching the blood of genetic twins.

Apparently she was "promoted" from there to the Puff, as it was called by the SS: a brothel for officers' use and, rarely, *Kapos* who had earned special privileges in the camp. Official SS records in Bonn note that Hans-Jurgen Sedlmeier, recipient of an Iron Cross second-class for pulling two men from a burning tank on the Russian front in 1942, was reassigned to Auschwitz because of a pronounced limp and was to report for duty in the spring of 1943. Russian documents returned to East Germany after the war were only recently returned to the Federal Republic of Germany last year. The fall of the Berlin Wall, and shortly afterward the collapse of the *Hauptverwaltung Aufklarung*, East Germany's secret police, eventually brought to light the name of the officer who ran the women of the SS brothel in Auschwitz. Handwritten notes of witnesses confirm a dashing figure in his SS tunic, white-blonde hair cut skull-close to the sides of his head; Waffen SS cap tilted rakishly to one side.

Haftmann thought of the bloated face decades later sans jackboots and military tunic. Chief John Millimaki, favorite son of the Jefferson-on-the-Lake Chamber of Commerce. Chief of police for the last two decades. War hero. Nazi pimp. Woman killer.

13

~ ~ ~

"So, Haftmann, c'mon, give. I was in that house with you. How did you know it was Millimaki?"

"You're a great vice cop, Wendel, but you have a few things to learn about homicide."

"Like what? Man, how did you know that an old lady's horoscope and a doctor's bill would lead you to Millimaki?"

"Just this: The time frame was too neat. The woman is released from the hospital and dead in a week. Coincidence? The killer had to be local. Furthermore, he had to know cop patrols and operations with pinpoint accuracy. He *kept coming back to that woman's house.* He wanted her alive. She was the last link to his past. She had something that could expose him. He kept her alive under that god-awful torture for weeks but she never gave up what she had. All these years thinking he was safe. Just one thing that could give him away, and he didn't know how to go about it until he read an article in the paper a couple years back about experimental surgery with lasers. You can remove a tattoo with no telltale scar.

"What scar, Haftmann?"

"The scar that would be left under his armpit in conventional removal of a tattoo. Laser surgery knocks the ink particles loose beneath the skin without affecting the skin's surface. All SS officers were tattooed under their armpits with their blood group numbers in case surgery had to be performed under battlefield conditions. Himmler's idea. They were too valuable as specimens of the Aryan ideal. How could Sedlemeir have guessed that one of the few women who survived the death camps – inmates themselves killed many of the women who were forced to have sex with the SS – would later turn up in this resort town?"

"So how *did* she know it was this Sedlemeir for sure?"

14

"She didn't. I spoke to the doctor in Cleveland myself. They both called in to have tattoos removed within days of each other. He just happened to schedule them on the same day. She went there for the same purpose without any idea she would meet a man who had terrorized her from her past. She wanted the number removed from her wrist. Doc Harris said she didn't have it removed, even though she had made an appointment to have it done. All I could learn from the dermatologist was that he had spoken to her over the phone when she made the appointment in late October. She told him she waited until this late in her life because she was terrified of knives."

Meldrum let that hang in the air for a while, then he said: "OK, so tell me this. The doctor had no idea he was putting these two people together? Shee-it, c'mon, man. That ain't right."

"Call it chance, fate, luck – I don't know."

"But how did she get the receipt from the doctor's office?"

"I'm not sure. She knew she had to have proof, and I checked her telephone calls from the day after the appointment in Cleveland. She called the Wiesenthal Center six times during the following week and another 12 times altogether. She knew a handwriting specimen wouldn't be enough to convince anyone, especially a false signature practiced for decades, and photos aren't foolproof. Everybody changes. Millimaki-Sedlemeir had the face he deserved but it wasn't the same as a newly commissioned Waffen SS officer in the photos Vienna faxed me. The tattoo was everything to her. She had to prove it and that was why Sedlemeir tortured her for weeks.

"That's why you kept yelling at old Doc Harris to look at her wrist, right?"

"Yeah, I knew that if she had her tattoo, something

wasn't adding up."

"The rest is guesswork, I suppose. She must have been a brave old woman. Imagine getting that receipt right from under the nose of a man who was part of her hell on earth. Tough woman, Haftmann. Very strong."

"She had to be, Wendel. It was Auschwitz."

"Makes me sick to be human sometimes."

"Feature it this way: she concocted her scheme when she saw Millimaki come in for his appointment. A horrible memory flashback burst free: Hans-Jurgen Sedlemeir right in front of her, fat, aged, gimp-legged, but him all the same. Everything in the flesh that made her life the terrible thing it was. She made a moment's agonizing decision. The receptionist in the waiting room said she remembers our woman. She saw her rip a corner out of a magazine – the one from the astrology magazine I found behind the Goya sketch. The other was that she doesn't remember actually *handing* the receipt to Millimaki after he wrote the check. She remembers there was the sound of a scuffle in the hallway – our woman confronted him, started screaming at him – and somehow she managed to get the receipt from him without his knowing it. It isn't possible to know. She must have learned some terrible survival skills in the camp. Could be she picked his pocket. She had too much experience in being close to males pressing against her."

"What happens now? With *him* I mean?"

"Millimaki may talk, but I doubt it. Mookie told me that the state attorney general's office has sent people to him all week. Maybe they're cutting a deal to save the state some bad publicity. Who needs real Nazis in Ohio with all the fake ones running around the countryside?"

At that moment a dispatcher approached him with a message. It was the same young woman he had confronted in the snow-filled parking lot that morning he and Wendel went to the Kneeling Woman's house. She smiled as she handed it to him. It was from the new Chief-of-Police appointee, Wilson Boomhower:

Thomas Haftmann, private investigations, assisting acting case officer W. Meldrum, pending homicide investigation of female decedent no. F-93-6. Call Harris/county morgue/Sheriff's Office, Jefferson ASAP.

"What's this, Wendel?"

"Oh, man, I forgot to mention it with all this other shit going on. This morning, they found your runaway. Mookie was looking for the methane probe."

"God damn it, Wendel, they're just kids." Haftmann folded the paper neatly and went downstairs to make the call.

No Escape, No Turning Back

I was fatigued from the long drive home with a sulky runaway teen. I had finally tracked her from one of the shabbier bars along Jefferson-on-the-Lake's notorious Strip (dubbed Little Minnesota by the locals) to another shabby bar in Marianna, Florida. Walking inside my own apartment through dust motes and stale Ohio air, I felt the same itchy foreboding that usually precedes bad news or an illness. I scanned my brother's letter first.

The letter was three pages and dated 23 June, which I remembered had been a Thursday because that was the day I found the girl and her lesbian lover in the trailer where they had set up housekeeping. Jarrell's letters were always faintly embarrassing. I don't know why exactly. He was my fraternal twin, and sometimes I felt I had his thoughts in my head. He had a disarming self-honesty that was never my strong suit.

Lately he was going through that bad patch married people speak of after they have settled differences or resolved grievances or, mostly, postponed revenge until another day.

Jarrell's handwriting was crabbed and ugly, a fact that got him tagged with the nickname Spider when we were kids. He owned a tavern in Wyandotte with a beer garden that ended on the Detroit River, but his house was on Grosse Isle, expensive and gaudy. I considered the place neurotic and very hard to like. In fact, the house was much like Edie, Jarrell's younger wife, a woman I also found hard to like.

He wrote:

. . . No, everything you said is true, brother mine. I can't be offended by the truth. The truth is that I think I am a coward when it comes to dealing with the consequences of putting a stop to my situation. If I move out she will begin to systematically use the children against me and spit more bile into their lives than they now have. I get sick of my own despair. Sometimes I think that even if I were divorced and separated that I would still have to carry the baggage. I just don't think she would let me alone. Would I have to move, abandon my kids and assume a new identity? All these thoughts go through my mind.

. . . Maybe all she really wants is to feel loved and respected and valued. I thought recently in this context that love is the only mystical force that does in fact touch everyone's life. What a hell to live in if you couldn't love someone and spent your whole life fighting and bullying the people around you to love you. The irony is that they did love you or could love you or would love you if you would give them half a chance. In Edie's case she will not listen to her rational mind and deal with the imbalances in her life. I can't deal with them for her. And you are right, it is killing me bit by bit . . .

He had signed off "As ever."

I saw him in my mind's eye: walking me to my car and apologizing for Edie still asleep upstairs, he hummed a piece of Schiller's "Ode to Joy," a nervous habit he had picked up when he didn't want to talk.

The second letter took moments to read; it was only a two-sentence paragraph, the date was 25 June and the letterhead announced Duffy, Fuqua, & Rosenthal, Attorneys at Law, with a bank building address in Wyandotte:

> *Please contact Sheriff's Office, Wyandotte, (313)-882-9864 as soon as possible regarding case no. M-92-8. Refer enquiries Det. Sgt. Thorpe, ext. 215, who is case officer pending homicide investigation of decedent, advised your brother, Haftmann, David Jarrell. DOD 23 May 1992.*

The cold, clipped syntax of the message burst in me like a sob and sent me staggering down the hallway. A spume of bitter, yellow vomit splattered the toilet seat before I could focus my eyes well enough to get the lid up and send the rest of my stomach's contents noisily into the bowl. Twenty minutes passed before the spasms ceased, but I was left half-blind by a searing pain rippling across my forehead in intervals that made dialing the Wyandotte Sheriff's office almost impossible. Finally I got it right and asked for Detective Thorpe's extension.

While I listened to the hollow clicking noises bouncing electric impulses from Ohio to Michigan, I thought of my last drunk and the reason for it: Micah, my then-wife, had set the letter ending our marriage on the coffee table where I found it after my shift. I wanted to be drunk fast and then I didn't want to be drunk at all, but it was too late, a pint of Jim Beam too late, and I couldn't get the shock of her words out of my skull – all the worse for being the clichés of ten thousand such letters written in trite phrases of self-justification to absent, beguiled or just stupid spouses oblivious to the coming disaster.

I had mercifully exorcised the words she wrote but not the effect, and I often wondered since that time which combination of dubious traits had earmarked my own failures and cost me such anguish over a woman I still loved and hated. The marriage was gone, and I wasn't a homicide cop any more. Since self-honesty is an easy casualty of survival, I had few professional ambitions or ideals left about human nature to worry over.

Thorpe was efficient yet human in his response, an unusual combination in a veteran detective. Wyandotte is small, pleasant, casual to the eye – no prevision of Detroit down the road – so maybe he had not yet seen his share of brutality to shed that note of compassion in his voice. He told me what he could, which was little enough: Jarrell had been killed during a hold-up attempt at his tavern last Thursday at 1:45 in the morning. One other patron had been killed, and a few hundred dollars were taken. The killer threw gasoline around the room after he murdered my brother and the customer, but his torch job was badly done – a lot of smoke damage but the structure of the bar was intact.

To my question "Why?" he had the cop's sense to know I wasn't questioning my brother's mindless killing but expressing bewilderment at the odd circumstance of a stickup man's delaying his escape to torch a place he just robbed.

"Makes no sense to me either," said Thorpe. It wasn't done to create a diversion because there was no need. The killer hit Jarrell's bar when there weren't many people in the place at that time: only six customers including the second victim, a biker type of no fixed address. Edie had seen it happen – saw her husband's brains blown out of his head. The others were serious drinkers, all locals.

Descriptions of the killer from the witnesses had gone out fast. Michigan's Criminal Investigation Division had faxed back a composite within hours and the killer's N.C.I.C. number and jacket were on Thorpe's desk by midmorning.

He was a Jackson State con named Richie Landross, only three weeks back on the street and a rap sheet of armed robbery convictions going back to his teens. His last trip to Jacktown cost him eight years of hard time when killers from the worst prison in the state were being steadily paroled through the system after four years. His parole officer died in 1989 while Landross was completing his last issue for holding up a bar on Livernois. Thorpe read me the telex Michigan C.I.D. had clipped to the rap sheet: Richard "Landy" Landross, age 39, last address on Gratiot Avenue in Roseville just above Ten Mile in Eastpointe. Rode with a biker gang in his twenties, tried to set up a Harley Davidson parts store but was nailed selling guns and dope out the back by Detroit vice in '81. Got his first nickel in '82 and became a regular ever since. Thorpe added:

"On his last job, a convenient store in Ecorse, he pistol-whipped a clerk so bad she had to have 45 stitches in her face. I'm looking at his rap sheet now. As he got older he got worse as so many of this kind do. More violence all around. All of it unprovoked. He'd get the money and stay around to beat on people. One of those kind that if he had been a dog society would have put him down years ago."

Thorpe called a few people he knew at Jackson State Penitentiary to get a lead where Landross might be inclined to hang out. Everything pointed to Detroit, some hole-in-the-wall biker bar where he could lie low until the heat cooled.

I thanked him and said I'd be coming to Detroit to help square things for my brother's family. He gave me a time and place to meet him at the precinct when I got to town.

Around dawn I collapsed, the bottle dropping like a lead weight from my hand, exhausted from the drink I

23

hated and needed, onto the floor next to the tattered velour couch I was calling bed these days.

When I awoke hours later, I had the right smoldering temperature behind my eyes. I was pure, seething hatred and my hate was named Richie "Landy" Landross.

I couldn't get my hands to stop shaking; my body's air-conditioning was working overtime. I thought of my father and how the sweat rolled off when his shift at the steel mill ended, and he'd down four, five beers at the local bar. He'd look up from his bar stool when my mother sent me or Jarrell to fetch him home, and I'd see his smile when I came in to the bar, blinking until my eyes adjusted and there's he'd be in his usual stool upending a salt shaker into his beer. I was glad that bar had burned down years ago. He died from a brain concussion inflicted by some professional wrestler from Cleveland passing through. My father went to defend a friend of his from this man. He lasted thirty-four days with a brain so swollen they had to cut open his skull. The man who beat him to death disappeared after the fight. I often wondered if maybe my becoming a homicide cop and Jarrell a tavern owner wasn't the same thing, after all—two sons looking to bring their father back. Now there was just a brother.

Back at the motel, I called Edie to see how she was doing. I don't know why I asked, but I did.

"How much insurance did Jarrell have on the place?"

"Oh, a million or so. The place was worth twice that."

"Did he have anything on himself?"

"That's personal, Thomas."

"Edie, answer me. The cops will be asking sooner or later."

"We both had million-dollar policies on each other. Jarrell took them out when we were married. If you're thinking—"

"It's just a question, Edie."

"It's a cop question, you sonofabitch—"

The click and the sob reached my ear at the same time. I had a way with women.

I had switched to Tanqueray when Thorpe called me.

"Could mean something, could mean nothing," he said.

"Give," I said. I was already bleary-eyed and half-asleep in front of a television show that featured obese toddlers and a smarmy host oscillating like a weather vane between fake pity and clucks of disapproval. The studio audience at this daytime freak show laughed and gasped at the videos of these overweight kids raiding the fridge and stuffing their faces with a pornographic fidelity to their gaping and masticating mouths. Their tiny hands had lines around the wrists like rubber bands.

"Did you hear me, Haftmann? She knew Carnes," he said simply.

"I—what did you say?"

"Put the fuckin' bottle down or whatever you're sucking on and listen because I don't have time to waste on a boozehound."

"Start over. I'm listening." He had my full attention.

"Your brother's wife knew Carnes. He used to pimp girls along the Cass Corridor eight, nine years ago."

Before I could ask what that had to do with Edie, I knew. Knew it in my solar plexus.

"Edie used to be one of his girls."

It's a minor miracle I made it through that viper's nest of bisecting interstate highways downtown Detroit that clotted rush-hour traffic and knotted Interstates 94, 75, and the Ford Expressway within a half-mile of one another. I was on automatic pilot and thinking of the questions tumbling around in my brain. Every guy I know who likes to bet always tells you they saw it coming, knew it was going to turn out that way all the time. None of those guys ever got rich from gambling, and I've loaned a few of them some money after one of their sure things fizzled.

But I still couldn't feature it: Edie was a cheerleader and a prom queen. Her father wasn't exactly rich, but he made a good living fixing the teeth of the kids whose fathers were very rich. Even had a house in Grosse Pointe once. Her mother was an accountant for a tire-purchasing firm.

Thorpe said she had arrests up to the age of twenty-five and then she goes off the radar—it was around this time she met my brother. She had several aliases when she hooked but her favorites were Bambi and Snow. Thorpe said she left Carnes' stable, but her record stops there. That's where my questions were going to start and so I eased off the gas a bit to get myself calmer. I had punched the sun visor off its track. Carnes and Landross. . . and now Edie, beautiful Edie. It didn't make any sense. Maybe she left Carnes after he turned crossdresser; maybe Landross made him an offer. Too many maybes. Edie had the only answers that mattered now.

I recalled Thorpe's last words when he dropped the bomb on me:

"Stay away from this from now on, Haftmann. You're an out-of-state private investigator. Landross is the kind penitentiaries were made for—impossible to rehabilitate, remorseless. He'll die or he'll get old but he won't reform and he won't quit."

"I hear you," I said.

"Haftmann, leave Edie to us. You don't know every—"

I was past Allen Park barreling down Telegraph and just missed fishtailing a Datsun. The exit to my dead brother's house was just ahead.

I wanted to be a private eye because I saw the uselessness of being a cop who had to follow protocol. I wanted to be my own agent of justice and pompous though that sounds, it's what I still believe.

I hammered at the door, and when she opened it in her house coat, I lost every question I had gone over in my mind. Something in my eyes must have betrayed me because she turned on her heel without a word and was heading back to the kitchen. I walked in and headed for her. She had the phone in her hand and was punching in numbers. One hand was tucked into her robe but one heavy white breast freed itself.

I grabbed her by the hair and jerked her head backward. She released the phone and gasped in pain. I turned her face toward me and gave her one hard ringing slap across the side of the head that flung her backwards into the kitchen island. Her legs splayed open and exposed her all the way to her pubis. She jerked spasmodically for a moment and I could see her eyes regain focus. Her mouth glistened with pink blood over her white teeth. I had hit her very hard. She tried to get up by bracing her back against the island but lacked strength and slumped down to the floor. Her bathrobe was open from chest to crotch, the belt uselessly unable to restrain the magnificent body. Her eyes were, however, clear now. She spat a gob of bloody mucous at me.

"You motherfucker."

"Tell me about Carnes first. How you met him. Where you were, how old. I'll tell you when to stop."

"You kiss my fucking ass, you fucking cocksucker."

"Reverting to your whore days, Edie? They weren't very far from the surface, were they? When did you leave Carnes?"

"Fuck you. You think you can beat the shit out of me, big man? I've been beta up by men before, and a whole lot tougher than you, faggot."

"I see. So Carnes being a crossdresser—"

"He may have worn a dress but he was twice the man you were. He had a cock like a mustang and he could fuck for hours—"

I reached down and hit her across the jaw just hard enough to rattle her head.

She opened her legs wider.

"Have a look, Thomas. I know you'd like some of this. Jarrell always thought you were jealous of him because you married that lawyer bitch. I always thought she was a lesbian, and I bet him I could have her licking my pussy inside—"

She flinched and held up her hands to her face. I don't remember raising my hand to hit her again, but my fist was closed and cocked over my shoulder. I was breathing hard.

"Just tell me about Carnes before the cops come. Maybe I can help. Not for your sake, you cunt. For my brother."

She stood up but when I reached out for the underside of her arm to help her, she threw my hand off. She leaned one hip against the island and covered the front of her robe with her hand.

"Well, why not? What's it matter now? Maybe you won't believe me, but I loved your brother."

"Spare me, bitch. Just start talking."

"I worked for Carnes a few months. I started tricking in high school to make money for drugs. I had a serious cocaine habit by the time I graduated. Nobody in my family knew." She laughed at some bittersweet memory I couldn't share.

"They'd comment on how good I looked when I lost weight but it was because I couldn't keep food down when I went too long without a fix. There was the fear of AIDS or STDs like now. I met Carnes outside Wayne State."

"Why there?"

"He said he saw me picking up college boys and professors. He said he could hook me up with respectable clients like businessmen, lawyers, other professionals. I wouldn't have to work the streets."

"How long did that last?"

"Couple years, maybe a few months beyond that. Then he went to jail. I found out later he sold me. I never saw him again until the—shooting."

"So you started tricking for Richie Landross?"

"Yeah, at first." She looked me in the eyes. "You know something? Jarrell knew your wife was going to leave you

29

before you did. He said you were one of those men who have no love inside them."

"You said 'at first.' What changed?"

"The clients were all rich. In fact, they were some of the biggest names in Detroit, too big even for the society pages. I saw the insides of more houses on Grosse Pointe than some of the Fords. I was very popular." She dabbed a finger at the split in her lip.

"Landross was your new pimp."

She looked at me. Her eyes were fierce despite the smirk.

"He was my husband," Edie said. "I'm done talking to you. Now get the fuck out of my house."

~ ~ ~

I guzzled more booze at my motel, and when the Tanqueray ran out, I found a party store and bought vodka, the highest-proof. I was passed out when the trilling of the phone broke through my dreams. All of us, Micah, Edie, Jarrell, and I were standing on a hill overlooking railroad tracks glistening in the sun. Micah, Jarrell, and Edie held hands and headed down the hillside to walk on the tracks. From my vantage, I could see black clouds of roiling smoke from a distant curve. It was one of those chuffing, old-time trains, not a diesel engine. Plenty of time to warn them, I thought. I started down the hill but the slope grew steeper and my shouts of warning couldn't penetrate their laughter. Then my legs were in muck midway to my thighs and I knew I couldn't get there in time. They were all going to die.

"Jesus Christ, Haftmann. I've been calling for hours." It was Thorpe.

The curtains were shut. I had no idea whether it was night or dark or morning of the next day.

"I told you to stay away from her," he said.

The booze fog hadn't lifted. "Who?"

"Edie. We found in her in the kitchen with her throat cut."

~ ~ ~

Thorpe waved me past the cops at the yellow tape. They had klieg lights from a portable generator pointed at the front door. They gave me a pair of cotton booties. I saw Thorpe in the kitchen standing above Edie's open, outstretched hands. Close up, I saw the beautiful blonde hair matted with blood and the jagged tears in her flesh. Her hands were lacerated with defensive stab wounds. She wore the same house coat I had seen her in but the rusty splotches showed where the knife had got through and there was a large pool of it beneath her body where it had flowed to equilibrium.

"None of the cuts were fatal," he said. Not deep enough from what the medical examiner can determine at this point. Looks as though she bled out, went into shock and died from blood loss."

Her ravaged body belied her face. It still held true to her bones and the lovely high cheekbones Jarrell used to gush over in his letters to me.

A detective near Thorpe said. "From the looks of it, he damn near exsanguinated her. You could wring more than a few points from what's left in the corpse."

Thorpe looked pained. "You believe it? *America's Most Wanted* called. They want to do a segment."

I looked at him.

"She'll be posted in Detroit. Wyandotte doesn't have the facilities. You can meet me there tomorrow. Go back to your motel, sleep. Your eyes look like a dog pissed in them."

"Where could he be?"

"I said go the fuck home."

I left him there haloed in klieg lights and blood spatter. They cops said Landross would be hiding in Detroit with the rest of the human rats and cockroaches. I wanted to see him in leg irons and a Kansas vest more than I wanted to see God.

The powder blue bed sheet had been changed and the maid had plumped the pillow in my absence. A touch of class in my flophouse dive. I could have fallen into a mine shaft as effortlessly as I fell into that bed. Then, as it always happens when you're tired to the point that your own eyeballs squeak from rubbing, the brain won't lock down for the night. My mind kept galloping ahead of my body, and I'd wake with a tremble unsure whether I was still in the bed or driving in the car down one of Detroit's unforgiving streets. My room smelled rancid from the reek of alcohol. I looked at my watch: 3:05 in the a.m. I had slept longer than I thought. But I wasn't going to sleep any longer because something I remembered from my first visit to Jarrell's new house kept nipping at a corner of my brain.

I took a cold shower and stepped out of the stall shaking. I put on clean dark clothes and grabbed a titanium flashlight from my travel kit.

I drove through the dark to the crime scene. All three houses on my brother's side were unlit. The outage didn't affect the other side of the street fortunately because I could see the shadow of a sedan near my brother's driveway. Probably a black-and-white standing watch. If the cops inside were cooping, they wouldn't see me from this distance. I had long since unscrewed the overhead car light from habit. I kept a tire iron under my car seat for emergencies. I left the flashlight on the car seat. Even dozing cops wouldn't miss that. I waited for clouds to scud over the moon's surface long enough to make my dash from the side of the road. I fixed the edges of trees, hedges, and house in my mind and hoped I could triangulate a path to where I wanted to go.

Near the atrium, I saw wisps of vapor rising up. It was the vent pipe from the bomb shelter Jarrell had inherited with the house. He showed it to me and laughed at the cold-war hysteria that made the original owner have it built. Warm air from the tunnel below met cooling air above ground. I honed in on the curling vapor once I knew I was close to the back of the house.

Near the French windows, I rolled my shirt into a ball and broke the glass to let myself inside. I let my eyes adjust. I had already mentally mapped the inside from memory. I walked toward the corridor through the kitchen where black blood was still pooled like glistening oil slick on the floor. Jarrell's music room was next, its white piano imported from Austria, barely visible in the light from the sheers. I moved past the family rec room and eased my way along the wall, ducking beneath windows as I came to them. I had my hand on the latch leading to the basement. The steps were carpeted. At the bottom of the stairs I waited listening for any sounds and felt my pupils stretch all the way to the rims, but nothing seemed to be moving and I could pick out no silhouettes in the perfect blackness.

I saw them but wasn't sure what it was—at first my eyes might have been playing tricks in the darkness. Little pinpricks of light; they danced and winked like radioactive dust motes.

I gripped the tire iron hard in my sweaty mitt and inched toward the filmy light. When I reached the place where the lights disappeared, I knew I was standing in front of the door leading to the bomb shelter's tunnel. There was no knob from this side. Jarrell had taken that out when the kids were young years ago, but he left plywood sheeting over the door and secured it with hasps. My hand gently scored the surface and confirmed their positions above and below. I placed the beveled tip of the iron into the lower hasp and as slowly as I could, I strained the screws loose, once free, I cupped them in my hand and loosened the bracket where it had been scored into the wood. I worked top and bottom, opposite pairs. The top was harder to part and the screws didn't part as quietly as the others. My heart was racing so hard I wasn't sure that I could tell inside noise from outside.

All I had now was planking over a hole. I could feel the change in air temperature. I thought about waiting for dawn, but I knew that was just my fear talking. There was nothing else to do now that I had gone this far with it.

I jammed the edge of the tire iron midway down the planking and jerked it free. The crack of splintering wood was out of all proportion and my right side was scored with splinters. I threw myself inside and felt cold concrete abrade the skin from the palms of my hand. At that moment, a bright light exploded with a spear of orange-blue-yellow flame. I smelled the cordite at the same instant I rolled hard to my left until my shoulder smashed into the foundation wall. Another terrible explosion of sound and light where I had been just a second earlier. My hunch was right and it was going to get me killed in another second, two at the most. I saw Landross's outline. He was backlit against a shiny steel surface and I could see from his motions he was jacking more rounds into the over-under Mossberg.

I got to my feet slower than I should have but the fist-sized chunk he had blown out of the wood had taken some of my flesh with it and I was nauseated and dizzy. My right side was raw but at least I wasn't holding my intestines in my hands, which was Landross's intent.

I heard the metallic clatter of the gun hitting the cement; then I heard an animal noise that must have come from Landross's throat because the next thing I felt was his body on my chest and his fists striking my head and neck. He couldn't see any better than I despite his time f\down in the darkness, but his punches were going to do their work if I didn't snap to. I couldn't get his body off my chest; he seemed to cling tighter the more I thrashed. Every time he landed a punch, it took me longer to shake it off. Soon I'd be helpless and he could take his time. I managed to deflect one of his blows and strike upward. I caught his jaw but did no damage. Then I felt his thumbs crawling up my face gouging tracks through the skin on their way to my eye sockets.

My right hand was on his wrist but I couldn't break his momentum. I was going to have jelly for eyeballs in moments and I had black, existential moment of letting go, letting it happen, but my hand must have dropped away because I felt a sharp sensation and closed it around a long piece of splintered wood. I took a breath and waited while he set himself for the plunge into my eyes, his forearms extended straight like pistons. In that pause before he bunched his muscles, I thrust my hand up and over his elbows at a point where I hoped his own eyes were vulnerable, staring straight down at my contorted face, neither of us able to see the other in the tumult. I felt contact, then liquid, then warmth roll down my wrist and forearm. I never heard him scream.

Suddenly I was weightless, floating in the dark. I heard loud sucking gasps of air and knew it was my own tortured breath. I felt a sob like a bubble erupt from my throat and prayed it wasn't vomit or I'd die because I knew without even trying to move that a black hole was already sucking me down into its vortex.

The cops heard the first muzzle blast, but they took their time securing the premises as good cops will always do regardless whether you're spouting blood from all orifices just feet away. It's training and protocol. I'm not complaining. They found me. They found Landross just inches from me with a broken spike of wood sticking into his brain and interrupted a Norwegian rat sniffing at the blood on the deck.

Thorpe met me at the emergency room where I was having stitches in my shoulder, arms, and neck. There was a foul-smelling plaster smeared over my battered side. A steel cup held fifteen pellets the internist and one nurse had plucked from my aching side one at a time. Their conversation seemed amiable and I heard the word subcutaneous at least six times, but then I was reeling from the dope they had given me.

Thorpe was not sympathetic. I could imagine the paperwork I was causing him.

As usual, he said, I was running around half-cocked and ruining the investigation. I blinked dizzily and half-heard. He seemed to feel it a waste of time. My eyes were nearly shut from the gouging Landross had managed to get in, but the doctor said it wasn't permanent.

He did have some good news for me, though. The state wasn't going to prosecute me. I was encouraged to leave right after the funeral. Edie's body wouldn't be released, however. She would stay in a cold-storage locker in downtown Detroit until all the pieces of the puzzle were laid end to end. That, too, was protocol. One grubby private investigator had killed the object of the state's biggest manhunt since Coral Eugene Watts. It was an embarrassment to Michigan law enforcement. I needed to go away quietly after deposing my statement. The *Detroit News* was going to be told that police "acting on an informed hunch" stormed the residence of murder victim Jarrell Haftmann, "whose brother was visiting the residence at the time" and come upon the deceased, "a person of interest in the ongoing investigation," according to homicide detectives on scene.

I was on my way out of town when I pulled over at another one of those party stores I would remember for the rest of my life as the saddest places I had been. I waited for a local dope slinger wearing a bandanna tied so low over his forehead it looked like rabbit ears bouncing every time he wagged his head. He saw me looking at him, scowled, and called "motherfucker" before sashaying off with paisley underwear exposing the crack of his ass. I watched him dash across the street through heavy traffic, his high-top sneaker laces untied, and wondered whether, if he got hit by a car, he'd call the driver "a motherfucker," too.

I asked Thorpe to meet me at a bar I saw across the street.

"What the fuck are you doing so far down Gratiot?" he asked. "You've got a death wish."

I was sipping my third scotch when he slid into the booth.

"I should know well enough by now not to ask if it's too early for that," he said.

I said, "I'm pretty sure I know all the story, but I'd like to hear it from you."

He sighed and made that pained face at me.

"I never said any of this," he said and leaned toward me.

"I understand."

"Tell me what you think happened. Maybe I'll listen to your theory," he said. A cautious cop to the end. But I suppose I'd have done the same if I were in his shoes.

"My brother tried to burn down his own bar for the insurance. It was a simple insurance scam. All those customers in the bar that night–you kept refusing to fill me in on them, but they were all bikers or ex-bikers. One was AB just out for a manslaughter beef a week before the robbery. Even a rookie cop at half your speed doesn't miss that."

"OK," Thorpe said, "I'm still listening, Haftmann."

"There was a snitch somewhere," I said. "One of them had a wife, an ex-wife, actually."

Thorpe nodded. "She hated her hubbie badly enough to talk. The man had a history of slip-and-fall schemes—"

"When my brother broached his plan, and the easy money, just for being an eyewitness to the holdup, it was too good to pass up. Maybe he told a friend who told a friend."

"That part we don't know yet," said Thorpe.

"My brother was a fool to think he could control a chain of maggot scum like that."

"It could have worked," Thorpe shrugged. "What else?"

"He paid off the witnesses, the place was doused with gas. My brother was supposed to be tied up and put in the cooler. I'm guessing somebody was paid extra to call it in so he wouldn't have to freeze in there. Perfect alibi."

"You're not getting all A's, but I'll give you an A minus for your sleuthing."

"Then there's the X factor," I said.

"Edie. Your brother's wife. The one thing he was sure of," Thorpe said. "Scorch the place, fuck the pocket change the 'robber' would get away with, and collect two million for the building and the business."

"What I haven't figured yet," I said, "was motive. My brother had plenty of money. That bar has been a gold mine for years."

"You don't live here," said Thorpe. "You don't see the meth labs popping up like toadstools after a rain. It takes a hundred thousand dollars to detoxify one of those places after some asshole amateur chemist gets done cooking his shit?"

I nodded. Jarrell must have seen the writing on the walls. Just one of those places could kill a neighborhood bar, destroy its reputation, flip a whole neighborhood in a month so you were stuck for good. Nothing but junkies and crank addict s."

"My brother turned to the very people who were known to market crank, the Aryan Brotherhood."

Thorpe nodded. "He just picked the wrong team. I checked on his life insurance premiums. He'd been upping the payout and paying those high premiums for years until the time was right."

"I can figure that myself. What I can't figure is why Edie tipped off that psychopath Landross—"

He shook his head at me. "That's why I've been telling you to stay clear. You don't know the truth, Haftmann. I've got to go. Nice talking to you. Stay the fuck away from my precinct. In fact, stay out of Michigan unless Ohio State's playing in Ann Arbor."

"You owe me, Thorpe," I said and held his arm.

"Listen, Haftmann, let it go. It doesn't matter now. Your brother's in the ground."

"I just want to know where it went wrong," I said.

"It went wrong," Thorpe said and shook himself free of my hold, "because of love. That's where your brother fucked up. Edie was still working for Landross. She'd been seeing him for months."

I watched him leave. He never looked back.

Back home I had time to think and piece it together. I thought of an idiot savant I'd seen on TV, a man whose brain grew so fast he could memorize a thousand books but couldn't pour piss out of his boot if the directions were on the heel.

I went back to Jarrell's old letters, years and months back, and I read them again. I read between the lines and I understood, finally, what he had been trying to confess to me all along. There was no doubt he loved her to the point of madness. But she wasn't the type who could give love back.

Thorpe broke down a bit and gave me a few more details and then I knew I had all the story. Edie would see clients for Landross, rich clients just as she had with Carnes. But these were men like Landross who belonged to a sexual netherworld. Edie "bottomed" for the very rich. She met discreet clients in Grosse Pointe, Birminhgam Hills, and often in the hotels of the Renaissance Center downtown. Sometimes she would "top" for a masochistic client, but she was better as the receiver of pain. After a while, she couldn't have hidden the scars and welts from my brother; maybe he saw one of those orange-size bruises on her skin and she confessed. Maybe he enjoyed it vicariously. It was clear that her money kept them in their lavish lifestyle, not his profits from a bar that was fast going downhill. I wondered how he could spend the money while his mind's eye must have been conjuring up those sordid images of men tying up his wife with silk ropes or leather cords, sodomizing her or inserting dildoes or their thrusting cocks, even defecating on her white skin or those beautiful cheekbones. How could he stomach that? Maybe the bar scheme was a way out of his private hell. With two million, she'd never have to squirm beneath some rich degenerate anally enjoying her and urging her to scream behind her silk mask.

Thorpe said they found a book of names and prices taped to the bottom of a chiffonier in the hallway. He brought one of those men in and winkled a confession out of him. I didn't want to know his name or what he used to do to my ex-sister-in-law. I thought of her frozen body, myriads of ice crystals covering her translucent skin beneath the heavy rubber bag where she was stowed away in that locker. I saw them on her long eyelashes and in the corners of her mouth. He thinks Edie used a wig and a false name to visit Landross in prison. The Brotherhood ordered wives of associates to smuggle dope in their vaginas. Was Edie that loyal? He was still lending her out to friends even while he was in stir. It's certain, Thorpe figured, that Carnes was going to get it at the robbery too. He was a bright thread leading to the whole sordid business.

I thought of my brother, pacing the hardwood floors alone at night, convincing himself he could handle sexual vermin like this and free Edie. No one was ever going to have Edie alone. Not the depraved scum in opulent homes along the shores, not my brother, and finally, not Landross. Edie's sexual needs were beyond them all.

The last bit must have come as a shock to Landross and set him to planning his revenge. All the witnesses that night described a slender man in a ski mask. Only Edie herself could have put cops onto Richie Landross so fast.

Once she heard that her husband was killed, her loyalty to him was over. I thought how curious love is sometimes.

I've got their kids with me in Ohio. They both have Edie's white-blonde hair and Jarrell's warm brown eyes. The boy seems to have a talent for the piano. It'll be good to hear a Chopin nocturne once in a while.

The Riding Boy

She looked sane. Sometimes you just never know. In private investigation work, you tend to get people at the ends of their tethers. But I also had fifteen years in homicide and that taught me to control my face, so she had no idea what I was thinking. Besides that, she must have been used to it, used to telling her story all around, and seeing all the reactions on the faces of the people she told her story to before me.

"He'll be coming through here today or tomorrow," she said. "The postcards always show the route. I just – I don't know where else to go, Mr. Haftmann."

This apparently made her realize she was implying something uncomplimentary about my one-man operation. I nodded as if to acknowledge the obvious.

She was no referral, certainly no local. I've been living in this resort town and drinking in the bars around here long enough to know that much. Not stunning, but a presence to her, the sort that made your eyes cut away from the person you were talking to if she were to come into a room. Like the corny line about Monroe in *Niagara*: she made an entrance walking away from the camera. About 40, five-eight, 130, brown and brown. Brown eyes with tawny flecks. That kind of brown hair with blonde streaks that shows well when it's put up. Fleshy but aerobics for maintenance probably. Simple clothes – too good for any hash house on the Strip except Mary's Kitchen. Too dark for the season, though. The navy blue fabric of her blouse was bunched at the neck, and there seemed to be a lot of cloth straining behind her crossed arms. Not the coarse types this burgh is used to. Her perfume was Obsession. I loathed it because it used to be

Micah's, my ex-wife's.

She got the story out, but I knew long before she ceased talking why none of the big outfits would touch it with a barge pole. And why I knew I would. I've become an existentialist in my old age. I expect the world to be absurd. One of my last investigations as a Jefferson homicide detective was the one the local papers still refer to as the "Kneeling Woman" case: a seventy-three-year-old woman who had survived a Nazi concentration camp and was living out her retirement years in Jefferson-on-the-Lake happened to discover one of her torturers in the same doctor's waiting office; both had read the same advertisement in the Cleveland *Plain Dealer* about the new sonic treatment for tattoo removal. She thought it was time she finally let the past go and came in to get her numbers removed via the latest technology. He must have thought the same, the difference being that his numbers were accompanied by the lightning runes of the SS beneath his right armpit. The papers always called her the *Kneeling Woman* because she was found on her knees – the result of a stroke. She was rotting quietly into the floorboards when the paramedics arrived. They had to cut the boards around her dead skin to bring her out. Turns out the man in the waiting room, a retired and respected Cleveland professional with a large family, had recognized her too and tracked her to her home where he found her in that condition. Too afraid of exposure to call for help, he came by every other day and gave her sips of water and bites of food. Her will to see him punished kept her alive.

I've seen my share of lunacy and mayhem in and out of a cop's uniform. One of my rules is *Don't make simple things complicated and vice versa*. And one of these days, I intend to follow it.

I told her it would cost her four hundred dollars (my *per diem* expenses), fifty per day for one assistant, and one thousand dollars as a bonus if I delivered the boy. She agreed and wrote me a retainer check for four days' work on the spot. I told her to check into the Windjammer Motel just off the Strip and wait for my calls.

First, I called Tico. He frequently picked up a few bucks as my assistant on the rare occasions when I couldn't do a job myself. Tico is an ex-welterweight who fought out of Youngstown and retired about ten years ago to become owner of Tico's Place, my watering hole of choice in these parts. I told him what I wanted, and I could imagine him methodically wiping glasses as he heard me lay out the scheme. Tico grunted an OK at me, but I could imagine him wiping the decal off the face of the glass. Tico's no existentialist like me, but he's addicted to excitement.

I thought of the last photo of the boy she had nudged across the desk toward me. He was almost ten years old now, but he was beginning to show the vacant look of the mentally deficient. Her eyes, I thought. His bare feet were evident and showed the effect of his bizarre confinement – the bottoms were curling up from disuse as the muscles atrophied.

I asked her why. She look ashamed and said, "He called me in a drunken rage after the divorce. Said he had a DNA test done. I knew then – " She looked up at me. "I never expected to get away with anything, Mr. Haftmann. I was going to tell him myself. The marriage was over before it started. But he was so determined to get revenge for my betraying him. When he lost the court case over having to pay me – it was his own pre-nuptial agreement – I thought he'd go berserk. He even attacked his own lawyer in court. An officer had to take him away, he was so enraged. I'll never forget how he looked at me. The names he called me. I can't repeat them."

"Who is the father?" I asked her.

47

She said, "He's someone I knew from high school. He married someone else after – I left. Just a boy I used to date. My own age. Mr. Haftmann, I wasn't looking for sex or an affair. I was just . . . lonely. My husband was always gone. Always making deals somewhere. Money was everything to him. I was never good enough or smart enough or had enough class to be with him. I was always wrong, said the wrong thing or wore the wrong dress for the wrong occasion. I knew he regretted marrying me right after the wedding . . . I was his little hillbilly woman to his friends and family."

It had started strange. He was thirty-five, a wheeler-dealer just hitting his stride, and he happened to be driving in a chauffeured limousine through Reynoldsville, West Virginia of all places, returning to Detroit, when he told the driver to pull over at a roadside cafe. She was seventeen, the local beauty. He must have been feeling like one of those men, those princes or feudal barons of commerce spawned in the wake of the greed of the last decade, who feel they can do anything. He scooped her up. In a week they were married. Practically bought her right out from under her family and the boyfriend with whom she would later have her only child.

The Riding Boy. A child driven from one end of the United States to the other in vehicles hired exclusively for the purpose. The boy grew up in automobiles. She showed me a fistful of postcards from her purse, all addressed to her in her mother's home in West Virginia in different handwriting styles, all showing various towns, big and little, across the United States. Bangor, Utica, New York, Ocalala, San Diego, Beaumont – his entire world was a blurred landscape of people, like him, all in cars or trucks or highway vehicles moving down freeways that flicked images onto his retinas but left no impression, no deep images of life lived or experienced. No concept of home, of family, of love. His father paid the drivers so well and gave them such meticulous instructions that they had to check in at various points in their cross-country trek. The boy never had the same driver twice. No one ever suspected that his rich, powerful father was having him driven back and forth across the major highways of the nation for the pure, sadistic pleasure of tormenting the child's mother. Punishing her for adultery. The postcards had been coming for years, she said, before she awoke one night back home in Reynoldsville in an icy sweat with the full knowledge *the boy was never going to experience anything of the world except what he could see from a moving automobile.*

She could never prove it, of course. How could you? As the boy's mind caved in from the numbing sameness of a world seen from the backseat of a car, his deteriorating physical and mental condition would be explained a dozen different ways. The doctors in various towns would prescribe medicine, and his life on the road would resume. *She would know*, however. The postcards would arrive at intervals like expected beatings. She would know *he knew* that she was powerless to stop it.

So she put the postcards together; she saw the itinerary and the hundreds of thousands of miles logged every year. Then she saw it: Route 90, our nearby interstate, deadheads in Seattle; it was the single common denominator, no matter how many towns or miles were consumed. This driver, she reasoned, grew sloppy and more predictable than most: the postcards were laying a route that would bring her son through town. She had tried for years to interest someone, anyone, to save her son, but her ex-husband's money and connections ensured that no district attorney's office or law-enforcement agency could come near him legally. Even if he weren't one of the richest men in the Midwest, the court had already awarded the boy to the father before it was known that he was not the child's natural father. Now, her one window of opportunity was about to close. Every prestigious firm she tried, every blue-chip freelancer, turned her down flat once it was obvious she wanted a snatch job who her ex-husband was. Chance put me at the other end of her tether, a long shot, divorced, ex-alcoholic private eye with an existentialist *Weltschmerz.*

Calculating the boy's travel time on the basis of the postcard's delivery date, she saw the pattern: her husband must be using the same driver as four years ago. She believed the route was identical and that would mean they would be pass by, at the earliest, midafternoon today or tomorrow afternoon. Not only that, the boy would have to come right through here because State Route 531 bisected the Strip at Jefferson-on-the-Lake, and a section of Route 90 just south of us was closed off for expansion so that the detour would have to take in this one-mile strip along 531. An extra bit of luck was Chief Millimaki's greed and the windfall of travelers accustomed to fast speeds; his men were picking them off like barnyard flies for flouting the posted maximum speed of 25 m.p.h.

The Windjammer was cater-corner to the Strip so that every window looked out onto the 531 turnoff. She left the office with my Zeiss field glasses and Tico stood his watch at Lake and Erieview with a walkie-talkie. Every car turning onto the Strip with one driver (in case he used women as drivers too) and a boy passenger was spotted once she alerted us. Tico had the photo and could come right up the window to confirm.

Eight hours crawled by. Every few minutes Tico would call me just to break the monotony.

At eight o'clock, as the traffic picked up for the nightlife, the walkie-talkie squawked once, then her voice screaming, "That's him! That's him! Oh my God!" I heard

Tico calmly ask her what car, lady, what car? He kept repeating it because she had become hysterical. Finally, she told him: blue Datsun, California plates.

I had a few minutes more than I planned because the traffic directly outside my office was bottlenecked. I looked down the shiny column of cars, already a patina of neon glitter reflecting from hoods and tops. Then I saw it.

When the Datsun was directly opposite me, I walked up to the window and saw the boy sitting in the back, then cut my eyes back to the driver who was staring straight ahead as if bored. Tourists were routinely jaywalking between the stalled traffic, so nobody took notice of me. I took the large crescent wrench from where I had it tucked alongside my forearm and slowly keyed the side of the Datsun. The *screee* of metal was loud enough for the driver to hear it, and his eyes bugged. He flung open his door in a second, and by the time he had cleared the door, I was bringing the wrench around in a short arcing chop that caught him flush behind his left ear. He tottered and started to fall to his knees, but I managed to muscle him back into the car; his head lolled backwards but I could see a vein in his neck pulsing like a gorged worm. Breathing.

I had the boy out of the car and by the hand and we were walking fast down the Strip just as the first blaring of horns erupted. We passed several cars and I could see drivers leaning on their horns, upset at the stalled vehicle ahead.

At the Windjammer inside her motel room, I gave the boy to his mother. Her eyes were already red, but when she saw her child, she burst into loud sobs and hugged him to her. Tico shifted from one foot to the other, not out of nervousness (he had no nerves) but because he was eager to get back to his bar. I pieced him off, added a little extra, and told him thanks. Then I waited a little longer for her crying to subside. The boy was quiet except for some guttural noises that I could not understand as speech. She kept kissing his face. Maybe it was the first time he had been held by another human being since he was an infant. I called a taxi that would take them back to town, where her car was waiting for her. "Stay away from your usual places," I said. "Change your name and habits for a while. Get out of state before you write any more checks."

Before she left, she wrote me the check for a thousand dollars. Then the taxi pulled up and we shook hands at the door. The boy, docile but eyes moving every which way, clambered into the back, as if he knew his part without having to be told. The mother looked at me once and waved.

Nothing's really simple. I've been known to screw up a two-car funeral in my time too. The driver I had attacked had been taken to the local hospital; it was feared that he had suffered a heart attack. Then I heard from one of the dispatchers at the station house, one of my best sources, and she said the guy was treated and released, but left a different name at the desk from the one he carried on a license in his wallet. The cop who showed up to do the incident report ran it through NCIC, and they discovered he was an ex-con from Nevada with a long rap sheet, mostly B & E and car theft. He had a couple warrants on him, and they brought him in. He talked to them. Then he talked to the FBI.

Yesterday I was eating my usual breakfast at the Log Cabin, and I noticed an item on one of the back pages: *Millionaire Detroit Entrepreneur Commits Suicide*. It began: "A multimillionaire businessman and stockbroker was found dead in his West Virginia mountain retreat called Hawk's Talon, police learned yesterday . . ." I skimmed the rest of the article. My stomach felt it before my eyes saw it. Near the end of the piece, I came to this part: ". . . in what looks to be a double homicide and suicide, his former wife and son were found bludgeoned to death in a room below the master bedroom. She was a forty-one-year-old native of nearby Reynoldsville . . ."

Sometimes I wonder if I've ever done anybody any good in my life. My grandmother was from West Virginia. She used to say, "If you think you're important, try sticking your finger in a bucket of water and pulling it out. That's how much you matter." I went to Tico's when I thought I couldn't stand it anymore, wanted to get good and drunk, but I saw him talking to his boy Enrique, a welterweight just like Tico used to be, and I saw how much he really loved his kid, and I knew I wouldn't get drunk that day. Tomorrow's another day, though, and probably another rock waiting to be pushed up a hill.

The Last Outlaw

"I exist on the foundation of something I do not know."
–Carl Jung, *Memories, Dreams, Reflections*

The bullet entered Robert DeMott just as he had been about to climax, so she slowly shifted her weight to reach for the Beretta where she had placed it under the bed. He drank prodigious amounts of alcohol and that usually made sex difficult, but tonight he expected to be serviced by her mouth; he held the back of her head with one meaty paw and thrust into her. When he was fully erect, she took it out of her mouth and sucked along the side to the head, a porno film trick he liked, and worked back down the other knowing that she would expect him to lick his bag–something else he liked his women to do for him. It revolted her but she was careful to keep him from suspecting anything different tonight. Instead of taking it back inside her mouth as he expected, she brought the gun up behind her back and looked up at him from her knees and said two words. Just a girl's name. His eyes were glazed slits of pleasure but with the name came a slow recognition and he blinked; then they widened in recognition. Before he could say anything, or even look down at her, she placed the barrel of the gun gently against the bottom of his sac, shut her eyes against the noise and recoil spatter, and pulled the trigger.

A small but mean little gun, it blew his testicles to pulp, punched through coiled intestines and perforated his liver before ricocheting against pelvic bone and coming to rest against the elastic skin of his abdomen wall. Even if paramedics had been standing outside the cottage door, the feces pouring into his bloodstream would have killed him if nothing else. As it was, he was to endure one final, insulting shockwave of pain when she reached over to his writhing mass on the bed and leaned her face into his curly pubic hair. She bit down hard on the glans until her gums and teeth were red. Her face at that moment was beyond anything DeMott had seen. She gazed at him lying there with his face twisted in to the pillow, teeth bared and one incisor cracked from biting down when the pain slammed into his body. He had a moment to live and maybe one animal scream left to erupt from his lungs when she put the gun gently against his temple and squeezed off another round that fluttered strands of greasy black hair. His left eye popped open in reflex action to the turbulence going on inside his brain but he was dead before it finished churning its scorched path through the meat turning pulpy gray matter to a frothy liquid stew inside his skullcap.

She stood wobbling on her legs, an icy bubble welling up inside. She retched once, hard, but nothing erupted from her empty stomach; however, it broke the panic before she was crazed by what she had done. She had now a slow-motion kind of inertia to contend with, the real beginnings of shock, in fact, but she could not break her gaze on the crisscross of surgical scars lacing the fat white flesh of his exposed knee. She forced herself to snap to and tried to wrestle his Levi's up but it brought forth another spasm from her stomach and she vomited yellow bile across his thighs. She gave it up. Calmer, she gathered her belongings into a neat pile and finished the packing that she had started earlier. It was almost three in the morning. The sky outside was still black but in an hour it would be pewter and then the sun would streak the clouds with pink and lavender frills. The gulls over the lake would shriek with hunger and dive for the shoals of yellow perch and shad. Time, she knew, would be the enemy now. DeMott's death was just the beginning, not the end. There were forces which would soon move in opposition to her plans, and she knew that she had a long way to go before it was over. She said the name again, a mantra to give herself strength and with the image of four more men out there somewhere, breathing, who would have to be made to stop, she whispered the girl's name once more, almost as if in prayer, not so much asking God for forgiveness as offering a sacrifice for good fortune.

~ ~ ~

The call from her came at five in the morning. When she told me about DeMott, I asked her where she was calling from. A payphone on the Strip by Otto's Miniature Golf. I told her to meet me behind the arcade across the street and to stay away from the light.

On the way over I thought about what she said. You might as well try to shovel smoke as understand a woman who could put a hot lead projectile into a man's body at that angle. Micah, a crossword nut, once told me that in the pride the female does the killing. Males are good for nothing but sex and death, she said.

She looked exhausted. Her bronzed skin under the bar's lighting was gone; her face was fishbelly white. She looked older than I realized.

"I can recommend a good criminal lawyer," I said.

"No. I don't want a lawyer, Thomas. Help me get away."

"If I don't turn you in, I'll lose my license. I'll go to jail."

"I can't do jail."

Do jail, convict slang. With some mascara and the right clothes she could lead the discussion at the next Zonta meeting.

"Then why kill him? Why not leave him, walk away?"

"You're a man. You wouldn't understand."

"Don't give me that feminist bullshit. This is murder two, if you're lucky. Or manslaughter at the least. The cops aren't completely stupid. They'll find him before he's cold. Get wise. I don't even know you."

Then she told me what I figured had to be coming, somehow, the thing that would get me out of bed and here in the street with her instead of dialing in a tip and going back to sleep. I told her we were going back there. We had to get her things. I didn't tell her that screwing up the forensics was a dangerous and foolish thing to do.

"I'll show you where he lives," she said. "He's got a cabin off by itself near the beach."

"I know where he lives," I said.

I had been there before. Last summer the Lake cops were so wrapped up in an FBI corruption sting involving gambling and the Youngstown mafia that the DA's office didn't want to contaminate the investigation into Bobbi Rae Phillips' disappearance and presumed murder if it ever went to trial. Micah was lead prosecutor. I did some discreet B & E at the time of Bobbi Rae's disappearance – her family was putting pressure on the cops and DA–one of my biker contacts had given me DeMott's name and told me what he did with some girls who didn't want to go to the cops. I had no Fourth Amendment constraints at the time, just a little trespass problem if anyone saw me, and so I told Micah I had seen what amounted to a rape kit inside his cabin. No probable cause but it was a lead to follow up. Bobbie Rae had been missing three days by then. DeMott was in jail on a DUI at the time but the Outlaws had rolled into town and were creating their usual havoc. One of the bikers looking at hard time had rolled over four of his buddies to cut a deal so the cops could put a case together. The five of them had drugged and gang-raped the girl after luring her to the isolated cabin.

The case collapsed around Micah when all the evidence was declared fruit of the poison tree. They found Bobbi Rae's body with a methane probe a couple hundred yards from DeMott' cabin. DeMott was a derelict academic, a hardcore alcoholic and boozehound, who had wandered into town after some scandal that cost him his reputation and career. He couldn't remember that he used to teach American novels at Ohio State for twenty-five years let alone recall which booze fog resulted in seeing five men digging a grave on a stormy night. The bikers' defense attorney shredded his testimony at the stand. That, more than anything, resulted in the bikers' high-fiving one another while Judge Sweeney banged the gavel for order and the dead girl's family wept and moaned. I'll never forget the look on my wife's face.

My eyes boxed the squalid room. What I saw was the wretched detritus of someone's last days: a ratty carpet strewn with beer cans, water stains on the wallpaper, a kit of crescent wrenches on the sill, on the floor a rusty pair of channel locks, copies of girlie mags mixed with some bondage porn, unwashed clothes smelling of must and body odor, urine in the toilet bowl. I found a shoebox of sexual paraphernalia in the small closet—three latex dildos of various shapes and sizes, a box of colored and ribbed condoms and a tube of cream "for the sexually adventurous." No evidence of a woman except for a tidy pile of clothes in the corner. The mass on the bed was not yet in full rigor. "Help me," I said to her.

"No," she said. "Not that, please. Don't ask me to do that."

I told her to meet me back at the arcade in two hours.

"Thank you, Mr. Haftmann. You'll never see me again or hear from me. I'll take an Amtrak—"

"I don't want to know," I said.

It's always your past that gets you. I was once a hard-charging Cleveland homicide cop. Now I am an existentialist in a shithole. I believe what Sartre said: Hell is other people.

~ ~ ~

After her disbarment, Micah went to work as a paralegal at a law firm on the Ohio River in Wheeling, West Virginia. She'll never practice law again but she loves it so much she can't stay away from it.

I gave Emma $500 and the keys to my car. I told her where to leave it at the bus station in the next town. I didn't give her much chance.

I went to my office, made some coffee, looked at my past-due bills and decided which to pay and waited for the cops. Lieutenant Millimaki and a sheriff's deputy knocked at four forty-five in the afternoon. I was half-asleep at my desk.

In the room Millimaki eyefucked me. "Knock this silent shit off, Haftmann. You called in the tip in the Bobbi Rae case. Everybody knows you wanted him after what happened to your wife. By the way, where is wifey now? She still a lawyer?"

"I told you that I never met DeMott. I didn't say I didn't know him. He's another greasy fuck in this subterranean shit-chute you call a resort town. He drinks himself blind, when his fuck beeper goes off, he's spun around and pointed at some teenage hooker. His death is a benevolent form of population adjustment."

"We're on this case good, Haftmann. You got anything to tell me, you better tell me now."

"Sounds like professional police work, Chief. Congratulations. May I go now?"

He ignored me. "OK. See what you can do with this name." He pulled another card from his coat pocket. "Forné, Emma. About twenty-five, thirty. Dancer at Annie's. Anyhow that dirtball owner says she filled the W2 with that name. Address and phone are fakes. No aliases, no known associates, no priors under that name, no jacket, nada. Zero. Zilch point shit. Prints all over the room but nothing from the computers just yet. Nobody's seen her."

"I saw her dance there a couple weeks back. It was late. I was drunk. That's all."

"You fuck her?" This from Schroeder, his face screwed up and leering like a gargoyle.

"No," I said. "I didn't know her except as a dancer. She was—"

"A nice-looking piece of ass, eh, Tommy," said Schroeder winking at me. "Real good-looking woman. Not a skag like that dump usually hires. Where'd she go—that is, after she did our boy?"

"I don't know. I never met her," I said.

"We'll get her, the psycho bitch," said Millimaki.

Back home, I was shaking badly. I sat in the dark and waited for time to pass.

Memories kept tickling the corners of my brain. Micah doing a crossword in the kitchen just days before she left me. A word I had never seen: *Cimmerian*. I looked it up: *Very dark or gloomy. One of a mythical people who inhabit a land of perpetual darkness.*

I called her house in East Liverpool and left a message with her law firm in Wheeling, a mile away, to call me back. She rang back at my office number.

"Hello, Micah."

"Hello, Thomas."

I wanted to choke out the words: *Come back to me.* Instead, I said: "You gave her the gun, didn't you?"

"Yes."

A .765 mm Beretta Tomcat Titanium model. I had given it to her for Christmas, our last one together. As far as I knew, she had never fired it, never even took it out of the box.

61

"Why?"

"Why ask now, Thomas? She came to me for help. After what those stupid cops did to the evidence in Bobbi Rae, I swore it wasn't going to happen again, not again, not another little girl raped and murdered by those animals. Sweeney would have killed it in a 404b hearing if we tried to show guilt – "

I thought: Just another runaway, another lost girl in a resort town full of lost teenagers. The country was full of lost kids. They blinked out like stars in the night sky.

"The law, Micah. The law. What happened to it? When did you stop believing in it?"

She sighed. "How do you know when you lose your faith? You just do and then all there is left is to act on it."

"She killed DeMott," I said.

"I know."

"Oh Jesus, Micah, what have you done?"

"Goodbye, Thomas. Don't call again, please." *Click.*

You make choices in this life. Sometimes you're the chosen. But there are moments when you're neither the chooser nor the chosen and that's when nothing makes sense–not your life, your character, your hopes, your dreams . . . not even your nightmares.

~ ~ ~

I found Emma née Thompson a.k.a. Emma Forné in her office at a community college in the next county. The sign outside her door said Business/Administrative Services. I noticed a small snapshot of Jennifer taped to her computer. It was the same one I had seen on flyers on the strip. The slit in her skirt was a raffish touch. I recalled the night I had seen her nude on stage surrounded by rogue males in a blue haze of smoky light.

"Hello, Emma," I said.

She knew my voice before she turned toward me. Unfazed, she said, "Hello, Mister Haftmann."

"That's a lovely outfit," I said. "They say anything yellow and black in nature will either eat you or sting you or kill you."

"Is that true?"

"Where is the gun, Emma?" I asked. "I want the gun," I snarled.

She stared at me a long while, bemused. "Let's go talk," she said, pushing herself away from her computer.

We walked over to the Commons down the hall. Students with backpacks were milling about in clusters, chatting, talking about classes, teachers, papers – normal life. She handed me a cup of black coffee from the vending machine.

I said: "Let's start with an easy one. Where-is-the-fucking-gun?"

"I have it."

"I'd like it, please. Now."

"No."

I hissed: "It's registered to me. It's my wife's gun."

"I know that. Micah said you'd come for it sooner or later, once you figured it all out." Some students at a near table looked our way.

"Micah said – what? What else did she give you?"

"Some court documents. The police files on the other four."

"She gave you sealed documents?" *My God, I didn't know her at all.*

I said: "So you're going after all of them?"

"Yes. Every last one of them." She sipped her coffee daintily; her long slender fingers were laced with blue veins. I looked at her face. Her eyes had tawny flecks the color of tea. I had never noticed. She was voluptuous, classically beautiful, except for the hard set of her mouth. "DeMott killed my sister," she said. "The Outlaws had nothing to do with it."

She told me how DeMott had fixated on her sister, followed her everywhere, begged and pleaded with her. At first she had brushed him as a harmless drunken letch. She let him bankroll her crack habit, charged him for her time and nearly always without sex."

"In the her last letter," Emma said, "she was charging him a hundred dollars for a half hour of her time. They'd meet for coffee in the morning when she was hung over." She began mocking him when he couldn't perform. She charged him more money for her time until he–couldn't take it any longer. He killed her in his cabin."

"How do you know?"

She unfolded a piece of paper in her hand. I read the faded handwriting, a childish scrawl with loops. It was dated the day before she disappeared. She described how she was going to "get free" of her habit and this "nice older gentleman" was going to give her the money, just a loan until she could get back on her feet.

Then I said: "Somebody will figure you for the killer. You're her sister, for Chrissake–"

"No one has yet. It wasn't hard to fool a bunch of drunks at Annie's, remember? I'll be leaving here tomorrow. I just have to stay ahead of the police."

"Which one's catching the next bullet?"

"Do you care? Did you care when my sister was beaten and kept half-alive in DeMott's cabin for days on end?"

I had to ask: "When did you decide to kill him?"

"I don't know. Maybe when I saw him and I knew he was the one who killed her." She had a wan smile on her oval face.

"Why bring my wife into it?"

"If you're worried about the gun, don't be. It's my insurance until–until I finish. Then I'll need just one more bullet. She can say the gun is stolen."

64

"You won't do it," I said, "not with a gun anyhow."

She smiled and canted her face to me. Her eyes were yellow, glittering with passion. "How do you know what I won't do?"

"The cops will have you before then," I said, but I was winding down, fading, beaten.

Suddenly she said to me: "Your wife is smarter than you, isn't she? Is that why your marriage failed?"

"It's part of the reason, I suppose." I remember Micah came home very late once, and I kissed her; I remember the smell of another woman's sex wafting from her hair.

"You should forgive her," she said softly, maybe reading my mind.

"I can't," I said.

"Love is terrifying," she said to me or to no one. "What it will make you do."

"Good luck," I said.

She paused a moment. "I told DeMott just before I shot him—who I was."

"Was it worth it?"

She had that same wan smile. She didn't say anything.

There was nothing left to say and so I said goodbye to Emma Forné or Emma Thompson, whoever this beautiful woman was, and left her sitting there with her thoughts.

I felt as if the ground under my feet had been sprinkled with lime dust and wetted until it turned to slurry. It seemed to take an hour to walk out of the building.

The sky had turned to a mushroom glow in the late afternoon. There was a water fountain outside in the courtyard, and some leaves were drifting down from a gingko tree—bright gold coins falling to earth.

Later, I thought there was something reptilian about Emma's revenge, not at all like a big cat on the savannah. Something older. Like a crocodile. They say it has a second heart valve that lets it dive deeper and keeps oxygenated blood pumping without a need to come up for air. Was it an old heart or was it the modern heart we will find ourselves evolving toward? I didn't have an answer then. Besides, I had a more immediate problem. The coroner's inquest was convening in the morning and I had to have some answers for the prosecuting attorney. Behind him was the glowering Millimaki waiting for his turn.

I drove back to Jefferson on I 90 and hooked a left for home on 534. A few stars dotted the horizon. I saw Deneb arcing over the haze from freeway lights, the brightest star in Cygnus, the Swan. *Winter coming.*

The classical station on my radio played Saint Saëns' *Carnival of the Animals.* I half-listened while my mind cavorted among bits of flotsam from my past. Too much guilt and shame, I thought, too many disappointments, too many people hurt and too few saved. Too many bad endings to promising beginnings. I was running out of time. The car seemed full of tinny notes bouncing around the car. Fragments nibbled at the edge of my consciousness—some names, mostly, but the usual cognitive farrago of despair's sad melody.

But it was crocodiles that I thought of finally as I turned off the highway and pointed the car home still undecided about my testimony in the morning. The big ones that lay at the water's edge with jaws able to lift a water buffalo by the flank or snout – diving deep, twisting in death rolls, snapping at prey, protecting their young–or eating their young – their ancient hearts beating with violence or repose. I slapped my palm in disgust on the steering wheel. The first sign for Jefferson-on-the-Lake flickered past and there I was again, back home, in that cesspit of lust and booze, broken dreams and a bad marriage, a tawdry little place of cheap thrills and commercialized greed like some dying bird with dirty plumage washed up against the sand at a place where melting glaciers had stopped to form one of the Great Lakes.

I fell into an exhausted sleep and dreamed of a brilliant

aquamarine and turquoise mountain of frozen water five miles high, something that had scraped its way south from the polar cap thousands of years ago and in its refracted light I saw the faces of the teenagers I had sought in lonely, deserted places. There in the midst of that warped imagery of my dream was Micah. Her beauty still enthralled me, made me raise my arms to her in a hopeless gesture. I saw her turn gracefully and there was another woman emerging from the ragged shadows. The women embraced. I saw Emma Forné holding Micah, their pale faces glowing, yellow eyes boring into me, accusing me.

The Slave Master's Dungeon

Her shabby motel, a squalid weekend trysting place for locals, was barely within township lines, so he knew full well this was an inconvenience. No apology, just the usual morose silence and grunts when he got into the car.

The good news was that she was going to wrap this up soon, with or without him, and get back to New York, back to what she was doing before he pulled the one big string he had left to pull to get her assigned. Now *that* was a whodunit. She couldn't wait to wrap this up, except for the paperwork that task forces like this generated, but today was the last time she expected to have to spend in Haftmann's company.

The squad car assigned overnight was gone but the crime scene tape was intact when she pulled into the driveway. Fortunately the owner had someone open the gate for them. She smiled at the thought of Haftmann trying to scale his big body over the cyclone fence. She indulged a wicked fantasy of him getting snagged on the razor wire at the top. Serve him right: this morning as she left the Freeway Motel, she had to step around the lineup of beer bottles in front of her door. Tokens from the next-door occupants' all-night party. She had barely slept.

The barrels in the corner were wrapped in plastic and duct tape. Five of them. They had to open just the one to know what they had. She hadn't worked a crime scene in a long time, but it came back to her effortlessly. Grudgingly she had to admit that Haftmann was a competent crime scene investigator. She wondered how long the man could binge drink and still be a good investigator. He must be dissolving brain cells like sugar in water from the looks of him. The darkened beard couldn't hide the unhealthy pallor of his skin or the bruised eyes set deep into their sockets. She told herself not to judge; crime-solving was an intellectual exercise to her, her computer and cell phone were her real weapons. She rarely had to look at broken bones or blood, although the Russians were a throwback to the Jamaican posses of the eighties. They killed with gusto.

"When are they coming for those other fucking barrels?"

"Cleveland's sending a HAZMAT truck. Jefferson doesn't have one."

"Jesus fucking Christ. Everything today has to be so complicated, doesn't it?"

He wasn't expecting an answer. She was checking the itemized list from yesterday to be sure they had all the evidence bags accounted for. The area in front of two vast storage sheds was littered with piles of junk, and it all had to be sorted and checked off against the list from yesterday. Most of it was worthless junk. It took every available deputy from the sheriff's office over seven hours to sort everything into piles and separate potential evidence. The man was a disorganized packrat for all his skills as a predator.

"Look at this, Cheng." He never used her first name.

She walked over to where he was rummaging through stacks of old newspapers.

He was holding a length of bright chain in his hands.

"Fucker devised it with the same kind of ratchet as the ones bolted to the wall, but he needed a bigger chain for the kind of weight and tension he expected to hold. That's what those little scratch pads with calculations we found yesterday meant. He was solving a design problem." He held out one end of the chain and worked the handle to show her. "Clever little rascal, huh?"

She scanned her eyes down each one of the thirteen pages of paper.

"Not in the inventory," she said. "We missed it."

Haftmann wasn't blessed with subtlety. She flashed back to a moment yesterday afternoon, after hours of tedious detail work, when the stale air and dropping blood sugar levels were putting everybody on edge. A young woman, obviously fresh from the academy, was bent over the drain plucking bits of debris from the trap and placing them into various bags with her tweezers. Haftmann saw her place something into a glassine bag and confronted her. "Don't use cellophane for that," he cautioned, "If there's an intact follicle on one of those pubic hairs, it'll degrade in cellophane and they might not get a DNA match later." He held it out one of his paper sacks to her. A tiny clump of matter containing a pair of corkscrew hairs slipped from the tweezers and fell onto her wrist. She looked down at it. Then she removed it with her fingernails and placed it into the bag, set it down next to the tweezers, got up and walked past Haftmann and the others working on their tasks. Annie could hear her loud vomiting – they all could, of course. No one spoke but out of the corner of her eye, she saw one of the older male cops wink at Haftmann and mouth the word *rookie*. She wasn't one to avow her feminism like some other women agents she knew, alpha females who champed at the bit, loved nothing more than to compete with their male colleagues to show how thick their skin was, but she burned with shame whenever a woman in law enforcement let them all down like this. Haftmann merely smirked and went back to whatever he was doing. She vowed she would never let herself get to Haftmann's point.

The Memorial Day weekend just ended, traffic was slowing down on the main arteries into town, but the crowds were a bothersome addition to the work. Just bad timing along with unnatural warmth at this time of the year. Northeast Ohio was experiencing a mini-heat wave before June. It was already ninety and her blouse was stuck to her back. She had taken off the blazer as soon as they arrived. Dry cleaning wouldn't take out certain smells, and at the back of the storage shed, well past the parts he had used as a barricade to disguise the goings on, there were odors wafting about that clung to your skin and leaked into your pores.

"The weasel chose the end of this building facing the traffic. Gave him an extra cushion of noise. They had seen the corkboard walls he had jerry-rigged against the back of the last shed as far from any passersby or casual traffic as he could get." Haftmann came up behind her. There wasn't room for two abreast. Pfeifer had used the debris as a bulwark to hide his activities and soak up any screams or sounds emanating from the rear. Haftmann came up behind her and she felt him close. The sounds of distant highway traffic ceased as if they had crossed a magic line. They were like two amateur hikers walking between boulders in an ever-narrowing crevasse. The air became fetid and darker.

"God damn it to hell." Haftmann swore behind her as he banged his knee against something. "He stacked some of this shit twelve feet up, straight to the rafters."

As slender as she was, she was tempted to turn sideways to squeeze past the last of this artificial barricade; she wondered how Haftmann had managed to do it yesterday, but he was the first one through. One of the deputies was arguing with him about "probable cause." Haftmann grabbed a slender young man with a goatee and spectacles and thrust him at the deputy. "He's from the fucking coroner's office," said Haftmann. "He doesn't need a warrant." The thin youth, half-terrified that the big cop actually intended for him to lead the way, almost collapsed with relief when Haftmann shoved him out of the way and started to bull his way toward the back of the facility. "Just write it up that way," he barked at the deputy. She went in right behind him, not waiting for a response, and wished she hadn't been so concerned about the fact that William Paul Pfeifer had acted entirely alone and this was a mop-up exercise, not a rendezvous with the "Dungeon Master," as the papers had started to call him. She was sure Haftmann had an ankle gun or one behind his belt but her Glock 29 was sitting in its shoulder harness back in a desk drawer of her motel.

The bloody mattresses had been removed by the officers who brought the HAZMAT truck. The walls were still streaked with blood. The hooks Pfeifer had installed against the walls were still there. The bondage equipment had been packed up, a catalog of its contents taped to the side of the boxes. The remaining barrels in their thick painter's plastic wrapping stood like sentinels in a row against the far wall. The women he brought here came to die. Whatever caused him to select some for killing was known only to Pfeifer; he refused to say a word at his prelim and had clammed up ever since, issuing statements through a lawyer.

Then the lights went out and they stood in the blackness. The smells intensified and before her heart could up its beat count, she breathed deeply, silently, mouth open in the practiced way of her power yoga exercises. She would not act frightened, not if meant dying in here to prove her courage, and immediately winced at the stupidity of that vanity.

"Where's that fucking generator switch, God-damn, motherfucking jizz-gargling, cocksucker . . . "

She had asked him, twenty minutes into their first surveillance of Pfeifer's house, whether he could get his Tourette's syndrome under control. His vocabulary was a continual streak of filth and pornography. It didn't offend her "delicate sensibilities," as he accused her of having, but it was bad, she argued, because it dissipated cognitive energy. "Well, let's just say it's my way of getting rid of bad chi, OK with you, Agent Cheng?" It was a long night, unbroken by much of interest from the darkened house with its one upstairs dormer room the sole light. Pfeifer was relentless. Even Haftmann said he was impressed by his sexual vigor. He was online or on his cell phone trolling for women all the time, continually. He was such a nondescript, ordinary-looking man quite the opposite of the flamboyant Russians she tracked back in New York. You wouldn't notice this unremarkable, balding man in his sixties if he were your next-door neighbor. They had followed him to several hotels in the area, everything from an upscale bed-and-breakfast off Lakeshore Boulevard with its houses averaging three hundred thousand to one of those Crazy 8 motels off Route 11 where the neon sign advertised adult films and a "massaging mattress." At first Haftmann found the number and kind of women he drew amusing, and as often as not, as soon one would come up to Pfeifer in a motel parking lot or wherever the rendezvous point was and greet him warmly, Haftmann would unleash a mix of filth or drollery about what the next hour or so was going to involve for her. They had seen his lurid web site often enough: The Dungeon Master, he called himself.

~ ~ ~

"Asshole!"

"What?"

"Not you, Cheng. That dumbass driver . . . OK, so there's your career to consider. This is a feather in your cap and you don't know about any list so just cut the goody-goody shit on that, will you?"

"It's evidence, Thomas."

"Cheng, Christ almighty, this case is a lock and that fuckface is going to Lucasville down by the river for the next twelve years until they put the syringe in his fucking arm. He'll probably die on death row writing his shitty, evil memoirs before then. Not like those women he shackled to the walls and tortured . . . for days. That place *reeked*. You smelled it, too. You're a good cop for all that you're FBI. It was rancid with fear and blood and decomposition. Those women, the ones in those barrels . . . "

She remembered the stench of the first barrel they pried open. It flooded out of the barrel and overwhelmed the sweet coppery stink of his torture room. Haftmann had picked up a shod foot in his latex gloves and the foot had come loose from the miasma of whatever gluey potion Pfeifer concocted to break down their bodies. "I can't afford to have any blowback on this. I just want out of this godforsaken state without the fear I'm going to be called back because of this little gambit – and all because some woman used to know your ex-wife." She finished up a little heated and had to watch so her voice didn't rise the way some women did, that annoying "California lilt" at the ends of sentences. The bastard was actually smiling at her now.

She didn't know what to say.

"You're thinking I should be Xeroxing the fucking shit out of that list and slipping it under every windshield in town. My revenge." He thought a moment and then repeated it: "My revenge." It seemed to her that his mind had gotten stuck at a crazy angle.

"She – the woman, her name is Roberta. I overheard my wife call her Bobbie. She's married, got a couple kids. Her husband never knew. I mean, about Micah, my ex."

"What about this . . . other with Pfeifer? Think he knows?"

"I doubt it. Aren't husbands and wives the last to know?"

"Look, Haftmann, I'm sorry about your marriage and all that. I don't mean to pry – "

"Cheng, it's not about my fucking bruised male ego. Believe me. I was . . . hurt, yes, isn't that the word, or should I have said, I was *devastated,* when she left me."

"Left you for another woman. So why give her a break?"

Haftmann laughed. "You're a tough little bitch, you know that?"

"Fuck you."

"Because . . . I loved her," he said quietly. "I honest-to-God loved her, deeply, madly, with all my heart and soul, my whole body and mind, everything."

"But it ended," she said.

"Yes, it ended," he confirmed and nodded his head as if that explained everything. "These women, the girls, too, that Pfeifer . . . met. I don't know why. I thought I knew her. I guess we don't really know each other when it comes down to it. What makes us tick, I mean. What it is we need to have fulfilled. What would make a respectable woman call up this psychopath and let him bind her hands and legs and then inflict pain on her. Some of them had to know he might not stop. They had to see in his eyes he was capable of going past the safe word. Yet they kept coming to him, dozens of them. Look at all those so-called normal women hooking up with this . . . monster."

If this was going to be some chauvinistic male bullshit about women's innate masochism, she was going to pull him short right now. "It's not about their motives, Haftmann!"

"Easy, Annie. I'm not judging them. I swear to God I'm

76

not. No more judging anyone for me. I just don't understand any of it." They pulled into the station house parking lot next to a lilac bush. Its heady scent enveloped them as soon as they got out of the car.

"Jesus Fucking Christ, smells like a French whorehouse. Look, I'm soaking wet," Haftmann said.

She looked at him. He was back behind whatever mask he had dropped a moment ago.

"Yes," she said; "you're all wet."

"That a pun, Cheng? Leave the idioms to me, OK? Your English isn't that good, and you don't handle English's nuances all that well."

"You're an asshole," she said. "Seriously disturbed."

She shook her head in dismay as they walked up the steps. The heat was ghastly, downright formidable, and for the first time since they were away from the storage shed with its nightmare horrors, she shivered.

At the top of the steps he turned around and said, "What's the verdict, Cheng?"

"I'm still deciding."

She knew that, despite his bluster, if she called it, he would abide by it – yes or no. It irked her. She didn't know why exactly. But why do this to her? He was waiting for his answer, calmly, idiotically, his face blank and composed despite the droplets pouring down his cheeks like outsized tears and his dark thick hair matted onto his head.

Then something from a long time back popped into mind. A memory of a crime scene in New York: a cold case of a child and his mother bound and tortured to death in a low-rent kitchen apartment near the Bowery. They found the husband, a dismembered floater, several weeks later in the East River near a jetty in the south end of the Battery. It turned out to be merely a revenge killing for an unpaid gambling debt. Nothing important involved, although she had a pretty good idea which one of her mobsters was behind it. He would leave many similar scenes of carnage in his wake, some more stomach-churning. These mobsters liked to kill. The little boy's face was so white. The stab wounds he had received were minimal compared to the mother, who was cut many times in different places, and with different degrees and angles of thrust to make sure she felt as much pain as possible.

She, however, not the homicide bulls in the kitchen, deduced something in the two deaths the others were confusing: the killers didn't do the mother last so she could see her little boy die. No, they did her first. He had to watch his mother being cut time after time after time until the blood leeched from his face at the overwhelming horror of it. The mother went to her death knowing she was leaving him there in that kitchen in their frenzied hands. It was a final, brutal sendoff into oblivion for her. It was how they think. The autopsy proved her intuition right.

That night she was watering her plants in her apartment. Satie's *Gymnopédie* was sending its liquid, silver notes around the room. Then suddenly she had to step out onto the balcony and suck some of the city's filthy air into her lungs. Before she knew it, a sob escaped her throat. There it was: an unbidden betrayal of her oath *never* to show her feelings, always to be like ice in winter – yet she had sobbed for that little boy's horrendous pain and the mother's ineffable sadness at a universe so wicked and vile it was better to be dead than live in it one second longer.

"OK, Haftmann," she said, without turning to look at him, opening the doors wide. "Now you owe me one."

She knew he was standing there wearing his stupid lopsided grin for her benefit. She took off her sunglasses and headed for her cubicle. There would be hours of report writing ahead of her before she could go back to that wretched motel.

Archangel's Daughter

The voice on my machine left a message more convoluted than a Chinese wedding in the Tang dynasty. Part had to do with some rich man's daughter. I drank lukewarm coffee, scanned the headlines for the usual carnival of grotesquerie my worthless little burgh by the lake presents, and called him back.

Mel said he represented the Donner agency in San Francisco. I have some old drinking buddies at Tico's Place who like to pull my dick. You see, my métier is runaways, teen girls mostly, and preferably those with fathers who pay well. Once in a while I do a skip trace for a bail bond outfit. You'd be surprised how many deadasses on the run come shambling into this cheapjack resort only to get caught up in the action and then, simply, caught. The place is like flypaper, especially for my lowlife clientele. But those infrequent, rich-daddy jobs, if they pan out, keep me solvent. The man wants to impress, fine by me. I'll goose the bill later.

I know some West Coast outfits, and I had heard of Donner before. Very exclusive in their clientele, which meant they shied away from the flashy celeb cases in the tabloids south in LA.

The girl was Carly Mixsell with a long *i*. The reason he called was that his client required a local contact for their agent because the daughter was last seen in our fair little shithole. That would have been the height of the silly season around here. Kids come and go – we get a million passing through each summer. Most go home after sampling the wares, which usually means binge-drinking,

79

sampling homegrown bud or the hydroponically grown stuff from British Columbia which packs a wallop. But dropping X or acid hasn't gone out of style around here, or it could mean finding sexual partners for the occasional coupling at one of our fine lakeside cottages (no extra charge for the vermin) with interludes of sunbathing by the shores of our PCB- and mercury-contaminated Lake Erie. We're not likely to make the executives at Disneyworld shit with envy because the word among bikers, transients, dropouts, and various miscreants has gotten us a sizeable underground reputation as a good place to get lost if you happen to be traveling or running. By Labor Day the crowds have gone and the locals can get back to brooding over lost revenue until spring. The paper said we have more meth labs in northeast Ohio than anywhere outside central California, and the combination of easy-to-make meth – a real sex enhancer until you start to tweak – has added to our tawdry allure. You see the crowds on the sidewalks inflated with a tougher, shifty-eyed sort amid the square johns.

Mel stonewalled me when I asked about his client, the father. He said I would get the full skinny from his firm later. Meanwhile he faxed photos and a C.I.'s report of her sighting here. Mel said I could be "invaluable" to the search as if I were just waiting for a call like his to add meaning to my empty life. He added that I could bill his firm at the same rate Donner charged its own clients. He made it clear by implication, however, that I was to assist whomever their field agent was. True, the per diem was more than I had ever made and the promised bonus for finding her was beyond generous, but for all of half-a-second I contemplated telling Mel to kiss my rosy-red gofer's ass.

Trouble is, I was poorer than a shithouse mouse at the moment thanks to my penchant t for online gambling and a certain PGA golfer who couldn't make birdie if he was looking down at the cup. I rolled up my shabby maverick image.

Mel didn't realize he had flunked the smell test two minutes into our conversation. For one thing, I don't get recommended much locally let alone from across the country and the Donner people wouldn't touch me with a barge pole if they did a background check.

"Let's cut the shit for a second, Mel," I said. "What's her story?"

"Carly's father is filthy rich, made his millions in real estate."

I did some online checking. Woodland Hills was swanky, not Beverly Hills swanky, but a secular nirvana – that is, if monster houses with landscaping to hide the infrastructure is your idea of heaven. I visualized a divorcée ghetto and Plexiglas offices advertising shrinks and counselors for precious diseases and stresses from post-cosmetic surgery to earthquakes. Places without sidewalks where drifters were encouraged to keep moving. Not like my little corner of the world.

Around eight o'clock I quit working. My cell was on for the field man's call and my cold coffee was turning gray at the edges. No doubt about it, Carly Mixsell was one shapely, whey-faced beauty. Not the California bronzed look, either. Maybe a slightly imperfect rhinoplasty that uptilted her nose a little too much, but the imperfection enhanced her fine-boned symmetry. As gumshoes say in the books, she was easy on the eyes. Brains to boot: graduate of Marlborough School for Girls in Los Angeles, Bryn Mar, *cum laude*, dual degrees in pre-law and urban studies, UCLA Law School.

Mel had used a black marker, but vegetable dyes are readable under alternate light sources so when I passed the infrared wand over the sheets, I could make out what they were withholding from me. Most of it was trivial personal data mixed with financial information, but the blacked-out portions were intriguing, even though I could make out fragmented and cryptic allusions to one other person. There was a string of numbers and letters in private code behind the inky murk on the sixth page.

I decided the sun was down long enough for me to go across the street for my first brew. I had a large bar tab to pay. It was no secret that Tico's wife Marta frowns on my ever-expanding credit line. I was just locking up when the pager vibrated against my leg. My caller was phoning from the pay phone at an intersection known as Little Minnesota, where young female transients hang out looking for older male tourists.

"Corner of Duquesne and 531," the man's voice said. "Hurry up."

He wasn't local. Nobody called the main drag bisecting the resort by its state route designation or anything other than the strip. I didn't like his tone, but I reminded myself of the money being a short-term gofer was paying.

He was a smallish man, barely a hundred-fifty, with a balding, peanut-shaped skull over the top of which he lapped a few long strands of greasy-looking hair in one of those comb-over jobs standup comedians loved to poke fun at. He introduced himself as "Agent Leo," although it wasn't clear whether that was a first name or last name or, like Mel in San Francisco, a *nom de guerre* for the purpose. Maybe they named themselves like hurricanes and the L's were next in rotation.

"What a dump," Leo said.

"Some people call it home," I replied noncommittally.

"I've been propositioned twice already since I called you — See that one?"

He pointed to a shorthaired blond in a Lycra miniskirt.

"I'm glad you resisted the temptation," I said. "His

name is Juan Carlos and he duct-tapes his package between his legs."

"You're shitting me," Leo said.

"You're free to check it out. Cost you twenty, though," I said. Juan Carlos was looking at us.

Leo opened his black windbreaker and tapped the butt of a .357 Ruger Blackhawk. "I'll give the little faggot something to put between his legs," he said and looked menacingly back at Carlos.

"Cover that up, you shithead," I snapped.

"Let's get this straight up front, Hartmann – "

"Haftmann."

"Whatever. You're working for me. You're my errand boy on this project."

My relationship with Leo went downhill from there. We walked across the street to Gino's pizzeria where I had to wait while he made the kid at the counter repeat the entire menu before ordering a sub. "Can't fuck up a sub," he said to me.

I suggested we find a bar to talk. He pointed back the way we had come where his rental car sat in front of Annie's. The sight of Leo masticating his sandwich and talking with gobs of food in his mouth was revolting.

As soon as we sat at the end of the darkened bar, a number of heads swiveled our way, took us in, and dismissed us as tourists. I knew a couple of them from other times. I had been in here many times over the years and knew the last three owners. The place was a moneymaker to me because it drew transients better than any other bar. For a twenty, I could buy top-notch information. Nothing is sacred in Annie's and it's understood by mutual consent of all the biker gangs to be neutral territory.

Leo stage-whispered, "More gangsters in here than they got locked up in Soledad."

It wasn't much of an exaggeration. The black hood, sombrero, and dagger symbol were already showing up on graffiti all over the Lake, as we call it. Someone had even tagged the Chamber of Commerce building with EME's logo.

The bartender set a couple cans in front of us, and I held my breath hoping that Leo wasn't going to make a scene by asking for a glass. There never was an Annie as far as I knew, microwaved meat-loaf sandwiches had always been the entire menu, and beer glasses had been banned since 1987 when two brawlers cut off various parts of each other's anatomies to the delighted applause of onlookers.

"Who is Archangel?"

"Oh shit, I knew you were going to be trouble right from the start," Leo said.

He slumped his shoulders and looked morosely in the mirror. It was warped and made his bald pate look triangular, insect-like shape. My face looked strange, too – like a mackerel with bulging eyes.

"What's he mean to the case, Leo?"

"Oh fuck me twice," Leo snorted. He sagged lower and looked more deeply into his beer.

"The answer's not in the can, Leo. Who is Archangel?"

Leo wasn't a hard nut to crack. His real concern was his macho image as a standup guy. He let out the story in dribs and drabs. I winked at the bartender standing in his conical halo of light midway down the bar. I had used this gambit on more than one weasel.

"You don't know what you're getting involved with, Haftmann."

"Tell me about Archangel," I said.

The sole advantage to being known as a fuckup is that you have little to lose, and you can do things others wouldn't who believe in the rules. The hackles on my neck were tickling as if brushed by tiny spider legs, and I was glad the dark interior wasn't showing the gooseflesh on my arms.

This ordinary-looking mutt on the stool next to me spun a story that you couldn't sell to Hollywood. My poker face might have cracked a bit because I saw Leo squinting at me through his own reflection. Right then, I'd have bet all I had left in the bank on the worst odds going that Leo's story about Archangel was false, every word of it.

For one thing, it made as much sense as a rat fucking a grapefruit, but I checked that remark at the door and instead replied, "That's quite a story, Leo."

"It's no story, believe me. Archangel is one for-real, scary motherfucker. We have to find this girl tonight and get that disk or we're both going to be in some very deep shit."

OK, now feature this: you have a club of rich white men in San Francisco. All but one is Caucasian, the exception being a Chinese, but Leo wasn't sure about that. Their ages ranged from twenty-five to seventy-five. All are as rich as Croesus with fortunes made or inherited. They keep their real identities hidden behind aliases because this club, Leo said, doesn't like publicity for the very good reason its membership has exotic tastes. They choose a derelict building, sometimes the Castro district, but they'll meet down by Fisherman's Wharf, not the trendy section either. A gym rat from Gold's is hired to keep the crackheads and huffers from loitering too close to the entrance and by a pre-arranged code, two or three times a year, he gets a check in the mail and is told where and when to show up, what equipment to bring. The eligibility for membership (here, I believed, Leo was garnishing the truth but how much I couldn't tell) isn't written down in the founding protocols, and the number of members changes. But what gets you in isn't money. Not even a lot of money. You just have to be willing to do certain things to get elected.

Leo described it this way: "You have to pass a challenge to be initiated." When I asked how he could possibly know this, he brought me up short; his agency was the best in California with a client list of heavyweights in society and politics, "including that muscle-headed governor and his rabbit-faced wife." He added grimly: "But nobody can do the freaky things they do without word coming to light eventually."

I thought Leo's choice of words drink-inspired, but I learned how wrong I was.

When I asked him where the proof was that these "probationers" had met their challenges satisfactorily, he said, "Simple. They have to film themselves doing it."

"You mean . . . actual film?"

"VHS, DVD, digital, CD-ROM, fucking infrared, whatever – Haftmann, it doesn't matter. They have to put their faces on film and we are talking about people who do not *want* to be seen on the society pages."

"Where does Archangel come into this?"

"Archangel handles the tapes for all the meetings. He's the one who's supposed to destroy them right after. They tell their pet ape to make sure a fifty-gallon drum and a can of gasoline is on hand so everybody can witness the burning."

"I take it that there's worse on those tapes than genteel art smuggling," I said.

"We aren't talking stupid shit like internet streamers of Tommy Lee banging Pamela Anderson on his boat, for Chrissake. Some of those 'challenges' are nothing short of snuff films – sickening, perverted stuff like you never thought people with money could be involved with." He was wrong: I never had illusions about people with money.

Leo himself had seen one of the DVDs. He described

the early part crudely, just routine depravities, such as an orgy in a Bangkok brothel, a ménage a trois with blonde Scandinavian sisters, anal sex with an under-aged prostitute along Highway E55 near Dresden. The last part wasn't so routine. He described a homeless man buried up to his neck in sand and run over by a giant truck tire – the cameras had been rigged to zoom in on his face.

"All you could see at the end," Leo said, "was his mouth opening and closing in these silent screams like . . . like dog-yips. Then . . . an explosion of red mist."

"You've suppressed evidence of murder, Leo."

He snapped as if snakebit. "You can't threaten me, Haftmann."

"You're working for Archangel, aren't you, Leo? It was never about a missing girl."

He sagged even lower on the stool. "It's worse than that, my friend," he said with some mix of sadness, guilt, and fear all rolled up. "We're both working for him."

On the day his agency was supposed to negotiate a settlement for the return of the disk, he found an envelope in his car with glossies of his wife and two daughters. They were unaware their photos were being taken. He recognized the Montessori parking lot. His twin girls were standing on grass, holding hands, waiting for his wife to arrive to pick them up. The wife was in three of the shots. In one she was bent over, stretching the fabric of her skirt while she put a bag of groceries into the back of her Navigator. There was no message with the pictures; Leo didn't need one.

"We were negotiating the ransom. The day arrived for the drop," he said. "Then it went sideways."

"What went wrong?"

"The fucking boyfriend is what went wrong, that cocksucker," he said. His voice raised a couple octaves above normal drew several heads in our direction.

"He double-crossed her, me, the agency, Archangel. Took the money – two lawn bags, exactly as she said. Put them into the second dumpster behind the right building."

"Something's wrong with your picture, Leo. Five million in garbage bags weighs more money than anybody can just walk off with," I said. His hands were shaking.

"No shit, Sherlock," he fumed. "The bitch – "

"Lower it. People are looking at us," I cautioned.

"She had it all thought out in case Archangel had another team staking out the drop, and I don't doubt for one second he did. For all I know, he could have flown in a commando team or professionals who do extractions in foreign countries and don't ask questions."

"How did she get away with the money?"

"There was a hole blowtorched into the second dumpster with a false bottom secured by a latch. The money dropped straight through into a basement of the building. They had all the time they needed to haul it off and exit. The warehouse was deserted, and honeycombed with exits. A division of Delta commandos couldn't have secured the location."

"So now that all that bullshit about a missing daughter is out of the way, let's cut to the part where you picked me out of the phonebook."

"Don't be so glib, pal. Archangel knows who you are. You go home tonight, I wouldn't be surprised if there's a special-delivery envelope waiting for you too. Just in case I haven't been clear enough for you, these people are fucking . . . *disturbed.*"

We drove to his cottage, a low-rent motel off Duquesne, a dog run of similar pastel shacks made of cement blocks far from the touristy areas of the resort.

Leo showed me his arsenal under the mattress: an S & W .45, a .44 Taurus Tracker, a SIG Sauer with rubber grips, a buck knife, over-under shotgun, a 30.06 deer rifle with scope, and a small Bobcat 25 caliber. The bed was covered with ten-shot magazines and assorted paraphernalia of violence, including an old-fashioned blackjack made of birdshot and leather and a retractable stainless steel baton.

"Leo," I said, "what army are we attacking?"

"I'm guessing you don't take many high-risk cases."

"That's right, and I don't intend to start now. You need to call the state cops right away. Screw your agency and whatever Mel told you to do. Look, I have a couple contacts I can make – "

But Archangel knew he got to him. It was in his eyes. The disk, the money, in that order, and without delay.

"Tell me what you want me to do," I said.

~ ~ ~

That evening we staked out the four cabins sandwiched between Lilac and Frangipani – the prettier the street's name, the lousier the digs.

Leo's tipster said a woman who looked like Carly was supposed to be in the third cabin, cater-corner to the one facing west. Leo wouldn't ID his source, but it was good enough to take him from San Francisco to Jefferson-on-the-Lake in a big hurry.

I had the Zeiss night-vision binocs trained on the window overlooking the lake, but it might have been the waxing moon's glow that lit the window. Leo was fidgeting in the back seat, twirling an unlit cigarette around and around in his fingers.

"I see movement in there," I said.

"I have to come out of there with the disk. You know that, right? I have no choice. We don't leave without the disk. That's priority."

"What about the money, Leo? She's bright enough to hide it in offshore accounts all over the world."

"You let me worry about that," Leo said.

Around two in the morning the light went out. No one had come out of the house.

We approached the cabin from opposite sides. The wet grass soaked up sound except for the buzz of traffic on the strip. Some bikers celebrated nearby. Normal night sounds. A single yellow streetlamp thirty yards from the cabins might as well have been on Mars for all the illumination it provided.

These ramshackle cabin doors had cheap plywood doors a child could kick down.

"Just make sure you hit the light switch fast," he growled.

Leo charged and buckled the door from its hasps. I flooded the room with light.

Before Leo could bring his gun up, I kicked out with my leg and sent his SIG clattering against the wall. His face registered disbelief, but he recovered and fumbled for his second gun tucked into his pants. That's when I pressed the front sight of my Glock into his forehead and barked one word: "Don't!"

He looked from me to the woman in bed, back and forth, wondering how we managed to get in cahoots. I took my plastic cuffs out of my jacket sleeve and bound his hands, drew the tie tight enough to make him grunt, and shoved him against the wall where the force knocked some cheap prints of lightning over the lake onto the floor. Then he followed them to the floor, sliding with his back against the wall, until he sat with his legs splayed out in front of him. His head down, his hands formed a supplicant awaiting alms or a benediction.

"You stupid cocksucker," he snarled from deep in his chest. "Archangel will kill us all."

"Tell me something," I said. "Why not just keep the money and let her run?"

"Fuck you."

Carly's mouth had been opening and closing soundlessly the whole time like a dim goldfish; she made a leap across the bed toward the door, propelled by an adrenalin jolt of fear. She hadn't bothered to cover up her nakedness. The fact that I was standing foursquare in front of the blackened rectangle where the door had been didn't faze her. I hated to do it, but I had no choice. There's a reasonable amount of noise the denizens tolerate before phoning Five-Oh. I clotheslined her in the windpipe going past.

As carefully as I could, tilted her head back and massaged the sides of her neck. I felt the strap muscles on both sides, no damage to the hyoid. Her carotid was bumping like a worm on steroids under her skin. I shifted my weight to pin her hands so she couldn't scratch me. She was dizzyingly beautiful. Her eyes opened wide and took me in. Not pinned like a junkie's, but wide and staring, with gold-flecked irises. She twisted her head and vomited a tiny spume of yellow bile.

I had to admire the girl's pluck. She was going to run nude into the wee hours of the night down a cul-de-sac full of partying bikers. She must have known what her fate would be if Leo, Archangel's designated assassin, caught up with her.

Something twitched in my limbic brain. Leo had an ankle gun, one of those nasty little deals that guaranteed the slug would punch the meat of your brain to stew without exiting or blow your knee cartilage to shreds so that it resembled the head of a mop.

My memory is probably not accurate, but I have a strong visual impression he had actually leveled the weapon at me first and then, for whatever reason, shifted it to Carly lying next to me on the floor. I twisted just enough to make his first shot miss, but I could feel the channel of air the bullet cut as it went past my right ear on its way through the faux wood panel through the drywall. As I jerked my head back and heard the *thunk* in slo-mo time, a second shot singed my eyebrows and scorched the air in its wake.

I planted my size twelve right in the middle of Leo's face.

I just didn't expect to see a nude female in a Weaver stance with my own Glock aimed at me in the middle of the night in a wretched fleabag. She obviously knew how to use it. Instead of the little popping sound of Leo's automatic, the shot had the unmistakable noise of a serious weapon. The bullet did its mayhem with authority. Leo's head was suddenly disarranged and wore a red stripe across the right eye socket like the zigzag of a lightning bolt. She drilled him again, in the forehead, and I watched his ridiculous strand of his hair flutter atop his skull and then settle back down like a bird about to take flight. I saw gore behind him outlined against the wall. I remained stock-still, didn't dare breathe, and thought about ditching my existentialism for a quick prayer. I didn't need peripheral vision to know she was aiming at my heart.

When she touched the barrel to my side, I flinched. It was white-hot.

"Move," she ordered. "Stand against the wall. Lace your fingers over your head. Face the wall!"

"I can help you, Carly," I said. "I know some good investigative cops. I know some lawyers – "

She laughed or maybe snorted. "Lawyers," she said. "I'm a lawyer or didn't you know that? My father gave me the best education money could buy."

"Your father is Archangel," I said.

"You're not as dumb as you look," she said.

I was getting old. My brain cells misfired more and more. I missed things I shouldn't have.

The spit was gone from my mouth. "I'm not with him,"

I said. "I was just hired to find you."

A second later I heard the sounds of her dressing in haste behind me.

"Leo betrayed you," I said.

She was sitting on the bed. I heard the mattress squeak. "This place has bugs. My ankles are all bit up."

"Chiggers," I said.

"Shut up. I don't know why I don't kill you, too. These hillbillies might not know the difference between backfires and gunshots, so be quiet. Leo got anxious when my father handed him the money. I think he knew then my father suspected it was me all along."

"Leo killed your boyfriend, filmed him being torn apart by sharks," I said.

"Leo? Leo couldn't pour piss out of a boot with the directions on the heel. Leo was out of his depth from the start. Like you, mister. When he dropped those bags of wadded-up newspapers instead of the five million into the dumpster, I knew what happened. He came here to kill me but only because he had no choice. He had to cover his tracks or my father would have known."

It was still hard to feature. The boyfriend in the roiling moil of red water – she filmed it.

She saw my expression.

"He was my challenge," she shrugged. "That's how I was able to get close enough to where my father kept the key to his safety deposit box. I broke the gender barrier on the all-boys' club."

I risked a look at her. She was dressed, smiling.

"Keep your face to the wall," she said. "Stay there five minutes and you'll live. Move before then, and I'll put a bullet in your eye. Leo should have shot me first. I missed qualifying for the last Olympics by five lousy points."

She was gone – out the door and into the night and the dark.

I stayed the whole five minutes and threw in two for good measure. When I lowered my cramped arms, I heard the sirens wailing, approaching, their Doppler effect telling me they were turning down the cul-de-sac even as I wondered what kind of story I was going to shape to get myself out of this fix. I looked around the dingy room smelling of mold and urine, a room stinking of cordite – it held me in an iron grip until the cops came in shouting and swearing, like clowns tumbling out of a Volkswagen. I was safer with Carly.

My license has been suspended, but I have hopes of getting it reinstated. I still have a few friends in low places. Meanwhile I still drink at Tico's Place. Martha keeps giving me the fisheye whenever the tab gets a little high. I haven't heard a word from anyone about the case. The DA isn't through thinking about what to charge me with but at least he's not hanging Leo's killing on me. After eight hours of interrogation in the precinct, I went back to my office and called Mel at his San Francisco number, and of course, there was nothing but denials at that end, no such employee had ever worked for the company, etc. Archangel's money worked fast. Maybe Carly found some way to get him to call off the dogs. As long as I was less than forthcoming, I wouldn't have to look over my shoulder for the rest of my life. I keep thinking how she played her part in the big Get Even. My right eyebrow has turned white where the bullet sizzled past. I call it a memento of the night I stared at Old Boney and he blinked instead of me.

A Woman with Tea☐Colored Eyes

"Idon't remember it. Sorry," I said.

"Three years ago," she said. "I was the blonde."

Her hair was shoulder-length, chestnut. She was early forties, attractive, dressed in business attire, a little too chic for Youngstown. I had been to her restaurant on East Federal three or four times because it's close to my office and the food is very good. It's called Alessandro's but there's no Alessandro. She thought the name had good drawing power for a place that specialized in Sicilian cuisine.

She was explaining Hollywood residuals. I tried not to watch the late-spring dust motes floating behind her left ear like a tiny swarm of gnats. I'm thick when it comes to money, which explains why I have so little of it.

The show didn't last more than a year; it was called *Profiles of the Paranormal.* Three men and one woman, all with psychic gifts investigating past unsolved crimes. She said she was added by the producer at the last minute because a show featuring all males was a Nielson no no. I nodded my head as if I understood the dynamics of that too. It was her break because she was working the fringes of TV and hadn't landed a good role in years. It was harder for a woman climbing the age ladder in Hollywood, she said, and it was just a matter of time before her agent dropped her. She auditioned within an hour of her agent's call and got the part.

"So you have no psychic abilities?"

"Good God, no," she laughed. "I don't know which end

of the Ouija board is up." She had a good voice, maybe some elocution lessons back there. Her eyes were light, almost tawny.

So far, all I had learned about the reason she was talking to me was that someone at her restaurant must have recommended me. They say the first things we say to each other are important clues to our personalities, but I must have slept through that seminar. My mother taught me it's rude to interrupt. I let people who come into my place take their time.

"It wasn't all fake," she said. "The two guys, Ben and Lanny, are genuine paranormalists. I think they were, but who knows? They worked in Vegas in the smaller lounges off Fremont. The producer got his big concept when he caught their act."

At Cardinal Mooney where I went to high school, we had different words for spiritual entities. "A team like Roy," I said, "and what's-his-name, the one that got chewed on by the tiger."

"I think that was Roy," she said.

"You said the program had three men."

Her perfume was citrusy, and my nose itched.

"Laurence van Vuuren, the producer, decided the show required scientific appeal, so they made one of their camera crew part of the show. They gave him all these fancy instruments for detecting ectoplasm and emo-peaks."

She said Laurence liked to jazz things up with words for the gee-whiz stuff. An 'emo-peak' was a place where someone was murdered and had left an emotional turbulence behind to measure. It was like wading in warm water when it suddenly turns ice-cold. To me, it sounded like karma for dummies.

"Can you just do that?" I asked her. "Be a technician one day, an actor the next?"

"Sure," she said and smiled. She flashed those baby dimples where the muscles were weak. "As long as you pay your SAG dues." My keen powers of deduction inferred SAG was their union.

"Barry was younger and better-looking than the other two guys," she said, "so Laurence figured he was giving the ratings a bump with the seventeen to thirty-four females."

"With all that going for it," I said, "I'm shocked it only lasted a year."

"You'd think so, wouldn't you? The trouble was Ben and Lanny wanted to renegotiate their contract. They were constantly arguing about who had more lines and time on the meter."

I let that pass. "But you didn't mind it?"

"Heavens no, I was grateful to be working full-time again. People have no idea how exhausting it is to go from one cattle call to another just to get into that three-second crowd scene."

"I'll bet," I said. We were getting to the end of the small talk. The corners of her mouth turned down a fraction, and her light eyes went from tea to amber.

"It started in Miami," she began. "The first one, I mean."

They were down in Little Havana filming. The granddaughter of a deceased woman inherited a house and discovered strange phenomena like dishes moving from one side of the cupboard to the other. The grandmother had been born in Haiti. This was the kind of "thermal aura" the show reveled in, Moira Brenneman said. The old woman's father was an importer from Port-à-Prince, apparently a member of the educated liberal aristocracy at the time of the notorious Papa Doc Duvalier and his secret police. Shibley Jean Talamas might have been working for the CIA, according to the granddaughter, when he was arrested by the Tonton Macoute, those killers in dark shades. The grandmother always believed her father was tortured to death in one of Papa Doc's jail cells. The grandmother was born in Little Havana two weeks later when her mother fled the island. The rest of her life was normal, Moira said. She grew up, married and had a daughter of her own.

"How did your part figure into it?" I asked her.

"Oh, I was strictly there to emote. I was told to look, quite literally, as if I'd seen a ghost."

"That would be the dead woman, right?"

"Oh no, Laurence said we should go for the big one." She made a tinny banshee noise for sound effect, and crooned in a low voice: "The murdered grandfather whose spirit can never rest." Laurence built the show around a triad of hoodoo, bayou, and Santeria as often as he could get away with it, she said.

The grandfather's spirit apparently had its own built-in GPS. He had followed his baby to Miami and lay dormant until his child died of pancreatic cancer at the age of sixty-two.

Moira said, "When the needle on Barry's machine went into the red, we were all supposed to react as if we'd all shared this one big cathartic moment together. Every episode, the same thing. We had the timing down so well we could anticipate everyone's moment of shocked surprise at the reveal."

"The reveal," I said.

Her pretty eyes grew round and her lips fluttered; she did a little nervous tango in her seat. "The revelation where we all finally *know*."

I was impressed. "That's very good," I said. "You said it began in Miami."

"The first letter. I have it here," she said. She took out a folded sheet of paper and handed it to me.

"Do you have the envelope?"

98

"No, the mail clerk at the studio threw it away," she said.

Ordinary paper, a single word-processed sentence: *You bitch stop looking at me.*

"There were others?"

"Three more. Each one arrived after the next three episodes. Then the show was pulled." She held out three more folded sheets.

"No envelopes with these either?"

"They were stuck under my windshield wiper."

"He followed you around the country?"

"No, we did final cuts and voiceovers at the studio in Culver City," she said.

Similar paper and motif in all three: *I told you to stop looking at me. I warned you bitch.* The fourth sheet just two words: *Last warning.*

"Why didn't the studio help?"

"They tried. The CCTV cameras didn't cover the lot where we park. You have to be on the A-list for that. LAPD has a special investigator for stalkers. She's very good, but there wasn't anything she could do except tell me to be vigilant on location."

I looked at her.

"Technically, I wasn't stalked." She made a frown. "In Los Angeles looking for a strange circumstance is like looking for a needle in a haystack of needles."

"How about your co-workers or the camera crew?"

"Studio security put surveillance on my car after the first note. They had their chief interview the cast. That made me real popular, believe me."

Out there she used her mother's surname – Ducent, on the hunch it sounded more "accessible," whatever that meant.

"I'm not making light of your concern, Miss Brenneman, but I'm assuming those notes didn't panic you at the time."

"You're right," she said. "It comes with the territory of being female. Every girl attracts her share of weirdos. Get your face on TV and the lid on the nut jar comes off."

I waited for her to tell me the rest.

She pulled a piece of paper from her blazer pocket. This one was hand-drawn in block letters with a black magic marker: *Fucking bitch I told you to stop looking at me now you're going to die.*

"This was put under my wiper blade two nights ago. I was going over the books and doing my next-day produce orders. Except for Emilio, my cleanup man, there was no one else in the place. There's a small alleyway where I park behind the back door. It's a metal door with an iron grate. I went out there around ten for my cigarettes. The note wasn't there. When I left the restaurant, I saw it."

"What time did Emilio arrive for work?"

"He comes at nine thirty every night. He was never out of my sight the whole time," she said.

"Have you mentioned this – stalker since you've been back in town?"

"Of course not. Very few people outside my circle even know I used to act for a living."

"You need a bodyguard, Miss Brenneman, not a private investigator. I know some retired police officers from YPD. I can recommend a few names."

"I can get a bodyguard on my own, Mister Haftmann. I want to know who this lunatic is. Will you take my case?"

I had never had a client refer to herself as a "case" before. *The Case of the Hollywood Psychic and the Voodoo Stalker.* Erle Stanley Gardner meets reality television. I do skip-trace jobs mostly. I'd even gone after a missing dog once. I was out of my depth. So naturally I said yes.

I spent a week putting her under surveillance. I must

have gained ten pounds dining at Alessandro's in the unlikely event her mystery writer wasn't the craftiest criminal on the block. I talked to Emilio and was satisfied. Moira's life was routine and predictable from the moment she entered the restaurant at seven in the morning to closing it late at night. No one hung around to watch her leave. No irate customers sent food back. I use the same Army-issue night goggles as the troops in Baghdad and made sure she wasn't followed right up to the time I saw her enter her condo at Lake Glacier.

After that I spent two more weeks chasing my tail in Los Angeles. I first interviewed her agent who had a hard time remembering Moira as a client. The LA detective assigned to her left Crimes again Persons and was working child-abuse cases. She met me in the center of that donut-shaped area downtown on Palos Verdes Boulevard at a Starbuck's. She couldn't give me much. For one thing it was an open case and any suspects' names were off limits to civilians. I tried the old cop-to-cop *shtick* and it got me zilch. She thought Moira's note writer was an insider, not a deranged fan of the paranormal show.

"Why?"

"People who stalk the stars go in for these long, convoluted messages," she said. "Their fantasies compel them. Man or woman, they see the victim as someone who's already intimately involved with them." The hostility, the low-class syntax and profanity – it struck her as JDLR: Just Doesn't Look Right.

I tracked Laurence van Vuuren, the show's producer, to a toney rehab in the Malibu Hills. He was by turns cooperative and bitter. I didn't know he used to be a filmmaker. His slide into oblivion included the paranormal show and a sitcom after that about a dysfunctional family. I tried to turn him back to Moira's threats, but he seemed oblivious to any treachery not directed at him. He also had the worst comb-over I had ever seen. The top of his head looked as if someone had pasted a huge furry black letter S to his pate.

We sat on a swing overlooking the surf. He dabbed his nose with a lilac-scented handkerchief. He said he inherited his mother's hypersomnia, a condition that made everyday smells anathema to him. He reminded me of some pampered aristocrat in his coach sojourning through the befouled streets where garbage, dead dogs, and steaming chamber pots were hurled from upper windows. He preferred scented handkerchiefs. He ordered a dozen bottles specially made for him at a shop in Cannes.

I couldn't budge him to remember much about the Haitian episode. I thought about the man Talamas murdered in a filthy Haitian cell only to be resurrected half a century later as a cheesy ghost by this self-indulgent narcissist for entertainment. Back in my motel I thought about Papa Doc's young thugs in their opaque sunglasses.

I struck out with everyone else who had anything to do with the show. Barry was back behind the camera but working indie films in Europe now. The security guard detailed to watch over Moira showed me copies of his reports to his supervisor. I saw no entries beyond the times where "Miss Ducent" was escorted. She led a routine life even then. I talked with the nutritionist in the canteen where Moira ate a fruit salad and yogurt on Mondays and Wednesdays and a braised tuna fillet with a spinach salad on Tuesdays and Thursdays.

My next stop was Vegas where I tracked down Ben of the paranormal duo. He was back to performing before live audiences. He and Lanny had split up for good. After the program folded, Lanny left him for some young stud in Brentwood. "That hypocrite Laurence made us keep our relationship hush-hush. Gay street and ghost street don't mix."

I spent my last day avoiding panhandlers and hustlers on East Chavez where I was staying and put my notes together in my motel room. It was a wash, I had nothing. I could have stayed in my office in Youngstown, made phone calls and gotten the same results.

I shagged the redeye back to Cleveland-Hopkins and hitched home on a commercial prop job to the Youngstown-Warren county airport.

I called Moira in the morning and arranged a meeting.

She came out from a back office when I arrived and shook my hand. Her gorgeous eyes buzzed me. She wore a carmine lipstick and looked elegant from her gold gladiator sandals all the way up to her loop abalone earrings. Her blouse was bone-white and made the skin at her throat glow. Under the palm trees and baby-blue skies of California, hordes of stunning women crossed the street everywhere I looked. Under the battleship gray skies of Ohio, she stood out.

She led me into her office. I handed her my report and watched her riffle the pages.

"I couldn't justify staying out there any longer," I said. "Too much time's gone by. I like to justify my fee with results. I'm sorry."

"I'll write you a check," she said.

"No hurry."

She insisted. I didn't blame her for wanting me gone.

Sunday's *Vindicator* on my doorstep made me giddy. Below the fold on the front page I saw a glamshot of Moira from about a decade ago. The headlines said local restaurateur Moira Brenneman, age 40, was found dead in her condo at Lake Glacier.

I read the rest between waves of nausea. The manager was called by Moira's employees when she didn't open up Alessandro's. He found her hanging from a terrycloth belt tied to a clothes hook behind her bathroom door. Her knees inches from the tile, a granny knot fixed over the decorative hook where her white bathrobe was hanging; the other end cinched around her neck.

I found Det. Sgt. Jerry Pruel at his desk in Robbery/Homicide.

"I was just gonna call you," Jerry said.

"You found my invoice," I said.

"Check this out," Jerry said.

He tossed photos across the desk to me.

She was nude, her face in profile was purple, the tongue protruded between swollen black lips; her right was glazed like a dead bird's. One photo showed a partial bowel movement. No dignity or secrecy from homicide cops.

"What did Elizabeth say?"

Jerry's smile grew wider. "A standard 'neck compression event.'"

Pathologist Elizabeth Bhargrava's been around longer than water, a grandmother with a singsong voice whose hands have been inside more guts than Attila the Hun.

"What are you saying?"

"Sexual asphyxia," Jerry said. "She just forgot one teensy-weensy item. You gotta make sure you can untie the fuckin' knot before you pass out."

"You're crazy," I said. I tapped the photos. "I knew this woman."

"You think she wasn't a freak?" Jerry leaned forward to look at me.

He wears a cowboy belt buckle the size of a canned ham. I said I was a long way from convinced that Moira Brenneman accidentally offed herself playing space monkey.

"Toxicology came back clean." He smirked.

"No alcohol, no nothing, is that what you're saying?"

"We found a stemmed glass on the floor by the tub."

Jerry took a working stiff's mean pleasure whenever one of our more upstanding citizens wound up on Elizabeth's slab.

"What about the threats?"

"We looked into them," he said. "Your report didn't dazzle us, by the way."

"What about the hard drive in her computer? You take that apart yet?"

"Working on it," he said. "The Samoan has it."

The "Samoan" was actually a Solomon Islander – Danny Gumataotao, a brilliant hacker who did freelance work for the police whenever their tech people couldn't untangle something. He was a chattering, wheat-haired, blue-eyed fragment of history, the seed of some English great-grandfather, a bo's'n who climbed the mizzen mast for Her Majesty's Royal Navy and then mounted as many island women as he could. How Danny had washed ashore in the rust belt of the Mahoning Valley was a mystery in itself.

"Elizabeth's slipping if she's writing this off as accidental."

A woman who had come to me for help was now a station-house joke.

"You got your fee out of her, right?"

That stung. Pruel snapped his notebook shut. "Stay out of this, Tom. It's no red ball. It's just an unattended death."

Crossing the street to the car park, I knew I had blown the case of a lifetime, the one every private investigator dreams of.

I called Danny. His voicemail wasn't taking more messages.

"You ever answer your phone?"

"Hey, uh, Detec – I mean, *Mister* Thomas Haftmann, what's up?"

"What's in her computer?"

"You mean the Brenneman thing, right? Pruel cleared this, right?"

"Don't worry about Pruel. Tell me what you found."

Danny whined until I reminded him why he was going to tell me. He had stolen one dollar from each of 28,000 MasterCard unencrypted accounts in Wilmington, Delaware. He lived in fear his fraud indictment would be unsealed and he'd be doing the backstroke in the state pen's toilet.

He lived in married student housing on the YSU campus. Another one of his scams. I called from Mahoning Avenue, which was a few blocks from Danny. I didn't want to give him time to think it over and bolt by the time I got there. In a few minutes I was knocking on his door.

He opened it. What flickered across his face was supposed to be a smile but it didn't reach his eyes.

He pointed at a bank of computers. "Over there. Help yourself."

I walked a zigzag line between stacks of technical magazines. Danny wrote a column for *Wired*.

"You ever clean this pig sty, Danny? I don't speak geek," I growled at the monitors.

He came up behind me, wringing his hands. "Play it, like, you know, I was out at the time," Danny pleaded. "You just happened to come over to visit, like, and you saw the screen so – "

"Just tell me what this gobbledygook means."

He hit a few keystrokes and brought up a website specializing in sado-masochism. The artwork showed a dungeon with manacles and ringbolts. Caricatures of women dangled from chains. A blonde, a brunette, and a redhead. One hirsute man, a polar bear with mange, revealed a crosshatch of livid welts on his back; the raven-haired beauty in skin-tight Lycra outlining her shaved pudenda stood next to a leather ottoman caressing a whip. Mild fare for the voyeur.

Danny hit a few more keys. Moira's last chat-room conversations.

The language was the oddly prurient text-messaging of horny teenagers. Abbreviations like LOL. Her online name was "Giselle."

Her male correspondents were proficient in the jargon of the lifestyle, the euphemism used by the website's promo.

One of the men who used the pseudonym "Ed Friendly" talked about a slave contract, 24/7. The other called himself "Arcturus." All three chatted about good times had in places called La Fuk, Lair de Sade, another place called Hellfire in Manhattan.

"What is COPAD?" It sounds like some urinary tract disease.

"Church of Perversion and Debauchery," he replied.

"You sick bastard."

"Hey, man, I had to look it up myself!"

"Where are their computers?"

"Hey, I bounced to their nodes from their ISPs, but that's as close as I can go."

"Dan-ny, oh Danny boy . . ."

"Pruel will totally kill me, man!"

Ed Friendly turned out to be his actual name. Ed Friendly from South Beach.

He didn't want to talk, but I twisted his balls hard over the phone. He begged me not to tell his wife. He was an elementary school principal in Coconut Grove. When I told him how Moira died, he sobbed into the phone.

Everybody lies. How much lying is sometimes hard to tell over the phone. Ed Friendly could stew in Florida while I checked out Arcturus.

I flew out to LAX that night. Danny tracked Arcturus'

computer to a server in West Hollywood. Lair de Sade was in Los Angeles. According to my Tom-Tom, van Vuuren's house and Lair de Sade were three blocks from each other, door-to-door.

Van Vuuren's rehab stint must have left him chipper because he sounded confident over the phone, although he wasn't very keen on seeing me again once he remembered who I was. I pressed hard for a meeting that night.

He answered the door of his bungalow in a white toga that made him look chubbier. He led me through the dark wooden paneling of his interior to the pool, a corrupt Horace banished to his estate after his noble struggles with the senate.

He made me an old-fashioned Horse's Neck. Then he asked me who the most famous citizen in Youngstown was.

I said, "Emil Denzio. He was a thief."

"Ah yes," Laurence said. He gave his nose a quick swipe with one of his scented handkerchiefs. "No one ever names a saint when asked that."

"When you insisted on coming out here," he said, "I did some research on you," he said. "My first film was a documentary about bears. 'The Bears of Kodiak Island.'" He said it as if it was in bright marquee lights over his head.

"That's where you adopted your Arcturus handle," I said.

He shrugged. It wasn't worth denying.

"What you told me about Moira Ducent, how much was true?"

He studied his drink as if the answer was in there. Then he looked out over the aquamarine square of shimmering water. The underwater lights rotated different colors every few minutes. He sniffed and made another one of those I-smell-excrement faces. He mumbled something in French.

"What?"

"Laissez bon temps roulez," he repeated.

"Huh?"

"Let the good times roll." He said it as if he had ashes in his mouth.

Then he spilled. Laurence had established a relationship with Moira/Giselle years before the paranormal series. A small part in one of his Dracula films led to an invitation to attend one of his exclusive parties. When her career was collapsing, she begged him to use his influence to hire her over the director's protests. Laurence had a stick to make him behave.

Moira used to work in the Lair de Sade and knew people, some very prominent in the film industry but a number were big in the other end, the money people who backed the moguls. Laurence provided the establishment with some homemade fetish films of his wild parties in the Hollywood hills. She informed him which playrooms at Lair de Sade made interesting viewing. She meant hidden two-way mirrors and peepholes where people performed acts of bondage and domination that could have ruined lives, marriages, and careers had they become known outside the fetish community. BDSM, to her, was a higher calling, flogging a way to enlightenment. She was a proud member of COPAD. Laurence knew how to keep a straight face. After all, he worked with actors every day.

Laurence introduced her to people, to men with power. With her California tan and her amber eyes, dressed in a Brazilian lace cami with boy shorts, she could humiliate millionaire tort lawyers and filthy-rich hedge-fund managers. Adorned in black spandex and wielding a leather thong, she transformed herself into the female Mengele of the selection ramp. Laurence described Giselle leading a political powerhouse from Sacramento in leatherhead mask without eyeholes, his testicles cinched so tight he yipped with every step. The memory made him laugh so hard he almost choked and spilled his drink.

"Moira played with fire," he said. "She took her clients to places where the mind is not used to going. Some men became obsessed. One committed suicide."

The pergola by the pool was garnished with vines bearing flowers with cerise petals. Their centers were crimson like blood drops. I thought of ghost drops – what homicide cops call when blood and sere separated. The red ball of sun tipped the bottoms of clouds like a fresco with gold flaking and brushed salmon and mauve strokes across the sky. Coyotes lived in the hills beyond. They had yellow eyes, too.

He leaned over and whispered a name.

"You know it," he smirked, "a fellow citizen of your town, I believe."

I remembered a tiny hesitation in Moira's voice when I asked her how she had saved the money to open her restaurant.

If you lived in Youngstown, it would be hard not to know the name. His family dated back almost to John Young, the man who founded the city. They were in timber and coal mining; then they designed and patented the machines to dig it from the earth. Back when the Mahoning Valley looked like hell without a lid on during the Carnegie years, they prospered and diversified. This scion was a legendary entrepreneur who started on Wall Street after Princeton and worked his way up as a senior trader for Sachs Goldman. He was a billionaire, a friend of the beautiful people in the entertainment industry and a man linked to powerbrokers in DC. He might not have made *Forbes'* top ten every year, but he had the private cell numbers of Warren Buffet, Bill Gates, and Mexico's Carlos Slim, the world's richest man, and if he wanted to get you, he could get five people above you and you'd never know what hit you. In Youngstown it once took the entire Lenny Strollo crime mob, a dishonest city government, and a corrupt courthouse to do that.

I felt like vomiting into van Vuuren's beautiful pool.

"Everything connects, eh, gumshoe?" Laurence said.

"I don't know," I said.

"Now that you know you aren't dealing with something banal like, say, some actor with a declawed gerbil stuck up his ass, what are you going to do?"

I flew home that night. My apartment was expertly tossed. It took me an hour to realize it. I drove down to my office about three in the morning. Same thing. Not a paper out of place, file drawers locked – except that the Brenneman file was missing.

I called Pruel in the morning.

"I'm off the case," he said.

"Listen to me . . ."

"It's over," Pruel cut me off. "Accidental death, ligature strangulation."

"Jerry, wait – "

"You talked to Danny, God damn it. You stepped over the line, Thomas."

"Forget Danny," I said.

"Finished, I told you. All the bears have exited the stage."

Jerry had read exactly one Shakespeare play in high school and this was the only line he remembered.

"She wrote the threats to herself."

"What the – what are you saying?"

"She wanted to make herself radioactive so he'd leave her alone," I said.

"He – who?"

I said his name.

"You're batshit, Haftmann, if you think that."

"He has a golden reputation to protect. He must have tried to get in touch with her again after she came back to Youngstown. She didn't dare confront him in the open," I said. I was aware my voice was cracking.

"Whoah – forget it," he said. "It's over."

"What – what am I supposed to do, Jerry?"

"Go take a long walk around the park, go fishing . . . You can't bring her back."

"Who got to you?"

He thumbed the connection dead. Nothing but Ohio air.

I waited for the sun to rise in California. I called van Vuuren's number all day.

The studio security boss sent me a couple articles two weeks later. The *Los Angeles Times* clipping of an elderly man's body found in the hills off Mulholland Drive. The man was identified by a forensic odontologist as Laurence van Vuuren, resident of Los Angeles. His body was ravaged by coyotes. Cause of death unknown. The second one was from *Variety*. It was more detailed but no less unkind:

'Aside from a forgettable documentary on Alaskan bears, Laurence van Vuuren mixed horror, banality, and trite philosophy in films like *The Gypsy Vampire* and the putrid *The Vampire's Caravanseray*. He was a pretentious Roger Corman without the master's campy touch. Beneath his schlock was more schlock. Hiscinema verité is always a hair's breadth away from risible – except in a single film, *The Devil's Deception,* wherein a jaded young screenwriter trying to make it in Hollywood falls in love with an equally jaded young nymphomaniac. Van Vuuren disappeared in 1983 after an unfunny and pretentious sitcom. Hollywood hasn't noticed his departure until now.'

~ ~ ~

Days pass, seasons, months. My license got yanked. Naturally. The process to get that ruling rescinded has taken all my time and most of my money. Three lawyers have dropped me like a dead Easter chick; none said why. The bureaucratic delays grind on and on . . .

I see his name in the paper all the time. Ohio's a big swing state. A vice presidential nod isn't out of line; his family influence had put *The Vindicator*'s editorial staff in the bag long ago, but it's even been mentioned in the *Plain Dealer* and yesterday's Columbus *Dispatch* as well. I've had hang-up phone calls every few days. Same thing – a breather at the other end. I told Pruel someone's following me around town. He just squints and looks at me with pity. I can read it in his mind: *paranoid delusions*. He said I was turning into Gene Hackman at the end of *The Conversation*.

Before I leave my house, I set my traps. I tell myself to remember the woman with yellow eyes . . . *One day I was sitting in my office and a woman named Moira Brenneman came to see me. She used to be in movies. She once played a psychic in a series about violent events that left an ectoplasmic turbulence in the air . . .*

The Long Bus Ride of Annie Cheng

Detective Annie Cheng gripped the sides of the door to hoist herself up, her height being a modest inch over five feet, and broke a nail on one of the rubber seals. The pain was like molten electricity shooting up her arm to her neocortex. She tried to change her involuntary gasp to a grunt, but Chief Millimaki, who was lumbering down the aisle already, turned to regard her. She often compared his looks to animals in distress. The look he shot her this time was decidedly ovoid, not as blank as a cow's, however, her favorite animal for him, but a sheep whose sideways mastication of its cud has just been interrupted by a sound it cannot recognize. Then it was gone and he was back to being the chief, all six-foot-three inches of shambling, cigar-smelling bulk. His high-school defensive tackle days so far gone from his bloat that not even muscle memory could lurk beneath a hide so well covered in excess tissue. She hated the sight and sound of the man with a revulsion that was almost palpable in weight and color.

Millimaki wasn't the first or only male to mistake her petite size for weakness. Det. Sgt. Annie Cheng had grown to puberty in Shanghai. It might be the most cosmopolitan city in China, but it was still China.

She was looking for an excuse to get him out of her way now that Doc Harris had pronounced the bodies and forensics was wrapping up. His interest could only be ghoulish at this point and he had to know, inside that confined space, he was an impediment. Their relationship might be different, more complex as it had become with

115

every other male detective in the precinct since the days of her first arrival, but she knew he would always be consistent in one thing: give him an opportunity to display his power, and he would do precisely that, all other urgencies secondary to his ego's demand for recognition of his authority.

Five bodies, all elderly, three male, two female. The men at the station called aged vics "Q-Tips" – but the tag would be a misnomer here. The two men were bald, their wives were both sporting expensive wigs albeit matted with blood.

"The driver, the husbands, then the wives. Popped them all right here. That how you see it, Cheng?"

She watched the last of the forensics people spear a shell casing and add it to a baggie.

"Looks that way," she said.

She hoped he wasn't looking for an argument over it. Millimaki was a political appointee beloved of the chamber of commerce, and he couldn't read a crime scene any more than he could read Chinese. In fact, she was pretty sure from the males' positions and eyeball hemorrhages that they had been done after the women. The driver was last to go. He was executed from behind; the slug had torn through his brain, exited his right eye socket and still had force to make a bull's-eye through the thick safety glass of the bus's windshield. His body was dragged to the back, and one of his shoes had come off. There were bloody scuffmarks where the killer had dragged him to the back. "He must have been a bloody mess when he got off," she thought. The man's head had been a geyser of arterial spray. She could see the spatter dotting the rows of felt seats all the way to the back. At one point the killer must have turned his body because the spray resumed more heavily on the other side about midway down. That blood was an overlay, however, so it was clear he was last to be shot. Maybe he thought the killer would spare him if he cooperated or he was still needed to drive. Plenty of time for theories later. Right now, she was winding up hour six of the first forty-eight and there were relatives of the dead to be called before they learned of it on television. She thought once more of the men having been made to watch their wives die. Neither man apparently had fought his attackers. Their faces betrayed no emotion; they both looked asleep, although the one called Charley had one eye at half-mast as if he were winking over a good joke. She thought of her sheep image again and banished the thought: she had no right to judge these people.

She glanced out the window and saw a crowd gathering at the yellow ribbon where state troopers had set up a perimeter. She hoped they share this with CID where she had some good contacts from the days before her transfer, although more and more, she referred to it as her exile.

Millimaki spotted the Cleveland WOIO logo on a van pulling up beside the local radio station's and newspaper's SUVs. He shoved past her to intercept them. His ego could also be counted on for mugging it up in front of the TV crews. Cleveland and Erie, PA were big time. She hoped he wouldn't offer up one of his half-baked theories, but she knew it was a foregone conclusion. She wondered why he never made vague noises about what he didn't know. Instead, he felt a compulsion to advertise every scrap of information to the media because his thick brain worked on facts like a fractured clam overwhelmed by too many grains of sand. When he picked one out to work on, it would be the wrong one.

She looked at the old men's faces again. Their jaunty summer clothes with belts worn too high clashed with their vein-rippled lean shanks. One of their ball caps found on the floor with loose casino tokens bore the name of a ship the Navy had mothballed decades ago; the other man's, Charley's, had one of those unfunny retirement slogans. She heard one of the forensics team call her name softly from the driver's seat and she turned to see a questioning look. "Sure," she said, "I'm done here." It was the one who had taken the photos. The odor was getting profound, well past the spoiled milk stage. Headshots evacuated bowels as well as turned brains to stew. The killers might have wanted to screw up forensics by leaving the air conditioner on full blast, a degree shy of morgue-air temperature, with the engine running–or they had simply fled once the bus was driven to its final destination.

"Detective – Detective Cheng!" She was stepping fast, head down, hoping to get to her car before anyone made her.

It was Mollie Barns, and she grimaced at the recollection of another memory jolting her from her necrotic images she had just left behind. There was something about the woman that filled her with squirmy distress. No secret why she was picked to anchor her station's nightly news. Her skin was alabaster, lightly freckled at the nose, and framed a face that was stunningly sensual. Her strawberry-blonde hair was parted in the middle. On any other woman, it would have looked out of style; on Mollie Barns, it was brazenly fetching and gave her magnificent blue eyes and long, arcing eyebrows a look that made women want to ask her if she'd ever been a model. When she looked deep into the camera, men would pant and forget whether she was describing a double homicide or the recipe for double fudge nut cookies.

"Annie, wait!"

She stopped. Might as well face her, she thought.

"What are you able to say at this point?"

"Nothing."

"Who are they?"

"We aren't releasing names yet," she said and immediately reddened at the thought of her own cowardice, saying "we" when all she had to say was "I." She was investigating officer and this woman was a nobody, just a good-looking newsie. Not quite, she forced herself to admit. Barns was looking at her, looking for the signal in Annie's eyes that said "I remember you, I know you." She wouldn't give it. Damn her. Damn her to hell and her lovely skin and that pouty face that tried to play her even now.

"Can you at least tell me how many victims?"

Annie looked from the mike Mollie had stuck in front of her face down to her thin wrist with its marbling of tiny veins up her fine-boned arm with that same reddish blonde hair dappling her bare arms and catching the last of the summer sun and forced herself to look into the eyes of the only woman she had ever felt a surge of sexual attraction for in her life.

"Five," Annie said and immediately hated herself for succumbing to the woman's allure yet again.

"C'mon, Annie, can't you give me a few minutes of your time?"

Annie's jaw clenched at the thought of Mollie making that pathetic, little-girl moue with her face. She saw a patina of sweat above Mollie's curved lips from the blast-furnace heat. She thought of sweat beads rolling between the freckled tops of her breasts down her cleavage. A scented waft of cinnamon and dough seemed to envelop her all at once, and she thought the woman vile for bringing her powerful sexual being so obviously into her own space. Annie stepped back as if she'd been slapped.

She wondered what her father would have thought of her distress and its origins, so very un-Chinese even for a liberated university professor. Perhaps he would have understood that, she thought, before he could ever have

understood her desire to become a detective, homicide no
less, and remove herself as far as humanly and
geographically possible from her natal country and all she
knew and cherished. As always happened at this time of
day wherever she was, she felt the pangs of memory
tugging at her, demanding she view those images again
like a box of old photographs that she must look at every
day.

"Not today, not now," she said but it was to that
mental summons she spoke rather than to the woman.

Her own car was long since out of the sun, and she felt
the sweat prickling her scalp as soon as she fished the keys
out of her pocket. She kept her hair short and rarely
attended to it during the day. A stray wisp had stuck to her
cheek and so she brushed it back. She remembered
combing her sister's glistening blue-black tresses and
giggling when they attended boarding school in Shanghai.
In those days, her father's exile from Peking University
seemed to be a blessing in disguise. They left the smoke-
filled skies of Beijing behind and reveled in the warmth of
Shanghai.

She played Satie's *Gymnopédie* number 1 and let the
interior of the car fill with his silver notes as she headed
north along Route 11. The killers must have had a car
waiting at the rest stop. They had to be local, too, she
knew. You didn't plan on finding a rest stop in a hijacked
bus with dead passengers especially along this barren
roadway. She thought of the incredible bravado or
stupidity of the killer or killers in driving a bus of dead
men and women down a stretch of Interstate 90, one of
nation's busiest arteries, in the middle of a summer
afternoon and turning off onto the Jefferson/Ashtabula
exit known to be patrolled by state troopers keeping an eye
on speeding gravel trucks who thought complete visibility
for ten miles ahead and behind was a license to speed. Yet

not a car or semi had noticed this bus or, if the drivers who passed it or bothered to think about it, guessed that it was any different from any other charter bus taking a bunch of senior citizens for a day of gambling. She hoped she could keep this detail solvent long enough to exploit it in the investigation. The words she would use to console the next-of-kin were shaping themselves into rows in some compartment of her mind. The music helped her unwind from the cramped bus and its former occupants.

They weren't killed at the rest stop, they were already dead. She put in a call to the precinct to see if she could get a line on her four; she told her partner to pay attention to the driver in case he turned out to be interesting. She was sure the victims were not randomly selected. From what she had learned so far from the rest of the charter group, Sam and Alice and their neighbors Fred and Mary Lou had decided to return to the air-conditioned bus before the rest. The killers were already inside waiting.

Every detective Millimaki could spare and a couple he was able to borrow from the Sheriff's were still on the interviews. She told Jimmy to stay on the computers; he was a whiz at it, but he considered himself an ace interviewer. The truth was he was too short-tempered to be worth a damn at it and she wouldn't trust him even with the meth cases, which were like interview-training sessions for rookies. She put in a call to Haftmann's office on the Strip to see if he were in. Nope. Sun over the yardarm, which meant he was probably at Tico's Place beginning another night of hard drinking. Jimmy openly scorned her using Haftmann as a source – "a fucking worthless boozehound burnout" was Jimmy's description of the resort town's most infamous ex-cop. But Haftmann knew things. He had taught her a great deal when she was new and even when he mocked her, before he became an open drunk, he was a good mentor and opened her eyes the way only a veteran cop can do for you.

Annie had just turned onto 531 when it struck: Jimmy had groused over the phone about not getting at missing out on the interviews. "The one old broad, what's her name, Mary Lou? Her grandson came in and I gave him the news. He went white as a sheet. He said – this is a quote now, Cheng, 'She was always lucky' end quote. Loved those all-day junkets to Detroit. Kept bugging her husband to take her."

"Where's the boy live?"

"Lives with her and the grandfather."

Annie used one fingertip to flick the notepad open to the victims' addresses. About five miles from the station house. She hit the gas and pulled into a Craftsman bungalow on Dorchester surrounded by a hedge. The boy answered the door. He was about fifteen; his red-rimmed eyes and puffy face suggested he had been having a long cry over his loss.

She sat on an old velour sofa worn down on the arms. He had the defeated look of so many relatives she had talked to when disaster or tragedy came home to roost. He never wavered or hesitated but he couldn't recall many helpful details, such as when Mary Lou and her husband Fred Stowe first made plans to visit the newly opened Detroit casinos. There was something about the crime scene that said it had been anything but random; this wasn't carnage left behind by a desperate junkie who saw an opportunity and took it. She was sure the murders were planned and the victims chosen in advance. The boy handed her a flier from one of the casinos advertising a senior's day buffet special. The boy Andrew said it came in the mail a week ago. Annie asked him if he knew of anyone who might want to harm his grandparents.

He looked shocked. "No one," he said. "They were kindest people on earth. They took me in when my parents died and raised me."

Back at the station she asked Jimmy to run a credit history.

"God damn it, Cheng. You know we need approval."

"Just do it, Jimmy. Something's really wrong here. Those people were set up."

"That's not possible. Those people just happened to return to the bus first from the restroom. It was pure chance. Some crackhead saw an opportunity with old duffers and held a gun to the driver's head. When a couple old ladies came back with their purses, he ordered the driver – "

"To drive off with four passengers? All he had to do was take the money and run. He could have stayed right there and picked them all clean one at a time as they came back to the bus. Instead, he shoots all four of them and orders the bus back onto a major interstate in the middle of the day."

"You're mistaken, Detective. And even if, for argument's sake, you're right about that part, it still proves my theory. Nobody but a dope fiend in need of a fix would do something as stupid as that."

"Just run the check, Jimmy. You owe me."

While her partner went off to his cubicle, she made a few more phone calls and came up with the name of Andrew's girlfriend, a sophomore at Jefferson High School.

Annie found her at the neighbor's babysitting; Carly was a typical, gum-chewing fifteen-year-old. Like the rest of her generation in the thrall of Britney Spears, she wore hip-hugger Levi's and showed too much belly flesh.

"Andy loved his grandparents. He was crazy about doing things for them," she said and popped her gum as an exclamation point.

"Did Mrs. Stowe own a gun?"

"Hunh?"

"Did Andy's grandmother own a weapon?"

"How should I know?"

Annie rode back to the precinct with her bone-white blouse sticking to her back. Upstairs in the muster room, she found Jimmy yapping to one of the women dispatchers known around the station house as "Deep Dish" for her extraordinary cleavage. She pulled him aside.

"Nothing unusual," Jimmy said before she asked. "They were both solvent, debt-free citizens. T-bills, and 401Ks, assets and cash, all together they were worth about three hundred forty thousand, minus about twenty, twenty-five if they liquefied – "

"OK, spare me. What else?"

"They were buying land in Florida, a lot of it. Apparently First Bank was backing up a mortgage on a property down there. Looks like they were consolidating for a big investment in a condominium on the waterway near Miami."

"Shit," she said. "I'm still convinced it's about them."

"Fuck it, Cheng. Be a cop. This isn't about women's intuition, you know."

"Fuck you, Jimmy."

At home, she made some green tea and put on a Chopin nocturne. The phone rang.

"Annie?" *Oh God, Mollie Barns.*

"Come on, Annie. I know you're home. Pick up. Your partner told me – "

"What do you want, Miss Barns?"

"I recall a time when it wasn't *Miss* Barns."

"Mollie, what do you want?"

"I just wanted to say hello. You looked so frazzled this afternoon."

"I've been hanging out with dead people all day so I'm a bit tired."

"I've got something for you, maybe it's nothing. Do you want it?"

The way she said *it* made Annie think of Mollie touching the tip of her pink tongue to wet her shapely lips.

"Go ahead," she said and waited.

"OK, maybe nothing, maybe something. Here goes. We're doing a story on teenaged abortion and I did a few interviews with local doctors. One of them, she asked me not to name her if we did this story, said she was alarmed at the high incidence of STDs in this area. It's getting to be an epidemic. Her word."

"What does that have to do with abortion," Annie asked, but she was thinking *me* when she said it.

"It's just . . . odd," Mollie huffed. "I asked her what kind of STDs, you know, just to keep her talking and we got into this discussion about teen sex and so forth."

"Mollie, I'm really intrigued but I have to lie down. My head is hurting me."

"Want me to come over and rub it for you?"

You bitch. Annie let the silence lengthen.

"OK, Detective Cheng, here's the scoop just for you. She said the disease that's showing up among her patients is – get this – syphilis. A dozen cases in the last six months. Nine of them are Jefferson High girls."

Annie clicked off with much of a goodbye. She heard the wall clock she had been given from her father when the family was ordered to leave Beijing. It had been her grandmother's on her father's side. Its *tock-tock* in the silence of the darkened room was not reassuring as it always had been to her.

She felt the surge at her temples would grow into a full-blown migraine if she didn't get into bed and practice her meditation. These headaches sometimes lasted for days. She looked once more at the inviting bedroom and said "Hell with it." Out in the subsiding heat of twilight, she buttoned up her damp blouse and headed for her car. It was still hot to the touch. This early in June, the heat was freakish and threw everything out of sync.

She made it to the neighbor's house where Carly was babysitting and was told by the mother she'd gone to the public library to finish studying for her physics final.

She found Carly at a table near the genealogy section.

"Why didn't you tell me you were being treated for a sexual disease?"

"Carly's gum-chewing ceased and she looked at the detective across from her.

"You're Chinese, aren't you? I thought you were maybe Sicilian or something."

"Who gave you syphilis, Carly? Was it Andrew?"

The girl lowered her eyes and seemed to sag a bit in the shoulders, but then, as if rejuvenated by some secret thought, she sat up straight.

"Promise me you'll keep this conversation private?"

"I'll do all I can to protect your confidentiality. But you have to understand this is a big, a very big homicide investigation."

"Andy's grandmother – she's old-fashioned, you know? Bunch of us kids from school, we have this kind of club, see? We meet at different houses and we have sex after school or on weekends. But it's no big thing. Or at least it wasn't."

Annie finished for her. "Until some of you contracted the disease. Do the teachers know what was going on?"

"Hell no. They don't know anything. All the kids know," she sighed. "Even the ones who don't get invited. It's like a secret. We'd make inside jokes about it and we'd be in the know but the teachers never had a clue what we were saying."

"How did you arrange the meetings and the places?"

"Oh, we'd pass notes in school, send emails, you know.

126

Then we'd meet up
    Somewhere at one of the guy's houses if the parents
would be gone."
    "Like, say, Andy's grandparents' house?"
    "Yeah, sure, whatever. Any one of us guy's houses – it
didn't matter. Their house, my house. My mom works
about like ninety hours a week. Big shot corporate
executive. She's never home." She looked up. "She always
calls me on my cell around now. Quality time." It was more
a sneer than a statement.
    Annie looked at her. She blamed her headache for the
trompe l'oeil that made Carly appear at one and the same
instant both a young girl on the threshold of maturity and
then a grown woman talking casually of sex. Carly's
nipples were clearly outlined against her lace bra, itself
brightly visible beneath the sheer top.
    "What kind of sex did you have when you would
meet?"
    "Well," she said perking up as if this were prelude to a
physics question, "we'd do different positions, try out
some things, ya know, if somebody had, like, the Playboy
channel. We'd watch that and a couple of us would go into
the bedroom and try it."
    She picked up a couple loosed pencils in front of her
and jabbed them at a paperback in front of her.
"Somebody thought up one called 'a sandwich,' where two
guys would go with each girl – " Annie put her hand gently
on Carly's.
    She didn't know how to ask the questions despite the
girl's frankness.
    "At first it was just a bunch of us from the high school.
Then somebody invited some older guys into it, and we'd
have sex with them, too."
    One time there must have been about twenty guys over
to Andy's and somebody dared Kelly Ingersoll to give all

the guys a head job. She did it, too, man. She came out of
the bedroom and there's like cum all over her hair, her
face, and she was bragging about having done it."

Annie thought it was one of the saddest things she'd
ever heard in her life.

"Why didn't you use protection?" It was the only
question she could think to ask.

"We did at first but it stopped. I don't know. The guys
didn't like to wear condoms. Some girls wouldn't do it
unless they did. I was one of the stupid ones, I guess."

Annie looked over Carly's head at the stack of books.
She could read some of the titles. They were passenger
manifests of ships that had carried the Irish across the
Atlantic.

Carly said, "It was getting crazy even before we
stopped meeting. That's the sad thing. It was all done with
because we found out we were infected. Syph, man, what a
bummer, hunh?"

"Yes," Annie said quietly and patted her hand. "A real
bummer."

She drove to Andy's grandparents' house and knocked
on the door.

"Detective Cheng, it's late and I've answered all your
questions – "

"No, you didn't," she said and eased her way past him
into the living room. "Tell me about the sex games. I want
to know the names of every boy and girl involved. If you
hold out, I'll tell a reporter friend of mine to put the names
in the paper for a story she's doing right now."

When he was done talking, he put his face into his
hands and sobbed. Annie felt like kicking him, but instead
she kept her voice even.

"So these other boys, these town boys, not from the
high school. Can you tell me their names?"

"We just knew them by their street names. One was

called Bic like the lighter, you know? The other called himself Philly."

"As in Phillip or like the city?"

"No, like the dope. Philly blunt."

She reached a detective on duty. Jimmy was long gone by now. He ran the names through their database and came up with a hit for the one called Philly.

"Name's Raymond LeShawn Targes." He spelled it. "However the hell he pronounces it. Got a juvie rap sheet. Nothing big. Busted on the strip for possession last summer."

She had a last address on the Strip but no k.a.'s. He was a transient at the lake like so many other lost kids or drifters who came through every summer in the thousands like migrating birds. Most went home. Some stayed for the action and a few got lost forever. Targes was twenty-two.

She parked about fifty yards from the cottage Targes had given authorities as his address. It was one of several down-at-heels shoeboxes rented out at high prices. Visiting families stayed at the other end of the Strip. These were strictly biker crash pads and a few were put to service as meth labs despite the close proximity to other cottages, where the cat-piss reek of cooking going on inside was a matter of minding your own business.

Yellow light bled out from under the cracked and splintered front door.

She drew her Sig out of her shoulder harness and tapped the front door.

"Who's there?" The voice was throaty, cracked from disuse.

"Police. Open up," she said and braced her back against the wall.

She heard glass breaking around back and ran.

A shirtless light-skinned black male was staggering to his feet. He had done a somersault through a small back window and through some miracle of gravity and physics had managed to land in the dirt without shredding all his skin to the bone. The arc lighting made him an easy target.

"Get on the ground!" she screamed.

He blinked a few times and seemed disoriented by the streaks of dark blood flowing from the gashes in his back, neck, and shoulders. His mouth moved but no sound came out. He reached down and started to take a thin knife blade out of his boot when Annie rushed up and kicked him between the legs. He made a whoofing noise as if air had been let out of him and crumpled to the ground. She kicked the knife away and held the gun on him in her Weaver stance. He rolled around on the ground, mixing up dust and blood, holding his hands between his legs and groaning in pain. She breathed out in great relief it wasn't angel dust or he'd have come at her in a blind rage without having felt the kick to his genitals.

She booked him in and did the preliminary paperwork. By the time she left the station it was two in the morning. She was supposed to meet Jimmy in the muster room to go over the case in four hours. Overhead Boötes with his two dogs chased the Great Bear and the Little Bear around the night sky.

By seven o'clock she was facing him in the interrogation room across a desk. Her hand gripped the paper cup to keep it from shaking. Her headache was back, had in fact regrouped for a better attack on her frayed and sleepless nerves. But she couldn't trust Jimmy to do this right. He'd brace the kid with his machismo, the boy would lawyer up, and that would be the end of the case. A cluster of detectives along with Millimaki stood outside or listened in from the next room.

"You may not have been the gunman," she started, "but if you don't give him up, he'll certainly give you up and then he gets the deal. You get the death penalty."

He scowled at her. His wounds had been dressed but his eyes glowed with fear. She was getting through.

"It was him, man. It was all Bic. His plan, he did the shooting. I was just there. I didn't know what was going down. The fool never said he was going to shoot them old dudes, man!"

"Raymond," she said in her softest voice, "it doesn't matter who did the shooting. You're a co-conspirator, not just an accessory before and after the fact."

"Fucking hell, man. Fucking shit fucking hell. He just fucking did it, the crazy cocksucker. How the fuck was I supposed to know a candy ass like him was going to go berserk."

Annie tensed. What did he mean "candy ass"? Edgar Antoine "Bic" Maldonado was a six-foot-three inch, heavily muscled California biker. Once they had his real name, for every DUI, drug arrest or possession of Targes, Bic Maldonado had a sexual assault or a deadly weapons charge in the NCIC database. She learned Maldonado had picked up the "Bic" tag as a spur-of-the-moment thing the summer he and Raymond hooked up over a drug buy at Targes' cottage.

"The kid, man, the kid. He set it all up. We was just supposed – "

Annie felt her stomach lurch. *Andrew, he meant Andrew, the grandson.*

She already knew the answer but she asked it anyway. "So Bic wasn't on the bus? He wasn't the shooter?"

"No, man, shit. Bic was all about young pussy. The kid brought us in for all the free quiff and then he started talking about how we could rob his grandparents and shit like that. How these old fucks had all this retirement cash and they'd just throw it away on the slots in Detroit anyway, so why not make a few bucks? Nobody was supposed to get killed."

"You and Bic were supposed to meet the bus at the rest stop?"

"Hell yes, just like he said. Only Bic's a no-show. "Don't need him,' the kid says. He was supposed to stay in the car and point them out to me. I'd get the money and we'd drive off. Instead, I turn around, there he is behind me with this fuckin' 9 mm in his hand like he's watched too many rap videos. I go, 'Oh fuck me, what are doin'? Get out of here before they see you. I said to myself, 'This is gonna be bad, Raymond' and sure as shit, it was."

She could feature it easily. The bus stopped there every time so the old-timers could relieve their bladders. His grandmother always had lots of cash. She had a knack for it, as Andrew said to her. It was so *cold*.

"Why did Andrew kill them? Why not just steal her money when she got back?"

"The fuckin' bitch was going to cut him off at the knees – no more allowance, no more new car, nada. He was going to be cut out of the will. She and the old man were going to give away all his college money to some charity for radioactive kids in Russia."

"And," she said, looking at him squirming in his seat, trying to keep the disgust out of her question, "you believed him?"

"Man, he said a lot of shit. I didn't know what to believe! I never fuckin' believed he'd shoot his own family! I never believed that for one second! The old lady, she saw, she knew. Man, he just popped 'em, one after the other, head shots, never hesitated like it was as natural as your stomach going in and out breathing. Bang! Bang! Bang! Bang! Every one of them looked him in the eyes and he did them all. Put the gun right into their faces – "

"All right, all right, easy, Raymond. Just start over. Tell me from the beginning how you met . . . "

They stopped for breaks and she brought him

McDonald's twice. Seven hours later they had it all or as much as any prosecutor would need. The day after Mary Lou Stowe and her husband of forty-seven years were coming back from the casinos, they had an appointment to meet with the principal. She was going to tell them about the sex parties in their house while she was off playing the slots.

Annie shivered while he poured out the rest of the sordid catastrophe into the tape. She thought about Andrew, the model student, straight-As, class president, honor society.

When she came out of the room with Targes, there was a dumbfounded look on most of the cops' and dispatchers' faces. They were wondering too how evil could pass itself off so benignly. She passed Millimaki's office and saw him gripping the phone with his back to the window, exhaling clouds of blue cigar smoke from his Swisher Sweets. The media, no doubt. Teasing them before the announcement of the big arrest. She hoped Jimmy had him collared and cuffed and was on the way here by now. There were BOLOS out for Maldonado. She dropped Targes off at fingerprinting while a uniformed officer stood just behind him and watched with more than usual interest. The slaughterhouse of the bus was still a big deal.

She went back to her cubicle and began typing up the report. Suddenly, a sob came out of her throat. She looked around to see if anybody noticed. Just nerves, she thought, and the constant drilling going on between her ears as the migraine blossomed into its usual ugly fragrance. She reached into her bottom drawer for some pills and almost passed out.

At that moment her partner walked past and gave her a thumb's up. Jimmy O'Keefe's sign of approval was another pang that reminded her of home and her most intimate losses – a sister, a father.

"Good work, Cheng. We nailed them. I just heard Maldonado was picked up. We've got a bunch of screaming parents and their kids coming into the station early so be here by six, OK?" He was gone like smoke.

The lack of sleep and her body's bone-aching tiredness weakened the floodgates of memory and they came pouring in on her consciousness. She'd leave the typing for tomorrow. On the way back she opened the windows and let the warm wash over her. The night sky was full of stars that her made automatically arranged into their proper constellations – Orion, Sagittarius, and there, bright against the black matte curtain was the summer triangle and its triad of Vega, Altair, and Deneb. She and her sister had memorized a different summer night sky so many years ago. She closed her eyes and felt the wind against her face and wondered who she was exactly in this country. Jimmy alternately envied her and mocked her; Haftmann, a sorehead and misfit, once praised her as a hard-nosed homicide cop, yet she felt like a little girl, a wide-eyed schoolgirl but not at all experienced like the young girl she sat across a polished oak table in a library talking of sexual positions.

She thought of the bus and its inert human cargo as she had first seen them. The young trooper first called out was standing beside the bus with a hand on it to steady himself as he vomited up his lunch. Dead bodies didn't affect Annie Cheng.

Then a memory, hot and sharp: she and her sister were riding in a cramped bus along the Outer Ring Road on their way to see their father in Beijing's Prison Number One. Ti'ananmen Square had just exploded across the wire services and entranced the world with the image of a student halting a tank in its progress. Her father's arrest was a matter of course. He would be released soon. The students admired him. He was a passionate man and a brilliant teacher. He had done nothing wrong. She smoothed Li Feng's white crinoline dress and hushed her.

Through the thick plate glass she could see how tired he looked, not defeated, just tired; she noted the chin stubble that always scratched her when she kissed him. After a few minutes she heard no sounds coming through the plastic headphones and watched her father's lips move lovingly around words she could no longer hear. Then a guard's rough voice came through ordering them not to discuss the case. They spoke of her grades and her plans to visit him again. They received the news of his death in an official letter months after in Shanghai. Through diligent but cautious research and contacting a number of her father's old friends and some who still had influence in the government, she learned that he had died of pneumonia in that prison. He had been without warm clothes or even a blanket to keep him warm during the frigid Beijing winter. His cot and waste bucket were taken away as punishments. His tiny cell was never cleaned of waste. She remembered holding Li Feng's hand and telling her that their father would be home soon. She could almost recall the exact words she used to comfort her. She remembered the look in her sister's anxious eyes and knew that, whatever she herself felt, she had to be strong for her. That night they counted the stars from the balcony of their spacious apartment, a privilege of her father as a valued university professor. She showed Li Feng, Lepus the hare and told her how he saved himself by hiding between the feet of Orion, the hunter. That night in bed, long after her sister's soft breathing told her she was asleep, she let herself weep. She dreamed of riding in a bus filled with people, all of them strangely silent. They were heading out of the city to the mountains, maybe as far as the Great Wall.

As they stopped at each village, the passengers one by one exiting, each looking back at her with a face of sadness. As they approached the mountain range ringing Beijing, she noticed the driver as someone she knew, had always known. It was her father and he turned back to smile at her once and began to whistle his favorite aria from *Tosca*. She must have drifted off because when she awoke in her dream, she felt the bus had stopped moving. She knew her father was going to die and there was nothing she could do to stop it; after all, she was just a girl. When she looked up, the driver was gone. There was nothing in sight for miles except stunted trees and scraps of litter clinging to the branches of birch trees. Beneath them was a shabby necropolis of tombstones. Li Feng gently slapped her face to wake her from her nightmare. Annie heard the caterwauling of car horns of Beijing's awakening traffic; then she knew it all over again and realized that even if she were to run as far from Beijing as she could go, she would always be ruled by fates as old as the constellations.

The Strawberry Girls

"In the past six years, 17 women have been found strangled, most of them dumped in vacant lots and abandoned buildings . . ."

– "17 Slayings, 6 Years–and No Answers," *Plain Dealer*, 24 Apr. 1994

"Many of the victims were all either poor or working class . . . Many of the victims were what police call 'strawberries'– women who sell their bodies for crack cocaine or other drugs."

– "Killings May Be Related," [Erie, PA] *Times News*, 30 July 2000

I was sipping coffee in front of Luigi's stand off Little Minnesota when I bumped into Tico. Tico doesn't waste words; in fact, he won't talk at all if he can get by with a grunt, so I knew his old lady had sent him out to me to see if I was going to settle my bar tab. Marta had the finest cleavage, and the shortest fuse, of any business owner on the Strip.

"Gracías, Tomás," he said when I mentioned I was looking at a big payday "tomorrow" and would settle up then. He shuffled from one foot to the other, unconsciously reverting back to his ring days. He grew up in a city garbage dump and spent his teenaged years running from Guatemalan death squads, but only his wife could make him miserable.

"English, Tico, English," I said to his departing back–
an old and stupid joke that neither of us seemed willing to
part with. The truth was I was badly strapped. The silly
season was long over, the tourists had gone home and so
had the job offers from concerned parents. I had to pick
and choose carefully now to avoid time-consuming cases
without much chance of success. I generally made enough
over the summer to see me through, but this year was
different. Long weeks of torrential rains and low-flying
clouds painted the sky dark, beat the surface of Lake Erie
to the color of hammered tin. The axiom in my trade is the
younger, the more rupees to collect at the end. That's why
my only case at the moment had me worried–the runaway
was almost an adult. I couldn't afford to get burned.

I was standing there waiting for Annie, sipping Luigi's
coffee out of a Styrofoam cup and wondering how he could
make money selling a brew that was better than the one
good restaurant. The guy's name, by the way, wasn't Luigi,
and he wasn't Italian. I like to know who my sources are,
so I ran the license of his Cutlass Supreme: James Roberts,
six two, 197, brown and blonde. He looked German or
Scandinavian, long sideburns and reddish-blonde designer
stubble on a face that looked more fox than pig. He wasn't
friendly but he was a good source and he knew faces
whenever I showed him photos of missing kids. He never
acknowledged the "Great coffee, Jimmy" or the twenty I
palmed him. But I don't know anybody who works for free.

As if the weather weren't souring things fast enough, a
serial killer from Cleveland had resurfaced and started
dumping bodies along the back roads of the county. A
fourth one had just turned up over the weekend. That's
why I was waiting for Detective Annie Cheng.

She was turning the corner near Eddie's Grill and I
watched her skip like a goat across the street. Her slim
body in black slacks, a show-pony swing of her blue-black

hair, and I was lusting for her all over again. I figured I would be lucky enough to get Annie Cheng into bed on the day the pigs ate my brother, and I haven't got a brother. Her petite Chinese beauty gave off sexual vibes that she herself couldn't control. We're both divorced. I used to work for the precinct she's been lead homicide investigator for the last three years. Annie wasn't the usual drifter blown by strange winds, the kind that brought me to Jefferson-on-the-Lake, the last resort of burnout cops and dope fiends.

She greeted me with that smile, and I asked her how the big investigation was going.

"Shitty," she said.

The fourth "strawberry girl" had turned up in Harpersfield a few miles west. Some boys on four-wheelers had demolished the township's new historical society sign, a tribute to R.E. Olds, one-time native son who shook the cow shit off his shoes and got himself to Detroit. The sheriff sent a deputy, who noticed a foul smell coming from the ditch, but it took cadaver dogs to locate the body fifty, sixty yards away in a small culvert where purple loosestrife

Plant grew out of the effluent. She was long gone to rotten and the decomposition too far advanced to reveal much about the manner of death. Some nicks on the spinal vertebrae suggested it wasn't very pleasant. Cleveland homicide named them "strawberry girls" when they started showing up dead in vacant city lots all over the east side as far back as the seventies. All whores, all crackheads, their clothes hiked up around their waists, some had their faces pulverized, and several were manually strangled. LaRonda Portis was a known hooker with an address in east Cleveland, just another crackhead whore, and in case anybody cared, mother of four small children, the by-blows of her wayward calling.

"We can't find the cabbie," Annie said. "I called every outfit in northeaster Ohio."

"You get a description?" I asked her.

"Yeah but the composite's not that good." She showed me the sketch.

"They never are," I said.

"There's one thing, though," she said and hesitated.

"C'mon, Annie, I'm not going to sell it to the papers."

"His body odor was ferocious."

I laughed. "Who said that?"

Annie didn't find the same things funny that I did.

"Three people saw her get in a cab, a white man driving," she said. "This was in the projects where a white man would stand out. A Dairy Mart clerk on Route 46 ID'd him when he stopped for cigarettes and some beer. Described him right down to the body odor."

"So you've got nothing but a cabbie you can't find and one distinguishing feature that goes away when he takes a shower."

She looked at me with that little tilt of her chin. She looked fourteen, like one of my runaways except she had no nose rings or tatts on any part of the skin she exposed. "He's a loose end we're looking to tie off."

"Cleveland cabbies don't charter fifty-mile runs to this shitburgh with a lone passenger. The guy was no cabbie and he's probably your perp."

"Thanks, Haftmann. I guess I can go back to the station and close the case now."

Sarcastic little minx, I adored her.

The she laid this on me: "The guy at Luigi's stand says he remembered her with some biker type."

"What?"

Roberts was *my* source. I don't mind sharing him, but it bothered me he was working for the cops too.

"Yeah," she said. "He gave me that big dope bust last

month. We weren't even close at the time. We knew dope was coming in regular because every kid on the Strip had a connection. This guy was clean. Forty-one, no priors in Ohio, NCIC didn't have him, nothing with drugs, surveillance never even heard of him. DEA thinks he was groomed by somebody down there. This has Mexican narcotraffic written all over it."

"How sure can you be?" I had to ask.

"As sure as three hours of intensive grilling can make it. He's up to his ass in heavyweight federal drug charges and he's willing to make deals with the DA's office, US attorney's, anybody's, to play ball, and if he had this to throw in for reduced time, he'd do it gladly. My hunch tells me he's not connected to the dead body in Harpersfield. He was flying back from Tijuana into Cleveland-Hopkins at the time the coroner says LaRonda Portis was breathing her last."

"So what's a twenty-buck crack whore doing so far from home?"

"That's the mystery of it, Thomas. But aren't you getting sidetracked? Your missing girl is all you should be worrying about."

"Yeah, I know. So give, Detective."

"That's you, Haftmann, always brimful of empathy for suffering humanity." She cut those gorgeous nut-brown eyes to my face.

"Suffering humanity be damned. I need to stay warm this winter. I need to eat. I need to pay my bar bill—"

"OK, OK, I get it. Here's all I can get you and you didn't get it from me," she said. She handed me a folded over packet of Xeroxes.

"Thank you, Detective Cheng. How about dinner sometime, a small token of my thanks? When's good for you?"

"Sure, Thomas, never's good for me." She swiveled

around smartly and blew me a goodbye kiss. She would tire of this game, I thought, long before me. An aging ex-cop on the wrong side of fifty with winter coming. I was afraid that I wore my own solitude like an ugly mist that kept people at a distance.

A beer at Tico's saloon would take the edge off and let me read the material she had grabbed from one database or another. I was *persona non grata* around the precinct and would be as long as Chief Millimaki held the reins and, I suppose, as long as people still remembered some of the fallout from my divorce from Micah, ex-prosecuting attorney for Jefferson County.

Laurie Tate was at the polar end of the social scale from LaRonda Portis. Her Syracuse family had real estate and businesses on both coasts. There was a manor house in Sarasota Springs, where the family kept thoroughbreds. Private schools. Her father told me she was debating whether to begin at Skidmore in the fall when her last contact reached him: a cheesy postcard, a beach scene circa 1980s, purchased from an arcade on the Strip and mailed from here. The card said nothing except she was "taking a year off" and would attend college next year. The parents confirmed the postcard's handwriting as hers. Nothing unusual in the style of phrasing. Until it arrived, they thought she was visiting girl friend at Dartmouth.

Marta hove into view, breaking my concentration. She wiped down the counter in front of me with a few desperate circles with the rag just inches short of my bottle. Her mighty bosom still shook even when she stopped wiping.

I went back to my musings. What would bring a rich girl to this seedy strip? I had asked that question many times before and never had a single or even a good answer for it. They seemed to drift, these kids, and many disappeared into a black hole, got themselves mangled and were spit back out—or were never seen again. It was my living, after all, but I didn't have to like it. For some it was the dope, for some it was passing through. Many kids rode in on the trains despite the danger because word on the grapevine was that Jefferson-on-the-Lake resort was a place to stop off for a while, relax, smoke some weed, make a little money; some girls freed from the constraints of home and status ran a little wild, some even tried hooking. In all my years here, the city leaders had never enforced the prostitution codes or run a sting for johns. Too many connected men, many of them local big shots, looked forward to a season of young female flesh. They made very sure no police chief would ever rock that boat by enforcing the laws against flesh-peddling and sex with minors. It created an environment that made you look beneath the surface of families and children cavorting on water slides and look hard at the beefy clown in greasy jeans with the anorectic, twitching young girl on the bike, whom he might have met an hour ago doing her table dance at one of the seedier bars.

I was still rattled by my guy giving up the dope house. The cops had practically tripped over it on their way to a dead-body-found call. A headlines-grabbing seizure they'd milk for months, but it made no difference to the illicit businesses along the Strip. Everybody who wanted to score, get laid, or buy a gun could make a connection in minutes. All of it could take place right under the tourists' eyes and nothing would be done about any of it. There was too much money and everybody had a hand in somebody else's pocket.

I used the payphone out front to call the girl's house and spoke to the parents; each was on an extension in the house. Although I had them send me the documents and photos I would need, you never get all the story so you to listen for the small evasions. Laurie Tate could be partying somewhere close by or she could be long gone. Both parents were adamant that she knew no one in Ohio, had never been there except when passing through along Route 90. "No, Frank, remember? She went to that concert last summer – the rap singer, wasn't it? – in Cleveland." "No, Helen, that was in Columbus." "Whatever," the mother sniffed. The papers Annie gave me mentioned property on the river.

"Could she have gone to see anyone in Pittsburgh?"

"It's worth checking out," the father said. "She used to visit cousins when she was little." I suppressed a groan. I wasn't keen on getting into wild goose chases just yet, but I promised I would go down there. They gave me the address.

I made a few calls, spoke to a few more locals on the Strip, and planned my itinerary for the rest of the week.

Dewey Brown, ex-Lake cop and full-time asshole, came in. I heard him but didn't bother to turn around.

"Hey, Haftmann. They let anybody drink here."

"Fuck you, Dewey."

"Never changes his bar stool or his brand. I know one thing you changed."

"I'm not interested, white trash."

"Well, shit, maybe your muffdiving lesbian of a wife–"

I broke the bottle right at his skullcap where the bone is thinnest. The light in his eyes went out and he imploded right on the bar stool–did a little shoulder jerk spasm– then crumpled in slo-mo to the floor. I watched. I shouldn't have. He had brought his redneck asshole buddies in with him, two of them. The Seymour brothers, Phil and Jerome. Phil and I were the same age, same height. Jerome, however, was five inches shorter and as many years younger than his bro, a whole lot faster. Tico paid Jerome to spar with his son, a natural welterweight, the summer before he turned pro.

Jerome hit me in the rib cage just under the heart. I don't think I had let go of the broken bottle at that point but it wouldn't have mattered. I did a silly imitation of Dewey's shimmy on the bar stool before I joined him on the floor. I was looking up at Jerome so it must have been Phil who kicked me under the jaw. I heard a bit of commotion around me, a dull buzzing that ceased, and though I tried hard to listen to the words, I found the impulse to slip into a black cave irresistible.

I came to with Marta holding a wet rag to my forehead. The brothers and Dewey Brown were gone. A pair of tapered legs merged in a vee beneath a woman's belted corduroy coat, and I realized Annie Cheng was looking down on me.

"Hi, Annie," I said.

"Hello, Haftmann," she responded. I thought the bells were still ringing in my head, but one of her black shoes was tapping the floor. I knew I was adding to her workload. She mumbled something about taking me home and then pairs of hands were grabbing at me in all directions. Then I found myself on my feet. Annie guided and frog-marched me through the door. Outside the sun was still gone behind scudding clouds and the streets were tinted with dark spots from rain that leaked instead of fell from the sky.

"How long was I out?" I asked her. She pointed at the nearby Crown Victoria.

"Twenty minutes," she said.

"Fuck me, a raving pussy."

"Yeah, well, get your head checked out."

"You mean that?" I tried out a leer that came off as a smirk.

"You know what I mean," she said and then said something in Chinese that was probably not complimentary to my character. She cut her eyes to me as

145

she drove in the direction of Harpersfield, the next township beyond the neon of the Strip. No bars out here that weren't on cement blocks.

"What's the hurry, Annie?"

"Shut up. I want to show you something," she snapped. Her hair whipped off her neck in the breeze coming through the open window. Annie always drove with a window down in case the car skidded into a pond or went into the lake. An old woman in Shandong had told her when she was a little girl she would die by drowning.

She drove to the dope house. The yellow crime tape was still intact.

"Fucking Millimaki," I muttered. Advertising his big coup to the masses.

She pulled up to the porch and got out without another word to me. I followed her to the front door where she pulled out some keys on a ring and opened it. I lifted the tape over my head without tearing it and followed her into the house.

It was an old Victorian, nothing special except for the wooden bannister to the upper floor; the dowels were all curlicued into twisted pretzel shapes and glowed in the yellow light streaming through the windows. It smelled musty and debris from the cops was still scattered around.

"Come here," Annie said glancing back at me, "And stop gawking like a rookie at your first crime scene."

We went down the basement. Someone, years ago, had decided to spruce it up with some bright blue paint—cement walls, brickwork chimneys, pipes, ceiling—the whole lot a cheery sky-blue panorama.

She took me into the washroom where an old coal chute had been sealed up. The walls here were unpainted, flaky with creosote and recent graffiti. It smelled powerfully of deodorant. Against the far wall near a cellar doorway, which obviously hadn't been opened in decades,

146

were scuff marks in the dust and a pair of chains dangling from rusted-out shackles dangling from ring bolts in the wall. I noticed the bolts, about twelve inches from the ceiling, looked almost new.

"What's this?" I asked her.

Annie stood there silently for a while, and then she said: "Jesus, look closer."

I reached out to touch one of the ringbolts and stopped.

"It's OK," she said. "We dusted."

There was dried blood, or what might be blood, along the seams of the cement blocks just above the floor where somebody had replaced the original fieldstone. There were thick smears of the same material against the wall about twenty inches from the floor.

"Look down here," Annie said and pointed. In a corner where discolored cardboard boxes had been stacked against the wall was a dull cascade of old brown paint–that is, until I looked closer and saw that it, too, must be dried blood. At the outer edges were the tails showing the direction of spatter. Too much for one human being to lose and still live.

"He got a lot of it on the walls," I said. I noticed where it had pooled around the drain and I saw where forensics must have taken scrapings.

"So what did your team find?"

"Besides the blood, you mean? Some brain matter, nothing around these scupper holes. A hose must have knocked everything loose and sent it out beyond the house."

Then I knew what hit me. "Your dead body, Portis–"

"Yeah," Annie nodded, "if you cut through the property this way, she would be maybe sixty, seventy yards from where we're standing."

If the strawberry girls killer was operating out of this

house, it was a major breakthrough. I remember when Annie just transferred up from Columbus; she hadn't been here a week before Chief Millimaki added her to the serial-killer task force, a token woman whose spot was earned because three bodies had been dumped in her county. That task force was about to get a jolt of adrenalin. She must have read my mind.

"Think, Haftmann," she said. "It isn't him. It can't be." She dug a little hole in the dirt and absentmindedly filled it in.

"Sure, he'd be an old man, but it's been known to happen. They do come out of retirement," I said.

"It's a copycat. Somebody's throwing dust at our faces." Now and then, Annie had a bit of trouble with American idioms.

I stared at her. It was time for her to tell me what I was doing here.

"We found an axe head behind those cartons underneath some newspapers. We're pretty sure it was used on LaRonda Portis. The three oblong indentations in the skull fit the dimensions."

"Come on, Annie, give it to me."

"What type blood is your missing girl?"

"O negative," I said.

"We typed two samples from the catch basin," she said. "O positive and AB negative," she said.

Schadenfreude—my old German grandmother had given me the word. A mix of sadness and joy. There's no English equivalent. It wasn't conclusive proof that Laurie Tate was not in the torture room with LaRonda Portis, but it went a long way toward that assumption.

I learned everything from what Annie could safely release from her files in the ongoing investigation. The house owner was interrogated for hours but he claimed to know nothing at all of what went on in the cellar. His house was never without people coming and going. Most of the bike gangs were his clients but anybody off the street and looking for grass was welcomed. If the owner was away on a buying trip, he always made sure one of his dealers was available to fill in. The cops had his ledger books. It was a massive business enterprise in marijuana. He had never felt the need to branch out. The cops were also looking at his substitute dealers going back three years, about the time the body dumping in the counties east of Cleveland started occurring.

"So how does a guy slinging hamburgers come by this information?"

"That's what I want to know," she said. "But Millimaki is putting a lot of pressure on me to lay off him. No taps, no surveillance."

"What the fuck," I shouted, "sweat him. Haul his narrow ass in—"

"Don't shout at me, Thomas," she said and glared up with her nostril wings flared for combat. "He's got a lawyer, and he isn't answering any more questions."

We drove back in silence. I had to keep focused on Laurie. Millimaki was Annie's problem, but I knew very well why she brought me there. She was asking me for some unofficial surveillance on our mutual CI, an all-too mysterious figure who knew more than how to make a great cup of coffee. Annie would never ask a favor directly, but she knew how to call in a marker. She also knew I'd oblige her.

I had to get that Pittsburgh thread tied off. The father was leaving voicemails two and three times a day. He wanted results. My instincts that Laurie Tate would not be found in Pittsburgh were wrong. I confirmed sightings in Pittsburgh, one from a storekeeper where she made a phone call and had asked for change. Time to see the Tate cousins.

Melissa Tate was a first cousin. She had last seen
Laurie three year ago, maybe longer than that. This Tate
had cultivated the languorous demeanor of a Chekhov
female, but she had that trophy-wife look I had begun to
notice from the photos of the females in the line. She said
that Laurie had seemed sad and had lost too much weight,
too thin for her bones; she even called her "cadaverous."

"Young girls these days, you know," she said.

"I'm sorry, " I said, but I don't follow you."

"They show everything they've got, deface themselves
with tattoos and nose rings, body piercings, they call it. All
that grotesquerie."

"Laurie was different?" I led her on.

She narrowed her eyes to see if that cretinous remark
had escaped honestly or was I being snide.

"Laurie was mortified throughout her adolescence. She
was raised to be better than that. She was a completely
normal little girl growing up except–she paused for a
moment–she had more money than most little girls. These
are difficult years for girls, especially today, Mr.
Haftmann."

"I know, I see much of it in my line of work."

"I'm sure you do," she simpered and smiled. This time
I narrowed my eyes to her. "I just don't understand why
she's . . . she's taken off like that and left my poor aunt and
uncle in a tizzy."

What did she mean? *Laurie is, well, you know,
sensitive about that . . . unfortunate business that
happened to her when she came of age.* At first, I didn't
understand; then it clicked: the photos her parents sent
me showed a young woman with chestnut hair down to her
shoulders. The shots of her in evening gowns for what
could have been proms were more revealing. Laurie was
not a big girl, but she was extremely busty–not in Marta's
league by a long shot–but endowed with a shapeliness that

150

would draw stares from men on or off the beach. The cousin mentioned that Laurie had spoken of a breast reduction to save her back in her old age, but she wasn't sure if that was a joke. To my question about eating disorders, the cousin thought a moment and said no, but her weight loss that summer only accentuated her bosom.

"Do you have any idea where she could be right now?"

"No, I'm afraid not."

"Does Laurie stay at a certain place in Pittsburgh?"

"Laurie has friends everywhere. She's been all over the world, as I'm sure you know from my uncle," she said.

"He told me she grew up in Boston before the family moved to New York."

"Oh my, yes," she drawled, "but Laurie's lived in many places. She grew up in Mexico and Los Angeles when the family import business expanded. She spent a year or two in Hawaii, and I think in Singapore–or Thailand maybe." "Laurie's quite intelligent as well as mature. She's not like the typical Tate women in all respects, you see."

I wasn't sure if she was alluding to Laurie's bustline or intellect so I didn't pick up whatever she was hinting at.

"Does Laurie ever come here? Your uncle mentioned a place down here that Laurie used to visit when she was young."

"Yesss," she seemed to have to think about this for a moment while she hissed the sibilants at me. "Grandfather Tate was a contemporary of Carnegie. He supplied all the glass for the steel factories in Pittsburgh. He built a cottage on the river in McKeesport. It's right on Point Vue."

"Can you give me directions?" I asked her.

"Sure, but there's no one there. No one goes there anymore. I'm afraid the area has declined since grandfather's time. The rivers are full of muck and filth now. When Laurie was a girl, we used to hike in the woods, then catch and eat the fish."

"Her father didn't mention she was a nature lover."

"Most young girls are like young boys in that respect. But girls at puberty draw away from those things. Laurie was a perfect tomboy until adolescence until nature cursed her." She made a moue at me. Only a woman, I thought, could consider big breasts a handicap.

Back home, I felt the need for a shower and a few beers. My mouth was foul tasting. I couldn't put off bracing James Robinson much longer. I had another stop at the end of the Strip, a lowlife dive where girls would sometimes go if they were desperate. The bar owner, a transplanted San Diegan and lifelong member of the Pagan motorcycle gang out there, didn't recognize the photo I had showed him weeks ago when I made the rounds. I told him to imagine her in a thong. That rang the nematode's three or four brain cells to get a reaction. "Yeah, yeah," he said tapping her face on the photo with a blackstained fingernail. She had worked through August. "Nice cooze, not like these fuckin crazy Goth bitches," he said. "She quit on me just before Labor Day. That's when I need chicks the most. All these bitches run off, go back to college or wherever, man, and I gotta use these slack-titted locals to get by."

"Know where she went?"

"Man, she coulda made a shitload in tips if she'd stayed just through the weekend. Great rack on her. Lyin'-ass bitch said she was good to stay around through October," he fumed. He made an odd image of an affronted businessman.

"Anybody pay special attention to her?" I asked.

"How the fuck would I know? I'm too busy pouring drinks and running the place."

"Any idea where she might be now?"

"Man, I just hire them. They come and they go."

He showed me her work records. She used the name

Laurie Griffin and gave the address of cottages owned by the Pehrla family on Lakeview that I knew to be fake because that street went into the drink during the last el Niño season. The cottages were left to rot and I couldn't see Laurie Tate living in filth and spiders even with the contradictions I was discovering.

Many girls who worked this dive never existed on paper and wanted it that way. A weekend gig, some dancing, maybe some prostitution if the customer were halfway respectable. Every now and then a local would hang out here instead of try to pick up runaways on one of the Strip's neon side streets called Little Minnesota.

What didn't jibe was Laurie's doing anything like hanging around a biker's shitbox for money from what the cousin had told me about her. Even if she had acquired a serious dope habit, her parents had the money to send her to a toney rehab or keep her in dope without anyone making a fuss.

The cousin said she had a backpack for a change of clothes but nothing else out of the ordinary. Nothing unusual in her behavior, no telltale meth twitches or runny nose or mood swings. Just plain old, dear cousin Laurie, a little thin perhaps . . .

God damn it, what was I missing?

Robinson was just closing Luigi's. It was too early to close even for these end-of-season days. I threw a photo of Laurie across the counter, and he caught it expertly before it skipped into the Fry-o-lator. "Good catch, Jimmy. How come you didn't recognize her?" He held the photo too long and the corners of his mouth twitched. I'd be a piss-poor private eye if I didn't see all the arrows of guilt pointing straight at him from his own reaction. He looked like a man in grief. He tossed the photo back to me on the counter and turned to start scraping grease off the grill.

"Look at me," I said.

"We're closed for the day. I've got to do my routine."

"Look at me, asshole. You'll do your routine in the county slammer if I don't get straight answers. He threw the spatula in the corner and turned back; his head was lowered and his eyes slitted like a man aware he was already confined in small space that could get smaller. He had to stoop to keep from hitting his head on the menu board.

"Look, I didn't recognize her. I see thousands of girls every day. What do you expect?"

"You recognized LaRonda Portis when Detective Cheng showed you her photo," I pointed out. Cheng's photo was a recent mug shot from Cleveland P. D. I knew this wasn't a fair comparison between a pretty, whey-faced white girl and a hard-eyed crack whore.

"Look, man, some I remember, some I don't."

"OK," I said and took the edge out of my voice. "Let me ask you something—where do you get that coffee?'

"He furrowed his brow a bit. "Whaat? What the fuck's my coffee got to do—"

"Where do you get your coffee?"

"What's wrong with the coffee?"

"Answer my question. I just wondered where you got it."

He mumbled something about a Youngstown supplier, so I flashed him some teeth, big smile for the mutt; then I crossed the street out of his view and found a seat near the miniature golf course behind some hedges. *All right, fucker*, I thought. *Let's see if that shakes your tree.*

I counted sixteen rock doves wheeling in their dive-bomber formation overhead—another sign of winter coming when you had more pigeons diving for scraps off the street than gulls. Fifteen minutes passed and I heard the shutters rattle down. In a few weeks more, when just locals stopped by on their way to work their city jobs, he'd

close down for the season and head off for warmer parts
with his mobile food and beverage stand. I saw him carry a
green garbage bag in his right hand and duck into a cul-de-
sac some vendors used for garbage collection, something
he must have done every night; a moment passed, I heard
the clang of the lid hit the metal rim, and he was back out
and fast-walking down a cottage-lined street opposite me.
I crossed the street and kept him in view all the way.
Ducking down that, I found the dumpster he used. I lifted
one of the covers and risked a quick look inside. There
were three bags so I grabbed them all and swung them
over a small fence and hoped some litter freak wouldn't
bother them.

I stayed about sixty yards back and kept some oak
trees in my line of sight in case he turned around. He
didn't. He unlocked a lime-green Cutlass Supreme in
vintage condition and drove off. I memorized the plate and
returned to collect the bags. They might tell me something
I was curious to know. Back in Tico's, I called Cheng for an
update and learned from a friendly dispatcher she was on
call at a disturbance at the Oak Room. "Imagine that," I
said, "all these shit-biker bars and some old-men golfers
with pants up to their nipples get into a donnybrook at the
most sedate bar on the Lake."

"It isn't the first time," she said; the she offered a stage
whisper: "They had to escort Chief Millimaki home from
there last Sunday." I told her I wasn't surprised and hung
up. Millimaki was the corrupt old soul of Jefferson-on-the-
Lake.

Luigi's garbage was all garbage. He had lied about the
supplier, though. The discarded coffee bags said premium
kola beans, not blended, as you would get from imported
coffee from Hawaii, but real kola beans. Because I am
addicted to coffee, have been all my life even as a boy, I
knew that this was ridiculously expensive. You could get it

for twenty dollars a pound on the Internet. This had come from a supplier in Houston.

Why lie about where you got your coffee or how much you paid for it?

Even cops and locals had problems with their kids and needed some private-eye work on the cheap. I still had one or two debts I could call in. I made some discreet calls to the station and left messages on a couple voicemails.

Marta wasn't pleased to see me but she managed to uncurl her bottom lip long enough to serve me a draft and a shot of Hennessy's. My jaw ached every time I opened my mouth and the bruising had turned a hideous yellow beneath the stubble where I still couldn't shave. A couple local men I knew slightly were holding down both ends of the bar with me anchoring the middle like a drinkers' relay team.

Tico came out of the kitchen and I asked him what he knew about Dewey Brown and the brothers Seymour. "I dunno, Tomás. They start palling around, like, last year."

"I know they're customers, Tico. I'm not asking you to say anything, right? Just nod or something. Is Dewey in business with them?"

"What business?"

"The dope business, what else? Is Dewey fixing things at the station with the brothers?"

Tico washed his hands in his apron. Was he thinking or just nervous because I had put him on the spot?

"Dewey and Millimaki, they meet here for drinks once in a while."

"Thanks, Tico," I said.

He couldn't have made it plainer that an envelope of bills was slipped between hands while they shared a chinwag and a beer. Millimaki had to fire Brown last summer because he was just too dirty, even by Jefferson-on-the-Lake standards. Too much was about to be revealed in a sealed indictment. I knew that from Micah, my ex, when she was still deputy prosecutor. Dewey was the sacrificial lamb to make it all go away. She was furious that Brown was going to walk away from six felony charges. He lost his pension, but he knew how to get it back and more with all his connections. I was cordially disliked there, so how much better must it be for Dewey Brown, who had taken one for the team? While I was down there on the floor after our scuffle, the powerful reek of cat urine was thick in my nostrils when I came to. Millimaki had dissolved the precinct's narcotics jump-out squad; no surprise that meth labs were proliferating throughout the county like toadstools after a downpour. The cat-piss stench was a giveaway.

Back home in my pied-à-terre–that is, a room I rent in a seedy motel not owned by the Pehrla family; the locals called it the Crazy 8 Motel for the collection of misfits housed within–I found a string of messages, including a few hang-ups, a warning that could have been the raspy voice of Phil Seymour to "watch your ass" and then a long message from one of my very discreet sources at the station.

Eric James Robinson, aka James Roberts, was indicted for sexual imposition with a 15-year-old girl in 1995. This had to be a knocked-down rape charge. The girl was two days from her sixteenth birthday. He served one month of a six-month term, did community service and paid a thousand dollar fine.

"The weird thing is," said my contact, whose son I had rescued from a junkie crash pad on the beach just before it was raided, "Millimaki wrote a glowing letter in his behalf to Judge Hague in the pre-sentencing report."

It was around 1998 that I first noticed the man at the coffee-and-burger stand. Just another mope and drifter doing scut work to survive–or was he? The Supreme was vintage, mint condition. Like the expensive coffee, it was an anomaly in a place where people sold you bad food, watered booze, and shoddy goods. Tourists griped on occasion when the drinks were too watered down but steelworkers up from the Mahoning Valley were just grateful to see blue sky and green water on their week's vacation and so didn't mind the overpriced goods and the ramshackle cottages.

My second source gave me more bit to add to the mix. This Robinson was rich enough not to have to work another day in his life. His parents left him a house in Maryland worth a quarter million and enough waterfront property to put him on easy street. He could sell off a little at a time and never work another day in his life. Yet there he was, every day, rain or shine, working that hamburger stand like a man down to his last dime. "Another thing, " said my guy in a nervous quaver. "The guy's a college grad, U of Michigan, architecture, magna cum laude, class of 97. Had a nervous breakdown or something. The college won't release the records. I have a feeling there's more to it, something they don't want to let out."

"Thanks," I said.

"Don't thank me, Haftmann. That's it. We're square."

He clicked off and left me wondering about a guy with this much going for him asking people if they want fries with their burgers. I remember once, in a mood of excessive generosity, I slipped him an extra five with the twenty for a tip that had helped me bag a runaway that hadn't gone back to Toledo as I first thought. The smile on his face, now that I think of it, was a sneer. He was laughing at me.

Intriguing as "Luigi" was turning out to be, the fact is that I wasn't any closer to Laurie Tate, and a quick trip to Ann Arbor wasn't in the cards.

I called her parents, and much as I dislike doing this,

it's sometimes necessary to get a little rough with parents. I told them to stop bullshitting me around and give me the straight answers I needed. I held their little girl's life up in front of their eyes and told them I had to know things, unpleasant things maybe, but time was running out. I fired off my questions and didn't give them a lot of time to think or explain. At the end, I was sweating and Mrs. Tate was sobbing. The father was on the verge of cursing or screaming or maybe both, but I eased them down from their stress and did what I could to reassure them both I was still working every possible lead. In my heart and in my guts, I believed she was already dead.

My hand was shaking when I put the phone down. I had agitated their worst fears and learned nothing new about Laurie Tate, debutante and missing daughter, except that she had delayed going to college after high school. "She wanted to learn about herself before she committed," said the mother. The father chimed in, "I approved her decision wholeheartedly. There was no rush to go to college. 'Take your time, Laurie,' I said to her. "See the world a bit. Hell, I spent a year hitchhiking across America when I was her age"

Tico phoned me at midnight. The Seymour brothers were in the bar and very drunk. Nothing new there. Tico had repaid me many times over for the help I gave him with immigration with a little judicious eavesdropping. He heard Phil tell Jerome to "Shut up, leave it be, little brother." But he heard the words *Escalade* and *Robbie* as he poured them one on the house.

Robbie Pehrla was the rich-boy son of the wealthiest family on the Strip; they'd started out in the forties in a post-war boom of building cottages and bars along this scenic strip of land on Lake Erie. The son was spending the inheritance as fast as he could. Robbie was rumored to be involved in everything he could get his mitts on that was

illegal or below-the-radar like servicing the Pagans with
sex slaves or brokering drug deals. He drove only cherry-
red Cadillacs.

I was in the middle of one of my insomnia periods and
so had no sleep to lose. I grabbed the thermos of coffee for
the stakeout and drove to Tico's Place and waited for the
brothers. Phil and Jerome were the last out the door. I
watched them stagger out just as the lights inside dimmed.

While Phil was fumbling with his keys and Jerome was
pissing behind the fender, I hit little brother in the neck
with the Taser and watched him drop to the ground with a
strangled moan; a yellow arc of piss splashed around his
thrashing legs. Phil was so drunk he didn't react until I
was right on top of him. I held the buck knife at his neck
and asked him, "Where is the girl?" His tongue lolled
obscenely before he brought his senses into control.

"Pehrla . . . has . . . her . . . "

"Where?"

"With Robbie . . . McKeesport."

God damn it.

I should have checked the place out when I was down
there. *Why had the cousin lied?*

I hit 90 and swung south on Interstate 79 for
Pittsburgh, hoped the staties were asleep in their cruisers,
and made it in three hours' time. I arrived in McKeesport
just as the sun was climbing over the green hills; it could
have been sunrise in Rio de Janeiro if you kept your eyes
fixed on the blue sky; it was muggy and going to be humid.
The harbor smells of rotting fish, waterlogged debris, and
acrid haze from the factories down by the river were not an
olfactory treat. It was going to take me forever if I couldn't
locate the cottage soon, and I hoped Robbie's bright red
Escalade would shorten the time.

I laid a simple story on the morning shift clerk at a
Dairy Mart and found the posh section easily; from there,

it was reading mailboxes and eyeballing driveways. I had gulped the last of my coffee and felt the corrosive burn on an empty stomach when the ass-end of Robbie's car hove into view around a bend where the houses were more discreetly laid back from the road. These weren't cottages but half- to million-dollar houses with posh arches, long driveways, backyards landscaped to the river's edge, and tiered walkways.

I parked the car where it wouldn't attract immediate attention. There didn't seem to be any private security system to contend with. I loped around the side where a stand of trees gave me a shielding. The sun was full up and the house's windows were lit like gold.

The house had an add-on Florida Room with French doors. I jimmied these and stepped inside. The a/c was on morgue-room temperature. Plush carpets downstairs and a curved staircase. I left my shoes on and headed for it. I had a Sig in my right hand. Robbie once sold guns out the back door of one of family's businesses; he had been a star athlete in high school and still wore his hair slicked back as he had in the disco days.

I sidled up the stairs and listened but the thrumming of the air-conditioning masked any sound the carpeting didn't already damp. There was the faintest whiff of something—ammonia, a cat litter box somewhere close. At the top of the stairs, a hallway led to three doors. I angled to the first and peered in. An empty bedroom faced the Monongahela. The second doorway opened to a second bedroom on the opposite side except a balcony had been built off it. *Let's see what's behind door number three.*

I transferred the gun to my left hand and prayed it wouldn't be locked.

Laurie was nude on the bed, on hands and knees, her ass high in the air. Slamming into her from behind was Robbie Pehrla; his thick back muscles taut and his buttocks clenching as he drove himself into her. Laurie's huge breasts swayed back and forth with the momentum of his thrusts. The room was redolent of stale cologne, sweat, and sex.

"Get off her, Robbie," I said.

"Jesus Christ, who the fuck're you, motherfucker?"

He had thrown himself off her to the other side of the bed; his phallus still erect and pointing at me with a long glistening string of ejaculate trailing from its red tip.

I aimed the gun at his stomach the lowered it. "Shut up," I said.

When I looked toward Laurie Tate, I saw that she had a smirk on her face that said she was a long way from terrified.

"So Mommy and Daddy sent you, huh?"

"That's right," I said. "Get dressed."

A small-caliber gun with delicate filigree engraving on the grip, a Lady Smith-and-Wesson, lay on the floor in the heap of her clothes. I picked it up.

"Any other guns?" I asked Robbie.

"Fuck you."

She made no effort to cover herself and reached across to a nightstand drawer; then she looked at me to see if that was all right.

"Just my cigarettes," she said. "I like to smoke after sex."

"Get your clothes on, Laurie," I repeated. "You're going home."

"What's your name?" she said and blew a long stream of blue smoke in my direction.

"Thomas Haftmann. I'm a private investigator working for your parents."

She laughed. She drew her knees up to her chest with an unashamed frankness that exposed labia and a trimmed stripe of tawny hair that reached almost to her navel.

She looked over at Robbie, who had lost his erection. "Maybe we should tell Hartmann here what you're carrying around in the trunk of your car," she said.

"Shut up, bitch!" Robbie snapped. His face was sweaty and his eyes darted between us.

"Robbie brought something down from the Lake–"

"Shut your goddamned mouth!" Robbie screamed; his eyes were big and his face showed real terror. He reached over to slap her face. I kept the gun on him in case it was an act.

Laurie looked at him and laughed. Then she whispered," Maggot food."

Robbie screamed and lunged for her.

I was going to wait for this little melodrama to play itself out. I thumbed the safety off the S & W and held both guns in the direction of their bed splitting the distance between them. When I stepped back to give myself extra room, I caught me heel on one of her sandals and stumbled backwards.

Robbie had shed weight since his football days, but his reflexes were still fast. I had brought the guns upward in trying to catch my balance when he whirled and hit my shoulder with his fist. The Sig went flying out of my hand, but the little gun went off inches from his face.

Robbie was lying on top of me; his empty eyehole dripped blood and sere from the burned-out socket where the slug had punched through his brain.

I heaved him off me at the very moment Laurie brought the base of the lamp down on my head. The blow was glancing, or she might have cracked my skull open. As it was, I bled out plenty and that–plus her own panic– saved my life because she didn't hang around to finish me off.

I wasn't out long, but long enough for her to be gone. Robbie's Escalade sat in the driveway, so there must have been a second vehicle in the garage.

I had stanched the blood and lost some of the dizziness. I couldn't drive but I had to see what was in the trunk of the Cadillac in case she forgot it in her panic. Somehow, recalling her words before Robbie leaped at me, I doubted that she was given to panic. This was not how runaways usually acted. Not all were happy to see me but some were glad their sojourn was over. I made it possible for them to go home whatever the causes of their own uprooting or wanderlust had been. She was the first one who had acted with complete indifference about her own rescue.

I found the keys on the floor near Robbie's damaged head. The two guns were gone. My wallet was open and lying on the floor but she hadn't taken any money.

Luigi was in the trunk. Or as I should have called him formally in his death, Eric James Robinson was in the trunk with a large part of his skull excavated. He was nude, his hands crossed demurely in front of his crotch, in full rigor; dark liver spots of collected blood on his back and lower torso meant he had been in and out of rigor, possibly 12 to 15 hours in the trunk, and he was getting ripe. Whoever had killed him had been prepared to kill him: green garbage bags had been carefully duct-taped to cover every inch of trunk space to catch the effluent. I pulled one end of the plastic aside and saw a Mossberg shotgun lying near the wheel well.

Back inside the cool house, I sat down at the kitchen table to think. My head was still woozy, so I swallowed some orange juice I found in the refrigerator with a half-dozen aspirin. When I was ready, I began the cleanup. I removed every trace I had been there except what Pittsburgh forensics was bound to find. I would be just a presence in the house but not enough to identify. I wiped down the surfaces I had touched and resigned myself to the fact I was giving Pittsburgh homicide a fast leap forward to Jefferson-on-the-Lake and one down-at-heels gumshoe who was going to lose his license anyway. Right now, though, I had something more important to lose: time. Laurie Tate had a four-hour head start.

I knew enough to know where I had to go and there wasn't much time before she would be long gone and no low-rent P.I. like me would ever get close to her again.

My hunger and my head wound almost overcame me on the long stretch up Pennsylvania's northwest corner. I pulled into a rest stop and leaned out the door to vomit, shocking one elderly woman who gaped at me from her SUV. I bought a couple candy bars to ease the hunger and drove on and risked a speeding ticket that would put me deeper into it once they had Pehrla's time of death pinned down.

Back at the Lake, I drove to my office and threw the gun in a drawer. I took out the Glock I kept in there for no other reason than it didn't rip the lining of my suit coat as much as the Sig Sauer.

I drove to the dope house. There was no sign anybody had been there, no car in the driveway—just the yellow crime time flapping loose.

I went down the steps into the basement and saw her in the corner opposite the drain. She was on her hands and knees as before but this time she was dressed in a pair of cutoff Levi's; her shapely ass moved with each exertion. I saw a stack of cardboard boxes scattered all around the floor where they had been used for camouflage. There were banded wads of large-denomination bills thrown haphazardly into a pair of suitcases opened beside her. My Sig was in one but her gun was

She sensed me behind her.

"Come out of there, Laurie. Make sure I can see your hands."

"Hartmann? Is it you, you fucking cocksucker."

"Haftmann, not Hartmann. Back out of there slowly. Show me your hands!"

She inched her way out of the cubbyhole and turned to face me. Her hands were filthy and her face was smudged from grime and sweat. The gun was tucked, gangbanger-style, in the front of her jeans. I motioned for her to take it out.

"Slowly, Laurie, because I will shoot you," I said.

She took it out with two fingers. "Drop it and kick it over to me."

She did so and rubbed her hands together to remove some dirt.

"Jesus, what does it take to kill you?"

"I lead a charmed life," I said.

Her laugh showed white, perfect teeth in a face that was stunningly symmetrical.

As if she could guess my thoughts, she said, "The smile was bought and paid for. But not these"–she hefted her breasts–"these are my own. All the Tate men choose women with big teats. Then they all divorce their wives and marry younger women half their age. I figure my mother's got about five years to go before she's replaced.

I held the gun at her midriff. "Why?" I asked.

"Why what? Why . . . this?" The question seemed to annoy her.

"You could have had all the money you asked for," I said.

"I suppose." She looked up at me brightly. "But then it wouldn't have been so much fun."

"Why kill Lui – Robinson?" I asked her.

"He was beginning to bore me."

"He–he was in love with you?" I guessed it and realized it at the same time. I had some of it figured out but not all of it.

"Love? I don't know what that word means," she said quietly. It sounded like the truth to me.

"What I haven't figured out," I said to keep her talking, "was why the year out of college."

"Yes, well, I had to tell them something, didn't I? I don't get my trust fund money until I'm twenty-five. What the fuck was I supposed to live on?"

"Daddy's money," I said. "You're a rich girl. You have everything except–" I didn't know how to finish the sentence. As odd as that struck me, seeing that the young and beautiful woman in front of me was as amoral and deadly as a viper.

"Except . . . this," she said and swept her hands over her body. She reminded me of some scantily dressed Vegas showgirl assisting a third-rate magician in a seedy nightclub.

"I have this . . . condition. I'm sure you've noticed it." Her eyes looked down and I could see that her face was flushed. She burned with shame. None of her beauty mattered next to this one irrevocable thing, this curse that whatever fairy godmother had attended her birth and seen to it that she had all the womanly gifts a baby girl could ever yearn for in this life. But she must have turned her head at the wrong moment because some evil thing had also stolen up to her crib and left her with a curse that would turn all that priceless femininity to dust. She gave off a gamey odor that no amount of scrubbing could cleanse.

She looked at me. "My condition has a name," she said, "but who cares what it's called. The day I started to develop breasts I noticed it. I washed with lava soap until my skin bled. Nothing would take it away. It's a chemical my body produces. I'd have to die for it to stop making it." Her eyes looked within while she spoke. "No French perfume, nothing will cover my own scent. At first it was

my family's reaction. That hurt worse than other people."
She looked at me out of her beautifully symmetrical face;
her eyebrows were left stylishly thick and arced in perfect
harmony of art and genetics. What a pair of fairy
godmothers to have at your crib, one to make you
beautiful; the other to undo it all with the sweep of a wand.

"Do you know what high school can be like to a girl
whose body gives off . . . a stench?"

"Do you want me to feel sorry for you?" I asked her.

"Fuck you," she spat out. "I don't need your pity."

"Why kill Robinson? He was obviously in love with
you. Robbie Pehrla didn't have any trouble with it."

"Robbie would fuck a snake. You wouldn't have to
hold its head, either. Just give him the snake. His dick was
always hard."

"So what happened?"

"That thieving nigger bitch is what happened. When
they found her body, the dogs led them right here. Cops
showed up asking questions. Somebody didn't like the
answers. The next thing you know, there's a task force
going over the basement and that's when they found the
blood."

"LaRonda Portis' blood, you mean," I said.

"Yes."

"She worked for you? She was skimming?"

"Jimmy gave me the idea. He works for the Lake cops.
We set it up with Daddy's money. I had the connection
from a contact in Mexico. I speak fluent Spanish. Daddy
exports coffee from Hawaii. I import my product from
Mexico and Columbia. It's business, Haftmann." "Why
here?"

"It has everything I need. It's in the middle of a resort
town where hundreds of thousands of strangers come and
go every day. The cops are used to picking up the
occasional drunk and disorderly off the sidewalk. No DEA

within a hundred miles, everybody's hustling or on the take, the average citizen minds their own business."

"How do the Seymour brothers figure in?"

"Jimmy had them running errands, pick up and deliver."

"Enforcement?"

"No," she said with a shake of her dark hair. "They're too stupid, disorganized." She looked up at me and smiled. "That's my specialty. They've been running a half-assed meth lab for a couple years. We just helped them expand. Most of the product goes to Cleveland and Detroit. We opened up Pittsburgh and Youngstown. Nobody pays attention to two rednecks in a pickup around here."

"No," she smiled. "I did. I tied that bitch to the wall and I went to work on her. I cut little pieces off her until she screamed so hard she passed out. When she woke up, she saw my face and I started all over again."

"So you were the cab driver?"

"I just had to hide these"–she grabbed her chest–"under a jersey, wrap my hair under a baseball cap, and voilà, a male."

"They noticed you . . . when you stopped to buy cigarettes."

She furrowed her forehead at that. "Portis was so stoned she didn't even recognize me when I picked her up. She thought it was just another dope run and then back to Cleveland."

"Why torture her?" It didn't matter why anymore, but I wanted to know.

"Her own crack habit killed her. I cleaned up a loose end." She crossed her arms and hugged herself. It wasn't the damp that made her shiver.

I didn't say anything, just held the gun loosely in the direction of her stomach.

"Don't ask me for an explanation," she said simply.

"But you fucked up, Laurie. You left the body out there too close to the house. You had to know the cops would canvas, maybe the dogs would leave them here to–" I hesitated. How odd to worry about the delicate sensibilities of a psychopathic killer, however beautiful the woman herself.

"The smell, you mean?"

Her eyes glittered. She emitted a girlish voice I had not heard that seemed to come from somewhere past her. "I wanted to be close to the smell."

I might as well learn what there was to know. "Was she the first?"

"Oh no," she said and giggled. "I did four of them. The first one . . . it was just to see if I could do it. The second one was more . . . instructive. She screamed a long time. Jimmy dumped those two together out off some county road because he said the cops were already looking for a serial killer, some guy who was out there killing black prostitutes."

"Jimmy wasn't going to help me anymore. He said he couldn't take it. He said I was plying him. I had to drag her out there myself."

"So you had Robbie kill him?"

"No, Mr. Haftmann, no. Robbie couldn't kill anyone. I shot Jimmy."

She swayed in front of me, a sleepy little girl in a woman's body, recounting the mayhem of her young life's work. "Robbie didn't want him stinking up his trunk. I made him do it. I wanted to see if he smelled like the others," she said.

My stomach was churning bile. She was beyond understanding or beyond understanding herself.

"Isn't that a curious thing?" she asked me.

"Yes," I agreed. "Then Robbie became your partner?" I had to keep her talking, get this finished before I lost my resolve.

"Yeah, Robbie's family is well off. 'Connected,' he likes to brag. He knows some 'big dagos' or 'big Jews,' or somebody who could launder the money for a small percentage. I told him we were getting too big and somebody would notice but if Robbie's got anything higher on his list of priorities than pussy, it's money." Her eyes were luminous and feral.

"It's time, Laurie," I said. I hoped she wasn't going to be hard about it, but I had no choices left. My shitty life and my shitty job were all that I had.

"I'll give you this money," she pointed toward the suitcases. "There's about five hundred thousand."

"No thanks," I said.

" I'll suck your cock."

She kept her eyes on me but her hands had been slowly moving to her blouse and she unbuttoned each one from the bottom up. When the top button was gone, she exposed her bra and lifted her breasts from the bottoms. "You like them?" She took a step toward me.

"It's this way or death row, Laurie. You know that, right?"

"You motherfucker."

She looked at me and I knew she was going to turn on the tears. Easy for a sociopath to do; they learn by imitating others. That's how they know how to respond but they're always one note or beat off. Her timing was poor, too, like the second-best part in a high-school drama and so when the tears started flowing down her cheeks, I saw only the coldness in her eyes and the dark pupils that were fixed on me.

"I'm sorry," I said. I reached around behind me and jammed the SIG down my back right up against my buttocks. I took her gun and hefted it, admired its scrollwork for a second.

The summer I was out of high school, I had worked in a factory and saw a maintenance man catch his hand in a fan belt; he tore it off at the wrist and goose-stepped past me in total shock. Laurie's tear-streaked and smudged face reminded me of that. She approached me until she was close enough for me to pull her toward me by the back of her head. Her heart was pounding as the animal instincts in that magnificent body started to kick in, but I held her tight and kept the gun directly in her stomach. She started to whimper.

"OK," I asked her. Her own face was just inches from mine.

"No, no, no," she begged. "Please."

"Shhh, OK? Is it OK, Laurie?'"

I brought the gun up her side so she could feel the barrel drag across her ribs and gently pried her lips open. I could feel her heart pounding beneath those magnificent breasts, and her body at that moment, in sync with her terrified mind, emitted a sharp odor that wafted around us, a final insult to her feminine beauty. I knew the loneliness behind those black pupils, empty spaces where she had been hurt and her soul eroded and finally disappeared. I clenched her to me fiercely so that she could not squirm free or grab for the gun. Our embrace was more obscenely intimate than hers with Robbie Pehrla that morning

"It's time, Laurie," I said.

She moaned softly, a thousand miles away, already calling out from some other dimension.

I removed my hand from the back of her head, grabbed her left hand dangling hopelessly at her side and put my hand over it; she let do that without resistance. I put her hand over the butt of the gun and touched her lips. She cried out in pain from the force of my hand on hers, but I was willing to break her bones rather than give her the slightest opportunity to turn on me. I pushed the barrel until the front sight touched against her soft palate. With her small, fine-boned hand crushed around her gun, I squeezed the trigger.

~ ~ ~

I didn't like the way Annie Cheng was looking at me. We were standing in front of Luigi's boarded-up stand, and I was half-listening to her summary of the whole "sordid catastrophe," as she described it.

"Are you listening to me, Haftmann, because part of this concerns your girl," she huffed.

I had a cup of foul coffee I was sipping from while Annie spoke. I had bought it from the Swiss Chalet across the street but it tasted like something warmed up from last night. I pretended to blow on it so she wouldn't notice my hands shaking.

"Yes," I said. "I'm listening. I hear you fine."

"The Pehrlas are lawyered up so we can't get all the facts, and I'm not sure how much they knew about their son's business ventures on the side anyway. It's clear he was hiding her out. The report from Pittsburgh homicide establishes her in the room when he died. Robbie was a woman beater. Both wives confirmed he knocked them around."

I nodded and looked up at the sky. "More fucking rain," I said.

"So Pehrla kills Robinson over a falling out in the dope business," she continued. "We'll never establish motive, but they were down there looking to dump his body in the Allegheny–"

"Or the Monongahela," I said.

"The what?"

"Or maybe the Ohio River," I offered.

"Whatever, Haftmann," she said. "It doesn't matter which river he was going to be dumped into, does it?"

"Well, I wouldn't want to drink–"

"The point is, he was deader than Julius Cicero."

"Caesar," I said. Then, catching the look in her eyes, "Sorry."

"That's all of it," she said. "She was a spoiled rich girl who got mixed up in drugs, found herself way over her head with a violent boyfriend, and so she decides he isn't going to hit her again, or do whatever he did to those poor hookers from Cleveland. She accidentally on purpose shoots him in the face. Panics, drives back to the scene of the crime. Figures even Daddy with all his money can't buy her out of this mess, so she put the gun in her mouth. Good riddance," she said. "Now all that's left is the paperwork."

"Spoiled," I reflected, an ironic choice of words to describe it. "Maybe she wasn't all bad," I said.

"Don't get sentimental, Haftmann," Annie said to me. ""That's an emotion you can't afford."

"You're right," I said.

"It's justice," Annie Cheng said. "Let's just leave it at that."

"Fine by me," I agreed.

"There's just one thing that bothers me, Haftmann."

"And what might that be, Detective Cheng?"

"You're too good at catching runaways not to have found her when she was right under your nose . . . What's so funny?"

"Nothing, Annie."

The sound that had escaped my throat was somewhere between a laugh and a sob. We were all actors with lousy lines written by one deranged playwright. "Nothing at all. Let's go get us real cup of coffee."

The Dog
Returneth
To His Vomit

I've worked for rich men before. They aren't all pricks. But the genuinely nice ones are as scarce as fleas on eels, and Mister Elliott S. Curran III wasn't one of the nice ones. Even his Corgis, Nigel and Bruce, were a pair of snobs.

Money's money, right? It spends whether it comes from a crack house or a rich man's mansion. When I mentioned over the phone to him that I could find his "house" easily enough, he corrected me. It was a "manor," whatever that means when it's at home, and his residence was on an "estate," not on a lowly street. His phone voice was as dry as desert air. After I hung up, I wondered why men with pockets full of money were so humorless. You would think life would be an endless circus for them instead of the grim business they make of it, but then, no one cares what I think because I don't have much of it.

The bronze plaque on the brick gates said Fox Run Manor and had some words beneath that, but I wasn't there to read. I drove through and followed a lazy S curve toward a massive white colonial with huge columns on the porch that might have been smuggled from the Acropolis. There were so tall that the architects had to fatten them in the middle to give the viewer the illusion they were straight. Curran hadn't said much over the phone that morning when I returned his message. He was a potential client and I was desperate for clients because this had been a disastrous summer for me – the time when I make what I call my "winter bread" in the slack season. It was the first time since I had the lettering done on the glass in Old English that I wasn't solvent enough to get to next spring when business would start to pick up. The rich daddies I count on to locate their runaway kids had been few and far between; one case in particular involving a Florida couple's child cost me time and money I was never going to recoup outside a court of law. I was barely paying the utility bills for my one-room office, which was originally a makeshift real-estate shanty, housing some file cabinets and a computer, all of it visible behind a plate glass window that took up the entire front of my building.

I parked my car and walked up the front steps. On either side of house, cultivated rows of grape vines awaited harvesting. The man had his own winery. Beyond were acres of private woodland with big maples and oaks predominating among the scruffy firs. Below the treeline, the ones that didn't make it to full height were bent sideways by the howling winds off Lake Erie.

A woman with coiffed silver hair let me in. She didn't look like a house servant and her perfume was that tangy kind older women favor. I introduced myself, unnecessarily, because she didn't return the courtesy and led me across a huge marble foyer. The winding staircase to the upstairs balcony was so wide it could have accommodated chariot races where it met the floor. I let my eyes sweep right and left at the rooms as I passed by. No one else seemed to be home. Her heels made a clicking noise until we reached a carpeted corridor at the back of a passageway that suddenly opened to a spacious modernized kitchen. I counted three industrial-sized stoves that would have done Mary's Kitchen proud. That's where I eat when I can't bear the sight of another microwaved dinner.

She told me Mister Curran would be downstairs to see me in a few minutes. I had a retort about Mister Curran's ushering me to the back of the house, but she looked like the type who borrowed glory from her master, so I bit back my wit just in time. A loud clattering of toenails on tile would have drowned it out anyway because two dogs came scrambling into the kitchen to greet me. That's when I met Bruce and Nigel. They took turns sniffing my shoes and then retreated, tails up, back to wherever they had come from.

I asked her if I might have a cup of coffee while I waited, but she fixed me with a look between arched eyebrows that made me wonder if there was something beyond a *faux pas* in that request that bordered on the obscene. "The cook's gone for the day," she said and turned on her heels and went clicking off in the same direction as the two dogs.

I had my pride. I would give this Curran exactly five minutes and then I would walk out the door. Five minutes passed. What's another minute or two, I thought. Pride wasn't paying my bills lately.

He approached from a different direction behind the row of wine cruets and crystal goblets. I never heard him until he suddenly appeared around the corner of the stove I was leaning against. My elbow banged some cooking utensils. Maybe that was how he did things – like make people wait for him, send in the dogs, and then sneak up on them. Rich man's humor.

He wasn't much to look at. I've never been to college but he reminded me of that look professors are said to have – scholarly. A little washed out in the features, nothing much in the face to latch on to, mid-forties, and attired in casual wear down to deck shoes with the laces you'd never want to wear on an actual ship. A few minutes of conversation with him and the scholarly image evaporated; it was replaced by one of a single-minded Big Ten football coach you'd be stupid to underestimate no matter how unexceptional the team he fielded. The kind who improvised at half-time and ultimately killed you with a better game strategy.

His twin blonde teenaged daughters, Lerryn and Ashley, came bopping into the kitchen behind us just then, chittering like a pair of squirrels and begging their father for money to go the mall – not the "dump" in town but the one near Cleveland where "the Jews" shopped. I never heard of it. They rattled off names of certain kinds of fashion wear in the staccato fashion of twins who read each other's mind, but whether they were talking about sandals, purses, or skirts, I could not have said. If they were carbon copies of their mother, I'd put her in the trophy-wife category. Except for their voices, which had a languid drawl at the ends of their sentences, they were like most of the seventeen-year-old girls anywhere – except that my old white-haired grandmother would have been shocked at the cleavage Ashley or Lerryn exposed to the public gaze of randy males, a class for which I still held a modest claim.

Curran winced at the interruption but didn't apologize; they ignored me completely. He pieced them off with a hundred each. They went skipping out the back door like goats.

The case was simple enough. He could have given it to me over the phone and saved me the trouble of coming to the "manor." The girls' third Corgi was missing. They were both heart-broken (he claimed) and they wanted him found When it was my turn to talk, I gave him my credentials in highlight, the usual *per diem* rate, and the odds and ends of a spiel so long polished by now I could have recited it backwards.

But I nearly lost my footing when he said I was charging him too much. He wanted to haggle over the money. I was standing inside a house that wouldn't go on the market for less than a million-and-a-half in a depressed economy, and he was telling me that my nickel-and-dime fee was too much. It was no more than I was trying to get from the Florida couple for expenses incurred, or what I had charged Pete Callaghan at the precinct when his son went missing two years ago. Curran believed that a case involving an animal meant I should charge less. I had a split-second hesitation about telling him to get some other "dog catcher" out of the phone book. Calming myself, remembering the little ogre Poverty hounding my sleep, I ticked off the routine expenses I would be exposed to whether it was a dog or a human being I was searching. In the end, he grudgingly agreed and asked me to fax him my contract that afternoon. I took one out of my pocket and we both signed it on the stove.

He handed me a photo of "Bob." He looked like his siblings except that he had whiter markings, including a bib that covered most of his chest. The photo was taken outside in the summer. I saw the shadow of the photographer's legs extend to the front of his stubby legs on the manicured lawn. Bob's tongue lolled out of his mouth like a capital Q.

We spoke for about fifteen more minutes, and I wrote down some things in my notebook, which is pretty much a prop for the client. I learned to listen to people when I became a Cleveland homicide cop years ago because it's what you don't hear that matters. Bob, it seemed, had had enough of the good life and taken off for parts unknown. Because his two companions were romping in the yard, no one missed him at first. By nightfall on the day he went missing, which was two days ago, a family emergency was declared, and that evolved into an all-hands-find-Bob search party conducted by the live-in house servants and a couple of guests. Nigel and Bruce apparently had no interest in searching for their lost buddy and proved useless. The backwoods were combed by the men. I asked Curran if the dog wore a collar or possessed any device that might cause him to get stuck out in the woods.

"You're supposed to be the detective. Don't you think we would have heard him baying out there if that were the case?"

"Let's keep the obvious options open first," I suggested, but I thought seriously about goosing the bill for his sarcasm. I thanked him and said I'd be in touch if I learned anything.

He looked disappointed. "Aren't you going to begin searching the grounds?"

"You've already done that, Mister Curran," I said. "Bob isn't lost on your property unless he's pinned under a fallen tree and you just missed him."

"I don't want you to consider this an extravagant . . . case," he said glumly at the door.

"I'll have an accurate accounting for you when it's done," I said. I tried to smile but the words forming in my mind weren't flattering to his character unless *Webster's* has revised "tightwad" lately.

"Done?"

"I meant," I said, turning around on the last step, "when we find the dog or whenever you decide to terminate the search."

Back in my office, I called Pete Callaghan at the station but he was out working a case.

"Sheila, is that you, sweetheart, light-of-my life?" I knew it was just as I knew there'd be a long sigh coming soon.

"Thomas, what do you want now?"

She never called me "Tom.'" It was always my formal name. On those rare occasions when she was out of patience with me, it reverted to my surname. We both knew she had long since repaid the favor that resulted in my getting the fat, cigar-smoking chief of police out of her hair. He was a notorious sexual harasser, and he expected Sheila to grant him similar favors when she was first hired. She was pregnant with her fourth at the time and her husband had run off with a girl half his age. That was one of the reasons I left the resort town's police force. As they say in the bible, there was enmity between us.

"I need a favor, Sheila," I said meekly.

"Golly, gee, damn, gosh, Thomas. Now what else would I have expected from you?" That was as close to cursing as she ever got.

"This one's easy," I began.

"You said that last time," she huffed into her mic and which my cell picked out of the ether, tone intact. The unspoken part never changed . . . *and nearly got me fired.*

"I need to know if there's any scuttlebutt going around about missing dogs, is all," I said.

"You mean like dognappers, ransom notes?"

"Anything with house dogs turning up missing."

"Not that I know of," she said. Then she paused. "The Randall brothers got busted again for another meth lab. That's all the big news right now."

"Didn't those two clowns just get out of prison?"

"Yep," she said. "All of three weeks ago. That's how long it took those dummies to set up another lab."

Our little corner of the state is the meth capital of the Midwest, although you'd never know it if you didn't read the local paper. It was still crack, heroin, and marijuana that had DEA's and Columbus' full attention. The sheriff's deputies were out scouring the countryside week in and week out closing down toxic sites which seemed to spring up like toadstools after a summer rain.

"Thanks, Sheila. Buzz me if you hear anything."

It looked as though I was going into the woods, after all. I borrowed a pair of waders from my favorite barkeep across the street, whose wife Marta was fortunately out of the country visiting her mother in Latin America, or I'd be getting the fisheye for my whopping bar tab. I changed clothes and shoes and drove back to Curran's estate.

I spent three hours tramping around the back acreage and then beyond that to the stand of woods facing the interstate. I used Zeiss glasses on the flat terrain and checked out swampy wetlands where Bob might have strayed if he'd caught the scent of a rabbit. I used to hunt woods like these in my youth, and I could still distinguish a deer print from another animal's, but animal scat all looked the same to me and one dog turd resembled every other one. But there weren't any prints to find out here that didn't belong to smaller varmints like raccoons or to crows and carrion feeders. I saw a set of tracks that might have belonged to a four-wheeler. All the landowners out here complained about the kids trespassing on their dirt bikes in summer and snowmobiles in the winter.

I drove back to my house, showered and changed, then headed to the station. Luck was with me – no Millimaki in sight. I was made very unwelcome when he was on the premises. I talked to a young patrolman who had just come in with the Randall brothers. They had gone through booking and were sitting in the basement caboose waiting for transport to the county's bigger facility. I asked him for a minute with them. I said I was working a runaway case for a worried father.

"It's a long shot," I said, when I noticed his brow wrinkle up. It was a big stretch to imply the Randall brothers knew anybody that could afford to hire a private investigator. But he shrugged and gave me the OK.

"Two minutes," he said and led me down to the area known primarily as the drunk-and-dumbass pen.

"Hi, fellas," I said.

"Fuck you," said Larry, the older one.

He was thin and bald but his brother Jared was fat and had thick reddish-blonde beard stubble. Their mother wasn't celebrated for her fidelity to her husband. Before a cirrhotic liver took her off to her reward, she had gone through five of them, the legal ones anyway. I myself had dragged her out of a couple bar fights and put her in the back of a cruiser more than once. The boys apparently inherited their mother's deep-seeded memory of me.

"Fuck ass," said Larry. "I know you."

"He's that nigger-lovin' cop," Jared said to his brother. Five years ago Jared rode with a biker gang that had skinhead affiliations with a chapter in Brooklyn called the Devil Dogs.

"You guys know anywhere I can put down a friendly bet?" I said.

The young cop stood behind me and couldn't see the fifty I let peek between my fingertips. These boys had done jail before, and though they weren't the hygienic kind who wore an extra pair of underpants and socks so they'd always have clean ones to wear in the slammer while they washed one set, they knew the value of cash to their commissary accounts. Jail food was jail food wherever you were.

"You can kiss my ass in the crack, boy," Larry said and came right up to the bars to face me.

"Step back, sir," said the deputy to me.

"I'm sorry, officer," I said and did as he said.

"We ain't snitches, motherfucker," Jared said. He glared at me but cut his eyes once, fast, to his brother, silently negotiating with his older sibling.

"Thanks, boys," I said. "Just thought I'd ask in case you know of a friendly card game somewhere around or, maybe, a little action on, say, dogs."

"Why should we tell you, fuckface?" Larry said.

"Oh, I don't know," I said. "I'm just wondering what to

do with my free time now that I'm not a cop anymore."

I manipulated the fifty-dollar bill between my fingers so that old Ben's bald head peeked up like one of those magician card tricks. Larry's eyes glittered like a rat's. He was my play.

"Well, I'll be going now. Anybody in town I can say farewell to for you boys while you're in lockup?"

"I thought I told you to kiss my ass with your tongue out, shithead," Jared said. Larry looked me in the eye and said, "Yeah, you can tell Danny Portis' wife for me she can come on over here and suck my big dick," he said.

"Suck mine, too," Jared said.

"Sir, you need to leave now," the deputy said and touched my shoulder.

"Thanks, officer. I do appreciate the time with these good citizens," I said.

I fumbled clumsily with my visitor's tag on my shirtfront and dropped it trying to hand it to him. He reached down to his feet for it and I gave it an accidental little kick with my shoe while he was bent over. "You need to keep this on until we clear the area," he said with a spike of annoyance. I had the fifty folded and creased so that it formed a vee-shaped pellet, which I flicked behind me. It shot through the bars and landed at Larry's feet and he quickly covered it with a shoe. The cop looked at me brushing my pants as if I were removing a speck of dirt but said nothing.

Danny Portis was another lowlife, piece-of-shit douchebag just like the Randalls. That knowledge was the promising part that told me I might not have just wasted fifty dollars of Curran's money on a month's supply of Cheetos and candy bars from the county vending machines. The second good thing was that Portis and the Randall boys were rivals in the dope business.

Portis, a transplanted Youngstowner, was big on crack

and Mexican tar heroin, for which he'd run down to the border near Nuevo Laredo every so often and bring back a stash. They shared some of the same customers. Danny's wife Leona was a crackhead who was passed along the daisy chain of bikers, dealers, and criminal misfits until she wound up with a loser like Danny Portis. Some biker sold her to him two years and she lived with him in his crapped-out trailer unless he was off doing time or making one of his deals in Mexico. Sometimes Danny would stay down there for months and take advantage of the cheap drugs. Unlike the Randall boys, who were known to stomp heads and sucker-punch victims in bar fights, Danny was non-violent and even likeable, in his own shitheaded way.

Three years ago the sheriff had busted up a cockfighting ring out by Danny's place. Portis had bonfires going in fifty-gallon barrels and about a dozen beat-up pickup trucks circling his trailer out in the woods behind the state park. It wasn't exactly inconspicuous, and a small commuter plane heading for the Jefferson airport called it in from overhead. He thought it was a marsh fire out of control.

Portis paid a six hundred dollar fine; the judge gave him six months and suspended three. Betting on fighting roosters wasn't high on anybody's list of crime-fighting operations. The paper printed a photo of a garbage pail full of dead roosters showing their feeble, drooping combs hanging listless amid the tangle; their talons, without the razor spurs attached, looked anything but lethal.

Of course, Larry could be playing me for the money. He had no reason to believe I wasn't a cop or working for them. My skill at reading people was waning; you lose your edge when you're off the streets. I called Danny's number and a female voice answered. I hung up.

Danny lived three miles out of town near an abandoned apple orchard. The rich soil that make the grapes flourish close to the lake was mostly clay out here. The dairy farmers were long gone. I drove past a few stunted apple trees that refused to die despite the yearly assaults of the Siberian Express coming down from the North Pole. Danny kept a pack of dogs out here, so I pulled as close to the trailer as I could and rolled down the window. A Rottweiler came bounding across the field followed by a mixed Shepherd; they were trailed by a loose pack of dogs that included a scruffy-looking Airedale and black lab or two with a few terriers bringing up the rear. No Corgi. I like dogs but whenever I encounter more than one at a time, I try to remember they were undomesticated wolves 50,000 years ago.

Fortunately, Danny's woman appeared at the door and took the cigarette out of her mouth long enough to make a shrill noise at the lead Rottweiler. He gave me a look as he rocketed past my car that I took to mean something like "Later for you, meat," and veered off into the overgrown field behind the trailer. I waited for the last terrier to fly past me yapping in chorus and head off in the same direction as his buddies before I got out.

"Danny ain't fuckin' here," she said and sucked in another lungful of smoke as antidote to the brisk country air.

"Where is he, Leona?"

"You fuckin' deaf? He ain't here, I said."

She looked me up and down. I stopped at the bottom of rickety steps leading up to the front door, which had boot-sized holes in it and looked as if it had been kicked in a few times. Leona and Danny weren't faithful viewers of *This Old House.*

"That's too bad," I said. I took another fifty out and snapped it in front of her. This was a crisp new bill; you could count the pixels on Ben Franklin's nose if you were bored. "I brought Danny some money I owed him from a long time ago."

"You can leave it with me," she said. She rubbed her arms together as if the breeze had turned suddenly cold. It was what she was thinking of poking into her veins at the crooks of those elbows that had her rubbing herself with anticipation. Leona was a dope fiend in the last stages. Her face was scabbed from scratching invisible crank bugs and she looked thirty years older than the last time I saw her riding in Danny's Chevy truck. She used to be a teen hooker working the corners of "little Minnesota" on the Strip in summers. She must have been about sixteen then and she was a real beauty in a Lycra miniskirt. One of those lost Appalachian girls on the run from sexual abuse or something bad who don't make it all the way to California but who get sidetracked to places like Jefferson-on-the-Lake. I looked at the lank strands of dirty hair hanging around her ears and remembered that luxuriant sweep of raven hair that once framed an oval face. Petey used to place her teenaged mug shots side-by-side with her most recent photos. The contrast never failed to produce guffaws in the muster room.

"Sure, Leona," I said. "May I come in?"

Playing a junkie is easy but sometimes it's like sipping a wave through a straw. You have to wade through a lot of bullshit to get at the truth. I put three more bills just like the first one on her kitchen table pockmarked with cigarette burns and dinged in a dozen places. I was surprised to see her gear lying in plain sight between a trio of mugs filled to varying levels with a gray scum that might once have been coffee. She scooped the bills up and put them into a cookie jar in the kitchen.

"I'll tell Danny you stopped by, Mister – "

"Jones, Mister Jones. Look, Leona. The truth is I need a little information. But nothing you say will hurt Danny so don't worry about that. I'm not a cop." I laid my ID on top of crumbs so she had to crane her neck to read it. She made an effort to do that while she absent-mindedly scratched at the back of her neck.

"So what do you want?"

I told her in short, simple sentences.

"You jest lookin' for a fuckin' dog?"

"That's all, Leona," I said. "It's a very special dog and the little girl is heart-sick over."

"You say this missing dog's name is Bob?"

"Yes, Leona, his name is Bob."

She digested that information slowly for whatever relevance it had in her dope-ravaged brain and blinked at me for a long two seconds. I had a pang of anguish, as I recalled the beauty she once had been but kept my smile pasted on. I could have been an axe murderer because her only goal now was to get me gone so she could get high.

"I don't know nothin' about no fuckin' dog," she said finally.

That was supposed to end our little chat right there, but I'm used to dealing with all kinds of lowlife, men and women, all ages, conditions, and backgrounds. It's a burden I carry sometimes as an occupational necessity. In my cop days, I'd probably have tried another gambit, and then we'd go round-and-round on that for a while; she'd say this, I'd say that – and so it would go until either I wore her down or she conned me.

Instead, I hit her in the solar plexus.

She double-up like a broken puppet. I know I can lose my license for a dumb stunt like that. But spare me the morality lecture, please, if you don't mind. As long as I'm not on videotape or there wasn't anybody hiding under the table pointing a digital camera or wireless videophone at me, it was just my word against hers. Leona was a station house joke. I had a slight edge in the credibility department.

That ganglia of nerves in the region makes you feel just terrible, but it doesn't leave lasting damage or a bruise. All of hers were old or healing ones provided by Danny or jab marks from her needle. I waited for her to get her breath. She wasted some of it on uninspired cursing in her patois of urban black and hill country. She made a move for something – a phone or a kitchen knife, whatever – but I countered it easily and took up more space between us. Leona wasn't convict dumb like the Randalls, but she had street experience and no doubt a few rough customers in her wake. I didn't want to get a hard kick in the pills as a return favor, so I stepped back a little and waited for her to come to grips with the reality of it.

"What you want with me, motherfucker?"

"I just want to know what Danny's up to these days," I said.

"I told your fuckin' ass I don't know nothin' 'bout no fuckin' dogs," she whined.

"That money says you do, Leona," I said.

"All's I know is Danny has some horses for his shows every oncet in a while. He buys some old farmer's horses what can't feed 'em anymore."

"What kind of shows?"

"That's what he calls 'em. Shows, horse shows."

"Do you mean he sics dogs on horses?"

"Yeah, I guess. I don't watch that shit. He brings some boys out here and they bet on the dogs, like, you know, how long it takes 'em to take down a horse."

"Don't lie to me, you crack whore," I snarled. I reached out a grabbed a greasy hank of it and twisted hard. I had to get her to finish it before she started troweling in the bullshit out of her greater fear of what Danny might do to her.

"A horse won't stand still and let dogs attack him!" I screamed at her.

She cried "Ow, ow. He – he spikes 'em through the hooves! Sose they can't run away from the dogs!"

"What do you mean – 'spikes them'?"

"Railroad spikes, I guess. Ow-ow-ow, you're hurting me, man," she pleaded.

I let go. You learn not to be surprised by anything human beings do. "Tell me about the dogs he's stealing, Leona."

"He gets them from the pound. Different places, he says. Hunters abandon beagles in the woods all the time. Danny says they's just throwaway dogs," she sobbed, broken.

"Does he use those dogs out there?"

"Them's pets," she said. "He keeps his pit bulls yonder in some coops he built for them back a mile that way down the road," she said and pointed through her faux wooden paneling just behind the tiny kitchen.

"Is that where he keeps the bait dogs?"

"I guess so," she said quietly.

I put another fifty on the table. "When's the next show, Leona?"

"Tonight, I reckon," she said but her eyes were pinned to the money.

"Buy some food, eat," I said. "You look like shit." I walked out. I took a walk around the trailer, listening for dogs, and saw twin ruts through the scrub where she had pointed. I'd need four-wheel drive to get back there.

I drove back to the office. I needed coffee but I wanted a drink and Tico's was too much temptation. I crossed the seat and found my favorite stool unoccupied. At this time of day, they all were.

"Tomás, what's happening?" Tico grinned at me. I had no idea why he was always glad to see me. I was his worst customer and I was probably the reason for most of the spats he had with his plump, doe-eyed wife.

"I've been interviewing a lovely couple for the next issue of *Country Living*," I said.

"Whiskey?"

"Whiskey," I said. I waited for the amber glass of Bushmills to restore some sanity to me, equilibrium to the universe, and cleanse some of the reek of Leona's filthy trailer clinging to my skin. Roughing her up had a price to be paid.

"Tico, is that your boy's Jeep I saw out back?"

"Tomás, you know I can't just let you borrow it like that," Tico said and I heard the too-familiar sigh, a preliminary signal before our usual negotiations. Tico could be stubborn when Marta was around.

"I'm on a job," I said happily. "I'll pay Cesar a handsome fee. I just need it for a couple hours tonight."

In the end, he gave in to me as he always did. I gave him a hundred for a retainer, which was the last of my mad money until reimbursement from Curran. I wondered if my second career choice was turning out to be as big a flop as my first. Tico was my only friend. When he first got here with his new family, he had worked and fought his way out of the garbage dumps of Guatemala to get here. I did him a favor when INS came snooping around rounding up all the migrant workers from Mexico who were overstaying their welcome after Welch's stopped hiring for the grape harvests. Tico was immensely proud of his boy. Cesar, however, was built more like his momma; when he boxed as a welterweight in Youngstown, they called him "el Torrito."

I was tempted to stay and drink. But I didn't. Danny wouldn't get started until dark and I had to get ready for my outing in the woods. At my age, an afternoon nap is a good thing no matter what the stereotype says. I kept a cot and an alarm clock in my office, and that's where I headed. I hadn't carried a gun on a case in five years. I made my cases with legwork and phone calls, but I kept a Glock as a concession to the image.

I drew the curtains, shut my eyes, and slept a dreamless sleep for three hours.

Tico had left the keys in the ignition for me. I tossed my duffel bag in the back and headed off to Danny's place. The road behind his trailer wasn't much better than where I was going. I drove a half-mile from his turnoff, put the Jeep into low, and bisected an angle where the road behind the trailer should lead to. It was slow going and I slewed into some thick dockweed but the big tires dug me out. I bulled my way to a clearing between some pines where I could make it the rest of the way on foot without being shredded to ribbons by briars. I saw no lights. I waited an hour by the front bumper and thought my thoughts surrounded by the effluvia of pungent odors of things rotting.

The first car approached around nine-thirty. Then they came in steady intervals every few minutes. I counted twenty big engines droning along. It was like waiting for the last kernel of popcorn in the microwave. It was five minutes since the last one. All trucks, Silverados and F-150s, I guessed – Danny's crowd, not your sporty SUV suburbanites.

I grabbed the bag and worked my way in the darkness toward the sounds. Truck doors slammed in the distance, loud men hooted. Finally, the dogs. Then I saw the lights speckling the blackness. Danny had rigged some wires with light bulbs dangling from them and strung them in a square. I could make out the edges of the plywood shanties he had constructed for the dog pens.

When I was about fifty yards to the lit square, I took out the night-vision binoculars. I could make out an area of churned-up earth bordered by the jerrybuilt cages of the fighting dogs. Nearby was a bigger plywood cage hut with chicken wire stretched across the front. That was where I guessed he kept the bait dogs. I detected a glowing, squirming, huddled mass of hind quarters, muzzles, and tails in the magma glow of my lens, but it was impossible to tell one kind of dogs from another.

I counted at least twenty men and five women. Nobody looked to be packing, but they were a rough-looking crowd. Some of the trucks had wire cages in the beds for their dogs they had brought to match up. The women were all around thirty, mostly hatchet-faced chain-smokers, and wore sweatshirts with goofy or obscene sayings on them.

Around ten o'clock Danny started the festivities with a prelim meant to lather up the crowd and whet their betting appetites. He grabbed a shorthaired dog by its tail from the coop and dragged it to the center of the pit. He held it between his legs and wrapped duct tape around its muzzle; the dog sat abruptly on its haunches in the center of the ring, jerking its head all around. A urine stream jetted from its nether region in a bright arc made fluorescent by my binocs.

The shouting grew a notch in volume and then a black blur streaked to the center of the ring. The action was intense, hard to follow unless you had the shutter speed of a fly. With the glasses, it was even harder but it was evident what was happening to the bait dog – it was methodically butchered by the pit bull, ripped from stem to stern. He tore open its throat with some lunges and shook it like a hunting dog trying to break a muskrat's neck. He remained clamped down on the dead dog's forepaw even when Danny beat the dog on the head to force its jaws open. I saw the slavering fangs appear ghostly white.

Another dog was brought out, a large poodle from the looks of it. This dog was equally terrified, but it ran from one end of the ring to the other before its attacker, another brindled pit bull, cornered it. The poodle thrust its own taped muzzle at its deranged enemy but that didn't deflect the charges, which drew blood or knocked the animal backwards. The crowd's cheering was heightened every time the pit bull took a chunk of flesh or fur from its helpless victim. The end came when the attack dog rammed the poodle into the corner like a linebacker sacking a quarterback and worried its dying body with shrugs of its bunched-up shoulder muscles. I watched the dying dog's legs spasm and twitch until Danny entered to pull the dog off the carcass.

The first match was between some bearded redneck's dog and the first dog Danny loosed into the ring. The betting commenced and the men's wallets opened for the contest. From where I was, I couldn't tell one dog from the other. The fight lasted twenty minutes. Neither dog wanted to quit but they were both bloodied and foaming blood and saliva by the time it was called off. The redneck's dog was declared the winner. He received a wad of bills from somebody acting as bookie and several claps on the back from a few spectators. I watched him take his bruised warrior off to the side where a piece of tarpaulin lay on the ground near some buckets. He emptied one of the buckets over his dog to clean him of blood and drool. The dog whipped its tight body and sent a drizzle of spray in all directions.

I heard a commotion near the opposite side of the ring and put the glasses on a cluster of men surrounding Danny. He moved away. I watched him slip a long-barreled Ruger into a holster tied to a post. The dog that lost the fight lay dead between the legs of the men who had witnessed the execution or the *coup de grâce*, although that was too good an expression for this spectacle.

I watched a second fight which seemed to be a replay

of the first one except that one dog was clearly more the aggressor. It looked like the dog that had killed the poodle, but I wasn't sure. It was obviously one of Danny's because he took the congratulations and pocketed a wad of bills just like the other man. He didn't bother to wash off his dog. He simple hoisted it by its stub tail and chest into a top cage behind the ring.

I didn't know how many of these I'd be forced to watch. My plan was to bellycrawl my way to the cages after the fights to see if Bob was inside one of them. If so, I had a large sack I'd slip over him and we'd haul ass back to the Jeep. Not much of a plan, but I was out serious money and I felt that I needed that dog on a leash to pry my fee out of Curran. I wasn't going to let him off with a donation to the sheriff's next Christmas party if I called in law enforcement.

My plan changed drastically when Bob was hauled out whimpering. I zeroed in on his white chest markings and saw the identical splotch as in the photo. The odds of an identical dognapped Corgi winding up here was just too remote.

"Fuck me," I said and pressed my face into the dirt. "Nothing's ever simple." I already knew there was at least one gun around. I had no time to call the sheriff's because Danny was already gripping Bob's muzzle. I saw the tape in his other hand.

I had my Glock out of the bag and then I was running, stumbling through the brush. I chambered a round as I ran toward the lights. I was giddy with fear – a real ass-puckering fear. You don't charge into a mob of raw emotions and violent men like that without feeling like a suicide bomber. They don't give medals to private eyes killed in the line of duty because we're mercenaries, and that fact makes us less brave than cops. Instead, the veterans of my profession get together to toast our brave, dead colleagues. I always intended to be one the toasters, never the toastee.

I'm so out of shape that I was fueled entirely by the adrenalin jolt. I accidentally squeezed off a round before I made my fool's entrance into their midst. It turned out to be a good thing. Danny's hand was still gripping the dog's fur to steady him when my shot ricocheted into the dirt at his feet. For all he knew, I was aiming for him – but it worked. I had his full attention. I also had the attention of everybody else in the squared circle and their silent, menacing stares, once the surprise vanished, will stay with me a long time.

"I'm taking that dog, Portis," I said as soon as I found my voice. I was about to add "Don't anybody try to stop me" when I recalled that's what the stooge in bad cop dramas always say before they get the shit beat out of them.

The problem was Bob. He didn't know me from Adam, and he was in such primeval fear that when I reached down to hoist him into my arms, he jerked free of the duct tape, whirled around and bit me on the chin. He put his low-slung body into high gear and bucked out of my grasp. I watched him bolt past everybody. He was gone like smoke, those little alligator legs churning like wheels.

Danny took advantage of my brief distraction. He threw out a fist that caught me on the side of the neck. It wasn't enough to take me down but it sent me tottering sideways. That was the signal for everybody to cut and run. Some fled this way, some tore off in the direction Bob had gone, and a couple bigger men balled their big fists and took a step toward me. I raised the gun and backed them off with that command voice they teach at the police academies everywhere.

The first shot snapped past me and thwacked into the plywood. I never heard the shot, but I felt the air sizzle beside my left ear lobe. This was getting into nightmare time way too fast. I saw myself in a gunfight with twenty hillbillies shielded by their trucks and armed with deer rifles and .357s. I took off between the dog cages and ran as fast as my legs could carry me, which is to say, not nearly as fast as my limbic brain was urging me on.

I took a roundabout way back to the Jeep, remembering the old woodsman trick of compensating if you're right-legged so I wouldn't wind up circling back where I started. I called the sheriff's office from the highway and gave them directions and descriptions of the place. The dispatcher sounded bored. Illegal dogfights didn't impress her as any kind of big-deal emergency. "You weren't there," I said and thumbed off. I left out the part about my weapon misfiring. If it came up later, I'd deal with it then. Meanwhile the adrenalin had subsided to a bad-tasting lump in my stomach.

I made it back to my office by two in the morning, bedraggled, muddy, with a dozen facial lacerations from stinging branches whipping at me from all directions, my clothes full of brambles, seed pods, and rips as well as a limp acquired from a gopher hole. I left the Jeep where I'd borrowed it and walked across the rain-glazed street to my humble digs. I crashed on the cot, too tired to drive home and shower. In the morning, I'd clean up, go in search of the fleeing Bob and hope he hadn't gotten permanently lost or gotten hit on the freeway.

I awoke at seven, an hour past my alarm setting. I called Curran's house and got the silver-haired woman. She said she would enquire if Mister Curran were "accepting" phone calls at this hour. When Curran came on the line, he sounded morose and impatient. I halted my much-abridged progress report in mid-sentence. I had a brain flash, a satori, whatever the Japanese call them. It never occurred to me, but I knew it before Curran finally said it: Bob, that brave soldier, had found his own way home in the dark of the night. He was reunited with kith and kin – and I was out in the cold, financially speaking.

"If you think you're going to charge me an arm and a leg for nothing, you'd better rethink your bill," Curran said.

"The dog didn't find himself, Mister Curran," I said patiently. "He had some help from me if you'd care to hear the details – "

"You're getting exactly a one day's fee from me, no extras, not a penny more. My lawyer is going over every line item you submit, by the way, so I suggest you bear that in mind and leave any creative writing out of your bill. I'm going to have to pay some veterinary doctor a fortune to sew up the gash in his paw. As far as I can see, you've done very little to earn anything – "

Pride, that miserable homunculus, was sitting on my shoulder urging me to tell the man to take my bill and shove it up his ass and his lawyer's too. But I politely let him rant at me and yessired him like any groveling house servant. I needed the money, the exchequer was drained, and I still owed Tico's boy for the loan of the Jeep, which I hadn't even washed of muck. He hung up on me before I had a chance to ask about Bob.

Tico wouldn't be serving for a couple more hours so I had some time to kill. I also had a personal score to settle with Danny, so I drove out to his place in a very foul mood. Every mile put my back up more and by the time I reached his dirt road off Route 531, I was in a towering rage. My anger boiled over and I envisioned smashing Portis' weasel head through the shitty walls of his trailer.

When I saw the flashing turquoise and cherry lights of the cruisers parked in front of his trailer and lining up both sides of the street, my rage evaporated. A deputy fast-walked toward me when he saw me getting out of my car behind the EMT ambulance, but I wasn't having it. As I said before, you lose your edge when you're off the streets too long. Danny's a nice guy in the way that some scumbags are nice. That is, they won't shoot you in the back to see if their gun works, but they almost all are cowards, bullies, small-timers, and they will lie their asses off to you for any question more invasive than what time of day it is. But people are like dogs and sometimes even a tame dog will bite. I used to ride with an old homicide cop from Cleveland who quoted this to me one night after we busted up a child-sex ring: *Homo hominis lupus est.* "Man is a wolf to man."

Danny killed Leona sometime during the night. Maybe he found the money and put two-and-two together in his tiny brain. I'll never know, but the officers acting on my call found her in the pit where she'd been ripped to pieces by the dogs. I hoped she was so stoned at the time she didn't feel much pain or horror. I walked down the four-wheeler path behind the trailer. That was probably how Danny had snatched Bob from the woods behind Curran's mansion. The treads looked similar enough for an eyeball match.

They were still snapping photos when I got to the pit. The crime scene tape was looped around some birch trees and stretched around the circle as far as the tarp where I had seen the bearded guy washing down his dog. I saw Pete Callaghan talking to a woman from the county animal shelter. By the time they arrived, all the dogs were dead or dying in their cages. They were all shot in the head. I heard whimpering and low moans from a couple still hanging on to life. They'd be euthanized because our county doesn't have the money it takes for surgery. "Better that way," I heard Callaghan say to her. "You can't give these killers to families with kids even if they do make it."

"Yo, Pete,"

"Ah shit, Tommy, I'm a little busy right now —"

"Where is she?"

"Over there, he said and pointed to what looked like a pile of muddy rags in one corner of the pit. "And over there. And there and there," he said. "She's all over the fucking place." Cop humor.

"Catch Portis yet?"

"No, but we've got BOLOs out. You know these jackoffs," he said. "He'll run around in circles for a while and then he'll fuck up. Danny couldn't find a skyscraper if it was standing right in front of it. What brings you out here so early?"

I was having a hard time focusing. I wasn't sure why that was. I've seen mangled bodies before. Kids' tiny bodies, old people's – you get used to it. You just get yourself into that cocoon where evil shit like this can't get through.

"Hey, you all right? You look a little green around the gills," Pete said.

"I'm fine," I said. "I didn't get much sleep last night." I threw in a yawn for theater.

"Christ, you got it made," he said. "Sleep in all you want, no bosses with wide asses the size of Millimaki's you have to kiss until your tongue's as tough as shoe leather. I really envy you," Pete said with a wink.

"That's me, Mister Easy Street," I said and returned the wink.

I got dizzy on the walk back and leaned over to vomit up a spume of yellow bile into the weeds. I badly needed coffee – something. I felt a strong pair of hands grip my bicep and I looked up at the young deputy's face who had escorted me downstairs to the holding tank yesterday afternoon.

"Sir, can I help you?" He looked at me strangely; he was still a young guy so he had genuine concern in his voice.

"Nobody can help me," I said to him. "I can't even find a goddamned missing dog."

His eyes bored into my back like an auger, assessing me. I walked over to my car more or less steadily by concentrating on the steps – one foot in front of the other like that, simple; toddlers do it all the time.

I drove back to the strip and parked in front of my office. But I couldn't bear the thought of walking inside it or drinking coffee in my usual swivel chair. My hands shook so I gripped the steering wheel hard to make them stop. I waited a long time until I saw the lights in Tico's Place finally come on and wondered if I could put that fake smile on my face long enough to cadge my first drink of the day.

Welcome to the Piggy Palace

It took me three days of drinking piss-warm beer before I made contact with Mace. He saw me shooting pool and challenged me with a twenty on the table. I scratched on the eight ball twice but I had to take the third game or he'd know I was throwing them. I handed over the twenties and we drank shots at a booth. He was wearing his colors in Annie's. It was supposed to be neutral territory among the Mongols, Pagans, and Angels but everybody knew the Angels ran things on the street.

"What's your fuckin' story, man?"

I told him in monosyllables mostly, mentioned a few people. Some places I'd been down South, out East and others where I'd done time.

He asked me a couple questions.

I gave him the answers and hoped they were the right ones.

He took a swig. "I'll check you out."

He got up and left.

The girl came over and asked me if I wanted another.

"Sure," I said.

Her eyes drilled mine, trying to read what I knew. The bartender, a baldie with a thick neck wrapped in a blue glyph, was reading the paper at the end of the bar.

I finished my drink, put a five on the table and walked out.

The waitress, Cindy, was still sitting on a stool at the bar with her back to me while she made small talk with the bartender.

It was after two when I knocked on her cottage door.

She was wearing a terrycloth robe and holding a drink in her hand.

"Want one?"

"No thanks."

I told her Mace wasn't going to open up just because we'd played a couple games of pool. It was risky being seen going to her place. Lights were on in several cottages and a loud party was going on at the end of the row.

"Never mind those meth heads," she said, indicating the party cabin down the lane. "They party every night."

Cindy's eyes were red. She'd been crying before I got there.

"Come in around four tomorrow," she said. "He's supposed to be meeting some people from out of town."

"I don't mind hanging out there," I said.

"I'm not paying you to shoot pool," she snapped.

"It'll look odd if I keep showing up just when he gets there." I was really thinking I didn't want her plying that big bartender with too many questions about Mace.

We agreed on a time and place to meet later that day.

I was shooting pool when Mace walked into Annie's at five o'clock. Cindy was on break. He told the two guys with him to take a booth.

He came over to me and jerked the cue out of my hands just as I was lining up a shot.

"What's up, Mace?"

"Hey, just fuckin' with you, dude."

"You thought over what we talked about?"

"Yeah, I'm interested."

"So?"

"Look, I got some people here right now I need to talk to," Mace said. "Some guys I know are throwing a little party out at this farm tomorrow night. Why don't you come over about ten?"

I pretended to think it over. "OK, sure."

"See that big fuck behind the bar? He'll give you directions to the place."

Mace went over to the booth. I had no choice. I went over to the bartender and told him I'd been invited to the party. He took a bar napkin and scribbled some directions on the back. He shoved it across the bar top at me without saying a word.

I called Cindy's cell. "What do you think?"

"I don't know what to think," she said. "Are you going?"

"I have to," I said. "Mace will know something's wrong."

"What does he think you're after?"

"I told him I'm looking to move some Canadian bud south. I have some contacts in Vancouver who know to cover me if he calls up there for a reference."

"What about Shannon?"

"I can't start asking him about your friend without raising his suspicions."

I said it with a little more heat than I intended. I used to make narcotics buys to get closer to a detective badge but I never liked it and I saw what happened to some cops who stayed under too long. They got addicted to living on the edge or they caved in to self-loathing.

I was having second thoughts about this kind of undercover work. I was a private eye with an office fifty miles south in the Mahoning Valley, and I wasn't sure fifty miles was far enough away to ensure my safety. I had a few contacts in this resort town still, but nobody, I was betting, who would ever cross paths with biker gangs. I had exchanged my Sig for the telephone a long time ago, and I was at least twenty years out of uniform, half that long out of homicide.

When Cindy walked into my office three weeks ago and told me her girlfriend and roommate was missing, I told her to go the cops. They worked for free. I specialized in finding lost kids for their parents and I admit to pre-judging Cindy's friend as a missing adult who didn't want to be found. This is America. It's OK to go missing.

But she wore me down with phone calls and pleading. I told her to keep her money. Nobody working in that biker's bar was going to get rich on tips. But phone calls led nowhere, and Cindy was convinced Shannon would never have just left like that without saying a word. She worked the bar at the Oak Room across the street from Annie's. No one saw her since she got off work that night. Cindy saw her bed wasn't slept in and figured she'd met a guy at the bar and stayed the night with him. It was something both young women did.

The idea to go incognito at Annie's was mine and it was based on a flimsy tip by a local drunk named Francis Beausoleil who claimed he saw Shannon in front of Annie's at two in the morning of the night she disappeared. The problem was that Shannon used to walk over to Annie's three or four nights a week to wait for Cindy to get off work. Francis wasn't all that sure which night he saw her in front of Annie's. He thinks she was talking to a man. He didn't know the man. He remembered waking up under a lifeboat on the beach the next day.

Flyers with her photo and description were tacked to poles or pasted in store windows up and down the strip. A tip line to the local precinct was listed at the bottom. Zilch, nada, zip.

~ ~ ~

The directions on the bar napkin were accurate. The farm was six miles outside the township in the real boonies. The local paper called it a "haven for meth cookers." Deserted farms overgrown with dockweed and stunted trees of heaven, trailers on cement blocks you wouldn't want your dog to live in, and coyotes who prowled the marshes for ducks.

Mace said the party wouldn't get started until midnight but the place was already rocking by the time I pulled in. I parked between a Fat Boy and a rusted-out Chevy pickup. I heard dogs growling from close by but I couldn't see the kennels.

I saw a couple tables loaded with booze and snacks and kegs of beer. Someone had rigged up a square of light bulbs that looped from two corners of the farmhouse to one limb of a birch tree and back again to a rusted pole that might once have held a home for purple martins. Inside the window of yellow light were dozens of people, mostly bikers and their women. I saw some probationers running around fetching beers. My face itched from going unshaven but most of the men here had heavy beards or elaborate moustaches. The patches on the cutoff vests bore the one-percenter's symbol and other signs of achievement for the ones who had put in the serious work of Angels mayhem. Greasy jeans, beards, ponytails, and tattoos – it felt like Altamont, 1969. I walked over to one of the tables and casually liberated one of the beers from its cocoon of ice and went looking for Mace.

I spotted him at the edge of the light talking to a blonde and brunette.

"Hey, bro," he said. He looked drunk. His eyes, however didn't smile. He pulled both girls to him and squeezed breast flesh hard enough to make the one on his left squirm and wriggle away. She fake-slapped him on the shoulder and said, "Ow, Mace, you bastard! That hurt."

They weren't the usual hatchet-faced slags on the backs of Harleys roaring down the strip on summer nights. I put them in their early twenties. Local girls probably. Some of them, like Cindy's missing friend, liked to play with fire. They sported too much cleavage and butterfly tattoos; sometimes they had boyfriends who dealt meth for the gang. Cindy told me Shannon liked to walk on the wild side with men and once had a serious drug problem. She had a kid back in PA being raised by Grandma. I wondered if these two knew Mace was the Angels' enforcer. He did a three-spot in Lucasville for a sexual assault; he was eighteen, right out of juvie. The judge didn't send him to a gladiator school, which told me it must have been brutal.

The girls giggled and bumping him with their hips. I thought of remora fish hanging out beneath the shark's belly.

Mace grabbed an ass cheek of the blonde. "Say hello to . . . hello to, what's yer name, bitch?"

More giggles, name-calling, laughter. Old Mace, some comedian.

Mace looked at the blonde and pointed an unsteady finger: "Alexis – no, Alicia." Then he turned to the brunette: "Jeanette."

Another chorus of giggles for the memory-challenged biker. "I'm Jeanette," said the blonde. "She's Alicia." Mace pulled a sad face; then he looked at me and grinned.

"Hey, you, bitch, whatever your name is, tell my friend here what it's like to have my dick up your dirt chute."

Alicia moved her head playfully under Mace's forearm, looked at me with a pouty, little-girl expression and said, "It's like taking a shit backwards."

Mace roared. His teeth were almost luminescent against the black of his beard: a wolf baying at the moon. He kept weaving drunkenly in and out of the light. I felt a knot in my stomach. Maybe they were all sharks and I was the remora.

Ugly people, I thought, *ugly lives and ugly language.* Why couldn't I get used to it?

The blonde reached around to press her hand flat against the front of my Levi's as I was taking a swig of beer. I didn't react. Mace tottered but regained his footing.

"You ever stick that old thing of yours in a girl like me, mister?"

"Not lately," I said. I tried to sound droll, man-of-the-worldly.

"From what I felt," she said, "be like stickin' a carrot in a big ole washtub."

Mace looked at me as if to say, *Can you believe this hoor's mouth?* Mace swung both girls into each other and put a bear hug around them. "Kiss, you crazy bitched!" The girls locked lips in a passionate embrace that was all theater for the onlookers who, hearing the commotion, were turning their gaze toward us.

I have this lifelong quirky habit of remembering statistics. One of them flashed across my mind: fifty men are killed annually in this country by their own cattle. They're always older men who think because they raised bulls from calves, fed them every day, and gave them names that the animals are pets. Mace's grin might have said wolf but in size and menace he was a bull. When I last did undercover at a biker kegger, I was twenty-five. Now I was over fifty, slower, with a constant buzzing in my ears. I was out of my depth and I knew it. Just like those old farmers when the bull paws the dirt in front of them, snorts, and lowers that massive head to explode into them. One thought for all: . . . *to be ground into the dirt by a thousand-pound wild animal.*

"C'mere, man, show you something," Mace said. He threw his arm around my neck and led me away.

"I thought we were going to talk some business," I said casually. One rule now: *Show no fear.*

"Fuck business," Mace said. He walked us onwards in the half-dark and I collided frequently against his bulk.

We were heading toward a ramshackle barn. I had seen it from a distance when I pulled in; it was spavined like an old horse.

The path we were on zigzagged through ruts. It must have been a four-wheeler track. I felt cockleburs sticking to my pants. Pretending to stumble, I cast a look upwards at the sky to get my bearings. A thin crescent of moon shredded passing clouds into dirty gray rags but away from the lights we were in blackness. How long would it take to set the dogs on me if I bolted now?

Mace steered me into the barn. The stench of cat urine was the first odor I was aware of – another meth lab. A chill ran up my spine. Mace didn't care I knew it.

The second was the rank smell of shit.

Mace said, "Bunch a them big fuckers yonder."

I couldn't see them but I could hear them moving and grunting in the dark.

The next thing I remember was coming to on my knees with a loud buzzing in my ears, like bees in a glass jar being held to my head.

Both my arms were gripped at the biceps and I was hauled to my feet.

I was still wobbly when Mace stepped into focus. He didn't look drunk anymore and his eyes bored into mine, searching for something.

Without saying a word, he snapped a hard punch that never traveled more than a foot straight to the bridge of my nose. My head exploded with fractured light.

Somebody near me, one of the men holding me upright, said, "Man, they musta heard that crack all the way back to the fuckin' party."

Blood poured out of my nose and down my chin like a broken pipe. I saw three Maces standing in front of me. I spit a gob of blood at the one in the middle.

I never saw the punch that knocked me out. When I came to, I was prone, bound at the hands and legs, and so nauseated I was terrified of choking on my vomit. I turned my head and regurgitated a brackish spume of bile or something yellow. At least it wasn't blood. The ringing in my ears was a demonic symphony.

A pair of boots stood in front of my face. I thought I was about to be stomped to death.

Instead, I was once again hauled to my feet and jerk-walked over to a stall where some hogs were thrusting their snouts through the boards. Shit, not domestic hogs at all. Wild boar. Razorbacks with curved tusks like scimitars. I had enough brainpower left from my recent drubbing to realize how fucked I was at that moment. *Of all the shitty ways to go . . .*

"Welcome to the Piggy Palace, motherfucker," Mace said.

"Finish me first," I said. It came out garbled because of my swollen face and the blood.

"No fucking way," Mace said. "We like to hear the screams."

"Yeah, it's fuckin' great," said one of the two.

"What about witnesses?"

"Speak up, asshole, I can't hear you!"

"Witnesses," I said and spat more blood.

"You're past it, old man. I set this up as soon as I heard you was lookin' into that Sharon girl."

"Her name was Shannon."

"I don't give a fuck what her name was, shit-for-brains," Mace growled.

"She's dead then," I said. Like saying rain is wet. The world tilted on a crazy axis. I thought of those ranchers before their bulls gored them into the muck.

"C'mon, Mace, quit jawin' at the cocksucker and throw him the fuck in," one of the thugs said. The other one made grunting noises like a hog.

Mace grabbed me by the shirtfront and jerked me so close to his face his beard stubble grazed my chin. He rammed me into the hog fence.

"Over you go, dude. Time to meet the boys on the other side. Sooooeee, pigs!"

The other two grabbed my legs and lifted. Mace's only mistake. I made my body go limp. As he bunched his fists into my shirt for a better grip, I slammed my head into his nose. I hit the floor like a dropped manhole cover and squirmed out of the grasp of the two bikers.

The blade cut a gash in my cheek and burned like a heated coat hanger pressed against my skin. Mace's enraged face loomed above; spit in the corners of his mouth.

"First I'm gonna cut your dick off and feed it to 'em!"

I'm a coward. I closed my eyes. I didn't pray.

The gunshot that hit Mace in the back dropped him on top of me. I smelled his rank two hundred fifty pounds of dead weight suffocating me – but tears were in my eyes: tears of bliss. The shouts and tumult in the barn were so familiar to me I sobbed with relief. Cops, a lot of them. Guns drawn and two dead-ass scumbags ordered to hit the floor with hands on heads.

"What the fuck, it's Haftmann," said one beet-red face looking down at me.

"You mind getting this big bag of shit off me?" I croaked. It was meant to sound cool, but it came out weird.

She wrote her signature on the check with a flourish – an ego trip.

"I should add a surcharge for mental anguish," I said.

She was bent over and I had a good view of the tops of her breasts.

"You tipped them, the cops," I said.

Her face changed expression, darkened, and the facial muscles around her eyes and mouth moved. She was getting ready to lie.

She stood up and seemed to make up her mind about something. "OK," she said. "I called them."

"It was damn close," I said. Two weeks and I still had

nightmares of those black bristles poking through the slats, their red mouths open and those white tusks thrusting toward me.

"I loved her," Cindy said.

"I know," I said.

"No, you don't," she said. "I loved her. I knew she was going out for a last fling before she committed to me – to our love. Do you understand?"

"I've never understood," I said. My wife, a Youngstown deputy district attorney, had dumped me ten years ago – for another woman.

I wasn't about to rehash what the SWAT team leader told me afterward. Cindy was a snitch, a paid informant; had been since she took the job at Annie's. It was a just another dope bust. It wasn't about me or missing girls. It was about busting another meth lab in Northern Ohio. If they hadn't reached the barn when they did, I would have been ripped apart. Mookie Brown at the precinct told me the muck in the stalls was still being sifted for bone fragments and DNA. In one stall they found an entire femur. Mookie described the tooth marks. Five bodies, so far. Four women, three of them street prostitutes, one teen runaway, and a male as yet unidentified. The biker who snorted like a hog turned state's evidence and identified Shannon as the last girl to disappear into the maw of the hogs. He never said why.

I had become something of a stationhouse joke when the cops heard about my solo undercover operation.

"If I'd – not made it out," I said to her, "would you have told the cops?"

She thought about that. "Maybe," she said.

I was bait to catch a shark. She called it love.

I said something, or muttered it.

"What did you say?"

"It was Latin," I said. "An old homicide bull I once

knew liked to say it at crime scenes. *Homo homini lupus est.*"

"What's it mean?"

"Man is a wolf to man."

An hour after she'd left, I couldn't get the citrusy tang of her perfume out of my office. I decided the best way to let in fresh air was to throw a phone book through my plate glass window. Some passersby in the street stepped around the phone book as if it were radioactive. The lights were on at Tico's Place across the street. I trotted over to get drunk as fast as I could.

Rock Me To Sleep

"**F**ucking faggots," said Millimaki.

"They do make a mess," said Petey Callaghan. We were in there pretty tight, what with forensics, me, Petey, and our fat-assed chief of police stomping around the room in his size twelves.

"I'll be at the station." Millimaki turned and paused, as if we might not want him to leave. He had already started to light one of his Swisher Sweets—just to irritate the new hire in forensics.

"Give Stiggy the report." He waved a hand through a cloud of blue smoke to remind us who was boss. I hated him, and I prayed he would slip on the stairs and break his neck and live out his days in a wheelchair sucking on small straws.

"What's Stiggy got to do with this?" Petey fretted.

"Just politics," I said. "We all done here?"

I was holding off on a three-coffee piss but a woman in the room made me uncomfortable with using the dead guy's bathroom while she was in there dusting. I gave Petey a long look. He nodded.

"Uh, hey, just the main room stuff'll be fine. We don't need anything in there." She looked up from her work, and gave him a nervous smile, cut her eyes to me, and began packing up her kit.

"Where do you want to eat breakfast?"

"I don't," I said. "Too early. I just want to find a head. My kidneys are bursting."

"Fucking fagbirds is right," he snorted. "They do make it easy, hunh? Nothing like a gay crime scene."

He started laughing while he drove us back to the station. I could imagine the scenarios he was watching. Petey had seen a few in Youngstown, where he had transferred up. I'd had only one other about five years ago, and it was even bloodier. It takes a long time to kill someone with a serrated knife. That guy then, the femme partner, had used three because the blades kept bending so he kept returning to the kitchen for a new one. The vic had awakened in the middle of the night thinking he was being stroked for some action until his lover slipped the blade beneath his pumping fist and severed it. When I got there, he was still in drag sobbing at the kitchen table, his mascara running in black snail tracks down his haggard face. The bloody trail led from his fuzzy slippers back to the bedroom where a coppery smell wafted in the draft and reminded me of the electric knives and the killing floor I had worked in years ago.

"What's up with these homos anyway, Haftmann?" Petey kept his eyes on the road, but we both knew what he meant. We were not friends though we had worked cases before.

"You mean, why not scream and yell, throw dishes, get a divorce?"

"Yeah, why the fuck do they have to trip out like that? Fuck Almighty Jesus."

"I don't know why anybody does anything," I said, but I knew Petey well enough to know that, once he had the scent of a weakness, he was going to worry it like a fighter who opens up a cut. I was used to it by now, the ribbing and sideways looks. I watched the scenery go past my window; another crappy autumn in northern Ohio, another season of loss. But I couldn't forget, not the job, not the parade of corpses and perps, not what I had become in the years since I thought justice was somehow involved in this sordid transaction we call "crime investigation." I felt like the last customer at an all-night freak show. I just wanted the show to end.

Petey was right about one thing. This one would be no whodunit. The killer was running but not for long. We had a name and a description to fax to the state cops. We knew his a.k.a.'s and his home address. My guess was he'd get bagged somewhere on a major highway running to nowhere or hiding out at a friend's who more than likely would rat him out eventually. *The dog returneth to his vomit.* Isn't that what the bible says? They'd love him in prison. Save them time switching him over. He didn't know it, but he was as good as bought, sold and married to some lifer; all that was missing was delivery to Lucasville down on the river. Nothing really changes.

I had run to this shitty little resort town to get away from all the slice-and-dice of a homicide cop's lot and it was back at me, steaming hot on a plate. *Yum.* Well, fuck this. I was getting out. I had begun looking into a private investigator's license, and I had a few start-up dollars that Micah hadn't stripped me of when she threw the dinner plates at the wall and walked out. Check that, I was the one who threw the plates. She was the one cheating. I was the one whose guts were twisted into little tiny knots.

I had brought two cases close to completion, this one was en route, and the remaining one had most of my attention. When it was over, I was gone, baby, and Millimaki was going to get my resignation letter in the form of an extended middle digit and a suggestion he kiss my ass right in the crack.

In the muster room Petey was gossiping with Mookie Brown about our "sad fairy" and "blowboy fudgepacker." I signaled him over for a quick discussion. We divvied up what was left of the case. I made a few calls, sent the BOLOs to dispatch, tidied up a few things on my desk and slipped on my shoulder harness. I kept the Glock in the bottom drawer because we have so many meth cases nowadays that it's just a matter of time before one of those shitbirds rips loose, grabs a gun off somebody's desk, and starts spraying lead around. Besides, I use non-regulation ammo and my piece is modified to hold a .224 BOZ round. I didn't mind that it would penetrate both sides of a UN helmet. There was actually a time when I relished the idea of charging into a room like a hero. Those days are long gone like so much else.

Outside I took in a lungful of air and felt my heart thump into panic mode. I never knew when these attacks were going to hit me, but at least I was outside – they were always worse inside – and I wondered if my mother's fear of small spaces was finding its way into my mind. Another reminder, if I ever needed it, that you can never escape your past. I popped a pill and waited a few minutes for it to kick in. Full circle: from catching dope fiends to becoming one.

I drove back to the strip and found my C.I. in the lakeside hovel where he squatted between gigs and fixes, rolling a blunt, which was what he did at dawn every day since I acquired him from an older detective; he's now spending his last days at an Alzheimer's clinic in Lyndhurst. Gerald's phone message was sitting on my desk when we returned from the crime scene. I could see he meant it to be urgent in his clumsy-assed code. "Urgent" translated as "I need to get high but I'm short of money." My weekly twenty was a retainer that saw him through the lean times, kept him in a little weed when he couldn't score crack or crystal, depending on what was available in town. The first time he gave me bad info was the day of his first lesson: I slammed his head against his cheap refrigerator and threatened to snitch him back to his buddies at Annie's. His eyes got big and I had his attention. Annie's Place is the hangout, and though the bike trash come and go all season long, when the Aryan Brotherhood is in town on business, the other gangs and wannabees show them respect their kind of royalty deserves. You did not fuck with them in prison and you did not violate their rules outside if you were in any way on their radar. You owed, you paid.

Gerald knew that better than most. He was doing two years on a drug possession in Conneaut's medium-security facility when one of the Brand enforcers got himself transferred. Gerald thought it was cool to have someone in the AB to hang out with and shoot the shit. He didn't know he was selling his soul forever once he got out. Gerald didn't give me half the skinny on his local assignments from his "brother" inside. He passed on what was safe enough for me to know, but never much I could trade to CID in Columbus or DEA in Cleveland. It was just a matter of time before he was found out. Being too small-time was keeping him alive, but he was frightened all the time and liked to stay stoned.

I found him curled up on a ripped-up Naugahyde La-Z-Boy in front of a TV playing an infomercial. His eyes were at half-mast so I knew he was coming down from the night before.

I shut the door behind me; the place reeked of cat piss and old socks. "You called, Gerald," I said.

"Hey," he said, acting annoyed, "I been tryin' to reach you all morning, man. Where the fuck've you been?"

"Unlike you, Gerald, I have a job."

"Good for you, bro."

"I'm not your bro, shitbag."

"I heard about last night – on the strip," he said.

That I doubted. It was three a.m. when I got the call. Annie's served after hours but the doors were closed and nobody gave a shit. Millimaki was paid off by half the bars for the same thing. Gerald loved thinking of himself as one of this crappy resort's leading nefarious citizens.

"Come on, give," I said. "I've got dead people all over the place that need tags on their toes . . ."

"OK, OK, chill, man, shee-it. Anyone would think you didn't like me." For a stoned-out snitch, he had delicate sensibilities.

"You know it isn't a really good idea for me to be dropping in like this." I waited a beat. Like most dope fiends, Gerald was keener when he was high; when he was between highs, like now, you had to draw pictures with big fat crayons.

"I ain't afraid of no narc tag," he said. He tried to sing it to the Ghost Busters tune. *Asshole.*

"A name, Gerald, if you please."

"I don't know his fuckin' name, homes. You don't just go up to a guy, ask his fuckin' name like you at a party. I ain't no nigger or Jew," he spluttered. Gerald had picked up the Brand's racist rant, but he would do meth or coke with anybody, including the Rainbow Coalition, if asked. I waited him out.

"My apologies," I said. "I forgot the convict etiquette. What does he look like?"

"Smooth, very smooth, good-lookin' motherfucker," Gerald said. "Got this big-ole tattoo on his neck."

"What kind of tattoo?"

"Jesus Christ, man, can I tell it my own way, you in-a-hurry motherfucker, you ..."

"Gerald, I know you're a little testy this morning because your drug-addled brain needs something. Now just give me what I need and I'll give you what you need."

"Fuckin' tatt was a de-sign, you know? Had some Chinese letters or some shit."

"Chinese. Do you mean symbols, characters, glyphs – what?"

"Whatever, man. Like this." He pulled over a stained

bar napkin and drew on it with a pencil he located beneath a pile of shaved beaver magazines. He started to fold the napkin, thought better of it, and handed it to me.

It looked like three strokes suspended between a pair of trapezoids.

"What it mean, like?" Gerald wasn't really interested. His eyes drifted back to the girl on TV selling some kind of back brace.

"It means I'm waiting for the rest of your goddamned the story," I said.

Gerald twisted around and put one leg under him. Micah used to do that.

"He was talkin' some weird shit, that's all I know. Looked like a fuckin' Messican or a halfie."

"English, Gerald." I waited while he flipped through the vast Rolodex of his vocabulary.

"Like a half-white, half-nigger, you know."

"What did he say, Gerald?"

"He said he was looking for this fuckin' cop, man, this *fucking cop*, somethin' about rigged evidence. Some brother got sent to prison on it, whatever."

"Did he name the cop?"

"No, no, no, man. Just that, he said, like, this fuckin' cop was in for a world of big-time hurt. Motherfuckin' payback, his exact words. I ain't lyin' on you, dog."

Gerald's absorption of rap culture made him oblivious to the contradictions of his borrowed hatred of blacks from his cellmates in the slammer.

"I had to call you, man. Dude had a serious look to him. Dude said that motherfuckin' cop was going to get his and his cunt wife, too."

Cunt wife . . . Micah.

I left him sitting in his chair with its goofy stuffing popping free in wisps and tufts. His eyes looked glassy in the smeared light of a new dawn.

Petey buzzed my cell. I was patched through, and he said that the PA staties had found our guy at a rest stop near Sharon. He had taped a note to the steering wheel and sliced his wrists with one of those same cheap kitchen knives. Petey was on his way now. I said I'd meet him, but he told me not to bother. This was a slam-dunk, thank God. Just paperwork now.

I was mildly curious about the note, but I would read it soon enough. I had seen my share over the years. Some were better than others; none ever explained the mess. Plato said we lived in caves and we could see only shadows of truth. I believed we lived in sewers like rats and we could see the cesspool clearly enough. Christ knows, I was weary enough doing the backstroke in it all these years.

But Gerald's hot tip did worry me. When Micah was assistant D.A., I was the county's lead investigator. Three years ago we had some scumbag biker dead-to-rights on the kidnap-murder of a fifteen-year-old runaway. I did a little B & E on his rental cottage on the lake because I'd been tipped off the girl was there, and there wasn't time for horseshit paperwork. The girl was already dead and buried in the sand because we found her with a methane probe. But it got out somehow in the forensics, what I had done, and that ruined Micah's case. The judge threw out all the evidence under a fruit-of-the-poisoned tree ruling. Micah was investigated by the state's commission on legal ethics. That put the first big nail in the coffin of our marriage. She started having affairs and finally walked out – straight into the arms of another woman. She shared a house with her down by the Ohio River. I went back to the Jefferson precinct in disgrace but nobody could prove it was illegal entry. I exchanged a cloud of suspicion for a booze fog and stayed drunk until it blew over. But it never seemed to be over.

Gerald's thug might be a typical loudmouth, the kind

that drift into Jefferson-on-the-Lake and drift away after the season. If the guy was AB, it could be a problem because the Brotherhood's tentacles had a long reach. Not a lot of my own brother cops would be saddened to hear of my premature demise. These thoughts tumbled around while I drove and searched for a stand open this early for my first cup of coffee of what was going to be a long day.

I checked out the sandwich stand on the corner of Little Minnesota where a guy with two-day stubble served good espresso and had an eye for young quiff. I was cultivating him for another stoolie, in fact, but he was so close-mouthed I never found the moment to set the hook. He grunted at me. When I asked if he'd seen a man in town with a Chinese glyph on his neck, he gave me a double-grunt reply. *Next stupid question*, it translated.

I finished the coffee and headed down the street past the arcade.

I'm not a lucky man and I've never been a lucky cop. Unlike cop shows, it's all legwork and writing reports, and mostly talking to the same lying assholes you spoke to earlier, but when you know a little more, you go back so you can tear down their lies.

Three chrome choppers rested outside. I squinted through the dirty glass like a Peeping Tom. Kurt, the bartender, was closing down, but I doubted he was serving coffee to his three biker customers. I said I wasn't lucky, but the last person I expected to see come strutting out, blinking like a baby bird in the light, was a guy that Gerald had just described to me right down to the shaved head and Chinese character. He cut his eyes to me and started a fast scissor-walk.

I've been eyefucked before; every cop knows that look. My radar had him locked. I trotted after him and shouted for him to stop, which did the thing you'd expect: he hauled ass, booked like a pair of angry Rottweilers were on his heels. My car was too far so there was nothing for it but to run after him. He ran with his arms pumping, head straight as a cheetah's.

He ran in the direction of a maze of narrow streets with rental cottages named for flowers that Ohio never grew; ultimately, I knew he'd wind up in a cul-de-sac. I just had to stay in sight. I watched his shirt whip out behind him as he tried to burn more speed. It was like a misfiring Plymouth 420 hemi being chased by a clapped-out Ford Escort with too many miles – the distance increased, and I was sucking air badly.

He disappeared around the corner of Lantana and Sago Palm. At the corner, I drew my gun and tried to control my ragged breathing; salt sweat burned my eyes. I approached, as they say, with caution. If he bolted inside a cottage – one of these ramshackle "resort suites" a rich family built and didn't waste an extra dime on construction – I might hear movement inside. This row of weathered cottages, sweat-blackened like an old baseball mitt, were mainly occupied by the strip's transients and many were dope fiends.

He appeared, magically, standing between the last two cabins. He held a knife at his side.

"Drop it!" I yelled.

He did the smart thing. I put a knee in his back, threw a nylon cuff around his wrists, hauled him to his feet, and led him back the way we had come.

"What're you ch-charging me w-with?" he said.

"Mopery . . . with intention . . . to gawk," I wheezed, but I almost passed out with the effort to speak.

"Man, I never expected – "

"What do you think, shithead, when you draw a knife on a cop?"

"Y-you started chasing me. H-How w-was I to know youse a cop, man?"

"You . . . get chased a lot . . . by middle-aged men in white shirts and ties?"

You halfwit, Gerald. He had left out the fact the guy had a pronounced stutter.

I Mirandized him. Then I pushed his head down to get him into the back seat. His eyes were red and his jaws were shadowed by beard. The stubble on his head was noticeable. But he didn't have a strung-out look to him.

He said nothing in the car. Upstairs in the precinct, I took down his stats and walked him over to booking. I looked up his priors from the NCIC database.

A uniformed officer led him past me. "What's it mean?" I asked and pointed to my neck

"It m-means 'd-danger' like, on all sides, b-beware.'"

He said his name was Dennis Smith. He'd just been released from the facility in Conneaut at the time Gerald was going up on his own beef.

He looked back at me. "Check it out, m-man. It ain't no alias. It's m-my f-fuckin' name."

I did. His real name was Michael Thibodeaux. His rap sheet said he was gang-affiliated with the AB and his moniker was "the Spoon" or "Mickey the Spoon." You don't get a name like that in prison for your dining habits. They give it to you for eye-gouging finesse. I didn't see any triple 6's, shamrocks, or Brand logos besides the single neck tattoo.

In prison the Brotherhood still favors the garrote and the shank; outside, they like overkill with over-and-under shotguns at close range, hydro-shock ammo and jacketed hollow points. They kill more than the mafia, more than any half-assed drug organization. They ran Lucasville.

I had my first interview with him before lunchtime.

"'One should die proudly when it is no longer possible to live proudly,'" he recited as soon as he saw me.

"So you've improved your mind in prison," I said and

smiled. "That's nice."

His eyes glittered under the fluorescent lighting and his bald head looked stippled. By then I had learned more about him. I knew he wrote the Brotherhood manual for other joints like Pennsylvania, West Virginia. It was more than indoctrinating new members. Tips on anatomy, for instance, what books to read so you could learn where the best places are on the human body to stick a razor-honed plastic shiv. I'd seen those manuals in a gang seminar years ago: *Knife fighting is like a dance. The smell of fresh human blood is overpowering in a first kill but it gets better.* The Brand's poetic gibberish comparing killing to sex, all for a holy cause. Scumbags with a tablespoon of literacy, I thought then, and still do.

"How were you supposed to do your assignment here?"

I looked at him to see if he flinched. His eyes never came off mine.

"I made it so they'd believe I was serious about the job. They'd kill my wife and kid in a heartbeat. They sent me photos of her driving, going shopping, visiting her mom – hell, they even had one of their guys on the outside wave at the camera while my wife was ten feet away putting the groceries in the car."

"Now tell me why you're here, Dennis or Michael. Why our little cozy neck of the woods?"

A pause, then he looked down at his hands, and the stutter intensified.

"I-I d-don't know, man. I s-swear it. I'm s-supposed to w-wait for orders."

I got him some coffee, and booked him on the third-degree deadly weapons charge, a kicked-down felony CCW, blade over four inches. On top of his parole violation, he'd get eight months, maybe a year, but my problem wasn't going away with him.

Failures were punished ruthlessly inside, sometimes
with demonstration killings in front of everybody. I read
Nietzsche too, but for my own reasons. Nothing like piping
a guy walking to his tier in full view of everyone to make
Nietzsche's point about bending space and reality to your
will.

I had little time before they would send someone else.
I had no doubt I was AB business, but Dennis' claim about
waiting for orders was a dog that wouldn't hunt.

~ ~ ~

I drove south past Austinburgh through fall colors and
giant colonials surrounded by massive oaks. These old
houses once held huge families that lived in their rooms
until they too produced children who would work the land
and then went into the dirt alongside their parents and
grandparents. I would never know. I was living in a motel
"suite," which is to say it came with a kitchenette.

I didn't let nostalgia sweep me away. Old John Brown
used to farm out here and stockpile weapons. He wasn't
known for kindness to wife or children. I was worried
because Micah had not returned my calls, and I was
waiting for the local cops in East Liverpool to acknowledge
my request for a drive by. Micah and her lover traveled a
lot, so they could be out of town. She told me she had
become a Wiccan about six months ago. I wondered if I
ever knew her at all. She was still practicing law but mostly
the *pro bono* cases and lawsuits against cops. It would be a
mistake to call that part of the state "cop friendly" because
police were notorious for harassing blacks and waiting
outside clubs to bag dealers and strip-search them on the
spot.

The dirt road ran in a zigzag loop around an empty
pond where cattails still bloomed. Their burst seedpods
reminded me of Gerald's forlorn couch.

T. J. was at home painting in what he called his

227

"Florida room," which was a clapboard add-on through which he punched holes with a crowbar to gain extra light. It was always chilly and dark inside. The half-light created a chiaroscuro effect on his canvases that he said he was cultivating in his art. He offered me coffee in a Styrofoam cup, which was thick as tar and tasted worse.

T. J. learned to paint in prison. His canvases reminded me of Bosch because they were busy with half-human devils and trolls or strange-looking machines that seemed designed for torture. I wondered if these infernos were based on his long sojourn across the landscape of America's prison system. He started his education at eighteen in a white-boy gang in Los Angeles, then did his first jail in Chino after one of their gladiator schools failed to show him the error of his ways. He worked his way up and east with stops at Marion, Illinois as a guest at their level-sex prison. He dipped south to Atlanta for a stint with the loose-knit Southern mafia, came back up north to Terre Haute and finished up in Lucasville doing ten to life for a passion murder when he caught his old lady with a cellie who was furloughed before him. He got old in prison and he got respectable enough to be left alone by the blacks and gangs. When he got so old that his health started to cost the state more to house him than to release him, they turned him loose – cleaned-up, reformed, and eager to rejoin society. Well, not exactly.

He hated the establishment with every fiber of his being and that was why I found our friendship, if that's the right word, strange. We clicked because we were existentialists of a sort, although T. J.'s was more, to quote him, "Sartrean than Nietzschean." He told me he had nihilistic spaces in his brain where I couldn't follow him. He was an old con who could spin a story if he chose, or he could tell you a hard truth that would wither the hair on your arms like a scalding liquid. I met him two years ago when he was being thrown out of a bar on the strip. Instead of booking him, I drove him here and put him to bed. Two days later I received a painting in the mail, which I still have. Instead of human souls in pain, his usual motif, he did a nude of Micah. He had lifted it from my coat pocket the night I drove him home. He returned it with the painting. Since the photo was taken when she came out of court one day, I wondered how T. J. had managed to do justice to her luxuriant bush.

He was grumpy but cordial enough to talk to me. We talked names. How he knew so much about prison doings still surprised me because he never again drank at Annie's. He didn't like the fact that every ex-con knew his rep and connections, so he chose the few bars that could be called "respectable." It meant putting up with loudmouthed tourists and horny college boys; sometimes the golfers' chitchat provoked him into leaving early, but he felt the tradeoff for his privacy was worth it. He wished cancer on the world and drank in his solitary corner.

He heard of Dennis Smith.

"He's not the hog with the biggest balls," T. J. said without taking his eye off a smudged corner of his canvas, "but he's pretty high up the food chain." He dabbed a few quick strokes in and squinted at the effect. From where I sat I couldn't see much of the composition.

"Somebody I know says he is," I said. I was pushing a button.

"Well, fuck him and you, too, because I know somebody that knows that stuttering, alligator-armed son of a bitch and it ain't so," T. J. huffed and gave me an icy stare.

I recited a few of the Spoon's stats to him.

T. J. paused and looked at me again but more thoughtful than challenging.

"Word I had," he said slowly, "that bastard's tall as he

is wide and can bench four hundred pounds."

"He's lost weight since then," I said. "He's not as big as he was in prison."

"Why you askin' me, hoss?"

I gave him some details from the biker case that landed me in the shit.

"The guy who probably gave the order is on the council in Lucasville. He'd be one of three brothers – not kin, I mean"

"I'm following," I said.

"One of them, the one I'd bet on, is downright fucking . . . *primordial*."

"What's his name, T. J.?"

He sat back in his chair staring hard at his work. It was tough to be a snitch. "Name's Dewey Longworth, fucking hillbilly with an IQ off the charts and no conscience. He's running the joint with them other two studs. They handle extortion inside and all the drugs going in and out."

"You have any idea why he'd take out a contract on me?"

"No, Thomas. No offense but you're small beer. They do reprisals on civilians nowadays, but it's always related to business. You pissed off somebody or you're related to somebody who pissed off one of the big boys. It ain't rocket science, man."

"My wife's career was ruined, it destroyed our marriage, and the killer wasn't even Brand, T. J."

He shrugged and went back to his canvas.

"Thanks for the coffee." I got up to go.

"I met Longworth," he said without turning around. "Once."

I waited.

"It was a year before they opened my cage door, about that. The place was the usual mayhem. You whack one of ours, we'll get one of yours, back and forth – same old shit, different day."

In the bad light he looked ancient. He was seventy, maybe older. His eyes were pale but not rheumy like old men's eyes.

"Longworth's a genius. Only a few can get made and the Brand still follow their blood-in, blood-out code. He saw how clumsy it was, what with associates and hangers-on, and all the running around you have to do to get anything done – shit, they want to whack a guy, it's impossible with a one-man, one-vote system. You have to send runners and lawyers, kite notes all over the fuckin' state to get permission. By then, somebody was sure to tip off the guy you want done."

He licked a fingertip and smeared a streak of paint. I could see it now: salmon-pink cirrus clouds above a river like hammered tin.

"So what's different now?"

"Longworth might be a half-educated peckerwood but he'd have made a first-class CEO. He told his boys coming up for trial anywhere in the state to represent themselves."

"So what?"

"So, if you was a damned lawyer, Thomas, you'd know what that means. It means you got subpoena power now and you can subpoena anybody you fuckin' well choose as a witness. Each time a Brand member sends out a writ, it means another Brand member is relocated to Lucasville."

He laughed. "Subpoena power unlimited. That's the law, my friend."

What used to take weeks now took a few days and you could meet openly in the yard to discuss operations.

The answer to my problem wasn't up here; it was down on the Ohio River. My guts churned.

I called the station and spoke to a dispatcher I knew. I gave her a plausible story for skipping out of town. I knew she'd cover me. She still hated Millimaki and would enjoy screwing him over if she could. The chief came close to a *quid pro quo* sexual harassment suit when she was first hired, but he had too many powerful friends. Get him drunk, and the pig will brag about the worn carpet in front of his chair. "That's where I teach 'em to pray," he told Petey.

I hit Route 11 and floored it. That stretch of highway is wide open – nothing for miles in either direction but a lobo wolf and a barbed-wire fence.

The dispatcher told me that, when they had Dennis empty his pockets, they found a folded-up letter from his wife. She wrote about their baby's teething and talked about husband-and-wife things. I told Sheila to go to the evidence storage locker and check the envelope.

"Get the letter," I pleaded. "Envelope and all. Look at it carefully. This is an emergency, Sheila. Call me back on your cell."

She called me back in two minutes. Her voice was scratchy from interference.

"Sheila, I need another favor, a big one."

"Golly damn, Thomas. This could mean my job if Millimaki – "

"I need you to look at the letter, see if there are any blank spaces. You're going to have to put a heating iron behind – "

"Whoah, sonny boy! Hold it right there. I could get fired for just touching the thing."

"Sheila, I need this."

"Gee whiz damn it all to hell. I just learned I'm pregnant again." A deep world-weary sigh.

"You men should have your balls docked like horses' tails when you turn thirteen," she said. I held my breath while she talked herself up to the edge.

"OK, damn you, but you better be there for me when the shit comes rolling down – "

"You'll see faint handwriting because it's in urine."

"Oh that's nice."

"Get it to the lab, use the wand – "

"The what?"

"A wand, it looks like one of those Halloween sticks. It has ultraviolet light – "

"OK, then what?"

"Write down what it says, word for word, and read it back to me as soon as you can."

"Thomas, it *better* be an emergency and not some pussy business you're up to."

Jesus, I had a way with women.

I drove on automatic pilot and tried to ease the tinny roar in my ears by not thinking. It seemed an hour had passed. I was sixty miles from East Liverpool according to the last highway sign.

I picked up. "Word for word."

"Now, dang your eyeballs, you don't have to tell me twice – "

"Sheila, for fuck's sake, just read."

"Here goes. First, I gotta tell you that there's a lot of gibberish with the letters *a* and *b* all over the one white space – like they were just filling it in with nonsense. Like it doesn't make sense."

"Just tell me how the *a*'s and *b*'s go in sequence."

"OK, now there's a sentence like you thought. Here it is: 'Well I am a grandfather at last my boy's wife gave birth to a strapping eight pound seven ounce baby girl.'"

"What else?"

"There's these little squiggles on some of the letters like little tails – curlicues, I reckon."

"Which letters?"

"Let's see – on 'baby girl' there's a mark on the *g*, the *n*, and the *d*."

"Thanks, Sheila."

"That's it? I risked my job for a lousy birth announce –

"

Shit, shit – this was bad.

I called T. J. *Pick up, pick up, you old fucker.*

"Who the fuck's this? Better not be some telemarketing bullshit – "

"T. J., it's Haftmann. It's important."

"Man, if I hadn't spilled that can of turpentine on my crotch and burned my tiny old dick, I never woulda left the studio."

"I've got a Brand code. Can I read it to you?"

"Lay it on me. Then call me right back," he said.

Five minutes later he rang my cell number.

"Well, somebody's in big trouble," he said. "They're not even trying to hide the code. Look how obvious one-eight-seven jumps out . . . they do love that Negro gangbanging lingo."

"What else?"

"'Baby girl' is a woman, the target's a woman."

"What about the *a*'s and *b*'s like that?"

"Son, weren't you listening to me? Longworth ordered one of his closest brothers killed for kissing a punk on the stairs – that's all. They traffic in fags, get blowjobs from them and they cornhole them, but if you get caught kissing a punk, you're violating code. Longworth gave the recruit who got assigned the job a gallon of pruno and his dead friend's photo to hang on his wall – a badge of honor."

I nearly collided with some gray-haired asshole in a Jeep Liberty turning into my lane.

I was twenty-five miles from Micah's turnoff. The house was in a valley and from a nearby hill I had a panorama of the rooftops and the river. I used to drive down here and park at dusk. Sometimes they'd come out with bread for the ducks and geese. I saw Micah kiss her once when no one else was around but me.

The hit wasn't on me – Micah was the target.

I made a few turns and reached the spot overlooking the house. I saw her car and another vehicle in the driveway. If there were other cars in front of the house, I couldn't see from this vantage.

Nothing looked out of the ordinary except for the fact that two professional women were home in the middle of the day. It was pretty country but hardscrabble poor where Appalachia's doorstep began. Most youth left home. Quite a few were serving in Iraq. The mines were closed. The glassworks factories stopped hiring years ago. I watched Canada geese fly over the river in a ragged vee. Every time a distant shotgun went off, my stomach dropped another inch.

When my beeper throbbed, I jumped as if I'd be bitten.

"I can tell you this much," said T. J. hacking up some phlegm. "You ever mention what I'm telling you, you'll be signing my death warrant. They're still using the same code as in my day. You use two alphabets, for instance, an *a* can mean a *d* and – "

"T. J., you have got to tell me what it says right now."

"It says, 'Confirm message to move on both.'"

I was out of the car and running, stumbling, down the hill. I hit a gopher hole and my legs went out from under me. I flew downhill like a rag doll tossed over a cliff. The ground wasn't frozen so I hit hard breaking some momentum in a half-assed shoulder roll. I managed to stagger back to my feet. My Glock was still there because my ribs burned as if a C. C. Sabathia fastball had been drilled into my side. The ankle holster, however, flapped empty and my 10mm Smith was somewhere behind me in the brambles. No time to go back.

I broke through the brush and wound up behind a faded white two-story house. A clothesline had been strung and bright colors semaphored in the breeze off the river. I was two houses from the big Victorian where they lived.

I saw nothing in the windows but sheers, no lights on. A small window directly above the storm cellar was their kitchen. On one of my voyeur trips down here, I had seen Micah's head framed in the windows as if she were standing there doing dishes. I was filthy with mud and debris from my crazed run, sweat-streaked and bleeding from a cheek where a twig had lashed my face. My eyes burned with a mix of tears and sweat.

I eased up behind the house and stepped onto the metallic cellar doors along the beveled edges where the dead bugs and pigeon shit made the footing slippery. I was almost at head height for peering inside. I gripped the edge and pulled myself up and looked in. Nothing – no sounds, no people.

I hunched down against the wall of the house to make myself as small as possible. No cars except my own on the overlook and nobody in their backyards putting away hammocks or summer furniture. I had to decide.

Skirting the house's perimeter, I kept as low as I could. I took a few steps at a time on the porch and risked passing the picture window – heavy curtains were drawn over it. A newspaper in its orange plastic skin lay in front of a door with an oval window. I turned the knob as gently as I could and found it locked. I jammed my gun into my belt in the middle of my back

I ran to the back of the house and lifted the handle on the cellar door: locked. These were built to cover the cellar steps, but they weren't bomb shelters. I hunkered down in a weightlifter's squat and jerked up until a trickle of blood flowed down my wrists where the metal edge cut. The small rod that acted as a spindle finally snapped.

I was down the steps facing a screen door, which I took off its hinges with a single jerk. Behind it was an unpainted plywood door secured by a hook and eye. I popped it loose from its hasps and squeezed past. Gasping for breath, I could make out an old fieldstone cellar built by men who were probably half a head smaller than most men today. I worked my way in the dark by touching the walls. There, faintly ahead, a glimmer of light in the darkness. Then a stairwell that led to the foyer upstairs out front. The steps were wooden, as old as the house, but their thick planking covered my sounds.

I pushed the door open and listened – still no sounds anywhere.

I was directly beneath the upstairs landing. I saw the television set from its position in the entertainment center. A patina of dust covered the screen. Plants, a bookshelf stacked to the ceiling with leather-bound volumes. Micah's law books. She was the bookworm, I was the TV remote-Nazi.

I left my shoes on the first landing where the stairwell turned – now the boards, though carpeted, gave out creaks under my weight.

Peering through the dowels, which twisted like candy licorice and were polished to a blond sheen, I saw the top landing. I held my breath and listened. This time I heard muffled sounds coming from a back bedroom.

Despite the high ceilings, a narrow corridor bisected rooms on either side. At the edge of the carpeting, tongue-and-groove boards led to the back room.

I sucked in a breath, and sprinted full-bore down the hallway.

Jodie, or what was left of Jodie's broken body, was slumped against one wall, nude and bound at the wrists, demurely covering her sagging breasts. A bullet hole had been drilled neatly through the center of her forehead. Her face was battered beyond recognition but her eyes were open, gazing sightlessly at me. Through the blurred lens of my brain, I had a fleeting glimpse of a shaved pubis.

Because he was bucking into Micah from behind, I was on him before he could react. When he turned to me, my lips parted in a bared grin, a mindless, all-consuming, rage-fueled violence. The growl that bayed from my throat didn't come from me. For a man so badly out of shape, I flew with an athlete's body across the room compressed into a single-minded mass of hate. I had forgotten Micah entirely. I took him at the edge of his jaw and drove his teeth into his lips.

We went over the bed and I was on top of him with my gun flailing down hard at his head, his shoulders, neck — anything I could strike. I heard the satisfying crack of bone again and again. The thin skullcap near the temple cracked like an eggshell. Even when he was unconscious, I kept hitting him with stronger blows. I just kept swinging. When I stopped, exhausted, his head was a red pulp, one eye missing from its jellied hole, and his jaw gaped open from being broken in so many places that it was practically detached. His teeth, what remained, were jagged red stumps.

I remember holding my ex-wife in my arms, or was she holding me — I can't recall. She was bruised, her face was beaten and her nose had been mashed to one side. Her cheekbones were her distinctive beauty, now all puffy and swollen. One of her eyes was completely shut. She said no words. I heard sounds again. The upside-down universe returned to whatever we call normal. I heard my breath rise and fall, rise and fall . . .

My hand, I later discovered, was fractured at the metacarpal above the knuckle so I couldn't have hit him again if had to.

How do you know when you've lost your mind — or when you've found it? There's no one left in the world you can communicate with and you're as alone as you'll ever be. You're like that escaped slave in the Winslow Homer painting on a raft far out to sea that's never going to make it through the next storm. And there are these dorsal fins cutting the water in circles around him. He's waiting to die, knowing he's going to die alone, and I think, as I thought then, there's a kind of resignation in his face, a knowledge that there is no God, there's only death . . .

~ ~ ~

Weeks later, when I was able to hold a phone with my right hand without whimpering. I asked her how she was getting along.

"I can come down there, help you move things," I said.

"That wouldn't be a good idea," she said. I heard a familiar weariness in her voice, my endless ploys to bring us back together.

Before we hung up, she said, "I'm moving out of Ohio."

"Where to?"

"I haven't decided whether to tell you," she said.

"You said something to me before, something when you pulled me off him. I'm just curious."

"You don't remember?"

"I don't remember that much, no, actually – "

"You said, I'm sorry, I'm sorry . . . you just kept saying you were sorry," she said.

I wasn't apologizing to the man I was clubbing to death so it must have been for me, for what I had done to us.

~ ~ ~

Some time after that I was sitting in T. J.'s studio watching him sketch. We weren't talking about anything in particular. I was drinking whiskey. Columbus CID had cleared me after a lengthy investigation. Because of the overkill in the room, I was told not to look for any commendations.

You could ask to see T. J.'s sketches but never ask to

239

see one of his paintings in progress. Not unless you wanted to pull back a bloody stump. I managed to sneak a look at the work-in-progress when he was off taking a leak. It looked like a rat with a child's toy.

He caught me scowling. His hand was still on his fly. Instead of the curse I expected, he said, "Art isn't supposed to be happy, Haftmann. Life isn't happy. It's dishonest to expect that."

I was tired from a long day of standing in the rain interviewing people. We'd had our second Dead-Body-Found call in a week that morning. A pair of lovers strolling on the beach found him. Nobody knew the guy, although it was clear he had been hanging around the resort. Just another drifter. Most of them move on and return like migratory birds in warm weather. A few decide they've run far enough, winter's coming, nothing's left to live for. We found him under a rotting lifeguard boat on the sand. I had walked past that spot a thousand times when I was young. I remembered how often Micah and I had walked along that stretch of beach and held hands and looked at the water. She loved how the light changed its colors.

T. J. was waxing eloquent again. My head throbbed from my aching sinuses every year at this time. I like winter more than I used to, more as I age. I like how it covers the filth and garbage of the landscape.

"People think that because old Thomas Jefferson said we have a right to *pursue* happiness means we have a right to *be* happy. Not so," T. J. began another discourse. I guess he missed those convict chinwags. He could go on longer than a whore's dream.

"You probably know this, Thomas. Even though you're a cop, I know you're not as dumb as you let on – "

Oh Lord just kill me now, end my pain.

" – Locke was an empiricist, who said in his treatise on

civil government . . ."

"Fucking cons," I thought. *Nothing else to do all day but plot mayhem, lift weights, drink, do drugs but I have to get one who studied law texts and read serious books.*

I imagined a clear, deep pool and stared into it. Then, unbidden, came Micah out of the water, as gloriously naked as Venus in her clamshell.

". . . the pursuit of *property*, not happiness – the motherfuckers have it all wrong, son."

T. J. babbled on – about politics, the great themes of life and art, or the future of the world.

". . . and besides that, I've never thought Michelangelo half the painter Raphael was, even when he was drunk . . ."

Lord, I believe. Help my unbelief.

"Yes, well put," I said. Micah, nude, in bed, waiting for me, was all I could think of.

"You lying sack of shit, you didn't hear a fuckin' word I been saying. And you better not be pitching that tent for me, faggot. One time in Marion this queer came at me . . ."

God Almighty. Whoever was it who put love in the mind of an animal?

~ ~ ~

Back at the station I had a call from the lead CID investigator. He told me the state's AG declined to press a conspiracy to murder charge on Longworth. I thought that would have been a no-brainer and said so through the veins in my neck.

"Easy, copper. Yeah, well, we did too, but it's more complicated than that."

"How the fuck could it be more complicated?"

"Jodie Barrett, your wife's . . . friend. She was Longworth's sister . . ."

~ ~ ~

It was a sordid tale. Two siblings raised in a one-story hovel built dog-run style in some backasswards hick town in the middle of the sticks. There were thousands in the hills like it America chose to forget every day. In these places life closed around people and hermetically sealed them off. Passengers zooming by on freeways or rubbernecking from their observation railroad cars always fancied these simple people's lives to be so romantically unfettered and stress-free. The truth was that it was more often a brutal existence.

As the factories and shops closed, it turned on itself in a kind of entropic ugliness like a dog in a leghold trap biting its paw. The mother died and she, Jodie Longworth, provided the domestic services for brother and father, which at puberty predictably enough now began to include sexual services. The father was a town bully in a place full of hard men, so there wasn't going to be any reporting to Children's Services, which of course, didn't exist anyway, even if it could be proven. At sixteen Dewey left off having sex with his sister to hook up with a motorcycle gang and was off to California, a fledgling biker and future AB leader extraordinaire. The old man finally left her alone when his pickup smashed into a tree on the way back from a bar. The timing was perfect: she was six months' pregnant and starting to show; she aborted the baby and set out to anywhere the little money she could get for the house an land would take her. It wasn't, unfortunately, nearly far enough.

She left town, changed her name, worked hard at a community college, and got a job as a paralegal. The lawyer she worked for fell in love with her, but she would never permit a male to touch her again. The lawyer, however, was a good man (if you discount the wife and kids at home) and he paid her way through West Virginia University where she graduated *doctoris jure* and was picked for the *Law Review*.

Years later she happened to be traveling through

northeast Ohio where a beautiful young prosecuting attorney of great promise had just experienced the worst moment of her career thanks to her stupid husband. Exit husband, enter beautiful lesbian lawyer – and *exeunt omnes*, chased by bears, as I remembered from a Shakespeare play from my youth. The farce of it, the ex-husband's ridiculing at the station, his drinking to forget, the people snickering behind their hands, his own doubts –

He accepted the fact he couldn't change much despite his existentialist free will. He could no more change the way he tied his tie ("One kind of knot is all a man needs to know," his father had said) than he could change the position of his basal ganglia.

The final chapter in Jodie née Longworth's life came when her brother stabbed a black inmate thirty-four times in his cell in Lewisburg, Pennsylvania and was transferred to Illinois to break up the AB's stranglehold. Longworth's mindless violence as an AB enforcer changed in degree but not kind. He began reading the philosophers and studying Sun Tzu. He adopted the warrior code and promulgated its values throughout prisons from coast to coast. He became a legend for his mind as well as his ruthlessness, and one day, after authorities in Marion discovered he and another con, a short man with a massive chest and a soft-spoken stutter that masked a killer's psyche, had set up an elaborate system of female pen pals outside the prison.

All wrote in the code Longworth and Thibodeaux invented, he was immediately sent to Lucasville. A bureaucratic snafu later sent his brother Thib to Conneaut, Ohio, where the two cons perfected "carnie" and developed a statewide retinue of loyal women acting as couriers and messengers for the brotherhood. Call it the Stockholm syndrome, call it misguided love, but these women would do anything for their lovers behind the razor wire.

In the snake pit of his heart, I knew there had to be a better reason for Longworth to destroy his own flesh and blood. Micah was collateral damage, as I would have been.

Longworth followed a tactic he made the AB subscribe to – do anything you could to get next to your enemy – something the AB had perfected even maximum-security environments. You sought to befriend your enemies (Sun Tzu here, no doubt) and get yourself assigned as their cellmates; then at your leisure, you "rock them to sleep." Longworth must have learned of his sister practicing law under an assumed name. The prison grapevine wasn't flawless but once he had her checked out, he knew he had a pawn to use. Her death was ordered, not by Longworth, but by Thibodeaux, who thought he was getting at Longworth through his own blood. Maybe Longworth had said enough about his past in some late-night conversation between cellies. That would put the Spoon on top of the Brotherhood pyramid, the most feared man of them all, if he could kill Longworth's sibling and make it dramatic.

Except that Longworth went him one better. While I was having the bones in my hand reset at the emergency room in East Liverpool, Dennis Smith was being returned to the Conneaut facility.

About a week after T. J. and I were discussing the great themes of life and art, the *Lake Erie News* published a photo of a younger, clean-shaven Thibodeaux under the caption "Slain in Prison Fight." It was a back-page piece worth only a couple columns.

When I snapped to, T. J. was looking straight at me with a strange light in his blue eyes.

"Haftmann, you were about a million miles away. I see I'm boring you with my scholarly disquisition on the relative merits of Pre-Raphaelite school."

"I'm enraptured," I affirmed. "Let me ask you something. I know it's bad protocol to ask a guy who's been in the joint anything personal – "

"Ah, fuck it, Haftmann, I'm too old to give a shit about that now. What can an old con who likes to draw and paint in his last days tell a fucked-up cop like you?"

"Do you believe God exists?"

"Ah, that. Pascal's bet. Now, old son, there are schools of thought to consider ..."

Oh fuck me.

I leaned back in the wicker chair and willed the throbbing in my head down to a dull ache. As I looked through the slats in T. J.'s studio at the barren landscape, my thoughts drifted about like the last leaves on the stunted pear trees in his so-called orchard. I remembered from somewhere far back in the abyss of memory that the Tree of Evil is always portrayed as dead and as hollow as the hearts of men.

The Last Case of Jimmy Revelle

"**H**ey, boss, know why God invented the orgasm?"

"Your stuff's getting old, Jimmy," I said.

"So white-trash hillbillies would know when to stop screwing."

Jimmy must have got out on his white-hating side of the bed this morning. Some days it was all about blacks, others it was "whitey" as the spawn of Satan in Jimmy's universe.

"Maryland farmer," I said. A silver Lexus had just cut me off at the light. "Whaaat? *Maryland farmers*, what the – " Jimmy gave me a look.

"I heard it on TV last night" I said. "The programmers substituted that for another expression. I'm trying to cut back on my swearing."

Jimmy looked disgusted. "Relax, dude. You just need a vacation."

"I don't know what I need," I said.

But Jimmy wasn't far off. At the top of the list of things I needed was more money. No decent-paying case in six months. The wolf wasn't howling at the door, but he was pawing at it and sniffing under it.

"Poon," Jimmy said and smiled up to his gold molars. His street badges, he called them. I doubted my faithful sidekick had ever been in a real fight in his life. Jimmy was glib of tongue and smooth when he wanted something, older than his twenty-five years. He was the product of a biracial relationship. His mother was from Kentucky, a "city goat," as he described her, and his old man was a violent, mocha-skinned convict with tatts who got a life sentence to go with his gangbanger ink. Maybe because he never knew where he fit in, Jimmy despised both races equally.

I hired him when a streak of good luck such as I had never experienced in all eleven years of private investigation in this town dropped fourteen juicy, pay-with-bonus cases into my lap in a single year, all of them in nearby Youngstown. I could have used three assistants in those days. Jimmy should have left when times turned sour. But he stayed. He never complained about the nights I stuck him in the cold or wet outside some straying hubby's fuckpad. Now I couldn't get rid of him.

He insisted that I never call him *James*. "That's a Negroid name," he said before I had let go of his hand. I was never sure if Jimmy's black-hating comments were a pose like his anti-Caucasian rants.

I pulled up to the curb on Mahoning. "I might be an hour. Keep an eye on our new toy." Jimmy liked to scour the Internet for the latest spook gadgetry and somehow he had talked me into buying the most expensive parabolic mic he could find.

"I be all right," Jimmy said, affecting a street spin.

"Jimmy, one of these days I'm going to pay for an intervention for you." I slammed the door.

Forty minutes later, I left the doctor's morgue-chilled office and walked back into the skin-prickling heat of midday. From a distance, I could see Jimmy snoozing against the seat rest. I got in and turned the A/C knob to full. We had a good hour before the husband I was following would be dropping by his freeway motel for his tryst with his sweetie on his lunch hour.

I cranked the starter and waited for the engine to fart, cough, and wheeze back into life. Jimmy was still nodding off.

"Jimmy, where do you want to eat?"

The tiny bump on his cheek was the slug that didn't have the force to punch an exit hole and so had come to rest there just beneath the skin. I touched his chin and swiveled his head gently toward me. His right eye looked up in that glazed look of the dead and the left eyeball was already black from hemorrhaging. The entrance wound wasn't large, just a puckered crater like a tiny volcano with black stippling of gunpowder where the barrel had pressed against flesh.

I breathed deeply a few times. I shut the engine off, got out, and stood by the car. I came to my senses and made the nine-one-one call.

People in violent cities joke about "murder" as a misdemeanor felony because it takes a lot to get the sirens going. Maybe we were heading back to the dark ages, back to a time when a mob guy used to sweat bullets on his forehead when he turned the ignition key in the morning, back to a time when "Crimetown, USA" meant us.

Then I heard them coming in that hi-lo wail just like television. Except that a guy who worked for me, a young man whose demons I didn't understand, was slumped over in my car dead from a contact wound to the temple. My roving husband was going to get a pass at his sleazy rendezvous on Route 5 this afternoon because I was going to be busy with the police for a long time.

I was telling my story to the lead investigator, a detective named Trubavich who seemed impressed I could pronounce his name.

"You were on the force," he guessed.

"No," I said. "I just pay attention."

The tightening of his lip corners told me he held that remark in contempt. How did I manage to miss this if I were so good at paying attention?

"Who were his enemies?"

"He never mentioned anyone to me."

"Did he use or deal?"

This part of Market Street was high-crime; all the businesses had burglar bars and gates. Residents were mostly elderly and trapped in their homes.

"I don't know what he did when he wasn't working for me."

Trubavich grilled me for a few more bits. My knowledge of Jimmy Revelle was so limited that I could put it inside the circumference of a shot glass with a fat crayon. I felt ashamed I didn't know more, but Jimmy gave out a happy-go-lucky side of himself and didn't invite confidences the few times I had tried to get to know him. I had enough experience with cops to know they don't like it when you try to play amateur criminalist. The murder police are an elite unit, and they consider private investigators little better than a nuisance – to a few we're rancid pond scum.

The golden forty-eight hours turned to seventy-two; then it was a week, two weeks, and Jimmy's murder file went on the shelf. I called Trubavich less often and knew he was up to his ears in other shootings because the long-expected, meth-lab invasion from central California had finally reached town like a dirty ocean wave. That kept homicide bureaus across Northeast Ohio jumpy and short-tempered.

I had wrapped up my last case, agreed to testify for the wife for a few bucks more, and was back to my normal round of alternating insurance fraud with adultery, the eternal dance of lust and greed of the working private investigator. But Jimmy's murder gnawed at me like a deer fly on an open wound. I stormed around my office late, irritable, kicking things that didn't deserve to be kicked. I told Revelle's unhappy ghost I couldn't afford to do his case even if the police didn't mind me nosing around.

"Nothing personal, Jimmy," I said to my nearly bare

office wall.

"Do what you think is right, yo," it shot back.

"Heck with it," I said. "OK, you win."

"My nigga," Jimmy's sly, mocking voice echoed in my head.

~ ~ ~

"Them crazy boys, shit," the grizzled old man I had halted with his shopping cart full of loose metal said to me, "they be drinkin' the wine of violence too got-damn much."

He bumped his head at me several times as if we were standing together in a church pew waiting for the pastor's call-and-response. But we were standing in the middle of South Avenue. The sunburst glinting off the sheet metal in his cart formed a halo around us. I noted some copper jacket bands on the sheared-off fittings; he'd get good money at the junkyard for his next dope blast from these. He wanted me gone, so he was jiving me with his rap, but my private investigator's license had made him leery. Maybe I was in cahoots with the real po-lice.

If you want to know what's going on in bad neighborhoods, find a junkie. Sure, they'll tell you anything at first, but if you're patient, you'll get some morsels. The old guy wagged his gray chin at me and squinted up at me and I thought of Jimmy's dead eyeball. The glare from the passing windshields around us added to the sunburst of sticky sweat. My day had begun at five in the morning. Being a dope fiend is a full-time job and they get up with the sun to begin prowling neighborhoods in search of capers to get the bread for the first fix.

When my informant left me, he was ten dollars richer whereas I had two new pieces of information about James Revelle. His other part-time job was dealing weed to college kids near the YSU campus on the other side of town. The second was that he was a pot pirate, a risky occupation in a town where 15-year-olds will shoot you just to see if the gun works.

Before I knew him, Jimmy made lots of cash by selling burn bags to the hillbillies in the valley. Baking soda in baggies for coke, cashews for rock. He wore new clothes to high school for a month and had six pairs of Jordan Retros and Nike LeBrons in his closet until a serious dealer showed up at his house and told him he was ruining business on his corners. If he kept it up, he'd never make it to ninth grade. Jimmy went to work for a car wash after that. Something about the joy of ripping off people thrilled him.

"Dude called himself Nine-Eleven. You believe that shit?"

I went through three more sources and forty more dollars before I had the name of the biggest grower in the county Jimmy might have been stealing from. His fields were out in the scrubland beyond Lake Glacier near a federal preserve. My informants were in agreement on one thing: the grower was a transplanted redneck from Alabama who left the state when the competition for space in the foothills of the Appalachians got too keen and federal agents began investigating him. He had moved up here to get closer to a steady supply of consumers. His biggest distributor was a local Crip staying with relatives; he was supposedly on the run from a murder charge in Compton, according to one source who bought from him.

I counted out my emergency funds and figured I could give it five more days, no more. That meant I had to put some of my rules on the shelf. I followed the redneck from his house in Smoky Hollow, a downtown neighborhood that borders the Youngstown State campus. He drank at a biker's bar on the old 165 Highway outside town. The neon Coors sign above the door sizzled out at one-oh-three in the morning, but he didn't come out until three-forty; then he climbed into his Dodge Ram and drove home slowly on back roads to avoid cops.

At four the next morning I saw him stagger out to his ride. Before he climbed in, he took a long leak against his front tire. From a distance, I watched the arc of his urine stream in the orange glow of the sodium light of the highway.

If he followed the same path home as last night, he would take the short dogleg off the road near Mill Creek Park. Providing he didn't keep an Uzi in his extension cab, it was where I planned to have my talk with him.

I pulled over and waited. When I heard the big engine growl at the turn, I flipped on the hazards. I headed across the road and ducked low near a guardrail smothered in damp fescue grasses. He slowed down for a look. At that moment I darted out from behind my cover.

I jerked the door open and him by the upper arm. Pulling him out of the cab was easy because he was a little man who liked to compensate with a big truck. I outweighed him by a hundred pounds, my heart pumped pure adrenalin, and I was the one blitzing him. As soon as he had his wits about him, however, that's where my advantage ceased. The little bastard was slippery as an eel and madder than a feral cat. He knew something about fighting dirty. I lost my grip on him and he was free. I barely missed having my eyes clawed out by his flailing hands. By the time I had regrouped, I was on the defensive. I saw him pull a buck knife from his boot, and I was the one running, fleeing into the dark.

An hour later I had worked my way back to the spot and saw my car windows smashed; my windshield looked like a gaping old mouth with jagged teeth. For good measure, he had taken a shit on my seat. "Sorry, Jimmy," I said into my pillow that night; "I'll do better next time."

On the third night, he never showed up at the bar. I drove to his house but his truck wasn't there. Information is everything in my business and I didn't want to brace the drug dealer without it, but I had no choice.

Melvin ("Yellow Shoes") Biggs had another claim to fame besides his drug business: he had fathered fourteen children. He also had an eclectic gang working for him, according to my best informant at the *Vindicator*. Dionte Woods and Lawrence Stokes were from Detroit, graduates of Young Boys Inc. Lorinzo Smith was a Cabrini Green product from Chicago, and Isse Dicoté hailed from Mauritania and spoke a polite, exact English. The paper did a piece on Dicoté a couple years ago for impersonating a Saudi prince. Smith was alleged to be the gang's enforcer and prime suspect in three drug-related homicides last year. His photo reproduced in color for the Sunday edition showed him smiling with a pair of gold incisors; the caption below said "The Golden Viper smiles for his mug shot." His gold-tipped fangs, dodging murder raps – it all gave him good street cred. To the cops, however, he was a sociopathic nightmare.

These boys were so enamored of their own publicity that Dicoté was assigned the task of "public relations" for the gang. I asked my contact at the paper to set up a meeting.

He didn't want to do it without knowing the reason behind the meeting. I couldn't blame him. You didn't want these thugs coming to see you later over some "misunderstanding." I didn't have to tell him and he knew why. He and I crossed paths on a case once, and I kept him out of a report that would have destroyed his career.

Biggs liked yellow, all right. His shoes were yellow; his do-rag was yellow, and his track outfit was yellow. It was the last time I would think of yellow as a happy, philosophical color.

"What you want, motherfucker?" were his first words.

We were in an abandoned warehouse down by the

Conrail yard. I had asked for the McDonald's on Mahoning. His boys were moving around behind us, gawking, goofing around or sitting on packing crates while their leader had his chinwag with the white boy. I wasn't in any doubt these idling dogs could be sicced on me in a heartbeat.

"My partner was shot to death in a car last week," I said. "His name was Revelle. He lived on South."

"Yeah, I heard about that halfie. What it got to do with me?"

"I want to know who did it," I said.

"Then you best go look. He ain't here."

"I thought maybe you could point me in the right direction," I said.

"OK." He stuck his arm lazily at the broken door we had entered by. His face never cracked.

"I heard he was stealing stash from your supplier," I said.

"Man, you are one dumb motherfucker to be talking that shit to me."

I suppose he gave a signal. I didn't see it. The next thing I felt were two pairs of hands holding me rigid, while another pair belonging to the gentle-spoken Dicoté were ripping off my clothes.

"Find the fuckin' wire," Biggs commanded.

"I am looking. I don't see anything yet," Dicoté replied.

"His pants, Negro. Take his fucking pants off."

"I would prefer not to," Dicoté responded while patting down my groin area.

"You lazy, prefer-not-to motherfucker. Get the fuck out of the way! Dio, Lawrence, take this motherfucker's pants off!"

That must have been the two ex-Young Boys holding me by the arms. Before my brain could finish asking how this was going to go, a lightning-fast punch clipped my jaw and toppled me sideways. I felt myself jerking about on the dirty cement floor like a fish on deck except that I wasn't doing the flopping; those two were each holding one pant leg and having a contest to see who could get me out of my pants faster. I think it was a tie.

"Fat boy here needs to lay off the Krispy Kremes," one of them said.

I was down to my shorts and socks. I hoped that was sufficient proof.

"Get him on his feet," Biggs said.

The one gang member who seemed uninterested in these antics was standing behind Biggs. Suddenly he stepped forward and put a blade to my neck and pressed it against my Adam's apple. "You feel like rising up, white boy," Lorinzo Smith said. "You go on 'n try." He was close enough to my face to hit me with some spittle.

"Let him talk, Lo," said Biggs. He used a softer tone with his tame psycho.

"Let's just do this Dockers-wearing motherfucker," Smith said. I was happy to see the blade retract and go back inside his white skivvies. He had five inches of BVD showing above his beltless Levi's.

"Why you want know?" Biggs asked me.

"He was my friend," I said and felt a little blush from the lie creep up my neck.

"Ain't no white man friend a no nigger," Biggs said matter-of-factly."

"He was killed sitting in my car waiting for me."

"That so?"

Smith, somewhere behind me, snorted through his own nostrils. A wrecking ball could hit me in the head right then but I wouldn't have swiveled my head an inch to look at him. I waited for what would come next.

Biggs looked at me a long time. "I don't know who did your boy. I don't give a fuck, neither."

Biggs turned without another word and walked off. His wolf pack peeled away, one by one, following. Smith was the last to go, lingering behind to fire up a blunt, but I had a gut feeling he was waiting for me to say something; then he could kill me right there. My clothes were torn rags. One ankle was bruised from the bouncing. I limped back to my car and told Jimmy, or maybe I said it to his unavenged phantom, I was sorry I had failed him twice.

~ ~ ~

The Vindicator gave it a front-page column next to a photo of a house in blackened ruins. The headline said "Wife Dies in House Fire. Prominent Austintown Businessman Told Wife Asleep on Couch." When the husband arrived to find his house engulfed, the fire department was carrying out her charred corpse where she had melted into the sofa.

It was the same tomcat husband from the last case Jimmy was working for me.

The photos of his motel rendezvous with his young blonde would have clinched the divorce. His alibi was airtight. His wife was an alcoholic. She was drunk on the phone every time I spoke to her and drunk in my office the two times I had met her there. But that wouldn't preclude a judge from awarding her half his earthly goods.

His secretary called back the next day and said Mr. Ĉipera had agreed to see me in his office at 4:15. My phone message was just vague enough about my employment by his ex-wife that I hoped he wouldn't blow me off. Curiosity works in people this way, too. The shrinks should hurry up and name it so I don't have to mentally refer to it like the childish singsong that goes: "I-know-something-you-don't-know-you."

It was a bluff. I was fishing. But something Jimmy said struck a memory chord just as I was getting out of the car, preoccupied by the prospect of my doctor's latex-gloved digit. "It's easy to con people out of their shit, you know why? They think they have it because they the only ones that deserve it."

I thought we were still talking about wealthy doctors. I think Jimmy was referring to me. He was talking about the MP 229 Parabellum microphone, the one I had let him talk me into buying but had refused to let him take on stakeouts. Jimmy must have thought it was because I didn't trust him. That wasn't the real reason. It was because the husband wasn't the average shmucko cheating on his wife.

My background on the guy had turned up some interesting stuff. His father had come to America in the aftermath of Czechoslovakia when it was overrun by Russian tanks in 1969. He sold hot dogs from a vending cart to the steelworkers and soon he had his own diner. That prospered and turned into a chain of hot dog and bratwurst franchises all over the Mahoning Valley. The son sold them all to a national chain and invested in car dealerships, which he sold before Youngstown's short-lived boom tanked. He then invested in the dotcom boom before they too nosedived. Backed by his wealth and his father's reputation, he built up a hedge fund of powerful investors around the state, which was reputed to be run by a man who headed the Hong Kong branch for Goldman Sachs. His name was on plaques at the Beeghly Medical Center and the Butler Institute of American Art. One local rumor had him as silent partner in the Youngstown Steelhounds of the Central Hockey Division.

His office suite was in a high-rise on Federal Street next to the new Courthouse designed by Robert Stern. His secretary told me to wait in the foyer. She didn't recognize me, but I had seen her often enough stepping out of the motel room five minutes ahead of her boss. At four forty-seven he came out and greeted me by first name. His bone-white shirt was rolled to his sleeves, the silk tie loosened, and the Presidential on his hairy wrist all added to the impression of a busy executive pinching off a few minutes for the little people.

I offered my condolences on his tragedy. He waved them off.

"She drank heavily," he said. ". . . unfortunate, really." The furrowed brow was a nice touch. But already the subject seemed to bore him.

"I'm curious what homicide thought of the timing," I said. "She would have taken half of everything you have."

That stopped him short. Our little pretend game over.

"I know she hired you to dig up dirt on me," he said. "If it's your fee you're worried about, I'll write you a check."

"I don't want money," I said. "I want to know why you had my partner killed."

"You're out of your mind!"

He drifted over to a window to look out over the plaza which had failed to materialize.

"His name, by the way, was James Revelle," I continued. "He recorded you with a long-range listening device. He wasn't supposed to do it but he did it anyway. He contacted you about it and asked for hush money."

"That's an interesting theory, friend," Ĉipera said. "Without evidence it's just that." He reached into a drawer, took his checkbook out, and scribbled on its surface with an expensive pen. He ripped it free and flicked it across his varnished desk. I turned it around to see the figure. More zeroes than had ever belonged to me.

"I don't want the scandal," he said.

"It's a lot of money," I said.

"Call it goodwill," he said, "if it makes you feel better."

"I haven't rendered you any services," I said.

He relaxed his shoulders. His eyes drew me into his

confidence. "Look, I'm planning to run for a congressional seat next year. I have the nomination locked up for the primary."

"Why not just divorce her?"

"I would have, believe me, if your entrepreneurial associate had stayed out of my life. My wife had signed a prenup. She wasn't going to get half. I got her cheap," he said.

So Jimmy was working for the wife, who planned to blackmail her ex.

"It must have been some kind of pillow talk," I said, "to generate this much killing."

"I couldn't trust the crazy, drunken bitch," he said to me. "That line about a woman scorned – well, you know how it goes if you've ever gone through a divorce."

"So she was going to get her prenup canceled in exchange for the recording, whatever," I said. "You could have written her a check. Why not just write her a big check, Mister Ĉipera?"

"She didn't want to – part with it," he said quietly, poking two fingers through the venetian blind as if something interesting were going on in the street. He snapped the cord and shut and muzzled the streaming light like God snapping his fingers.

I understood. She wanted to bring it into court, expose him to the public, ruin his reputation and his political career before it ever got going. My testimony was just to prepare the way for Jimmy's grand entrance. I could imagine the triumphant look on his face as he came strolling into court and stared at me. Maybe she promised him enough to go into business for himself. Jimmy had the confidence for it. Too much confidence. I had told him just enough about Ĉipera's driver to keep him quiet – or so I thought.

Ĉipera had picked up this bulked-up ape of a former

pro wrestler with a prison record and dressed him in a nice suit – but a monkey in a suit is still a monkey. An Internet search of public records told me the driver had a long history with illegal poker video machines. My one friendly cop in the PD told me the man also had mob connections to the Sebastian John LaRocca crime family in Pittsburgh and West Virginia. Ĉipera dressed him up, gave him a new name and even used his downtown connections to obtain a CCW permit for him. Old habits, as they say. I felt bad about exposing Jimmy to even that much danger – stupid, stupid. How is it that I missed so badly what lay behind his smirk?

It wasn't much of a surprise when the ape himself walked in the room with a look on his face that he must have practiced a thousand times for those redneck ringside audiences in VFW halls.

"Take the check from him, Leonard," Ĉipera said to his Igor. Then, without looking at me, he said, "Leonard will escort you downstairs to your car. We don't need to speak again."

I hadn't anything left in my quiver but a few ragged, bent arrows. "The cops might be corrupt in this town but you can't buy off everyone, Ĉipera. The Revelle murder is going to stay open until somebody, maybe CBI, maybe the feds, somebody puts your wife's corpse and Revelle together with the evidence – "

"Leonard."

I was out the door and moving fast. Leonard's big mitt circled my bicep. He squeezed until I winced. We fast-walked to the elevator and he threw me against the back and turned to punch the button. Challenging a Neanderthal to combat inside an elevator wasn't going to make it on to my agenda that particular afternoon.

He kept his vise-like grip on me all the way to the parking deck and threw me against the side of my car.

"Thank you, Leonard."

"Kiss my ass, shitheels."

The fabric of his suit across his back was stretched taut like the skin of a drum. It probably cost more to outfit him than it would for Cîpera's own suits. His massive back disappeared around the corner and I was alone in a dim parking deck with my thoughts and my failures.

Cîpera's fraud election was engineered so skillfully that he came in with 77 percent of the primary vote that year. His general election bid set a record, even in corrupt Mahoning Valley. His name turns up in *The Vindicator* once in a while – appointment to this committee, chair of that, kissing this bigwig's shoes or that foreign dignitary's ass, taking junkets abroad as a Presidentially-appointed "goodwill ambassador." One photo in the Sunday paper showed Cîpera standing before a village atop the Bandiagara Plateau, in Mali, somewhere in West Africa, talking grandly about a "UNESCO World Heritage Site," as if his heart bled pure milk for those poor, suffering Africans.

I'm still here, still working small cases and scratching out a living, if you can call it that. Jimmy Revelle's been dead a long time. People forget. Lenny Strollo and his "Youngstown tune-ups" – that's long gone now, forgotten. You know what I think? I think Youngstown's latest golden boy is all the hero and savior we deserve.

She Played Bach In the Piano Bar

"**I**'m sorry," I said. "I didn't hear you."

I'd heard him, all right. I just needed him to repeat what he said.

"She's playing the piano, see? The whole time she's playing, she's eating another girl's pussy."

I let my mind work on that for a second. It's a sign of my age, I suppose, my first thought was the kind of music being played. *What the hell . . .*

"What kind of music – "

"Classical shit," he said. "Beethoven, Mozart – who knows? The whole point is she don't miss a note while she's going down on the girl spread across the top of the piano."

He didn't smirk. I wondered whether to follow this up but before I could open up my mouth again, he said, "All I know is when I hired her, she said she went both ways. Everything but anal, she says."

He handed me his card as an afterthought: Mr. M. Garrison L. Graziadie. Pres., Fortune Films, Sexcitement Media, Ltd. There was a phone number and a Youngstown address beneath it. It was about fifty miles from my office on the Strip on Lake Erie, which is in this flyspeck of a resort town halfway between Cleveland and Erie. But as far as the L. A. sex industry is concerned, anyplace in Ohio might as well have been Nome, Alaska.

"Like I said," Graziadei rolled on in his scratchy voice, "Nikki plays piano in this bar, see, and she meets this girl. The girl's boyfriend is jealous because Nikki is giving her the eye so when the girl climbs on top of the piano – "

"Why does she climb on top of the piano?"

He looked at me as if I had asked about the nocturnal mating habits of the nine-banded armadillo. "Why does she – so Nikki can get at her snatch, why else?" He resumed his plot recital despite my obtuseness. "Then he, the boyfriend, starts pitching a tent so he climbs on top and teabags her – "

Even Mickey Spillane had to be rolling over in his grave by now.

"I can guess what happens next," I said. "The piano collapses under their collective weight, bodies are flung everywhere. What's left of the baby grand is kindling. Nikki, in a fugue state because her Chopin étude was so tragically interrupted, knocks over the candelabra causing a fire. Everybody in the place burns to death. The cops spend weeks identifying femurs."

"Tell me you know what a porn film is," he said.

Maybe another sign of my age. I had a case once that involved an illegal gambling den in nearby Conneaut. A VCR with a porno tape was left on in one of the rooms but nobody paid attention to it. The gamblers were the degenerate sort, all mesmerized by the crap tables. The credits came on and I noted the title: *Private Dicks*. An ugly, skinny man an enormous penis had starred in it. Someone told me later that was John Holmes before he had his teeth straightened and years before he developed a heroin habit and did gay sex films to support it.

"What exactly can I do for you, Mister Graziadei?"

"I do a sideline business with some big hotels," he said. "DoubleTree, Marriott, lots of big chains. Not these Crazy-8 places you see off the highway. They want soft-core packages for their adult menus. I can make two, three of these in a month. Quality stuff, not the amateur shit Vinnie LeVoyeur Vincennes grinds out with bar whores and Romanian runaways."

Runaways were my stock in trade, actually. I do skip traces, matrimonial work, as Jack Nicholson likes to say in *Chinatown*, and yearn for that wealthy parent to come through my door to hire me to find a missing child.

"Pardon me for asking, Mister Graziadei, but why come all the way up here to the boondocks for an investigator? Youngstown's not big but it's big enough to offer several private investigative services right in the yellow pages. Cleveland's straight up Interstate eighty from you. Plenty of top-notch outfits. Me, I'm in the middle of nowhere."

"I know that," Graziadei said. "I useta come here when I was in college. This was a rockin' place for college kids from all over the Midwest."

He was right. But that was two decades and my bitter divorce ago. I had hung my shingle at exactly the time Jefferson-on-the-Lake was about to nosedive from families, college kids, and tourists to bikers, runaways, and dopers. The college kids showed for the big summer holidays but not as many. The kids are younger, harder, full of tattoos and Kool-Aid-colored hair, some on the hustle. I've pried several teen prostitutes from their black pimps or the Pagans Motorcycle gang who owned them. You can smell reefer up and down the Strip on summer nights but what goes on in some of the low-rent cottages is worse: heroin, cocaine, gang rapes, a bloody gay-sex murder or two. Nowadays it's mostly meth, Ecstasy, and crack turning the kids on. Below them are the Da-Glo huffers and the fiends who search for veins between their toes because every other vein is as shriveled as a slug in a box of Morton salt.

"I still want an answer to my question," I said.

"It don't matter. Nikki's missing. I want you to find her," he said.

"How 'missing'?"

265

"What do you mean, *how* missing? She's fuckin' missing, man. We were scheduled to finish the shoot two days ago, so I got to pay the bar owner for two more days rent, and she don't answer her phone."

Before I asked the obvious, he said, "I send one of my techs over to get her ass out of bed and he says she don't answer. I go over there myself and wake up the manager and make him open her apartment door. She ain't there. Vamoosed."

He made one of those whistling sounds with his lips meant to approximate somebody leaving in a big hurry. It reminded me of Daffy Duck bursting through the wall with Elmer Fudd chasing him with a shotgun.

I had to stifle my dislike of Graziadei. He was a small, thick man with an unpleasant raspy voice. Some people are born with a second coat of skin over their voice boxes and they sound as if they badly need to clear their throats all the time. He wore a black silk shirt beneath a beige sport coat despite the warm weather. The gold chain around his neck had a gangbanger-sized medallion. His cologne was too heavy, acrid, and he kept picking at his crotch as if he could not settle his package down. Maybe he couldn't; the slacks were tight fitting. I was afraid to look at his shoes in case my reflection stared back at me. Youngstown didn't get the memo about the mob's demise.

"What I meant to say," I began, "was that maybe she got tired of the porn business or had a better offer or wanted to rush home to be with a dying relative. Maybe she just forgot to leave a message."

He scowled at me. "Nikki's family kicked her out years ago. They tried one of those – what do you call them things?"

"Interventions?"

"Whatever."

"Did she take her personal things with her?"

"You think I know when these girls are on the rag?"

"I meant her purse, car keys, items she'd never leave behind if she went out the door."

"Look, I'm tellin' you, Nikki wouldn't just up and go off like that. That's not how she does things. She thinks things through. She's very smart, not to mention fuckin' gorgeous with big fun bags, all natural. Let's forget the Doctor Phil bullshit, OK? You just find out where she is."

The way he said it made it sound as if all I had to do was get off my fat lazy ass, step outside and point her out on the street.

"You do that," Graziadei said; "I'll take care of the rest."

This time it sounded like a TV hit man setting up an assassination. Graziadei had one serious *Sopranos* fixation, but the job seemed routine enough.

I gave him my standard line about involving the police; it was free service, after all, and they had the resources and manpower. He gave me a withering look.

"At least file a report," I suggested.

He nixed that too and asked for my rates. I gave him a standard contract. He didn't want me to explain it. He signed it with a flourish, left me a deposit in cash, all fifties, and we talked for twenty minutes more, although he seemed impatient to get going and I had to pull the necessary details out of him.

With his outline of Ms. Nikki Ingersoll, sex entertainment worker and classical pianist, I had what I needed to get started. I told Graziadei I would report at specific intervals unless I had something definite.

"Just don't drag it out, man," he said at the door. "I'm paying a huge overrun on this project already. It's costing me a shitload and I got nothing in the can to show for it."

He wasn't the first client who whined poorhouse out the door. And he didn't take all his cologne with him. I have big picture windows with my name in Baskerville script across the glass but no windows to open. I used a Kafka paperback to prop the door open. This close to the lake, you can smell rotting fish from the annual shad die-off: hundreds of thousands like tiny silver dolphins beach themselves to death at once. It makes you question the purpose of existence.

Coming all the way up here to JOTL, as we locals say, didn't make much sense, but working the phones can be done from here as easily as Youngstown and that's what being a modern-day gumshoe means: surveillance, internet, phones, and a fax. For all his bravado, Graziadei must have had his reasons for preferring my one-man outfit in an out-of-the-way locale to find her. I guessed Nikki Ingersoll was more than a moneymaker for Graziadei Films. It wouldn't affect my search. This was the off-season to the off-season, and I was short of clients. The alternative was to go across the street to Tico's Place and tie one on by noon. I got to work instead.

I started making calls. I'm something like a homicide detective, which is what I used to be in Cleveland years ago. The difference is that the body's there on the floor and it isn't going anywhere so you don't run up to it like a rookie cop with your mouth hanging open. It'll stay dead a long time. Your best clues are sometimes in the periphery, so you circle it, and get closer until you see what the body has to give you about how it got there. There's no body in front of a private investigator, and despite Graziadei's insinuations, I wasn't likely to catch her on a street corner waiting to be found. But she wasn't a ghost; like every straight or slightly bent citizen of the realm, she had a trail of numbers in her wake – we all do. We live in cities, pay taxes, apply for every kind of license to drive a car, own a gun or a dog. We have credit cards, debit cards, and we use ATMs. Best of all, we use our cell phones. Pay a fine or go to jail, they've got you. Everybody's in dozens of city, state, and national databases we wish we weren't in or can't get in. She might have boyfriends or ex-lovers, girlfriends and acquaintances, some who know her well, some who want to talk about her and some who won't.

I did a little checking on Graziadei. He had worked for LeVoyeur Productions five years ago before returning to Youngstown to start up his own production company. His website claimed he wrote, directed, and produced all the films his company made. He liked seeing his name in the credits. Besides the big chores, he listed himself as script editor, gaffer, electrician, and best boy. In *Bangable Bar Sluts* and *Cum-Swapping Hoes*, the films before this one, he was listed in ten or eleven different capacities. He said he would email me some jpegs of Nikki's glam shots. I was tempted to ask for the outtakes of *Bang Her on the Piano Slowly*, the film Nikki abandoned halfway through, but I thought better of it.

Nikki Ingersoll never used her real surname. She had a rolodex of stock aliases: Misty Canyon, Dasanna, Candy Barré and some that didn't rhyme or pun with smutty references. Between STDs and perverts drooling over her DVDs, there might be a local nutjob or three stalking her. I recalled Graziadei's description. I couldn't rule anything out yet, least of all the likeliest possibility that she had simply done what all porn actors do eventually, which is to leave a sordid business behind. I read somewhere that the average actor in Hollywood with a SAG card makes $30,000 a year. It's not much. Unless Graziadei lied, Nikki wasn't even close to making that. She started at three thousand for the first films, he said, and was making seven thou apiece when she disappeared. No residuals to collect and she would have to pay into FICA. Graziadei insisted to me he was a reputable businessman and did everything by the book.

She had her own website, a standard G-rated, aspiring-model-turned-actress-seeks-work with thumbnails of poses and some attractive shots done in a studio. She included links to her *Facebook* page and a couple other social networks. No hint anywhere of her real profession. If she were soliciting money for off-the-books or illegal work, I didn't get a whiff of it from the text she put out there. Crossing over to mainstream film work was a long shot, and if she was half as smart as Graziadei said, she'd know that. Even I knew of Traci Lords. I checked out *craigslist* but didn't see her there under her name or any of the aliases I found. Two girls bore a strong resemblance but they were operating from New Orleans or San Diego at the time her piano movie started to shoot.

Nikki did know how to play classical piano. She had gone to the prestigious Dana School of Music at Youngstown State on a full scholarship six years ago. It took me fifteen minutes on the phone with somebody in the Registrar's office to wheedle out the name of one of her former piano teachers. The recent privacy laws have put a crimp in my business the way Miranda once did to me, but a cop learns fast how to get a suspect to talk in the interrogation room. You can't legislate human nature; it's a matter of finding the right button to push. Her senior recital was a Bach piece. Something that goes with a sarabande, the professor said, a stately dance, he called it.

I traced Nikki's family in Chicago but I couldn't get anyone to return my messages. Graziadei said she was a switch-hitter but he didn't know the names of any current boyfriends or girlfriends.

I try to exhaust all the usual lines before I resort to asking for favors. Most cops like taking a private investigator's calls as much as vegans like strolling through third-world slaughterhouses. At YPD I'm down to one cop, Det. Sgt. Jerry Pruel by name, and he's tougher than a two-dollar steak when it come to granting my requests.

"Jerry, amigo, long time no see, no hear."

"Oh Christ, Tom Haftmann. I was wondering when I'd next hear from you."

"Got a favor to ask thee, laddie buck."

"Gee, really? I thought you called because you were concerned about my hemorrhoid operation next week."

I groveled a bit more, played the fool, and waited for him to get through jerking my chain. It comes down to this: Jerry and I worked cases at Youngstown Homicide before I finally quit cop work for good and moved up here. That's an exclusive club with a lifetime membership. Cops know it. We did a red ball in the late eighties involving three murdered construction workers in a home invasion that had the mayor calling the police commissioner every day and an anxious lieutenant looking over our shoulders every hour for new developments. Jerry doesn't panic.

"Looking for a girl named Nikki Lynne Ingersoll," I said. "Porn starlet in a minor key. Five-four, one-three-five, blonde and blue. Missing three days now. She was employed by Graziadei Films. Know anything?"

"I know that goof," Jerry said. "He operates out of vacant offices downtown whenever he can get away without paying rent. He moves around a lot and I hear he's always getting evicted or some landlord is threatening to sue for property damages."

"He make any real money with his films?"

"My guess is no, but I don't know that for sure. We've never had a reason to do a financial background. He doesn't break any laws that get on my work tray. His problem is, see, he's got a Napoleon complex and he doesn't know when to shut his big yap. He's been involved in a couple bar tussles but no charges filed on him. He likes to countersue anybody who's suing him. Probably spends everything he makes on his lawyers."

"You have anything hard on him like assaults on women?"

"No, nothing like that. Just a pain in the ass. His record's clean, no arrests. He acquires a harem of skanks now and then and shows up at a Kelly Pavlik fight with four or five in tow. Big stud act for the locals. He finds them in dives like The Rare Cherry downtown. Hell, you remember that shithole. Makes 'em big promises, but the girls who complain to us never have anything in a contract so it's his word against theirs."

"IRS ever do a deep audit on him?"

"I don't work for the IRS, Tom."

"He said he's got deals with big hotel chains to distribute smut."

"I wouldn't know a thing about that. Are we done here?"

"Thanks, Jerry."

"Don't mention it and lose my fucking number."

"Not a chance. You're my best friend. How are your hemorrhoids, by the way?"

"Fuck off."

After a few more obscenities and cursing his fate for even knowing me, he clicked off. I didn't learn much, but I wasn't willing to rule out Graziadei as a harmless creep in a nasty business.

My work requires patience. You sift for nuggets and sooner or later, a pattern emerges. This might be a free country but nobody disappears like smoke. We're still wondering which fender in which junkyard or fifty-gallon drum in a landfill holds the secret of Jimmy Hoffa's last resting place.

~ ~ ~

I had arranged to meet Nikki's piano-bar playmate at ten that evening in a Youngstown bar off Commerce. She didn't want to meet at her place, she said, because she didn't "want to be involved in whatever the fuck was going on."

Alexis Webb wasn't her real name but it was the name she used in Fortune Films. As an icebreaker, I asked her why she didn't go in for lots of names like Nikki.

"Some girls do, I don't." That was all she had to say about it. I left it there. The bar girl came over to take our order. I asked Alexis about a Florida connection but she shook her head emphatically. "Nikki never mentioned Florida."

"Alexis, I'm being paid to look for Nikki, as I'm sure you know. No one is talking about crimes of any kind," I said. "It's not illegal to go missing, no matter what Mister Graziadei might have told you. I'm just trying to get a line on where she might be right now," I said.

She was younger than Nikki by a couple years. She missed being pretty by more than that. I thought of a high-school cheerleader gone to seed before her time. She had a rough vocabulary but today that means nothing. Maybe twenty-five years ago sailors would have run out of the bar to hear her call the woman who had performed such adroit cunnilingus on her as "a stuck-up douchebag cunt," but nobody within earshot of our booth gave us so much as a glance. She asked for another Screaming Orgasm and that should tell you I was in a bar catering more to her age group than mine.

"Was Nikki seeing anyone in particular when she didn't show up for filming that day?"

"No – well, I don't know. I mean, like, we were making a film. I didn't ask her who she was fucking and she didn't ask me."

"I see." I didn't.

"Was anyone mad at her? Following her to work? Anything like that? Did she say anything about being in any kind of trouble?"

"No, no, no, nothing like that, man. I mean, we just made a couple films together. That fuckbucket Gary said he'd pay me the same rate and of course that turned out to be a big fat lie. He said Nikki insisted on more money so he had to take from my share to do the film, but he promised me next time I got top billing and the same money."

"So Nikki just didn't show up one day?"

"Right, man, liked, fuck, you know? Like, she just blew off the film, you know? Like, everybody's standing around with their thumb up their ass, as usual, waiting for the queen bee to get her own royal ass out of bed, and Graziadei's running around screaming like a lunatic having his usual hissy fit. Yeah, like he's Quentin fucking Tarantino, that two-bit, cheap-ass wop fuck."

"So it's normal for Ms. Ingersoll to arrive late for filming?"

"What's this Miz Ingersoll shit? That fuckin' bitch sticks a plug in her twat same as me. She ain't no goddam thing special, man. She expects everybody to do cartwheels the moment she shows up. Even Graziadei – he's, like, 'Where is she? Where is she?' The next, he's like, 'Oh, Nikki, honey, baby, can I get you some water, sweetie?' Fuck me, it's enough to make a person puke listening to him kiss her golden ass like that."

"I take it you and she didn't get along?" Why not toss a little more gas on the flame, I thought.

Instead of throwing another rod, she calmed down, shrank a bit in her seat, and appraised me coolly. I noticed her nose was asymmetrical. We're just monkeys. We look in one another's faces for validation, love, hope – anything but the truth.

"Look, man, she knows how to play a piano and eat pussy at the same time. You wanna give her the Nobel Prize for that, be my guest."

Right then, some tall, buffed male came over with a couple drinks in his hand and slid beside her. He eyed me the whole time. "You got any more questions for my girl, you ask me, man," he said.

I had noticed him when we sat down. He was sitting at the bar on one of those tiny metal swivel seats that reminded me of diners from the fifties. He kept swiveling our way. The fabric of his shirt was stretched taut every time he craned his thick neck.

"Shut up, Ronnie. This guy's just askin' me about Nikki."

"Oh yeah," Ronnie growled at me. "Well, fuckin' let him ask me his fuckin' questions then."

They made a cute couple, I thought. It turned out Ronnie was the jealous boyfriend in the piano bar film. He was billed as Rodney Clitflick. When it was clear neither one had a clue, much less any interest in the fate of the missing member of their recent ménage a trois, I paid for the drinks, put a ten on the counter for the drinks girl, and left these two silver-tongued soul mates nuzzling and cooing in the booth.

I called Graziadei from the road around midnight. He had mentioned he was a night owl, but it sounded as if he had just awakened. I gave him a brief report.

"That all you got? Shit, what am I payin' you for?" I bit off the retort and asked him about Nikki's relationship to the rest of cast and crew.

"Ah, them bitches are jealous. You seen her photos, right? Pretty fucking obvious why they hate her. She's fuckin' beautiful."

I started to wonder whether children in Youngstown elementary schools were ever made to conjugate regular verbs the way we used to.

"What about the rest of production crew? Any males pay her special attention?"

He saw through that as I expected.

"Don't go listening to everything Tina Barnes says. That little bitch is nothing but a troublemaker. I should never have promoted her."

Tina was obviously Alexis, although I had not mentioned driving down to meet her. I wondered how one got "promoted" in the world of cinematic porn. Graziadei satisfied that small curiosity with his venomous diatribe against Tina Barnes and her ilk. It was in the context of what a fluffer is supposed to do for male actors off camera that I deduced her skill set prior to co-star billing in Fortune Films.

I was driving back along Route 11 in the dark; it's an empty, fifty-mile stretch of road – nothing to see even in the light except for rotting barns and overgrown fields of scrub with scraps of plastic caught in the barbed-wire fencing. The only traffic besides me was a trio of Sidley's gravel trucks heading for Ashtabula Harbor. I was bored and tired of his oafish invective, so I cut in.

"You knew Nikki was planning something – some scheme or hustle of her own. I don't know what that is yet but I'm following a lead. Why don't you just lay it out and stop wasting my time and your money? I'll have a much better chance of locating her if you tell me what she was up to before she left."

Silence. I thought maybe the service had cut out.

Graziadei's phlegmy voice resumed: "I dunno. I know she had somethin' cooking in that big brain of hers. Right after the film, I was going to – "

He paused, looking for the right expression. Maybe he was afraid I would read something sinister into his words.

" – I was gonna ask her to, to marry me."

That I wasn't expecting.

Love in the pornography business. Who'd have thunk it, right? People performing sex acts on each other but

276

none of it means anything. The ringmaster of this sexual circus himself falls in love with one of his performers.

I suppose it was cruel of me, and maybe it was payback for his brusque manner, but I asked anyway: "What made you think she was interested in you? No offense, Mister Graziadei."

"Like fuck, man, there's plenty of offense in that question. I resent it. You're goddamned lucky you're on a cell phone in a car somewhere – "

"Then I apologize for asking," I said, "but I think the question needs an answer from you."

"Like hell it does. Fuck you, Haftmann – "

I made the exit to JOTL under a starless, blacked-out sky. No moon for the coyotes to bay at. Or was that only wolves? Nothing seemed to be alive in the world. My batting average on the day was not very impressive, so I debated whether I would have that tumbler of Glenfiddich when I got home. I wasn't sure I still had a client, but it could wait until morning. I had a sick feeling in the pit of my stomach. It's a nameless dread that doesn't mean anything; it's what happens to me sometimes when I have to deal with too many unpleasant people or hear too many sordid lies. Crime scenes never used to bother me as a cop. The blood's already spilled. It's all over but the shouting, and that only comes at the tail end when the cuffs get snapped on.

Nikki's secret website had an email address, and when I checked my email the next day, I found a reply to my request to meet her. I tried to sound like what I thought a rich but not-too-bright widower would sound like when he fell headfirst into a honey trap.

The response was curt, just a couple semiliterate sentences. *Go too Mickey D's on Market St., corner of Rt. 322, noon tomorrow, wait. I can meet you their.*

I called Pruel at the precinct and was told he was out. I

left no message. If Jerry was at a crime scene, I could forget my next request. If he was at home, he'd be grumpy, but I might have half a chance. His wife remembered me and called him into the house for me. Imagining Jerry with a trowel in his hand planting flowerbeds made me smile. He'd look for beetles drawn to a corpse's stench before he'd put the first petunia in the ground.

"Kemo Sabe."

"What did I do in my last life to deserve you?"

I checked my watch while he ranted. This one could be a world's record. When he finally ran out of gas and cursed me and all my ancestors back to Adam, he agreed to do what I asked. He called "the mad Samoan" and put him at my disposal. Danny Gumataotao isn't a Samoan, by the way; he's a Solomon Islander and looks it every inch: walnut-brown skin, natural blonde hair a California surfer boy would kill for, and eyes as blue as a larkspur. He's also a brilliant freelance hacker who works for YPD on occasion and writes a column for *Wired*. In brief, Danny knows computers.

I gave him a two-hour lead when I hung up and called Danny at his YSU student apartment.

"Yo, Half Man, say, how's the ex-homicide-cop-turned-private-dick doing up there in the frozen north?" Danny crowed it with an emphasis on *dick*. He despised me because I held a little blackmail item over his head from one of his nefarious computer scams.

"Jerry told you what I wanted," I said. "Did you get it?"

"Sure, sure, I got it for you. Jesus, anyone would think – "

"Danny, stop chattering like a brain-dead guinea pig and give it to me." Danny wasn't all bad, but there was something about him that made my teeth clench.

"I believe it's squirrels that do that, *Mister* Haftmann, and I think it's *chittering*, not chattering," he said.

"I'm going to drive down there for the express purpose

of squeezing your neck until your eyes bulge."

"Whoah, I can see that being a private citizen has done nothing to improve your temper."

"Once more, Danny, and then I'm hanging up and bringing my gun with me."

"Man, you – all right, all right. Chill, huh!"

Danny found a second website under the alias Becka Ann Call. It would have taken me the rest of my life to sift through cyberspace's porn sites to try to match up the photos Graziadei had emailed me from Youngstown. I had a hunch Nikki was casting her net for the depraved sugar daddies of cyberspace. There's a thin layer between the sleaziest of sites, like the out-and-out pornographic and the pay-to-view-me-naked of the webcam entrepreneurs. A warmer layer, in effect, between the colder layers of the depths where no money in exchange for services would be hinted at, but people looking for something special and exclusive could find what they were seeking. A smart, sophisticated woman in a high-end call-girl business did not want to invite cops or FBI cybercrimes unit by blatant advertising and she didn't want to waste time with lowlifes jumping their pay grades.

Danny was bragging how his program of robot zombies brought back the goods, but I wasn't interested in his computer jabber about "necromancers," "clusters," and "botnets."

"Danny, listening to this is making my ears bleed. Just send me what you found."

One emailed photo, an artsy pose in a chair, showed her *au naturel* with the chair back covering most of that voluptuous body she so freely displayed in her films. The photographer had used light from a window and shade to obscure as much as reveal. A large print of a sad clown hovered over her shoulder. Polished blonde flooring in tongue-and-groove, distressed red brick walls. Somebody's loft, maybe a rich man's fuckpad. It wasn't the kind of place Jerry had described as Graziadei's usual venue.

He sent me a follow-up email on the clown photo. Danny couldn't resist showing off. It turned out to be Emmett Kelly as "Weary Willie" and he said it was taken at the winter quarters of the Barnum and Bailey Circus in Sarasota, Florida. John Ringling had left a fabulous mansion and museum down there. Nikki's text said she was interested in making contact "with youthful minds, hearts, and souls to explore passion's horizons." It sounded like new-wave horse manure to me, and I wondered how geezers with cash and a yen for young women would be drawn to it.

The IP address of the computer Nikki used was in Canfield right next door to Youngstown. When I saw the house address of the one used to reply to my message, I had to call Danny back.

"Yeah, I'm sure," he said. "Erieview Road, Jefferson-on-the-Lake. Your turf, man."

My turf, hell, it was walking distance from my office.

"You positive about this?"

"Hey, man, it's me you're talking to here," he said.

"I believe the correct case form should be *I*, not *me*," I said and clicked off.

Another sign of galloping senility, I suppose – nothing was simple anymore and I was getting slapped in the face with my own blindness. I felt as if somebody had strapped ankle weights to my legs. It wasn't quite ten but I was owed a drink. I locked my office and walked across the street to Tico's Place. His Budweiser sign had been winking messages to my brain from across the street all morning long.

As soon as my eyes adjusted to the dark, I sensed trouble ahead. Tico's wife Marta was washing dishes behind the bar. Things were usually dicey when she showed up early. I had no doubt she thought exactly the same thing about me. We smiled at each other, hers was more grimace. Tico came walking in from the kitchen; apparently his radar was working overtime, too. Marta surprised us both and left without a word. The way she threw the towel on the top of the bar was a pretty accurate expression of her feelings.

"How are things in the House of Gutierrez?"

He set a beer and a malt whiskey in front of me. I usually had to ask for the second. Maybe he was projecting his own stress onto me. "Tomás, don't ask. You hear about the fire?"

"What fire?"

"Three cottages burned down last night. You didn't hear all those sirens?"

"No, I was out of town. I got back late. What time was this?"

"About eleven, maybe later. The fire trucks woke us up. Even Cesar, and you know how that kid likes to sleep." Cesar was Tico's boy but he was thirty years old and three years retired from a professional boxing career at welterweight. He used to spar with Pavlik at Jack Loew's Southside gym in Youngstown. What he said next reignited that gaseous little puddle of dread sitting behind my solar plexus.

"They found a body in one of them."

"Was the fire on Erieview?"

"Man, how you know that if you wasn't even here?"

"Woman or man, the body?"

"I don't know. Beer guy, he come in at eight, he say they found a body. Crispy critter, he say. Can't tell if it's a man or woman. That's all I know."

I left the malt on the bar. Tico's eyes must have been bugged. Halley's comet will be back before he ever sees that twice.

I jogged over to Erieview, which is just a gravel lane that deadheads at the Lake. I had a nodding acquaintance with the owner. He spent most of his time caring for his invalid mother in Sharon, PA, but the caretaker was a regular at Tico's. I knocked on his door.

He had a pretty name, but Charlie Beausoleil was about as poetic as a wall sconce in a latrine. He had the last cabin opposite the three smoldering ruins. I knocked.

"Charlie, what happened?"

"Huh, I don't know. I woke up when I saw the flames in my bedroom window. I was sound asleep, man. Gene's on his way up from PA right now."

"Cops say what happened?"

"The arson investigator just left. He was here all night. Look, I got to get down to the Jefferson Sheriff's to make a statement. I was just about to lock up."

"I heard they picked up a biker," I said. "Some guy from Annie's." I was fishing.

"No friggin' way, a biker! It was them kids. I seen 'em coming and going all week. It was one of them little assholes sure as shit set the match. "

Charlie spent a few useless moments trying to tuck in a shirt below his mountainous belly but gave up. "Fuck it, I got to go."

~ ~ ~

I drove to the Jefferson Sheriff's precinct. The holding cell in this resort town is nothing but a drunk tank. Real crime goes six miles south to Jefferson, the county seat. There's no Medical Examiner so they'd have bagged up the corpse and sent it off to the Cuyahoga M. E. in Cleveland. Elizabeth Bhargrava was still doing most of the cutting as chief pathologist. I had a long-standing in with her.

That was less than hour's drive, but I had an hour and fifteen minutes to make it to that Youngstown McDonald's by noon.

I've had my share of speeding tickets on Route 11, which begs a driver to feed some speed to his ride. Truckers are pretty good about flashing lights to warn of staties sitting in the grassy median like lions in the savannah waiting to pull down a luckless antelope. Three of them saved me from getting tickets and I made it with five minutes to spare. I parked at the far end where the employees park. No sense in giving anyone inside a look at my car. The note said nothing about how I was supposed to recognize my contact or be recognized, for that matter. This was going to be straight acting without a script.

I ordered a burger from the dollar menu and sat down in a booth near the back. The burger was a prop but after a couple minutes perspiring in the air conditioner, I had to unwrap it. The olfactory sense took over and I devoured it in three bites. If you discount a stale donut and my brew at Tico's, it was all I had had in my stomach besides Ohio air for the day.

"You look like you're really enjoying that sandwich." The kid who slid into the seat opposite me looked about fifteen. I was about to tell him to go cadge money somewhere else when I realized from the smirk on his face he was my contact.

"You bring money?"

"You didn't name a price in your email," I said. I had no idea what I was negotiating for.

"Three bills," he said.

"How do I know I'm getting the real goods?" I asked him.

He lifted up a Metallica t-shirt. I saw a crescent of silver next to a belly button. So I was buying a disk.

I took a big chance: "Nikki gave me a lower price when I spoke to her," I said.

His eyes narrowed a touch. "Nikki ain't running the show. I am. Price is three hundred. Pay it or fuck off, man."

"OK," I said. "I'm good for it."

"That's better." He relaxed a bit but I noticed his eyes cutting from one side to the other, sensing a trap. He had a blue glyph tattoo around one skinny bicep. The place was packed: office workers on lunch break, single mothers with little kids, retired men gabbing at tables and hopping up to get a refill for their senior coffee every few minutes.

"Look," I said, "if I like what I see, I'm going to want a lot more." I pushed a wad of fifties across the table at him.

His eyes popped and he snorted. "Shit, man, what's the matter with you?" He palmed the money and swept it toward him. It disappeared under the table and went into hiding in his BVDs next to the disk. He leaned forward and rapped my knee with the edge of the disk. Everybody watches the same films, I guess.

"For future reference," I said, "don't call a meeting in a public place like a McDonald's." "Don't tell me what to fuckin' do," he snarled. Youngstown manners again.

"Sure, fine, sorry," I said in as contrite a voice as I could muster. I was relaxed now; it was amateur hour with this young bozo, but I had no clear fix on how Nikki fit into this. Bootleg porn made no sense in a sex-drenched society; it had to be something beyond the pale. I followed another hunch.

"When I met Nikki in Sarasota last winter, she said she could get me a steady supply. We were supposed to go wholesale. Didn't she tell you? I have the contacts all lined up. Doing this one at a time for chickenfeed is a waste."

"Let me think about it," he said. "Give me your cell number. I'll get back to you."

"I don't know you," I said. "I feel I have an obligation to Nikki. After all, it was her set-up." I was trying to stay within the lines without knowing where the lines were. I think that made him suspicious.

I wrote the number of Tico's Place on a napkin and handed it to him. "I'm going to check you out, asshole." He got up to leave. "You better be who you say you are."

Decision time. Brace him now or follow him. He was a lanky, wiry teenager. I was a middle-aged two-hundred-fifteen. I decided to follow.

He strode across the parking lot straight for a beige late-model Civic driven by a girl with a shaggy mop of dirty-blonde hair. I didn't have to look at the plates to know it was Nikki Ingersoll's car.

I followed them to through the 422 interchange and into Niles. Some president was born here, maybe McKinley. Ohio has sent more mediocrities and corrupt politicians to the White House than any other state.

Niles is a small burgh; it wouldn't be possible to stay behind them for long without being detected if they were looking for a tail. I was hoping the girl driving was every bit as naïve as the boy.

They turned into a driveway in front of a small, shabby house across the street from a Dairy Queen. I kept driving past. I turned into a strip mall where dentists, insurance agents, and chiropractors offered services and parked close to the street end.

My field binoculars were back in my office, but I keep a Zeiss riflescope in the car. I had a clear view of the Civic's rear fender.

I called Elizabeth Bhargrava's office and left an urgent message to call me back. I was counting on her memory of me with a bit more affection than the mad Samoan's.

An hour later the Cleveland pathologist returned my call.

"Doctor Bhargrava, this is Tom Haftmann. I'm a private investigator nowadays and I'm working a missing person's case."

She said something rapidly in her lovely singsong

voice that convinced me she did remember me.

"Was the body found in the rubble up at Jefferson resort a female?"

"Yes, a girl. Very young," Elizabeth said. "Maybe thirteen or fourteen at most. Barely into puberty, I think."

Before Elizabeth could wax eloquent on pelvic angles or tibia length, I thanked her and rang off. I had seen burn victims before. The boxer's pose from the contracted muscles, the burst skin from the intense heat – most of all, the hideous barbecue smell which you can't dry-clean out of your clothes.

Nikki was twenty-four. Those teens I followed had sun-bleached hair, not dye jobs. Ohio isn't hot enough to do that. There was a Florida connection. The boy didn't bat an eye when I mentioned Sarasota, but everything else put him on edge.

I took my laptop out of the trunk and put the disk in. I was pretty sure by now what I would be looking at, and two minutes into the film, it was confirmed. Three teenagers, a ménage a trois. The McDonald's boy, the dirty-blonde girl in the car. The same piano bar, the same piano. The action was a duplicate of the Graziadei film except that Nikki wasn't in it. I watched the teenagers ape their professional betters in their own clumsy style and it was anything but prurient. The stick-thin girl atop the piano was almost certainly the girl found in the middle cottage. I waited another forty-five minutes and called Elizabeth again. This time, I got her.

"Elizabeth, I have something for the detectives investigating the girl you just did the autopsy on," I said.

"One of them just left," she said. She gave me his name and number at the Jefferson precinct. I knew him slightly.

"One last question, if you don't mind," I said. "Was she dead at the time?"

I heard what sounded familiarly like a tongue clucking

and remembered her from my detective days at the autopsy tables. The pathologist emigrated from Madras in India when she was a girl that age; now she was with a kindly grandmother with a long iron-gray braid who spent hours on the phone with the victims' families. She was also a stern taskmaster for her crew of assistant pathologists.

"No, no," Dr. Bhargrava said and her voice dropped a full octave. "She was alive." More tongue clucking. "She was very much alive when she was burned. I found ash in her lungs."

A child burned alive. What could she have done to deserve this fate?

Fifteen minutes later, the Honda backed out of the driveway. The boy was behind the wheel and he was alone. Another decision.

I drove straight for the driveway and pulled in. I banged on the door. Maybe she'd think her boyfriend had forgotten something and was back.

I heard the chain lock come off and the door cracked open. I kicked it all the way with my foot and put her on her ass in the middle of the floor. I stuck my P.I. badge in her startled face before she could get off her haunches. Cops have to worry about this sort of thing in court, not me.

"Where is she?"

"Wh-Who – I don't know – "

"Listen to me," I put a little basso-profundo in my voice to complement the blitzkrieg. It doesn't work on everybody. "Where is Nikki Ingersoll?" I hauled her to her feet.

"Ow-ow-ow, you're hurting me," she said.

What I said next wasn't especially polite or G-rated, for that matter, but it worked on her.

"She – she's in the basement," she moaned. "I didn't do it."

My stomach, sour as spoiled milk all day, felt the adrenalin jolt her words produced. The acid burned all the way up my esophagus. My Sig Sauer was in my trunk inside a gun safe. The ammo was on the other side of the trunk as the law requires. I never bothered to get a CCW license to carry. I didn't know when the boyfriend was returning. Yet one more decision in a day full of them.

"Show me," I said.

She led me past the kitchen, my fingers still tight on her upper arm, and down a narrow set of stairs into a dank basement. The walls were fieldstone but some homeowner had lain down plywood sheets. They were streaked with spray-paint graffiti in a variety of colors. My brain refused to read whatever the words said. I was concentrating too hard; the flooring was spotted with the same colors, a huffers' meeting place.

The girl led me to the other end of the basement. We had to go single file because the litter and debris on the floor reached past my knees. There was too much stuff and the smell was too rancid for this to be the sole work of a pair of teenaged renters. My right foot went into something soggy and I pulled it out.

"Jesus fuck," the girl said, stopping to turn toward me, "what's that fuckin' smell?"

"Never mind," I said. "Take me to her."

"There ain't no light back here," she said. I had to resist an urge to break her neck right then.

There wasn't enough cleared space at the end for anyone to turn around in, and the accumulated smells from the corner wafted upward into my nostrils no matter how hard I tried to breathe through my mouth. There was one small rectangle of smeared window that shone a bar of light in front of us. I was too mesmerized by the seething mass of squirming maggots on the floor to notice; then something, some instinct told me to look just past the horizontal bar of greasy light.

The crown of Nikki Ingersoll's head was illuminated like a blonde halo. I noticed squirming going on there too. Maggots were crawling in and out of a scalp wound. I could make out the hands bound behind her back. Her long legs were duct-taped in front. She was nude. Black worms of dried blood from the scalp wound crisscrossed her face. I couldn't see her eyes.

If it weren't for the barrage of smells, I might have detected more easily that one unmistakable odor of death, but it would have been like trying to pick out a Flutophone in the midst of a symphony warm-up.

I'd seen enough. "Let's go," I said.

"Look, man, I didn't do it!"

"I don't care," I said. "Move."

"Man, I'm tellin' you, Dollar did her – he did Melissa too!"

"What's Dollar's real name?" I asked her. I had to keep shoving her forward. She kept turning around to plead as if this was a police station or a court of law.

"I don't know. He goes by Dollar. That's all I know," she said.

I was used to it. Mindless fornication, nobody knows anybody's real name. It didn't matter to Nikki Ingersoll. It was all cop business now. I wanted out. My stomach was on rolling boil.

As we got to the huffers' spot, I noticed a pair of skinny hairless legs on the bottom of the stairs.

I looked up just in time to see the gun in Dollar's hand. It looked like a Glock and he was aiming it between the two of us. Before she could form a word with her open mouth, he said, "You cunt." He fired. I was still clutching her bare arm.

Her entire head exploded in a red mist. My face felt the velocity spatter. *A fragmentation round* – that was my last coherent thought because the rest was pure instinct. I hurled myself backwards into the dark basement and plowed through the litter as fast as my churning legs could carry me. I heard two more shots and I heard the whizz of air molecules being ripped apart next to my head. Whatever the rounds hit burst into pieces and chunks as if somebody had tossed a handful of silver tubes into the piles.

I was frozen for long terrifying seconds in that dream where your legs can't move because they're sunk in mud or wet cement. Running and stumbling through that muck was like running in waist-high water except that I felt sharp objects ripping into my flesh. I felt nothing. Another shot smashed into the timber just above my head and sprayed me with splinters. *A goddamn automatic*, I remembered. I would be trapped in the corner and he'd have a whole bunch of bullets left in the magazine.

I was almost back to Nikki's corpse in the chair. Nowhere to go. That window wouldn't allow a man half my size to get through it. He was much closer now, although I could hear nothing besides the sound of things being thrown to one side or another as I bulled my way deeper into the basement. The next shot blew a hole into the cement wall over my right shoulder; the blowback of stone fragments cut my jaw and cheek. I felt warm blood flowing down my neck. Before another shot left the barrel, I dove headfirst into a pile beside Nikki's body and hoped he hadn't seen me.

I tried lie as still as possible and curled myself in to a fetal position. I heard him coming toward me, cursing and growling like an animal.

He fired a cascade of shots all around, spraying the basement from one corner to the other. Slugs cut channels through the debris in front of my face and close enough to my tucked-in legs that whatever was hit ricocheted off something hard and smashed me in the middle of the back. I had the insane thought he was using a Louisville slugger to drive me out of hiding.

Then I heard the blessed sound of dry fire. A big decision now: reveal myself, go for him before he has a chance to stick another clip in there. Or stay where I was. I chose the cowardly option.

I heard a litany of unoriginal cursing just a few feet from where I lay curled. He spat out one last "motherfucker" and then he left. My sense of sound was about as rarefied as a blind man's at that point. I heard him going fast up the cellar steps. I got up. I had to use all my willpower not to vomit right there. I moved in the same direction as fast as my wobbly legs could go.

I held on to the walls as I went up the stairs to keep from fainting. At the top someone had spray-painted: "I got all the virgin tickets in my homeroom." It was signed Megan D. in big loopy schoolgirl letters.

The Honda was gone by the time I made it to the porch. It was the middle of the afternoon and cars went past the road in front of the house. It was a beautiful late summer day with a baby-blue sky and birds chirping in the trees. I stood there feeling the sticky blood on my face and neck and smelling the garbage-truck reek of my clothes and wondered why it wasn't pitch black with gobs of fiery rain pouring down from the skies.

~ ~ ~

I was in the Jefferson station house for eight long hours. Fortunately, they let me clean up first and get some food on my stomach. I wanted a drink, however, many of them, actually, but I knew better than to ask. Chief Millimaki, who disliked me from years back, stopped by the interview room to tell me a couple CID investigators were coming up from Columbus and to make myself available. I nodded. In the old days, he'd have a Swisher

Sweets sticking out of his mouth and he'd make wet, smacking sounds with it. Maybe his doctor finally got him to quit smoking. I assumed he'd want to live long enough to enjoy all the bribes and kickbacks he took from the power brokers on the Strip in his retirement.

I'm cynical enough to admit that I thought seriously of calling Graziadei to get the rest of my fee before the cops got to him. In the end, I let it go.

The trial was pretty sensational and both the Youngstown *Vindicator* and the Cleveland *Plain Dealer* covered it in lurid detail over the two weeks it lasted. In the end, the prosecutor couldn't make all the accessory charges stick. Dollar, whose real name was Jordan Hyslop, was a Florida runaway, a juvenile delinquent who sold himself under the piers around Miami and Fort Lauderdale. He moved up north to Sarasota with an aged gentleman who took him in and gave him money for sex; that's where he met Nikki Ingersoll, who traveled the state cruising for young boys and girls for the porn films she and Graziadei were making and selling.

What they didn't count on was Hyslop being more than an actor in these films featuring girls between twelve and fourteen. The state's psychiatrist called him a sociopath once you peeled away the rest of the mumbo-jumbo. Two days short of his sixteenth birthday at the time he poured a gallon of gas over a Michigan runaway named Felicity Monroe, however, was the reason they didn't try him as an adult. They figured it was too controversial at his age and he'd get a conviction overturned on appeal. As an ex-cop, I'm used to the antics of lawyers. It's always about lawyers, never justice. Hell, I was once married a lawyer. The kid will go away until he's twenty-one and he'll be re-evaluated. It won't even make the newspapers once he's released. Ohio will kick him across the state line and he'll be somebody else's problem.

Graziadei managed to get a pretty good lawyer. His trial date keeps getting put back on the docket. In a couple years, he might plead to the lesser child porn charges but even that's not a sure thing. His lawyer keeps referring to Nikki Ingersoll as the "inspiration for this diabolical business" and calls her "the procuress." I can imagine what the jurors' faces will look like if he manages to get the piano film into it. Her family sent someone in from Chicago to claim the body and they put it on a train for the ride home.

Two days ago I had a call from him. He's back in his office in Youngstown. His lawyer convinced the judge he wasn't a flight risk and bail was set at two hundred fifty thousand. Graziadei paid it in cash. It made me wonder whether he was mobbed up after all.

"I'm sending you a check, Haftmann," he said as soon as I answered. "I pay my bills."

"I'll send you a receipt," I replied.

"I loved her, you know," he said after a long pause. "I had no idea she was into this – this other business with teenagers. I swear to God."

"I don't care," I said.

"Did she – did she suffer?"

"Why don't you think about that over the long winter nights ahead," I said. I had no reason to give him any consolation about anything.

"I'll toss in a bonus," he said.

"Pay me what you owe," I said. "You send me a dime more than my bill and I'll give it charity. That's after I wash it off." I don't know why I was being so melodramatic. Maybe my adventures in that basement in Niles were still troubling me at some deeper level. I had no trouble sleeping at night. It was something else.

"What's your problem?" He sounded more like the arrogant clown who walked into my office that hot August morning.

"She played Bach at the piano bar," I said suddenly. I don't know from what abyss in me that came welling up, but it seemed important at the moment.

"What? What did you say? Go fuck yourself." He clicked off.

I have an old-fashioned Bakelite phone in my office; it's black and it weighs a ton. I don't know why I keep it. I picked up the receiver and mashed it on the toggle button as if I were crushing a bug.

It was a scorching hot summer day, ninety-five degrees and the humidity was almost as bad. I was sweat-soaked and I had barely moved all day except for checking my email. The calls on my answering machine were routine, one smelled like money. My life was going forward at its own pace. I had a little money coming in from a skip-trace so I paid my bar bill and kept the frozen smile on Marta's face from turning to a scowl. Elizabeth told me Nikki had been dead twelve hours; she was just coming out of rigor. Pathologists have their own gossip network like cops and everyone else.

I don't expect to be called to testify whenever Graziadei's attorney finally runs out of delays. For one thing, I'm not likely to be helpful to either side. It wasn't a crime to hire me, although a first-class outfit in Cleveland or Youngstown might have gotten to her while she was still alive. When Dollar and his girlfriend abducted Nikki, it was a spur-of-the-moment thing. A jealous girl wanting her lover to prove his love for her by killing the runaway they used in their threesome. Graziadei used Nikki to rent the cabin. For a man who loved seeing his name, they won't find it on anything incriminating. The Strip was a good place to go trolling for kids who might want to make some money for doing what they did for free anyway. I've tracked runaway girls in cabins like that going to parties and openly having sex in front of people.

I have two images of Nikki. I see her playing on a gleaming black Steinway. Her long, shapely fingers glide gracefully over the keys. That image blurs, refocuses like a camera lens being twisted, and then I see her slumped over in the chair in that basement. She was down there for almost five days, surrounded by stink and crawling insects; they never fed her or gave her any water. The wound on her head came from Dollar hitting her to subdue her to get her into the trunk of her own car.

Five days, five long days in that basement. I'm no believer in hell or heaven, but Nikki Ingersoll paid for her sins of the flesh in a way that even Dante and the medieval church fathers would have approved a worthy form of expiation. Sartre said it: Hell is other people.

The Bride from Paradise Park

You're likely to think there's no connection between the assassination of JFK and my decision two weeks later to become a private investigator, but you'd be wrong. Everything fits together. Maybe I'm just another lost baby boomer creaking toward old age. I held on to my conspiracy theories longer than most, but even I finally had to admit to myself that Lee Harvey Oswald acted alone. One misfit without money or powerful friends changed the world.

Jason Kotila walked into my office one day in early May because he wanted me to investigate his fiancée's background. Her name was Mandy Boyle and she was, as he said unoriginally, "from the wrong side of the tracks."

"I'm doing this for my family," he said up front. "My parents don't approve of divorce. We're strict Catholics," Jason said.

"Do you have a palimony agreement with her?" I asked him.

"Of course not," he said. "My father's rich, not me. He'll live to be ninety-five if he's anything like the rest of the men in my family."

"So there's nothing – "

"Nothing," he said. "Mandy won't get anything from marrying me. Look, I just want to get my dad off my back. I love her."

He blew air out of his cheeks out as if reliving his last unpleasant conversation on the subject with one of them. There were cousins and aunts sprinkled into his exasperated references to the "family" opposing his plans to wed someone born and raised in the Paradise Park, but I gathered his father, mother, and sister were the principal antagonists to the marriage.

"You know Paradise Park," Jason said.

It wasn't a question. If you lived in town longer than three months or read the local paper once a week, you knew the Paradise Trailer Park off Capital Road. The place was notorious for drug raids, domestic violence, and child abuse. Seven of twelve murders in town last year occurred in "the Park." Cops visited the place at least once a week without fail and take someone to jail or arrest somebody hiding out from a bench warrant. Local cops use their own slang for call-outs there: ". . . Hey, got another one over to Cesspool Road." That said all you needed to know.

He gave me the particulars of what he wanted. I gave him a couple of options involving my time and expenses. Most of my clients choose the economy option because they think they can do my job better than I can and a day or two is all it takes anybody to know a person's deepest secrets. After all, TV cops get it done in an hour.

Jason had met Amanda Boyle in a sophomore biology class. She attended his parochial school on a church scholarship. Mandy, as everyone called her, finished as class valedictorian, he said, whereas he himself barely managed to squeak out a diploma and attended the local community college for an associate's degree before he entered his dad's lucrative insurance business.

She graduated in three years, magna cum laude, with a double major in physics and chemistry and had plenty of fellowship offers to go to grad school. She could have worked with some prestigious professors at Case Western in cancer research if she wanted, Jason added.

What she did, however, was take a job at a local pharmacy as a technician to help support her mother in the trailer park where she had grown up.

"My family thinks she's nothing but a jumped-up hillbilly," Jason said, head bowed. I watched him twisting his hands together as if he were kneading dough. His hair was styled long on top. The word *preppy* had started forming in my mind when he first walked in. I learned two things since tacking up my shingle: first, everybody wears a mask. The second thing I learned is that everyone who comes through my door wants me to take something from someone else or I'm supposed to keep somebody from taking something away from them. I might as well be a damned lawyer. "My folks went ballistic," he said. "They had no idea I was that serious about her."

"What about her folks?" I asked.

He hesitated no longer than an eye blink. "Your classic trailer-park lowlifes. I begged her to get out of there but she insists she has to be with her mom. I told her I'd pay for an apartment for both of them but she won't take a dime from me."

After he left, I learned Mandy's father was doing serious time for killing some guy in a bar fight over drugs and got sent to Youngstown. The pen on Coitsville-Hubbard Road was opened fifteen years ago and houses some of Ohio's most violent offenders.

Jason told me Mandy once said he had sent her a tape of him reading Doctor Seuss when she was a little girl. Some prison program to help fathers reconnect with their kids. I knew a few men incarcerated there. They like to join prison programs like Aunt Mary's Storybook Hour to shorten their sentences or gain privileges.

Mandy also had a brother who was a total juvenile delinquent. He sold bags of parsley for weed in junior high. He assaulted a teacher in his sophomore year and dropped out at sixteen. According to Jason, Mandy's mom was high all the time. An occasional derelict of a boyfriend might stick around long enough for sex and to pay a few utility bills. I imagined Mandy herself would have to dodge some of these losers who'd try to molest her as soon as her mother passed out.

Mandy's sisters were "chips off the old block," Jason said; "both knocked up at sixteen. No telling how many abortions before then."

Jason's narrative of his future in-laws sounded like *Tobacco Road* meets *The Beverly Hillbillies* without the oil wells.

One of my contacts at the state pen works for David Bobby, the warden. I left a message at the switchboard for him to call me.

My contact told me Wayne Marvin Boyle, putative father of Amanda, was currently in administrative segregation.

"Gang affiliation?"

"Brand," he said. Short for Aryan Brotherhood. "He rocked some guy to sleep, but it was supposed to be a just beat-down. GI knows he's Brand so they got him iced down in ad seg." Prison argot: Wayne Boyle was an Aryan Brotherhood enforcer who garroted his cellmate. GI was the Gang Intelligence Unit. It's an old AB trick: get yourself assigned to the guy you've been ordered to hit. "Hard candy" was a serious beating as opposed to "soft candy." "Being rocked to sleep" – well, you don't need a dictionary for that one. It all had to be a public demonstration so everybody on the cellblock would know what's up.

"Now he's in deep shit with the big boys who run the tier," Chuey said.

I worked the phones all afternoon. The former Mrs. Boyle was an open book. Born in Wheeling, West Virginia at the tail end of a litter of thirteen. Hitchhiked up to Ohio at fifteen, worked in topless bars when cities were falling apart under the siege of crack cocaine in the eighties.

Besides dancing and stripping, she turned tricks to support herself and her habit. A typical story from grass to heroin to crack with an occasional interlude of sobriety. By the time she began breeding kids with various males, she was a long-gone dope fiend.

Mandy grew up in that depressing row of bucket-sized, first-generation trailers barely bigger than campers. Stunted, wind-bent trees line both sides of the entrance and give it a look like some cheap Halloween slasher movie set. Summer or winter, you can see plastic Mattel riding toys littering the postage-stamp of dirt yard out front. A few lack doors or have plastic duct-taped over broken windows. The more I learned, the more I admired the girl; she had grit and smarts.

It must have helped she was gorgeous. Jason showed me a photo of her sitting on the breakwall in summer blouse and white shorts. Her full bottom lip was like a curled wave about to break. All the parts were assembled just right. Go figure. Nature can build a palace in a place of excrement. Jason was marrying beneath him, but I could see a whole bunch of rich men more than willing to trade the checkbook to have her as their trophy wife.

Amanda's mother's mug shots showed the degeneration when she discovered meth or meth discovered her. Northeast Ohio is rotten with "Nazi-style" meth labs, Googling the Internet. A month doesn't go by before one blows up. We made national news when one blew up in a nursing home – *a nursing home*. Feral cats run loose in Paradise Park, but that cat-piss smell is more likely to be meth fumes blowing in the wind.

No doubt about her family; it was a slow-motion holocaust. Mandy's brother was biding time in a youth detention center for a home invasion. Her two sisters had different surnames and both had spawned a trio of children by different fathers.

Valedictorian or not, nobody's squeaky clean. If she so much as shoplifted a pen, I was going to find out. I planned to put the binocs on her and see what she did for entertainment when Jason wasn't around.

Jason told me he was going to clear Mandy's name and announce the nuptials for August. He and Mandy had to schedule several counseling sessions from his parish priest before the wedding can be blessed by his church. Jason's father was a millionaire several times over. Mandy would land in tall cotton with this marriage. I disliked the thought of her as a gold digger, but my clients pay the bills, not the people I investigate.

I drove to a small leather goods outlet store adjacent to the trailer park. The owner once told me he had to get a good security system or the "welfare rats next door" would strip him down to the drywall.

Her trailer was at the far end of the lane leading off the main entrance. I'd have the scrub brush behind her trailer for cover.

At nine o'clock, I got out of my Jeep and made my way through the field. Except for one rusted-out piece of barbed wire tearing a patch out of my sleeve, I had no difficulty finding a good spot.

Mandy came home at nine-fifteen, just as Jason said. She parked her Honda in front and went in. Unlike her beach photo, her chestnut hair was tied back in a bun.

According to Jason, the mother stayed in the back bedroom watching the television Mandy paid for and eating the supper she made or brought from the deli on her way home. At ten-ten Mandy walked out the front door of the trailer. She walked at a brisk pace but I kept her in sight all the way. There was one trailer set off by itself at the far end of the lot. I got up in a crouch to follow. The field was going to run out in another fifty yards. I worked my way to the edge of the field and hunkered behind a crabapple tree. I watched Mandy go inside the trailer.

I looked at my watch. She had been inside for sixteen minutes. I managed to creep up behind the trailer's window hoping none of those barking dogs I heard were running loose. The dark shielded me from the adjacent trailers, but I wouldn't want to get a face full of birdshot from some trigger-happy redneck.

The last trailer looked newer and bigger than most; it had a satellite dish on top. I went around back toward a sliver of yellow light where curtains hadn't been fully drawn. I crept up to the window ledge and looked in. I saw the magma glow of computer terminals in the center of the living room. I noticed cameras mounted in the corners and one large camera on a tripod pointed at the computer desk.

That was unusual. But not half as odd as the two nude women walking around. One was slathered in tattoos in helter-skelter fashion. The other was younger, smaller, undeveloped in the chest, and possessed of a thick pubic ruff. Her thatch extended almost to her belly button. Tattooed Girl scratched herself between the legs and lit a cigarette. She had one hand on her hip and seemed annoyed. She picked up a half-smoked blunt from an ashtray. Her bony companion spoke to her but I couldn't hear the words. I didn't see Mandy anywhere.

It might have been a low-rent porn website, one of those web-cam deals you subscribe to on the net. I ducked back into the weeds and waited. About ten minutes later, I heard the front door of the trailer creak. I angled my way to get a glimpse of Mandy walking back the way she had come. Two trailers back from her mother's she turned into the nearest one. The air stank of a concoction of smells, mostly frying grease and swamp muck.

She came out of that trailer thirty seconds later and returned to her mother's. I had to decide what my client was renting as far as my safety and my reputation went. We're like cops that way: humdrum boredom until the code comes over the radio. Most of the day is spent making phone calls and worrying about my ass getting wider, but then there are moments like these when a pit bull could be clamping down on my leg in the next five seconds or some drunk comes reeling out of his trailer with a .357 magnum mistaking me for a window peeper.

I had to know whatever the risk. I crept forward and saw Mandy tapping the inside of her mother's scrawny forearm with two fingers trying to bring a vein to life. Then she held up a needle and flicked it with her fingers. I didn't know what goods the spike was about to deliver, for the reason that Mandy's mother had a slew of convictions for heroin, meth, and crack at one time or another.

I jogged through the field back to the Jeep and drove home. I hadn't actually seen Mandy commit anything illegal, and I missed seeing her expression all through the surveillance, which was a frustration. But, no question, it was a sordid business from start to finish and there wasn't any good explanation to put to any of it. I wanted a shower and a drink in that order and that's what I had.

The next day I had a collect call from Youngstown State Penitentiary; it was Mandy's father and he wanted to talk to me about his daughter.

"I thought you were in isolation," I said.

"I got out this morning," he said.

He had a voice that was a low-pitched growl, a smoker's voice box caked with years of toxins.

"How did you know I was working a case involving her?" SHU is total lockdown. One shower a week, one hour exercise in a box the size of an upended coffin.

"I'm Brand, motherfucker. Didn't your boy tell you that?" *Chuey, of course.*

"I'm paying for the call," I said, "so tell me what you

have to say."

"Stay the fuck away from my daughter. I ain't ever getting out of this shithole, but I know people outside."

"So you know people," I said. "I know people." I made it sound as if we were a couple people persons having a friendly chat.

"Anybody can be got to," Boyle said. "That's all I got to say to you. Ain't gonna be no second call." He clicked off.

Anybody can be got to. JFK told a reporter two weeks before Dallas that killing the President of the United States was no great feat for a would-be assassin. A man just had to be willing to trade his life for the President's.

The Aryan Brotherhood isn't like any prison gang. The FBI almost broke their backs a few years ago when they cracked the Brand's secret code and rounded them up; they sent the top echelon of the AB off to different prisons. But killing a few sewer rats doesn't mean the rat population goes extinct. I read somewhere that every person in a city has the equivalent of four rats beneath him in the pipes and sewer tunnels. The Brand are the Norwegian rats of the sewer world.

Something wasn't passing the smell test. Wayne Boyle's call was one thing. Every con except a new fish knows phone calls are recorded, so if you don't want to hear your words being played back to you in court, don't say anything stupid on the phone. Law enforcement refers to the outside people who do the Aryan Brotherhood's bidding – which can range from warnings through beatings all the way to murder – as "associates," as if minor thugs and their whores are the junior associates of a law firm. But they don't warn you that they're coming.

I called Chuey.

"I don't know the guy except by his rep," Chuey told me. "Boyle is one dangerous sonofabitch, let me tell you, but he ain't stupid."

"Lifers have nothing to lose," I reminded him.

"That's just it, man. He ain't no lifer."

I spoke to Warden Bobby right after. I knew he wouldn't confirm anything Chuey said about Boyle getting off on a pending murder charge, but he did say they were looking into the phone call he made to me as a possible felony.

"What can he get?"

"Aggravated menacing? With his priors, he'll die in this institution," the warden told me.

I called Jason and asked him if he'd fund another day's investigation.

"No," he said. "This is as far as you go. You haven't got anything else on her by now you won't find it, so I want the report as soon as possible."

"You don't think what I saw in those two trailers warrants at least another day's surveillance?"

"Mandy's old lady has AIDS," he said. "What you saw was her giving her a cocktail of drugs to fight infection."

"The two nudes?"

"They're her sisters. They do this Internet porn bullshit to make a few extra bucks for what their kids need. So what if some old perv with a MasterCard in Bumfuck, Montana wants to whack off watching some girl sitting on the crapper?"

I was wondering how Jason's parents would regard this kind of capitalist initiative from their prospective in-laws.

"That's liberal of you," I said, "considering you asked me to dig up whatever I could on her."

"That's right, on *her*. I don't give a good goddamn about her trashy sisters or what they do to pay the rent. One more thing."

"Yeah?"

"Don't try to goose the bill," he said. "I'll stop by your

office tomorrow afternoon to pay you and pick up my report.

Clients. They can be such weasels sometimes.

I typed the report in three pages, single-spaced, and printed it out. I attached some Xeroxes of documents I had located from various agencies and institutions. Public records, mostly. The sort of paper trail everybody leaves behind. Mandy had nothing even close to incriminating and the testimonials I had gleaned from phone interviews purporting to be inquiries about her character for one pretense or another yielded only the highest praises. Nobody had a grudge against this girl; nobody had anything remotely bad to say about her, although everybody made a passing reference to her "unfortunate family circumstances."

Saint Mandy Boyle. *God damn it*. What was I missing?

Jason was inside my office at five minutes to noon.

"You're early," I said.

"Where's my report?" He picked it off the corner of my desk and riffed the pages.

"Pretty thin," he said.

"You told me not to goose the bill," I said.

"You take a check, I assume."

He glanced at the invoice, made a sour face; then he took out his checkbook and wrote out my payment. He tossed the check onto my desk and I watched it flutter in a shaft of sunlight streaming through my office window. It reminded me of baseball cards we used to flip on the playground.

"What's so funny?"

"I was thinking of Mickey Mantle," I said. "If I'd kept all those rookie year cards of his I traded away, I wouldn't need to work."

"He died of liver cancer," Jason said as if that were the sum of the Mick's legacy.

"We all die of something," I said.

~ ~ ~

One week later, I picked up the local paper and nearly threw up. The headline was all about the murder of a mother and daughter, residents of Paradise Park. The cops wouldn't comment but the reporter didn't hesitate to theorize; Amanda's mother's long history of drug abuse "might have been the motive" behind the burglary and the two murders. Apparently the killer, looking for drugs, caught Mandy as she was coming home from work and he surprised her before she had time to remove her coat. The mother was found in her bed with puncture wounds to the chest and a crushed hyoid bone. Mandy had fought her killer for a long time. The kitchen area was trashed and there was overturned furniture. She was badly beaten in the face and had been kicked so severely in the stomach, kidney, and abdomen areas that she died of internal hemorrhaging.

Three days later a man of no known address with a long string of felony convictions and a past history with the Mongols motorcycle gang was found with half his head missing in a deserted cabin in northwest Pennsylvania, just about thirty miles across the state line.

~ ~ ~

His office was like most on the Strip – just a shoebox with a desk and a computer. Maybe a sideline business in case this resort town takes off again the way it used to be back in the swing band era. Now it was mainly runaway or troubled kids, biker bars, and meth cookers. Tommy Dorsey isn't even a memory to this generation of teens with Kool-Aid colored hair and nose rings.

The door was closed and the blinds drawn. I'm not usually given to mad impulses like this, but I kicked it open and walked inside. That's me, Sam Spade.

There was a tiny back room and I could see the green

shade of a banker's lamp on a desk.

"Hello, Jason," I said.

"Fuck you," Kotila said.

The gun, a Sig Sauer, was lying in the middle of the desk between a couple stacks of manila file folders.

"That won't fix anything," I said. If that was the weapon that had killed the ex-biker, it was probably loaded with fragmentation rounds.

"Maybe I'll take you with me, fucker," he said. It was said just like his greeting, without much heat, so I was pretty sure it was a hollow threat and I felt the air go back into my lungs. A suicidal man with a big gun is a dicey prospect under the best of circumstances. I wasn't about to leap across the desk to get the gun away from him in any case. Sam Spade can kiss my ass. That happens in movies and the gumshoe is usually half my age and cruelly handsome. Being my age, I have the reflexes and face I deserve.

"I love her," he said in a weak voice.

He meant the blonde back in his condo on the lakeshore, of course. The one his family didn't know of. I didn't put her in my report. Jason never expected me to include him or his comings and goings in my background search, but there was something about him from the day he walked into my office that rubbed me all wrong. The rich, frat-boy smugness. The expensive haircut. The oh-so tender feelings for the girl from the wrong side of the tracks, his hound-dog look of despair, and all that guff about his heartless family – he laid it on with a trowel and that was the problem. I was born. I just wasn't born yesterday. I knew there had to be more to it than what he was telling me.

"My family . . . was going to make me marry *her*." This time I knew he meant Mandy.

Then it clicked: *she was pregnant.*

"How far along was she?" I asked him.

"Seven months, eight months – who cares?" he whined. "My father said if I didn't have the marriage certificate by the first of August, before the baby came, he was cutting me off."

"What about an abortion?"

He laughed bitterly. "Mandy was a true-blue believer," he said. "She fell in love with the Catholic church lock, stock, and barrel from the day she set her sights on me."

"Who's the blonde?"

"She's the woman I love, you moron. Haven't you been listening to me?"

"You murdered your pregnant girlfriend so that you could marry another woman. What am I missing here?"

His face held the same crooked smile. Who knew where his mind was at that point? It was all tumbling down around his ears like a house of cards under strobe lighting.

"I didn't kill anyone. I told him . . ."

"Told who?"

"I told him not to hurt her too much. Just to . . . work her over . . . you know, in the stomach. Cause a miscarriage."

"You're the one who contacted Boyle in the joint," I said. "You told him I was digging up dirt on his daughter. You told him I was working for your family, not for you. You made him think I was going to ruin her marriage, her only chance at happiness."

He sat there and shrugged. "Who could have known," he said wearily, "that a scumbag convict like her old man cared that much for her? He barely knew her."

I said, "I played my part like your stooge, didn't I?"

My report was supposed to *discredit her* to his family, not the other way around.

"They didn't care," he said. He barked out a laugh as if

it were a big joke at his expense.

"They actually wanted to force me to marry her," he added as an afterthought – or maybe a rationale. "Some gutter-trash bitch I had a fling with and knocked up and all because she didn't practice birth control!"

"So who was the hired thug? Who killed them, Jason?"

"He – Boyle told me . . . he gave me a name. Some guy. Somebody he said would do the work for me. Somebody he knew from up here. He was supposed to – "

" – somebody who was supposed to beat me up or get me to back off," I finished for him. One of Wayne Boyle's outside contacts. A Brand associate. Jason made the contact to have him "visit" Mandy in the trailer park, the perfect setting for something like this, make it look like a burglary gone wrong. Only it went way wrong.

"I told him to hit her, you know? Just to hit her . . . and now look, God damn it. My life is over!"

He looked as if he wanted to bawl and I wanted to grind my heel into his pretty-boy face. Mandy must have fought hard for herself and her baby. The mother was no threat but the killer had to take care of witnesses.

"You know, don't you, that the conspirator is as guilty as the trigger man? You're going to get the needle. It might take fifteen years but you're going to get a date with a tiny steel room the size of this office down there in Lucasville on the Ohio River, you motherfucker."

He didn't look at me. The hand of God Himself couldn't wipe the slime off this one.

The papers gorged on the story for weeks. Connecting the killer to the dead man in a cabin formerly owned by Jason's real estate company was the clincher. The prosecutor said Kotila did "a Jack Ruby" on his own assassin once he found out what the man had done instead of what he was supposed to do. Jason lured him there for the payment and then put a Glaser round into the back of his head while he was counting the bills. A loose fifty-dollar bill with brain matter on it was found at the scene.

I still have the photo of Amanda Boyle in my desk drawer and I take it out once in a while to look at it. The papers said Jason's lawyer, a big mouthpiece from Cleveland, requested another motion to delay. By the time Jason does go to trial, surrounded by his loving family and his big shot lawyers, he'll look like the victim. Mandy will be painted by the defense team as nothing more than a gold-digging slut from notorious Paradise Park trying to get her greedy hooks into a fine, upstanding young man. Trial lawyers, they can find an explanation for everything.

Mandy had a Catholic mass and burial. In the end, she got hallowed ground and that's all she got.

I learned a new word during the week of JFK's assassination: *catafalque*. It's what they rested his casket upon in the East Room. The military honor guard did a strange thing at that time at Jacqueline Kennedy's request. They're supposed to surround the casket and face outward. It's military tradition: guard your fallen leader from attacking enemies. Jackie asked them to turn around to face the casket. It was a most unusual request, but they obliged the grieving widow. "He looks so lonely that other way," she is believed to have said.

Thank you for reading.
Please review this book. Reviews help others find
New Pulp Press and inspire us to keep providing these
marvelous tales.

If you would like to be put on our email list to
receive updates on new releases, contests, and promotions,
please go to NewPulpPress.com and sign up.

About the Author

Robb White lives in Northeastern Ohio close to the house where he grew up. Many of his crime stories feature private investigator Thomas Haftmann, the protagonist of two earlier novels: *Haftmann's Rules* (2011) and *Saraband for a Runaway* (2013). A third novel, *When You Run with Wolves*, was published in 2015. He has a collection of short stories titled *Out of Breath and Other Stories* (2013) that mixes mainstream and crime fiction. Until he retired from college teaching this year, White wrote book reviews and conducted interviews for the print magazine *Boxing World*. His short story "Frotteur in the Dark" was selected by the editors of *10,000 Tons of Black Ink* of Chicago as one of 6 Best Of for 2009. *Special Collections*, an ebook crime novel featuring a female detective and an obese academic book thief, won the Electronic Book Competition of 2014 hosted by New Rivers Press (Mankato State University at Moorhead, MN).

NewPulpPress.com

www.ingramcontent.com/pod-product-compliance
Lightning Source LLC
Chambersburg PA
CBHW070544260626

47161CB00002B/502